THE HERO COMPLEX, BOOK 2
HERO IN HIDING

Aug. 2011	DATE DUE		
SEP 1 3 2011			
OCT 1 1 2011			
OCT 2 1 2011			
FEB 2 4 2012	DISCARD		
FEB 2 4 2012			
MAR 2 0 2012			

Demco, Inc. 38-293

HERO IN HIDING by Mitchell Bonds
Published by Marcher Lord Press
8345 Pepperridge Drive
Colorado Springs, CO 80920
www.marcherlordpress.com

This book or parts thereof may not be reproduced in any form, stored in a retrieval system, or transmitted in any form by any means—electronic, mechanical, photocopy, recording, or otherwise—without prior written permission of the publisher, except as provided by United States of America copyright law.

MARCHER LORD PRESS and the MARCHER LORD PRESS logo are trademarks of Marcher Lord Press. Absence of ™ in connection with marks of Marcher Lord Press or other parties does not indicate an absence of trademark protection of those marks.

This is a work of fiction. Names, characters, places, and incidents are products of the author's imagination or are used fictitiously. Any similarity to actual people, organizations, and/or events is purely coincidental.

Cover Designer: Kirk DouPonce, Dog-Eared Design, www.dogeareddesign.com
Creative Team: Jeff Gerke, Dawn Shelton

Copyright © 2011 by Mitchell Bonds
All rights reserved

Library of Congress Cataloging-in-Publication Data
An application to register this book for cataloging has been filed with the Library of Congress.
International Standard Book Number: 978-0-9825987-4-0

Printed in the United States of America

DEDICATION

To the awesome patients and staff of Gritman Medical Center
For being the best non-authorial job I've had
And to Patricia C. Wrede
for being my muse

And in memory of friendships lost
and never recovered

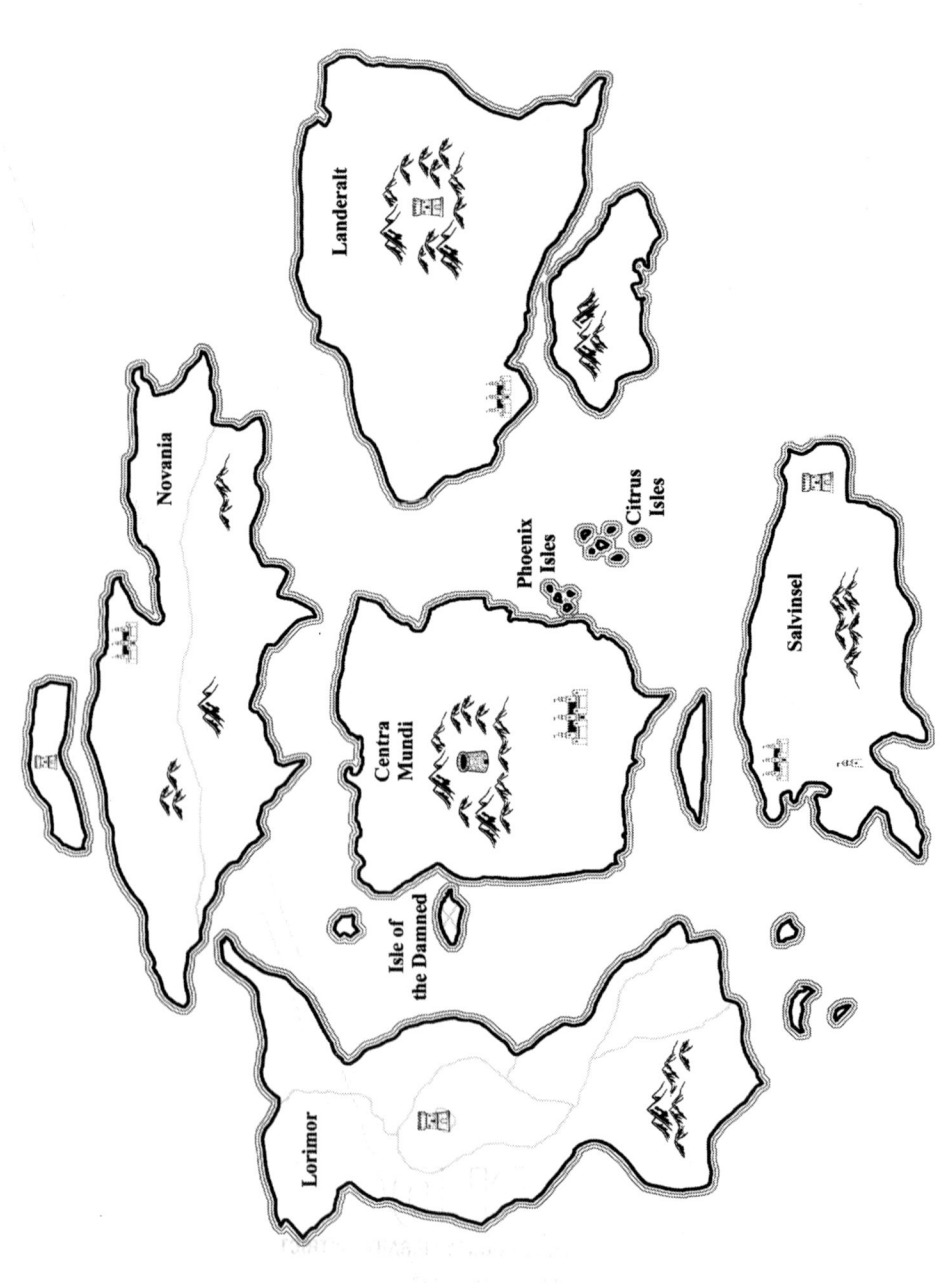

Part I

Chapter I

REINTRODUCTIONS AND PIRATES

*In which Readers have yet another Recap Inflicted Upon Them
And there are Pirates to Make Up for it*

IT WAS A dark and stormy morning. The night had been dark and stormy as well, but saying so at the beginning of the chapter would have been copyright infringement. Rain slashed out of the stormclouds and onto the soaked sails and deck of a cargo ship that struggled through the whitecaps.

Down in the corners of the hold, men and women in rusted armor sat on crates and leaned on broken swords and shattered dreams. These were the legendary Heroes, formerly of the International Heroes Guild, and currently on the run from the near-total annihilation of their once proud guild.

In case the reader is unfamiliar with the somewhat lackluster book entitled *Hero, Second-Class,* which preceded this one, there is in fact a reason for brave Heroes to be fleeing for their lives on a rickety boat hastening south away from their home base.

If the reader is actually familiar with said book, he or she need not read this section, but it may amuse nonetheless.

Our protagonist, the young red-headed Hero pacing the unsteady planks in the aft starboard corner, was Cyrus

1

Solburg, a strapping young lad who had just managed to attain full Hero status. His unique brand of unintentional magic use, which involved some small amount of damage to the underpinnings of the world every time he used it, attracted the attention of the sinister Voshtyr Demonkin, who came down on the International Brotherhood of Heroes like the proverbial ton of bricks.

Except that the bricks were evil. And any Hero worth his salt would have been able to lift said ton of bricks if it were only a ton. So the analogy breaks down.

But at any rate, the aforementioned evil bricks fell, thanks to Cyrus's unwilling betrayal of the Guild to Voshtyr in order to save his mate, Kris, the lovely leopard Katheni who currently sat in a wet and miserable ball near where Cyrus now worriedly strode.

If the reader is unfamiliar with the Race of Katheni, he or she is directed to either check the glossary in the back or, for the love of the Twelve and One, to *read the first book*. Seriously.

Shortly after their marriage came the slaughter of the Heroes in the Vale of Dreams, an event forever after referred to as the Vale Massacre. Kris and Cyrus were forced to flee, and they had spent the last two days on a ship, huddled in a damp and cramped cargo hold.

It had not exactly been the best honeymoon ever.

After the fall of the Heroes Guild, Voshtyr, assisted by his accountant, Lord Roger Farella, took over most of the continent at the center of the world, Centra Mundi, and began his campaign against the rest of the world. This ended the Age of Heroes and began the period of time known to some historians as the Age of Darkness. To others, notably the ones working for Voshtyr, it was the Age of Glory, and since history is written by the victor, this "glory" spread to the corners of the world, save a few.

Cyrus and Kris fled for one of those few places Voshtyr had yet to touch: Cyrus's home of Starspeak, Citrus Islands. Hence their current boat-encased, rain-soaked, and downtrodden state.

And so it is here that *this* story begins, on the stormy Sharkwater Sea, tossed like a boat-and-Hero salad, tracked by Forces Most Sinister.

Onward, dear reader, for the worst is yet to come.

Cyrus ceased his pacing and sat down next to Kris. The smoky lanterns of the hold seemed to make his hair glow. "I talked with the captain. The storm is blowing us a bit off course, but we should make it to Starspeak not more than two days late."

"That's two days more than I want to be on this boat," Kris said, burying her face in Cyrus's chest.

Cyrus smiled and held Kris. "I'm sorry, Kris. A boat was the easiest and least conspicuous way to get off Centra Mundi. I didn't think how it would affect you."

"It's all right," she said, giving him a weak smile. "But how do you keep your stomach from going all roily?"

Cyrus chuckled. "I'm used to boats. I've been around them the whole time I was growing up. Living on an island does have its benefits, after all."

"I suppose so . . . Cyrus, what's your family like?" Kris asked, leaning against her new mate.

"I don't exactly know how to answer that question," Cyrus said. "They're good people, if that's what you mean. Uncle Jacob is a hardworking guy, and Aunt Catherine is nice. She bakes the most delicious bacon-apple-cheese muffins you've ever tasted.

My cousin Marco's a bit of a twerp, but he might have finally grown up a bit. I've been gone for five years or so now . . ."

"That's not really what I meant," Kris said, tracing a furred finger across Cyrus's chest. "I mean, how would I fit in? Do you think they'll like me?"

"That's a silly question, Kris. Of course they will. I mean, their initial reaction might be a bit odd, and they might take a while to adjust to you, what with you being of a different Race and all."

Kris sighed. "I just hope I don't cause too much trouble for you."

"Well, we'll cause a stir, no doubt about it," Cyrus said. "The yokels on Starspeak don't get that kind of gossip fodder every day. But let's worry about that when we get there, all right?"

Kris nodded. "Fair enough. I am sure Starspeak needs a Hero just as much as anyone else right now."

Cyrus paused. "Um, actually, I'm thinking about giving up the Hero business entirely."

"What?"

"Well, if the Villains are serious about killing us off, I'd better lay low for a while. Anything resembling a Quest, or even magic use, would tell them where I was."

Kris frowned. "Yes, I suppose you'd best not use it for a while. If you break one ley-line, the Villains will find you in a heartbeat. So what will you do instead, once we reach your home?" She curled up at Cyrus's right side.

"*Our* home, Kris," Cyrus said, hugging her. "You're going to live there too. Oh, I don't know. Odd jobs, maybe." He gave the ship's hull a faraway stare. "Anything as long as it's not fishing."

Kris nuzzled him, a smile on her face. "Why not fishing? Don't you like to fi—"

The boat lurched to one side as if it had been pummeled by an enormous wave. A barrel pulled loose of the overhead nettings, smashing open and spilling clothes everywhere.

Kris clutched her stomach and moaned. "Remind me, if I ever foolishly dream of traveling again, that I despise the sea."

Cyrus staggered to his feet as the boat shuddered again. "That wasn't normal, not even for a storm. I'll be right back," he told Kris, and started climbing the suddenly unsteady stairs up to the deck.

"Well, give them another ssshake, then," ordered the captain of the *Windslasher*. The wind blew his oiled cloak around the scales covering his legs and tugged mercilessly at the peacock feather in his tricorner hat. "Let usss sssee if we cannot wake up the sssleeping Heroesss."

"Aye, sir," the gunnery sergeant said with a salute. The fat reptile looked as if he'd be more at home terrorizing a meat pie shop than on the deck of a ship. "All right, you two. Give that boat another wallop," he barked at two pale-skinned Humans who stood on either side of a deck-mounted device, a silvery bracket containing a head-sized spheroid of multifaceted crystal.

Dozens of crewmen ran about on the decks of the black-sailed corsair vessel. The overwhelming majority of them were Ransha, lizard-folk of the coastal variety. They growled and paced back and forth on the rain-slicked deck.

The rain fell sideways in the storm as one of the Humans standing at the silvery device shook his head. "This is a tool," he said, "not a weapon."

"I don't care if it'ssss your great-grandmother's underclothessss, you're going to use it to give that ship another wallop!" the sergeant shouted in the pale man's face, pointing at the ship that pitched and rolled not a furlong from them on the rough waves.

"Sssergeant, I think you've misunderssstood our guesssts," the captain hissed, his fangs showing from beneath his scaled lip. Captain Vesuvius Ypsilon smiled. His reputation might be that of the most infamous and merciless Ranshan corsair to ever sail the Five Seas, but he did know when to use tact rather than force. "We do not asssk that you use your devissse for attack," he said, his tongue flickering in and out of his mouth. "What we need isss for you gentlemen to gently lift the other boat, and then carefully drop it again. They mussst know that we mean businesss."

The pale man nodded. "I believe that I understand you," he replied, glaring at the sergeant.

The sergeant shrank back. The pale man's eyes were uncanny, as colorless as his skin. Muttering something about checking the ballistae, he scuttled down to the lower deck.

The two pale men returned to their crystal and placed their white hands upon the orb. Closing their eyes, they moved their hands about on the surface of the crystal. It glowed brilliantly for a moment, but it went out as they raised their hands. The other boat shuddered, and lifted itself partially clear of the water before slamming back into the choppy sea.

Vesuvius smiled, the wind and frigid rain billowing his oiled black sea-cloak about him. There was nothing in the world like a storm at sea to chill you through your scales and make you feel alive. Unless you could be in a storm at sea and feel the warm blood of your foes trickle through your claws at the same time. Now *that* was truly living.

And Vesuvius hoped to be truly living very soon . . .

Cyrus tumbled across the deck as the ship slammed back into the sea. Something was most definitely wrong. They had either hit a whale, or . . .

"Solburg! Thank the gods!" yelled the captain, salt water dripping from his beard, which was stained and brown. "Get some of those layabout 'Eroes out here. There's a military boat of some kind come alongside, and it's most definitely 'ostile!"

"Military?" Cyrus asked, clutching a rail for support and staring across the furlong of water at the looming vessel. It was almost twice their size, and judging from the number of ballista ports in the sides, it was hardly a merchantman. "What device are they flying?"

"Two flags," the captain replied, peering through the rain at the unidentified vessel's mast. The sky above was a thunderous black, tinged with orange and red, presumably from the setting sun above them. "One's a fanged red skull on black. The other looks like a gauntlet with somm'at in it."

Cyrus shook his head. "*Bok* in a bucket. It's one of Voshtyr's ships. I'll go get whatever Heroes are in fighting shape. Try to contact their captain and see what he wants. And *don't* tell him there are Heroes on board, or they might sink us."

"Aye, lad. That was me intention. Now, stop givin' orders to yer captain, and get them 'Eroes out 'ere, just in case."

Cyrus nodded and ducked back down the hatch to the common room.

Within minutes, he returned with five Heroes, sallow-eyed and grim. The Swift Strike, a Human male in his early thirties, held a matched set of longswords, one shattered beyond repair. His tight, stretchy purple costume had rents in it where more than one attack from a Villain had gotten through. Beside him stood an Orc in armored robes, the Burning Sky, listlessly rolling a tiny ball of magic flame between his hands. Behind the two of them stood a female Elf in a breastplate and a dented holy emblem of Brian, the god of beauty, around her neck. Blond twins, a male and a female Human known wide but not far as the Gold Star and the Silver Star, backed the group with an oversized axe and a gargantuan shield, respectively.

"These are the only ones with any fighting spirit left in them," Cyrus told the captain.

The captain snorted. "They'll 'ave to do, then, won't they?" He turned back to the railing and raised his speaking trumpet. "Ahoy the man-o-war! Steer clear of our ship! We've armed 'Eroes aboard!"

Cyrus knocked the speaking trumpet from the captain's mouth. "Hey! Didn't I just say not to tell them that? The whole reason we're on this boat is to get away and hide! We can't do that if you tell people we're on board."

The captain glared at Cyrus, and picked up his speaking trumpet. "Don't tell me what to do, boy, and don't touch me tools. I'd gladly sacrifice every 'Ero on board if it came to a choice between them and me ship." He turned from Cyrus and hailed the other ship once more. "Ahoy the man-o-war!"

• • •

"Captain, the fat one is shouting at us," the leftenant remarked.

"Oh, isss he?" Vesuvius hissed, flicking his forked tongue in and out. "Well, what isss it that he isss ssshouting?"

The leftenant shrugged. "Just something about how they've Heroes on board and how we'd best bugger off."

"That iss mossst unfortunate," Vesuvius said. He handed his assistant a longbow. "Give the man something to ssshout about, Leftenant."

The leftenant nodded and took the weapon from his captain. He drew the bowstring and aimed for the portly, bearded man on the opposite ship's deck.

"I don't think they're going to respond to us," the bearded captain of the refugee ship said, pushing his hood back from his face.

His first mate shrugged. "Chances are, they're just here to kill all of us and take whatever valuables we have."

At that moment, an arrow took the grizzled captain in the shoulder. "Nine Torments!" he shouted, losing his footing and collapsing to the deck. "What the blazes . . . ?"

There was a note attached to the shaft. Cyrus snatched up the note, which read thus:

> To the Captain of the Vessel alongside us:
> Please heave to and prepare to deliver over all Heroes you may have in your possession at this time.
> Cordially,
> Captain Vesuvius "the Violent" Ypsilon

Cyrus snorted. "I think it's for you, Captain," he said in disgust. "All right, gentlemen, listen up!" he said to the handful of Heroes who had come up on deck. "The other ship has nothing for us but a load of hurt. I say we board them first. Anyone with me?"

"You're insane, boy!" the captain said, yanking the arrow from his shoulder. "That's Vesuvius the Violent, a fearsome pirate if there ever was one! Discretion be the better part of valor concerning that one. We can outrun them if you'll give the ol' ship a chance!"

"Oh, really?" Cyrus said, glaring at the captain's bleeding shoulder. "I was under the impression that you'd sacrifice every Hero on the boat if it'd save your blubbery hide. Here's a better idea: you get us within boarding range, and we'll take care of this problem. Come on, fellows. Let's teach this pirate a thing or three."

"I thinks ve can handle it," the Burning Sky said, allowing his pet ball of flame to flare up a bit. His tusks showed as he grinned. "Ships is made of woods, and woods burn."

"Not so much in the rain." The Swift Strike sheathed the half of a sword and brandished his remaining blade. "But if we keep them off the deck, we'll stand a better chance at getting away."

Cyrus nodded. "You're probably right. You two, the Stars, get grapples ready. Swift, take the center. And Elf priestess, you keep everyone alive while our magic Orc tries to set their boat on fire."

There was silence for a moment.

Cyrus looked confused. "Okay, listen. I know I'm not a commander, and I'm not even a full-fledged Hero yet, but do you have any better ideas?"

The Heroes shook their heads.

"All right, then," Cyrus said. The rain collecting in his hair dribbled down across the tears in his tunic. "You get that ready. I'll be back here just as soon as I make sure things are all right belowdecks." With that, he ducked back down the hatch.

Kris greeted him at the bottom of the stairs. "What's going on?"

"Looks like one of Voshtyr's warships," Cyrus said. "The other Heroes and I are going to try and hold them off. You stay down here, all right?"

Kris frowned. "But I can fight too. You bought me that shield because you wanted it to be *useful*, remember?"

"I know you can fight, Kris," Cyrus said. "You're a brave warrior of the Kath Sul. But as good as you are, you're not Hero caliber. Besides, you'll do better down here at the choke point." He gestured at the stairway. "In case any of them manage to board and get past the Heroes, you can defend the rest of the passengers from here."

Kris growled, but nodded. "Oh kay. If you say so. But you shout if you get into trouble, all right?"

Cyrus hugged Kris. "All right. And then you can rush in and save my scrawny hide." He let go and stepped back. "Now, I gotta get back up there before the fighting starts." Cyrus started up the stairs, then turned back for a moment. "Hey, Kris?"

"Yes?"

"You know I love you, right?"

"Absolutely."

Cyrus smiled. "Awesome. See you when we're safe." He skipped stairs on the way back up, and arrived just in time to see the refugee ship veer toward the corsair vessel. The Heroes readied grappling hooks as the boat drew nearer. "Brace for impact!" Cyrus shouted down the hatch to the frightened passengers.

The refugee ship indeed veered, but instead of a cataclysmic crash, the ship shuddered and slowed to a halt.

"What in the Black Plains is going on?" Cyrus demanded.

What was going on was the concerted effort of the two pale men on the corsair ship as they hovered over the large crystal. "The fools keep trying to ram us with that tub of theirs," one of them said with exasperation, sweat mingling with rain on his forehead.

"Well, let them get clossse," Vesuvius said calmly, "but keep them from damaging my ssship. If the Heroesss want to throw away their livesss, we'll let them!" Raising his voice, he shouted to his Ranshan crew, who were all armed to the teeth and scaled to the tails. "If the Heroesss want a fight, we'll give them one. Aye, ladsss?"

The crew roared and hissed in agreement and promptly began to sing. Fourscore hearty lizards with their rough, throaty voices, stomped their scaled feet and thumped their heavy tails on the deck.

> Pirates Stamp and Pirates Tromp
>   Pirates Dance the Pirate Stomp
> Feel the beat upon the Decks
>   And go to break our Victims' Necks
> Hey, Ho! Hey, Ho! Hey Ho Harrr

We're Pirates and Ransha
    Most Feasome of Races
Give in, for we've Gotcha
    All Hands to the Braces!
Hey, Ho! Hey, Ho! Hey Ho Harrr!

See the Glinting of our Scales
    Hear the Thumping of our Tails
Feel the Pain of Fang and Claw
    Taste the salty Ocean's Maw!
Hey, Ho! Hey, Ho! Hey Ho Harrr

Fire Ballistae!
    Keep Steady the Rudder!
On Target with all, aye?
    So fire another!
Hey, Ho! Hey, Ho! Hey Ho Harr!

We bring you Death, We bring you Doom
    The salty Sea will be your Tomb
No mercy, no quarter, dead to the last man
    So Run! Give in! Give up while you can!
Hey, Ho! Hey, Ho! Hey Ho Harr

The lives that we've taken
    The treasure we've hoarded
Resolve never Shaken
    Stand by to be Boarded!
Hey, Ho! Hey, Ho! Hey Ho HARRR!!!

With that, the scaled pirates threw grappling hooks into the Heroes' ship's rigging, and swung across the gap between ships with roars of reptilian glee.

The Heroes promptly abandoned their own grappling hooks and readied their weapons.

"What's with the singing?" one of the Heroes said, watching the Ransha dance about. "Is it a battle cry or something?"

"All pirates all'ays be a singin' an' a dancin'," said an older sailor with one blind eye and a scar on his left cheek. His wooden clog tapped the deck in time with the Ranshan battle song. "That just be the way they do things."

The first wave of Ransha, five or six of the scaled humanoids, swung out on their ropes. With a roar they landed on the deck in front of the stalwart men.

That roar was all they had time to do. With grace born of years of training and strength born of being Heroes, Cyrus and the other six men and women on the deck slew the intruding lizards, staining the merchantman's deck with their black blood.

"All right, now they know what we're made of!" Cyrus shouted. "It's just going to get messy from here. Let's keep them off the boat this time!"

His companions nodded grimly.

"We're not going to do much by ourselves," the Swift Strike said. "If only the captain of this ship wasn't such a coward, or even if I had another longsword . . ."

"Here's one." The ship's cabin boy offered a plain grey longsword to the Swift Strike. He was very young, perhaps twelve years old, but Cyrus could see the excitement and hope in his eyes.

The Swift Strike nodded. "Thank you, boy. At least there are still some stout hearts on this vessel."

"More than ye'd think, actually," said the old sailor with the wooden clogs and single eye. Several more sailors stepped forward in ranks between the Heroes, wielding boathooks and oars.

Cyrus smiled grimly. "Great. Looks like we might stand half a chance after all."

The one-eyed sailor chuckled darkly. "Aye, sir. Takes more than a few swashbucklin' lizards ta scare me."

"Glad to hear it," Cyrus replied, rainwater dripping off his nose. "Look out! Here's the next wave!"

The second wave of Ransha swung over the railing, but the hardy sailors of the merchant vessel stepped forward and braced their assorted weapons.

Oversized lizards slammed into the oars and boathooks and fell flailing into the sea. But there were simply too many for the few sailors to deal with, for then the third wave landed. Then the battle truly commenced. Seven Heroes and fewer than a dozen seamen faced over fourscore trained and armed Ranshan warriors, and the victor was anything but certain.

In case the reader is unfamiliar with the Race of Ransha, he should probably both read the following section and avoid swamps. That is, unless the reader has a death wish involving being consumed raw by tribal lizard-folk, in which case nothing written in this book will help, and it is recommended that the reader rub lemon pepper and garlic on themselves before entering said swamp.

Ransha are the second-least human-looking of the Nine Races. The only similarity lies in the placement of head and limbs in relation to the torso and the general shape of the torso itself. There, all resemblance ends. Ransha have broad, wedge-shaped heads, dominated by a mouthful of fangs that put sharks to shame. Their eyes are most often pale colors and are protected by transparent scales.

There are two common and distinct breeds of these curious lizard-folk: the swamp-dwelling hunter/gatherers of Centra Mundi and Lorimar, and the coastal ocean-fishers that live scattered around the beaches of all continents save Novania, which is too frigid for cold-blooded creatures. The only differences between the two are that the saltwater Ransha have webbing between their toes and lack hind claws, while the landlocked lizards lack gills, but can walk on dry land with much greater ease.

There is another, rarer breed of Ransha, the Darkfang Ransha, a particular subspecies bred and raised in captivity by the Hereditary Evil Empire. They are bred as heavy troopers for the Army of Darkness™, and it is said that any two of them working together are almost a match for a Hero. They are like the swamp Ransha, but they have denser black scales, are larger and stronger, and are reportedly dumber than a stack of bricks.

In general, Ransha physique is unlike that of Humans. None of the vital organs are where one might expect them to be, and their musculature is entirely different. Ransha have special muscles designed for grace and speed while swimming and for their heavy tails, which narrow out to a point for swamp-dwelling Ransa and terminate in a flared fin for their oceanic cousins.

But above all, the Ransha's greatest strength lies in his scales. The scales of an adult Ransha rival those of dragons in toughness and impenetrability, while still remaining supple and flexible. Thus the hardy lizard-folk are more than a little difficult to kill, as a common weapon is of limited use against them. Fortunately for the other Races, most Ransha are more or less uninterested in conquest and tend to stay in their native areas revering the elderly and their ancestors.

But not all of them keep to their scaled selves. Vesuvius Ypsilon, called Vesuvius the Violent for his fearsome berserk fury, was a Ransha well-trained in arms and leadership. With his hardy crew at his back, Vesuvius styled himself "Lord of the Southern Waves," referring to the expanse of ocean between Centra Mundi and Salvinsel. And now that the opportunity to expand his territory even further had arisen, he had conquest on his mind.

Cyrus swore in frustration as his borrowed sword struck one of the pirates' scaly shoulders and glanced off. The none-too-clever Ransha lashed out at the young Hero again, but Cyrus dodged under it, seizing the flailing lizard and heaving him bodily into the sea.

The other Heroes were hardly having better luck. Only those with an Enchanted Blade or better were doing any real damage. More Ransha swung onto the boat every moment. The Heroes would be swamped in their foes in another three minutes.

"Captain!" Cyrus shouted. "Take us out of boarding range!"

The merchantman's captain scowled as he held bandages against his shoulder. "First you want me to close with 'em, and now you want to back off? Make up your mind, ye indecisive fool!"

"Just get us away from them," Cyrus snapped. "I paid fare for two to Starspeak, and I don't mean to arrive there as a corpse."

The captain grumbled, but he put his weatherworn hands back on the wheel and tried to veer away from the enemy vessel. The wheel would not budge. "What devilry is this?" he said, scratching his soaked brown hair. "Wheel's stuck!"

"No, it isn't. Look!" said one of the other Heroes, pointing across to the other ship. Two men stood around a large glowing gemstone on the pirates' deck. "Mages!"

The Captain spat on the deck. "Mages got no place on a ship. 'S not a good sign."

Cyrus gritted his teeth. "All right. Captain, I'm going over there to interrupt whatever they're doing. As soon as you feel the spell break, veer away. I'll get back on board as best I can."

The Captain scowled, but nodded. "Go on then, Solburg. Gods be with ye."

"Yeah," Cyrus said with a half smile. "I think He is."

Cyrus wasted no time in rushing to the forefront of the fight, slashing at the thick-scaled reptiles with his borrowed sword. Unfortunately, the cheap longsword snapped after the twelfth blow. Thanks to Cyrus's ill-timed weapon breakage, a Ranshan pirate was atop him with an axe before he could react. Cyrus threw his arms up to protect himself, but help appeared from an unlikely source.

"*Dime of the Ancient Mariner!*" shouted the one-eyed sailor, throwing a silver piece at the offending Ransha. The coin spun faster than any object had a right to, and crackled with electricity as it smacked into the lizard's head. The jolt threw the Ransha off-balance and off-guard, allowing Cyrus the opportunity to relieve him of his axe and kick him overboard.

"Thanks!" Cyrus said, then threw his newly-acquired axe over the old sailor's head, catching a sneaky Ransha in the chest with it. The lizard flew backward, skidding across the deck and leaving a streak of black blood on the planks. "Where'd you learn that trick?"

The sailor shrugged. "Spend enough time becalmed, and you'll take tiddlywinks to an extreme too."

Cyrus laughed. "I'll try to avoid that, thanks. What's your name, sailor?"

"You do that," chuckled the sailor. "And thanks fer the save. Me name's B—"

At that moment, a Ranshan pirate let go of his rope, rolled across the deck, and came up with the points of a wickedly-barbed trident through the old sailor's chest. The sailor coughed once, and gave Cyrus a wry smile before falling to the deck.

"No!" Cyrus shouted. "He was about to tell me his name! He could have become a recurring character!"

The Ransha shrugged and tried to pull the barbed trident free of the man's back. It was just a little stuck.

Cyrus's face flushed with rage. He picked up the old sailor's boathook and swung it with all his might.

The Ransha realized a little too late that barbed weapons were probably not the best thing to use in close combat. The boat hook, swung with such strength behind it, penetrated scale and muscle, sinking deeply into the Ransha's shoulderblade.

The Ransha roared in pain, but had no time to react as Cyrus spun, hook firmly embedded in the lizard's shoulder, and heaved the boat hook, Ransha and all, into the sea like a throwing-hammer.

The young Hero's face was now set. It was time to get out of here before anyone else died.

"Thossse Heroesss are very ressssiliant, are they not?" Vesuvius said, leaning on the railing of his ship, watching the ongoing fight through a wrought-gold spyglass. "It almossst ssseemsss a ssshame to kill them."

"Speak for yerself, Cap'n," the leftenant said, picking his fangs with the tip of a dagger. "I'd as soon see 'em dead and at the ocean's bottom than keep 'em in our brig for that Voshtyr fellow."

"And misss out on a thousssand-gold-per-man bounty for live capture?" Vesuvius said, scoldingly. "You're thinking with your clawsss again, not your brainsss."

"Which is why you's the Cap'n, and I jes' helps kills things," the leftenant said lazily. "We going to break up their bitty ship now, or jes' keep sending our boys over?"

"Give the boysss another five minutesss of fun, and then we'll sssink their sship."

Just then, the leftenant spotted a patch of flame-red hair working its way through the melee, drawing nearer and nearer to the side of the merchantman. "Sir," he said calmly, "it looks like our bonus is about to come to us."

Vesuvius looked over the side, spotting the young Hero as he made his way through the Ransha pirates. "Excellent," the

Ransha said, rubbing his claws together. "Let him aboard, then dessstroy the other vesssel."

Another Ransha swung across the gap between the two vessels, intent on wreaking havoc. His havoc remained unwrought, though, as the moment he crossed the gunwale onto the merchant ship, Cyrus stepped forward and thrust his palm upward into the pirate's jaw. The Ransha fell to the planks, neck snapped, twitching slightly.

Cyrus took hold of the rope, and pushed himself off the ship. The wind whistled around him as he swung through the air, the chill rain stinging his face.

And then he was on the deck of the opposing ship. Cyrus let go of the rope and slid across the wet planks, knocking down one of his scaled antagonists and stealing his weapon, a flat-topped, wave-bladed sword.

Then his foes were atop him. Cyrus lashed out in all directions as Ranshan pirates stabbed at him with pikes and blades, trying to find a gap in his guard.

I can't use my magic, or they'll know who I am, Cyrus thought as he embedded his blade in an opponent's skull, then spun and used the corpse to block an incoming spear. *But it sure would be handy right about now if I could . . .*

"Cyrusss Sssolburg!" someone bellowed from across the ship.

Cyrus kicked another pirate over the railing, then looked across the deck. A Ransha head and shoulders taller than the rest dressed in an oiled cloak and a magnificent tricorner hat stood on the opposite deck, pointing a cutlass at him. His scales gleamed dull silver in the frenzied patches of light cast by the ship's lanterns, and a thick tail with a flared fin stuck out the back of his cloak.

"Cyrusss Sssolburg!" the lizard repeated. "How nice of you to join me on my fine vesssel!"

"Couldn't help coming over," Cyrus said, catching the wrist of his current opponent and throwing him over his shoulder to knock down three more. "You keep rocking mine, and I came over to ask you to stop. You're making my mate seasick."

The large Ransha chuckled. "A sssenssse of humor even on the cusssp of defeat? You are a rare man, Sssolburg. A pity we mussst deliver you to our employer."

Cyrus blinked. Wait a moment, this Ransha knew who he was. He grinned. That meant he could use his magic without giving anything away. Cyrus reached into the sky, and snapped off the leading end of a conveniently-placed ley-line.

Thunderstorms are a naturally occurring phenomenon, both in Cyrus's world and in the reader's. But in a world where magic is part of the natural order of things, sometimes even a natural phenomenon can do something supernatural. In the case of a Thunderstorm, rather than a regular storm, cloud burst, or rain shower, the air becomes highly charged with elemental Air, as well as rain and lightning. If a mage is expecting such a boost in power, he or she can use it to devastating effect. If he is not, however, unexpected boosts in power can lead to odd consequences.

Cyrus was not expecting it.

• • •

The bolt of lightning Cyrus pulled from the sky was several orders of magnitude larger than he had been expecting. It struck him and split, scattering into a dozen smaller bolts that struck the Ransha surrounding him, blasting them off the deck or slaying them outright.

It also wiped Cyrus from the deck, or, rather, through it.

"By the Ssseven!" the Ransha swore. "Leftenant! Find the Hero!"

"I'm right here," Cyrus said, crawling out of the smoking hole in the deck. The bolt had knocked him down into the ship's interior. He felt his hair steaming from the contact with the heated air around the bolt.

He saw that he'd caused quite a bit of damage. More than he'd meant to, actually. The lightning bolt had punched him through three of the ship's six decks and charred twenty feet of planking in every direction around the hole. A half-dozen twitching Ransha lay outside the blast radius, their electrocuted spasms made worse by the pouring rain. To add a Cherry of Malevolence to the Cake of Destruction, a portion of the blast had even put a crack in the vessel's main mast.

Cyrus climbed the rest of the way out and stretched his arms and neck. "Now what were you saying about your employer?"

"Ah, in good time, Sssolburg," the Ransha said. "Firssst, allow me to introduce myssself. I am Vesssuviusss Ypsssilon, Ssscourge of the Ssseven Ssseasss."

"Takes a lot of time and hissing to spit that out, doesn't it?"

"'Tisss worth it for a proper title," Vesuvius said, planting his clawed feet squarely on the deck. "Now, I have ordersss from

Vossshtyr Demonkin to bring you in alive. I would humbly asssk that you not resssissst to the point of mortal injury."

Cyrus groaned. "Wonderful. When is that half-demon going to give up? He's becoming a grand pain in the posterior."

"I've no idea," Vesuvius replied. "All I know isss that I mussst deliver you. Now fight me!"

"If you insist," Cyrus said with a shrug. He launched himself at Vesuvius in a flying leap across the ship.

Vesuvius met him more than halfway with a leap of Heroic proportions himself, and with his heftier weight, he bore Cyrus straight down to the deck, splintering planks as they landed.

The Ranshan Captain wrapped his clawed hand around Cyrus's right wrist and slammed his hand against the decking. Simultaneously, he opened his fanged maw and snapped at Cyrus's face.

Cyrus cried out in pain as the shattered wood penetrated the back of his hand, causing him to lose his grip on his sword. The wave-bladed weapon skittered across the planks and fell off the side of the ship.

It hurt. Cyrus's hand throbbed like it had just been stung by a Plague Hornet, but without the swelling and painful death. Not that there was any less pain, thanks to the salt spray of the storm stinging the wound, or any less chance of death because of the scaled pirate about to gnaw his face off.

Cyrus's left hand closed around another piece of splintered wood. An improvised weapon was better than none. "Get off!" he yelled as he swung the plank with all his Heroic might.

The plank cracked in half over Vesuvius's skull and knocked the reptile clear across the deck.

Cyrus stepped out of the shattered wood crater in the deck and planted his feet squarely on the solid planks. In a flash, a hazy halo of mist coalesced around him as he discovered the Water ley-line running beneath the boat. "All right, Scales," he said, calmly making a *Come on* gesture with his bleeding hand. "Have at ye."

Vesuvius snarled, losing all of the civil façade he had maintained earlier, and sprang at Cyrus once more.

Pure, cold energy filled Cyrus, and he thrust a hand forward. With the roar of torrential currents, sparkling water burst from his palm at high pressure, checking Vesuvius's leap and knocking him back to the deck again.

Cyrus's fight was not the only piece of action on the decks of the two ships. Ransha from the corsair vessel had managed to slam down a boarding plank between the two ships and were charging over it to overwhelm the defending Heroes and the stalwart sailors. Other reptilian pirates swung over the lines of defense on grappling hooks to attack from the rear. The Heroes were individually more than a match for any five Ransha, but the ratio was much steeper than five-to-one. The battle was not going well.

"Ssso it isss true," Vesuvius said as he picked his sodden self up from the planks. "Magicsss without control, without finesse. I can defeat you with a sssingle ssspell, Sssolburg." He pulled an oiled vellum scroll from his belt and muttered an incantation off it.

Cyrus felt the tension in the ley-lines build, specifically the second Air line a mile distant. He understood somehow that it was a spell designed to block his access to magic.

Cyrus reached up and swatted the energy away from the partially formed spell. The spell fizzled and collapsed without the power to hold itself up.

Vesuvius blinked. "What wasss . . . ?"

The Ransha finished neither his sentence nor his spell, as Cyrus spun on a heel and kicked Vesuvius in the side of the head. Vesuvius crashed to the deck. The rain beat down on his oilskin as he pushed himself up on his arms and tried to look back at Cyrus, but by that time, Cyrus had him by the tail.

"And now," Cyrus said, "I'm going to do you one favor." He began twirling, Vesuvius held in his grasp like a throwing hammer. "I'm going to give you a flying lesson."

"Graah! Release me!"

"Oh, fine, if you insist," Cyrus said, letting go of the Ransha's tail.

Vesuvius rocketed across the deck and crashed into the mast, shivering the base of the already damaged timber into toothpicks. The entire mast teetered crazily for a moment then fell to the port side of the boat.

"Lesson one. Don't land on anything harder than you are," Cyrus said with a sad shake of his sodden skull.

"'E took down the Cap'n!" someone yelled through the hammer of the rain on the deck and the residual rumbles of the toppled mast.

Cyrus whirled to see where the voice had come from.

On the aft deck stood a grizzled human pirate and two tall, pale men, standing around a large chunk of what looked like a glowing diamond. The crystal rested in a silver frame wrought into the shape of a thousand malevolent eyes and distorted hands.

"Kill that *pic!*" the pirate yelled.

"No," said one of the men. "Voshtyr wants him alive. Besides, this is a tool, not a weapon."

"*Agzina sicayim*, you albino *pic!*" the pirate swore. "If you won't do it, I will!" He reached out and slapped his palm onto the diamond's surface.

"*No!* Don't touch—" the pale men yelled in unison, but it was too late.

The pirate's face registered first shock, then intense pain as he screamed aloud into the storm. He turned his wild-eyed gaze on Cyrus.

A blow like a Titan's hammer smashed into Cyrus's stomach, sending him hurtling across the deck, through the guard railing, across the gap of choppy water, and through the planks of the ship he'd started out on. His body punched a hole near the waterline. When the ship rolled back to starboard again, the boat began taking water.

"Stop this madman, quickly," said one of the pale men. He gestured at the wide-eyed and gibbering pirate sergeant. The light from the crystal blistered the sergeant's hands, but he seemed unable to let go of it.

"I cannot," replied the other, looking into the pirate's twisted face. "His mind has broken. If I touch it now, he may harm my mind as well."

"*I'll kill all of 'em!*" the sergeant yelled, choking as the veins in his face and neck began to stand out. "*GrraAAAH!*"

Three things happened simultaneously. First, hairline fissures appeared like a spiderweb across the surface of the oversized diamond device, prompting looks of horror on the faces of both the pale men. Second, the ship bearing the Heroes shuddered, and with a splintering crack, rent itself in half, spilling men and cargo into the stormy water. Last, the sergeant's eyes went from wide-eyed fear and fury to frozen open and so bloodshot that there was no white visible in them.

The sergeant gurgled something incoherent and slumped to the deck, blood oozing from his tear ducts.

The fissures in the diamond spread farther, turning the transparent crystal opaque. Both the pale men ran to the sides of the ship and dove off just as the crystal shattered in an eruption of light, sending sharp fragments tearing through the crew of the pirate vessel and punching a hole clear through the hull. Water gushed from the hole and broke through the other section of hull where Cyrus's bolt of lightning had weakened it earlier.

The merchantman ship sank . . . followed immediately by the pirate ship.

Kris shrieked as the impact of a heavy projectile rocked the boat.

"We're taking water!" a sailor yelled as he ran through the passenger hold. "Everyone grab a flotation device!"

Kris latched her claws into one of the crates that had come loose during the repeated battering of the merchant vessel, and she held on tight.

The ship split in half a few handspans from her. The deck tilted downward at a crazy angle, and the crate to which Kris clung slid across it and plummeted into the sea, Katheni girl still attached.

The water was cold, shockingly cold, mind-numbingly cold, like a frost spell designed specifically to lower body temperature, such as *Induce Hypothermia*. Kris spat out the frigid saltwater and sunk her claws further into the wood, hanging on for her life.

"Kris!"

Kris's ears barely picked up the shout as they swiveled toward the sound. She turned her head to see who had yelled.

Cyrus swam toward her, pushing a damaged life raft. "Get in and raise the tarp!" he shouted.

Kris released her grasp on the crate and struck out across the waves toward the boat. Reaching it, she clambered inside and began setting up the foul-weather shelter included with most life rafts.

Cyrus heaved himself in beside her and lay on his back, breathing heavily as the rain pounded down on his face.

The lifeboat was no more than twenty feet long and five feet wide. It was more like a longboat than a lifeboat, but it had a collapsible tarpaulin over the stern for bad weather and a footlocker helpfully but unimaginatively labeled TOOLS in large red letters. Beside it was another locker labeled, just as bluntly, FOOD. Water two inches deep covered the floor and was seeping in from somewhere Kris couldn't see. Its surface rippled constantly from the pounding rain and rocked off the boat in the waves.

Cyrus looked like he'd been drowned, smacked with a gigantic meat tenderizer, run through a laundry wringer, set on fire, drowned again, and then used as ballista ammunition. "Are you all right?" Kris asked worriedly.

Cyrus shook his head. "No," he groaned. "I just got punted through the side of the ship. My back hurts like the Ninth Torment."

"Here, let me get this set up," Kris said, looping a bit of rope about the gunwale of the boat to secure the tarpaulin before kneeling down next to her mate. "Can you move to under the shelter?"

"No, I need to—agh, my spine—I need to help the others." Cyrus pushed himself up to look out over the water. "I can't even see most of them from here. Can you steer toward the wreckage?"

"No," Kris said. "I think the steering thing is broken." She pulled on the wooden handle at the back of the boat. It did nothing to change their direction or alignment.

"It's a rudder, Kris, and it doesn't work if there's nothing pushing the boat forward," Cyrus said. "I'd row, but I don't know if I can even sit up straight."

"But . . ." Kris looked over the right side of the lifeboat. "Well, I hope the crew will be all right. I mean, I saw other lifeboats out there."

Cyrus slumped back into the boat, sloshing into the water collecting at the bottom.

He nodded, then winced. "Yes, but we have to plug the hole in the back end," he said, gesturing to the stern of the boat. "It's starting to fill up already."

Indeed, water was leaking into the boat every time it rocked to port, from a splintered plank just above the waterline.

"How do you patch a boat?" Kris asked. "I don't do boats, remember?"

Cyrus struggled to one elbow and turned his head to look at the leak. "I can fix it with a mallet and bit of tarp," he said. "Help me up, and I'll get it."

Kris pulled Cyrus up to his feet. He gasped, obviously in pain.

"Sheesh," Cyrus said. "My boat is leaking, my back is broken, and I'm using a half-drowned cat as a crutch."

"Keep up that kind of talk and I'm throwing you back in the water," Kris said. She helped Cyrus over to the box labeled TOOLS. "What do you need?"

"A mallet, some nails, and a tarp."

Kris dug around in the appropriately labeled box, and moments later came up with a steel-capped wooden mallet and a box of spikes. "Will these do?"

Cyrus nodded. "Perfect. Is there a bit of spare tarp and some rope in there too?"

"Here," Kris said, handing a folded patch of tarpaulin and a coil of hemp rope to Cyrus. "But you're patching the boat, not making a sail. What do you need with the tarp?"

"Ever had the hull cut out from under you by a Pyrradorsal?" Cyrus asked, threading the rope through eye-loops on the four corners of the tarpaulin.

"No, what's that?" Kris asked, kneeling, then sitting atop her legs. "A Villain device?"

Cyrus chuckled. "No, it's a fish. And don't you go licking your lips over that," he said, pointing at Kris, who retracted her tongue. "They're a real *kaltak* to bring in, and they kill a lot of people." He handed two of the rope ends to Kris and dropped the tarp into the water. "A Pyrradorsal's a big fish with a blade ridge growing out of its back and one longer one on the tip of its snout. They can shred a shark in a split second."

Kris giggled. "Your fascinating fish is all alliteration."

"Har har," Cyrus said, giving Kris his *I am not amused* expression. "Hang on, I need to get that rope." He dove into the cold water again. He resurfaced shortly with the two other rope ends in his hand.

"Oh, I get it," Kris said, looking at the water in the bottom of the boat. "If you put the tarp on the outside, the water will be pushing on the tarp from the outside, holding it on, and less water will get in!"

"Right on the m-money," Cyrus said, his teeth chattering from the cold. He clambered back into the boat, grimacing as he had to bend his back again. "It s-should l-leak s-slower n-now."

Kris frowned as she sat under the tarp of the weather shelter and watched Cyrus tie the ropes to the gunwales to keep the makeshift patch in place. "So, you've done this because of a Pyrradorsal before?"

Cyrus nodded. "Yeah. One g-got Uncle J-jacob's boat once, and he h-had to t-teach me real f-fast."

After Cyrus finished securing the patch, he climbed beneath the shelter and sat down with his head resting on his knees.

Kris scooted over next to him and began rubbing his back, shoulders, and arms vigorously to restore circulation. Cyrus merely mumbled something, a dazed smile on his face as she worked. When she finished, Kris wrapped herself around Cyrus's back.

There they sat for a time as the rain became a true storm and raged against the outside of the shelter. Cyrus fell asleep in Kris's arms. She smiled. She might not have been the one leaping over to the enemy vessel to sink it, but it was nice to know that she could still do some things for her beloved Hero.

Chapter 2

PURIFIRE

In which Cyrus and Kris Make Landfall and Meet a Wise Old Man

CYRUS WOKE TO three sensations. First, his back hurt like the Ninth Torment. Well, scratch that, it had hurt like the Ninth yesterday. If there were ten Torments, this would have hurt like the tenth. Or maybe it was just the stiffness that accompanied the pain. Either way, the ache in his back was hardly pleasant.

Second, although he wasn't entirely dry, he was warm. This was probably thanks mostly to Kris, who lay beside him on their makeshift bed of sailcloth salvaged from the TOOLS bin. The Kath still had her arms wrapped about him, and her head lay on Cyrus's chest. Cyrus smiled. He could get used to this. And probably would eventually.

But third, the familiar sound of surf reached Cyrus's ears. The sound of waves rolling up and crashing onto a sandy beach was all around them. He frowned. Surf meant land. And land meant that, well, they had landed in the night.

Cyrus kissed Kris gently on the nose. She stirred with a puzzled "mrr?"

"We hit land, Kris," Cyrus said, poking his head out of the shelter to see where they were.

Before him lay the beach of a tropical island. Sparkling white sand reflected the morning sun in a dazzling display of light. A thick cluster of palm trees rose from the low horizon, along with a single magnificent mountain peak of red stone. This sure wasn't Starspeak. Strangely absent were the cries of seagulls. Instead, Cyrus heard an occasional three-noted warble from somewhere above the boat.

He looked up at the weather tarp above them. It certainly wasn't that making the warbling sound. As Kris sleepily dislodged herself from Cyrus's side, Cyrus stood up and walked out from beneath the shelter. Interestingly, the boat was not just nudging the shore. It was run firmly aground, as if it had been pushed.

Cyrus stepped out onto the warm and grainy sand and looked around. Specifically, he looked up at the soaring spire of solid stone dominating the center of the island. More correctly, it sat off to one side, but the fact remained that it looked like quite the climb, with multiple small caves in the sides and cliffs that looked unattainable from the ground. At the top of the spire was the opening to a cave that looked large enough to provide good shelter, with a group of what looked to Cyrus like some kind of fruit tree growing next to it.

"Spire Island," Cyrus said to no one in particular.

It was a good thing he hadn't been addressing anyone, because the only other person there was Kris, who had just jumped out of the boat and sprinted gleefully across the beach. She appeared to stumble and crashed to the beach in a spray of sand, but she soon came sprinting back. She stopped just shy of pouncing on Cyrus. "Does your back still hurt?" she asked, coyly weaving her fingers together in front of her.

Cyrus shrugged. "Not hurt so much as really stiff. It just— Ack!"

Kris completed her delayed pounce. She lay atop Cyrus and kissed his jawline briefly before sitting up and looking around. "So, where are we?"

"Well, I think this is Spire Island," Cyrus said, sitting up as well, reaching behind him to support his aching back. It had been worth it. "There's only two island chains we could be near. You get one guess which it is."

Kris thought for a moment. "Well, I have no idea, but I would guess Spire Isl—"

At that moment, a reddish-orange bird of prey fluttered down and perched on the gunwale of the lifeboat. A golden tuft of feathers between its eyes flicked about as it bobbed its head and gave a curious three-noted chirrup.

" . . . the Phoenix Islands?" Kris said with a grin.

Cyrus was not so amused. He scooted slowly away from the bird. "Kris," he said softly, not taking his eyes from the bird's, "as gently as you can, get back in the boat."

"Huh?" Kris looked at the red bird then at Cyrus again. "What's wrong?"

"Nothing, if you enjoy being burned to death," Cyrus said, carefully standing. He crossed in front of the boat to take Kris's paw and lead her away from the phoenix. "Phoenixes are very territorial, Kris. We stay off most of the islands because anyone who strays onto them gets burned to a crunchy crisp. Get away from it, please . . ."

The bird chirruped twice, then hopped along the gunwale to rest in front of Kris and Cyrus once more. It gave a scolding whistle and ruffled up its feathers.

'

Cyrus mentally reached out and took hold of a Water line, just in case the bird attacked them.

"I guess it doesn't want us to leave," Kris said, leaning over to get a closer look at the bird.

Cyrus started to speak, but then something unexpected happened.

The phoenix leaned forward with a short whistle and bumped its beak against Kris's nose.

Kris giggled. "He seems friendly enough." She reached out and stroked the bird's tuft of yellow feathers. "Wouldn't he have shot fire at us already if he was going to?"

"Well," Cyrus said, scratching the back of his neck, "honestly, I don't have a clue. I've never actually been in contact with these things before."

"Little Magnus will not harm you," said someone from up the beach.

Cyrus turned his head slowly to the right so as not to spook the phoenix, and he saw an old man strolling down the beach toward them.

The man wore a robe of what looked like old sailcloth decorated with red and gold phoenix feathers. In one of his hands, which were deeply weatherbeaten, he carried a long driftwood staff. His skin was a healthy bronze cut through with a mesh of wrinkles. His eyes were the most remarkable thing about his face. They had neither color nor pupils. It was as if his eyes were nothing but white. Above them rested two of the thickest white eyebrows Cyrus had ever seen. They looked like giant fuzzy caterpillars. His beard matched his eyebrows: thick, bristly, and larger than life.

"Magnus, come," the man said. The phoenix chirruped and flapped over to perch atop the driftwood staff. "So, are you hungry from your trip? Being wrecked at sea tends to give one an appetite."

Cyrus blinked. "How did you know that?"

The man chuckled. "Well, I do not get many visitors here. The birds discourage tourists, you see." He took a few steps closer to Cyrus and extended his hand, far off to Cyrus's left. "Call me Conrad. And welcome to the Phoenix Islands, Cyrus Solburg."

Cyrus stepped over to the left and took Conrad's hand. "Thanks," he said grimly, putting more power into his grip than a normal Human could muster. "How in the Nine Torments do you know who I am?"

"Divine Inspiration," Conrad replied calmly, meeting Cyrus's grip with more than equal force, then easily pulling his hand free. "And the lovely lady must be Kris."

"Pleased to meet you," Kris said warily, giving her paw to Conrad.

Conrad jumped. "Oh, a Katheni! I hadn't anticipated that one. Or should I say I didn't 'see it coming'?" He chuckled. "Well, no matter. Come," he said, "I am certain that you, at least, hunger somewhat."

Kris made to object, but the rumbling of her stomach overcame the beginnings of her protest.

Cyrus was full of misgivings. What if this man were a Villain? What if he were lying about being Divinely Inspired? Worse yet, what if he were telling the truth? Cyrus shook his head. "Listen, Conrad, we can't go anywhere until you tell us who you are, why you're on an island full of phoenixes, and what is going on."

"I understand your apprehension, and I dearly wish that I could assuage your fears," Conrad said, shaking his head. The phoenix perched on his staff squawked and took wing, fluttering out into the trees at the end of the beach. "It must be hard to be hounded no matter where you go, especially for a young Hero used to reknown and praise, not assassination attempts."

"You're not helping," Cyrus said through gritted teeth.

"My apologies," Conrad said. "I was once a Hero myself, before my ambition blinded me and drove me to attack a holy place. Come with me, children, and I will tell you more. My home is just this way." He motioned with his staff and turned to walk straight into the ocean.

"Um, Conrad?" Cyrus said. "That's . . . uh . . ."

"It's right here, past this stand of . . . Wait a minute," Conrad said as the waves began slapping at his feet. He turned a hundred and eighty degrees. "It's just *this* way," he said, now headed toward the trees.

Cyrus looked at Kris and shrugged. He was hungry too. Kris slipped her paw into Cyrus's hand, and the two of them followed the strange man as he recounted his tale.

"In the depths of my blindness, the Creator made me see my arrogance," Conrad said, sweeping the tip of his staff out in front of him like a blind man's cane. "In that moment, he exchanged my blindness to the truth and my earthly sight. I lost the ability to see the hand in front of my face, but gained sight of events around me and the will of Him who made all.

"My companions did not fare so well. Some died in the retaliatory attack shortly after we'd attacked the temple. One suffered a horrible fate, a sort of living death that exchanged the magics of life and death. And one betrayed us all and became a foe beyond our strength." Conrad sighed, and stepped over a moss-covered log at the beginning of the treeline. "Forgive the rambling of an old man, children, but I do not get visitors here often."

"No, it is Oh Kay," Kris said, putting a paw on Conrad's shoulder. "I don't mind listening to you. You are feeding us, after all. It's the least we can do."

Conrad chuckled, a sad, raspy chuckle that sounded like he had sand in his lungs. "It is very nice of you to say that, young lady. But that is enough about my past. It is your future that I would speak of. Here is my home. Enter if you will."

They stood outside a nearly invisible entrance to a cave. It was shaded by the branches of multiple palm trees and overgrown with a curtain of leafy vines. Conrad stepped inside, parting the vines and holding them open for Kris. She stepped inside, retaining her hold on Cyrus's hand and pulling him in despite his apprehension.

Conrad seated Kris and Cyrus at a simple, hand-crafted wooden table inside the cave, which was lit by a number of what looked like emergency candles. He then proceeded to set the table with tin plates and forks that seemed to have been harvested from ration kits. The plates weren't the only thing that indicated salvaged living. In fact, the entire cave seemed to have been furnished in "castaway chic," with ship's lockers against the walls, benches made out of large oars, and what appeared to be a hat rack fashioned from an anchor.

Cyrus eyed it all with suspicion, cursing his inability to simply trust this old man who had not done them any harm. The fact that all the contents of the cave looked like they were from the Best of Shipwreck Decoration stylebook was not helping. If he was a shipwreck survivor, where were the others?

Kris's stomach rumbled once more. She looked sheepishly down at her white belly fur. "Shh," she told her innards.

"Fear not, young lady," Conrad said. "Food is on its way. In fact . . ." he tilted his head to one side as if listening for a far-off sound . . . "it is coming as we speak. Sit back from the table, children."

Cyrus and Kris scooted their chairs back and leaned away from the table. Within moments, Kris's ears twitched backward toward the entrance of the cave.

"What is it?" Cyrus asked.

Kris's face bore a mildly puzzled expression. "It sounds like wings," she said. "Lots of wings."

"Indeed," Conrad said. "They come twice a day to bring me sustenance. And today they bring food for my guests as well. Behold!"

With a rush of wings and a flutter of feathers mixed with a chorus of chirrups and chitters, a dozen or more phoenixes burst into the cave.

Cyrus threw himself over Kris to protect her from the magical fire the phoenixes trailed as they flapped about. But to his surprise, the birds did not attack. On some unheard signal, they flew by in a line, dropping foods of various kinds on the table. Cyrus rose from his protective crouch and felt the warmth of the tendrils of fire swirl about him, harmless and strangely pleasant.

"Dinner is served!" Conrad said. "Thank you, my little friends, and thank You, O Creator, for this feast. Children, children, come and eat of this bounty!"

Cyrus looked with vague apprehension at the items on the table as the flock of phoenixes flew out the cave mouth. Kris sat up and sniffed at the food as well. It was an interesting assortment of things, all in various stages of being burnt. There were burned oranges, flame-broiled red meat of some kind, blackened fish, roast pineapple, and a flagon of some steaming light brown beverage.

"The phoenixes cook it all by accident," Conrad said, feeling about the table until he found the meat. He lifted it onto a plate and stuck a knife in it. "They naturally produce so much heat that it tends to char whatever they carry. Cyrus, would you be so kind as to slice this, please? My carving skills suffer from lack of eyesight."

Cyrus took the knife and carved a slice off the roast for Kris, trying to avoid both the charred sections and the ones that appeared raw. *Cook* was apparently a relative term to the birds. He cut two more servings, one for Conrad and one for himself.

"So," Conrad said once they had begun eating, "I have been told three things about you. First," he raised a finger, "I know your names. This I have already told you."

"Yes, we were in doubt about what our names were," Kris said, putting a paw in front of her mouth to hide the giggle. "Thank you for setting us straight."

Conrad scowled good-naturedly. "You are the very soul of comedy, young lady. Second," he said, putting a particularly crunchy piece of meat in his mouth and making a wry face, "I learned from the Great One that your use of magic, Cyrus, is causing damage to the world and also making you a veritable beacon for your enemies to find you."

Cyrus sighed. "Isn't that the truth. What can we do about it?"

"He has shown me how to curb your destructive energies to ensure that your tremendous power causes no *unintentional* damage," Conrad said with a wink of his sightless eyes. "Tomorrow I will teach you." Conrad sat back in his chair and offered a bit of charred meat to the little phoenix he had called Magnus. The bird daintily took the morsel from between Conrad's fingers, then gobbled it down.

"Last, He imparted to me a message that at first I did not understand," Conrad said. "He told me that this day, the Light from the Fallen would come to my island and with him would be the Huntress."

Kris started and leaned forward in her chair. "Huntress? Someone called me that earlier," she said, peering intently at Conrad's face. "An old woman said I was the Huntress of the prophecy. What does everyone mean by this?"

"As I said," Conrad said, holding up a hand, "I did not understand at first either. The Huntress, you see, is part of the Prophecy of the End of the World. She will be the bride of the Light from the Fallen, his helpmeet in the trials leading up to the End of All Things. She will be mother to the Two of Balance. And she will not be of the same Kind as the Light."

Magnus hopped down from the back of Conrad's chair to perch on the table and begin eating the contents of the old man's plate. "I did not realize that the different Kind would mean a different Race," Conrad said. "When I met you down at the beach, it became clear to me. I do not understand the ways of the Creator, but you, young woman, are the Huntress. It can be no other way."

"Wait just one minute," Cyrus said, standing up and slapping his palms onto the table. Conrad and Kris jumped, and Magnus hissed at him. "Are you saying that Kris is going to have children? Whose?"

"Cyrus!" Kris said, standing up as well and scowling at him.

"Yours, of course." Conrad soothed the ruffled feathers on Magnus's head. "Fear no infidelity, Cyrus Solburg."

"But it's impossible!" Cyrus protested. "Humans and Katheni, Orcs and Elves, you name the combination, it doesn't work! I can't believe that, old man."

Conrad shook his head. "What you believe has very little bearing on reality, boy. What is, is. And what the Creator wills, happens. Your belief or unbelief changes naught." He sighed, looking even older than his wrinkles indicated. "I suspect you will find out soon enough. At any rate, my task was only to tell you. You must figure it out for yourselves."

"H-how do you know all this?" Kris asked.

"The Creator gave me this gift—and curse—to further His ends," Conrad said, rising from the table and turning to one of the ship's lockers that sat against the wall near the table, the feathers in his robe rustling. "Occasionally He sends a wayfarer or lost soul my way, and they leave with a tale to tell others. I believe I am known elsewhere as the Phoenix Prophet."

"The Phoenix—" Cyrus said, stopping abruptly and looking confused. "Wait, I know about you. Uncle Jacob used to tell me stories about the Prophet who feared no fire and lived among the phoenixes. So those stories are true? I can't believe it. Are all the legends true, then? Even the one about the mermaids?"

Conrad shuddered. "Ugh, those . . . creatures. Just about chewed my legs off, they did. I pity the sailor who actually falls for their beauty. Lucky for me I could not see. But I digress." The old man pulled a stuffed patchwork blanket of sailcloth from the cabinet and shook it out. "Much of these matters are the subject of tomorrow. Here, this will keep the two of you warm and dry during the storm."

"Storm?" Cyrus said. "But it's a clear blue sky out th—"

A reverberating crash of thunder drowned out Cyrus's last word, and sheets of rain began slashing down through the tree canopy.

"And now I must depart," Conrad said, picking up his staff. "My true home is atop the mountain. I shall meet you on the morrow on the beach."

With that, the Phoenix Prophet went out into the rain. Cyrus stepped forward to say something, but a swarm of phoenixes swooped out of the surrounding forest and clustered around Conrad. Within moments, the birds carried him off into the air, through the pouring rain, and up to the now-obscured spire of stone from which the island got its name.

Cyrus stepped back into the cave and sighed. "I don't get him at all."

"I don't think you have to," Kris said. "He said it was for us to figure out. And he only had good things to say about our future, right?" She gingerly put her hands on Cyrus's arm. "Right?"

Cyrus turned and wrapped Kris in a hug. "Don't worry, Kris. That sounds like the most impossible thing this side of Voshytyr opening up an orphanage and religious academy." He held Kris out at arm's length. "But if it is true . . ."

Tears welled up in Kris's eyes. "I don't *want* to be in a prophecy. I just . . . I just want to live a normal life with you. I chose you because of you, not because I wanted to be mixed up in such big things. I'm no Huntress. I . . . I . . ."

"You're my mate, Kris," Cyrus said, tilting her chin up. "Huntress or no, nothing changes that, okay?"

Kris sniffed and wiped at her eyes. "Oh kay." She hugged Cyrus again. "I wonder if 'Two of Balance' means twins . . ."

"Whoa, let's not get ahead of ourselves," Cyrus said. "We've been through a lot in the last few days. We're alive. Let's start with that. The more complicated things we can worry about later."

"Even if our boat gets sunk out from under us again," Kris said, putting a paw on Cyrus's shoulder, "we'll still have each other to help figure things out."

Cyrus kissed Kris. "Yeah," he said. "It's just too bad that the best thing that ever happened to me happened in the middle of the worst thing that happened to me."

"Are you worried about Reginald?" Kris stepped back and sat on one of the rocks in the cave. The rain continued to slash down outside. "I'm sure he's Oh Kay."

"It's not just him." Cyrus sat down next to Kris and rubbed her back. "I mean, we survived that ship battle. But what if that doesn't throw Voshtyr off? What if he keeps coming after us? I can't fight all his forces if he really sets his mind on getting us. Well, me, anyway. I think he only grabbed you last time to get at me."

As the rain fell, the two were silent. Cyrus wasn't sure how to broach the awkward subject of a truly impossible occurence involving the two of them.

"I mean, what does he even want with me?" he said after a minute or two. "I'm nothing special. I mean, I can shoot magic around willy-nilly, but that doesn't make me any better than one of his mages. What's so special about me?"

"Well, you're special to me," Kris said, nuzzling his chest. "But I doubt he wants to capture you for cuddles."

"Eucch," Cyrus said, picturing all the grotesque fan-fiction. "No. Just . . . no. I guess we'll have to wait and find out, eh?"

The discussion dropped there, as they fell asleep, lulled by the sound of rain on a tropic island.

Chapter 3

CONTROL

In which Cyrus learns the Secret of Controlling his Power and takes a Phoenix-Powered Boat Ride

THE RAIN STOPPED by midmorning the next day. The air felt hot and muggy to Cyrus, like he was trying to breathe underwater. In fact, the humidity was so intense he could probably have swum through the air just as easily as the ocean.

Kris looked miserable too. Her fur was frizzy and unkempt, even though she'd been brushing it all morning. She growled something about how water should stay in the sea instead of the air, and gave up.

The two of them headed down to the beach, where they found Conrad standing on the sand staring out to sea. "Hello, children," he said without turning around. "I take it you want to learn about your magic, Cyrus."

Cyrus squeezed Kris's shoulder, then stepped forward. "I don't want to call attention to myself or the people around me," he said. "I don't want to cause damage I can't repair. Go ahead and teach me, Conrad. I'm ready to learn."

"Without incessant increasingly bad puns?" Conrad asked with a smile.

Cyrus chuckled. "I promise nothing."

After Kris walked away to attempt to catch various forms of sea life in a tidal pool not too far from the shore, Cyrus squared off with Conrad. The old man planted his staff in the sand near a pair of jutting boulders. The waves crashed onto the sand as the tide swirled in, bringing with it seaweed and bits of broken ship, probably from the merchantman and the pirate vessel.

"So," Conrad began, looking up to the sky, "what you normally do is take hold of the lines and break them, using them to bludgeon your opponents into submission, yes?"

Cyrus nodded. "I hear that's not good for their long-term stability."

"No, since there are only a hundred or so of each type of line throughout the world." Conrad looked back to Cyrus with sightless eyes. "Every time you break one, it's one less time you can do it. And each time you do, unless you break them in even proportions to each other, you may cause an imbalance in the Elements themselves."

Cyrus started. "What? Like I could break the planet that way?"

"Why do you think the Creator sent you my way?" Conrad asked. "He rather likes His creation the way it is, unbroken and still functional."

Cyrus scowled. "All right, so since I can't do it the only way I know how, where do I start?"

Conrad took a step forward and touched Cyrus's forehead.

The world exploded into five colors and a stunning lack of scenery. All around him was the landscape of where he had been standing, but all bleached out to pure white and naught but outlines of boulders and trees.

Most astonishing was the net of colored lines that crisscrossed the sky and ground in golden yellow, flaming red, crystalline blue, and solid brown. Their pattern was orderly, not quite equidistant from one another, but they stretched out in all directions, interconnected and stretching from horizon to horizon.

Cyrus gaped. "What . . . what is all this?"

Conrad, now standing beside Cyrus, laughed. "You are seeing what every mage and elementalist dreams of seeing, young man," he said. "Those are the ley-lines. You see their locations and relative strengths. And . . ." he said, pointing above the ocean to the west, " . . . you can see what damage you have already done. Look there."

Cyrus saw two of the lines, a blue and a yellow, snapped off and frayed, floating free in the white sky and ground. "By the Twelve . . . I did that?" Cyrus asked, barely audible against the humming of the lines and the crashing of the pure white waves. "But look at the yellow line. Is that one splitting and unraveling?"

"Yes, child, it is indeed deteriorating," Conrad said sadly. "You have yet to realize that your callous use of the lines in your accustomed fashion does not just break them. They eventually unravel and disappear."

Cyrus sank to his knees. Hadn't the Creator given him this power to use it for good? Why then was it destroying a vital part of the world? He shook his head. "How can I fix them?"

"Funny you should ask," Conrad said. "There is no way to repair a damaged or destroyed ley-line. Ah, but do not lose hope. You cannot fix lea lines. But there does exist, in a form now lost in the annals of time, one way to *redraw* them."

A way to undo the damage he had already caused. Cyrus paused for a moment. If he could still use his unusual power to help the remaining Heroes and then fix the damage afterward . . . He collected his thoughts and looked back up at Conrad. "How?"

Conrad walked a few steps to collect his staff, then turned back to Cyrus. "Have you heard of the Heartstones?"

Cyrus shook his head.

"Well," Conrad said, "there are five elements that can be—"

"Four," Cyrus said. "There are four elements."

"Five, boy. I care not what those Highseekers told you. There is a fifth, but it is so obscure that no one, save Sorcerers, really knows how to harness it—and sorcerers do it wrong and poorly."

Conrad gestured at the lines floating in the air and ground and sea. "If you find all the Heartstones, one that corresponds with each Element, you can trace new paths for the ley-lines, or even access their full power without fear of damaging one. Each stone is kept in a tower where that Element reigns supreme. Each is an imbalanced object: it contains no trace of the other Elements. The Fire stone is pure, ideal Fire, the Earth stone, ideal earth, and so on. Combine the imbalanced stones, and you will achieve true balance for your own use. If you are to continue to use the gift the Creator has given you, you will need the Heartstones to do it properly."

Cyrus sighed. "I don't know where they are or even how to do real magic. All I do is throw raw magic around. This is too much to take in."

"It's not too much to take in. And you can worry about the Heartstones at a later time," Conrad said. "Only when you must face a great enemy will you need their power."

"What?" Cyrus said. "You mean Voshtyr? Or are you being cryptic on purpose?"

Conrad smiled. "That comes with the territory of being a seer. Now, back to your magic use. Casting a formulated spell isn't that much different than throwing raw Elemental energy. This is something a young mage would learn in MAG101."

"No it isn't," Cyrus said. "I had a very abbreviated course in Magic 101 from Halmer Blackfence in the last book. All he told me was that the Elements existed, something about 'counterspelling,' and the Capital Letters and Arbitrary Numbers."

Conrad frowned. "Hmm. Seems they've changed the curriculum since the last time I checked then. Well, if I cannot teach you the course, I can at least give you an object lesson." Conrad gestured into the air with his staff. Threads of golden light separated from the Air line and swirled downward to coalesce around the head of Conrad's staff. The threads twisted together into a hexagon filled with triangles.

"What is that?" Cyrus asked, staring in amazement.

"A spell," Conrad said. "More specifically, this is *ArcBolt*, a spell that hits one target and continues on to another. Observe." He threw the hexagon forward with a gesture of his hand.

It leapt forward and latched onto one of the outlined boulders. The triangles that had been contained in it scattered out into a chain, striking another boulder, a tree, and finally grounding out in a tide pool a few yards away from the one Kris sat in front of. She jumped and gave Cyrus a dirty look.

"So that's how it works," Cyrus said in amazement. "If I know the form, I can fill it up, and it works! Like a pie!"

"What?" Conrad said. "No! Not like a . . . well, I *suppose* you could think of it that way . . . You are a very strange child."

Cyrus chuckled. "It's one of my defining character traits. So, what next?"

Conrad sighed. "I wish I could see what you are seeing, child. Magic has always puzzled me as well. But to return the subject to your magic, try taking magic from one of the lines. Fire, if you please."

Cyrus reached out and took hold of a pulsing red line.

"*Careful!*" Conrad shouted.

Cyrus dropped the line. "What? Is it not supposed to bend toward me like that?"

"A short distance, yes," Conrad said tensely. Cyrus could see sweat beaded up on the old man's brow. "But be more careful. Take hold of it, but do not pull. When you pull them, you break them. Let it flow into your hand . . ."

Cyrus frowned. He reached up again and *touched* the Fire line. To his mind, it felt like the dry heat of the Mir desert, dehydrating to the skin almost, only solid and flowing, like sifting hot sand through the fingers. It bent toward him as he touched it, and Cyrus relaxed his mental grip. Curses, the thing was fragile. "So how can I use it if I have to hold it so lightly?"

"Instead of gripping it like a sword, try pulling it into yourself, like you did when escaping the Vale."

Cyrus nodded and concentrated on the palpable heat of the line. As before, it set his world on fire as energy poured down from the red thread above and filled his body. He happened to glance at his hand, and he started. It was turning red, like a bad sunburn, and wisps of smoke drifted from his fingertips. "My skin!" Cyrus said. "It's . . . it's all . . . !"

"You've an imbalance of the Elements," Conrad said. "All things are composed of some mix of the Elements. The Nine Races are fairly balanced in composition, especially Humans. Right now, you have disrupted that balance in favor of Fire. While this would have destroyed most people, it will not harm you. You could walk through fire and fear no harm, breathe in water and never drown, catch the falling lightning or bury yourself beneath the earth and never be hurt, for the Creator is with you. It is a gift."

Cyrus relaxed, and yellow-gold flames licked all around him, bathing him in flickering light against the white backdrop. "Yeesh, I almost look like an Elemental."

"At this moment, you *are* an Elemental," Conrad said, nodding sagely. "A Human perfectly in tune with the Elements, despite a lack of magical training. And as long as you do as I have told you," he added, pointing a finger off to the right side of Cyrus's face, "you will not damage another line. Your body will be your weapon, and you will not need to bludgeon your foes with shattered bits of creation."

"Um, question," Cyrus said, raising a flaming hand. It set the palm tree behind him on fire, and Conrad quickly doused it with a Water spell. "I've busted more than one kind of line before, and twisted them together into something more powerful. Can I do the same thing with this absorption thing? More than one line at once?"

"Perhaps," Conrad said, a slight smile on his face. "I would advise against it until you learn how to adequately control a single line. If you do not control it, it will overcome you and dominate your emotions and actions. And one more thing . . ." Conrad gestured broadly at the scenery, which began fading back into its proper colors and textures. The vibrant lines of energy in the sky, earth, and sea disappeared, but Cyrus could still feel their presence. "As long as you have stored energy from the lines in yourself, you will never be hampered by a magic suppressant field. Remember this well."

The feeling of extreme overheating gradually faded as Cyrus released his grasp on the ley-line and let the stored energy bleed away. He wiped sweat from his brow. "So that's it? I won't draw attention to myself anymore?"

"I wouldn't say that, child," Conrad said. "You still create a draw on the lines more powerful than any three Arch-mages combined, so of course someone will notice. But at least you will no longer shatter the underpinnings of creation every time you need magic."

Cyrus rolled his eyes and chuckled. "Gee, that helps a lot. So now what?"

"So now you go home," Conrad said. "I am certain that you have much to do there, such as finding something to do for a living instead of Heroics. The world is unsafe for such things right now."

"Yeah . . ." Cyrus looked down at the sand. "I spent my whole life training for being a Hero, and now all this happened. I betray the Heroes, and they get wiped out. My mentor won't even speak to me anymore . . ."

A clout to the skull interrupted Cyrus's self-blame session and knocked him to the sand.

"That is certainly enough of that," Conrad said, shaking his staff at Cyrus.

"Ow," Cyrus said, rubbing his forehead. "How can you not see me most of the time and then hit me on the head like you can see me just fine?"

Conrad smiled wickedly. "Ah, now that is a Mystery. But back to your Party of Pitying. What you have done can be easily attributed to ignorance rather than malice toward your brothers in arms. And perhaps even that is part of the Creator's plan."

Cyrus's head throbbed. "How is that a plan?"

"It is much like pruning away bad branches from a citrus tree," Conrad said. "Heroes have reigned unchallenged for the last two thousand years. Perhaps Balance had shifted too far, and is now on its way to the other end. Heroes have learned that they are not invulnerable titans who can do whatever they choose in the name of good. Perhaps now they will regroup as something stronger. My only fear is that this time Balance has tilted too far."

That evening, Kris, Cyrus, and Conrad sat around a fire on the beach eating a dinner that had been air-delivered by phoenixes. The phoenix called Magnus seemed to have decided that Kris's lap was the best place to relax, and he sat there preening his iridescent red and gold feathers. The bird's choice of perch was cocky, certainly, but probably because between himself and his relatives, he had enough firepower to glass the entire Mir Desert.

Waves lapped the shore on their way out, and a warm and gentle sea breeze ruffled Cyrus's hair. He was not exempt from phoenix occupation, as a hatchling so red-orange that it almost exactly matched the shade of Cyrus's hair had made itself at home atop his head, and would not be dislodged even by offers of bits of meat and fruit.

"Well, I agree," Conrad said, popping a morsel of toasted bread into his mouth. "That lifeboat of yours will hardly get you safely to Starspeak. You may certainly take mine, if you wish."

Kris groaned. "Not another boat . . ."

Cyrus rubbed her back between her shoulders. "Hey, no worries. Small boats are easier to control. I didn't know you had a sailboat, Conrad."

"I do not." Conrad pointed at the bird on Cyrus's head. "My boat is powered by the phoenixes. They push it about when the Creator sees fit to send me somewhere beside this island. After all, it is not as if I can navigate it myself."

Kris cocked her head to one side. In her lap, Magnus did the same. "They push you around? How?"

"I shall show you." Conrad rose from the sand and gestured toward a copse of trees on the shoreline. "Come with me."

Cyrus and Kris followed Conrad to a small cove neatly hidden by aquatic shrubbery and the trees on the shore. In it rested a sleek, narrow boat with an elongated and weighty prow. It seemed to be leaning forward, as if it had a hole somewhere in the front but was not taking enough water to sink the boat. The hull was entirely made of metal of some kind, with gutters down the outside edges like the groove in the side of a sword to divert blood away from running down onto the handle. Attached to the stern was what looked like a tapered box, with a small, nozzle-like hole at the back. The whole apparatus at the back was large enough to perhaps fit a small dog in.

"What kind of boat is this?" Cyrus asked, kneeling down to examine the hull. "I've never seen one like it."

"Well, I've never seen it at all," Conrad said. "All I know is that the phoenixes do something in the back, and it moves forward quite rapidly. It took me less than a day to make it from here to Sharkwater Channel one time."

Cyrus whistled. "That's incredible! So you're going to take us to Starspeak in this?"

"No," Conrad said, "I'm going to have the phoenixes do that. I don't provide the power for the boat—they do." The old man looked tired as he turned away and began walking back down the beach. "When you get there, just tell the phoenixes to go home, and they'll bring the boat back to me."

"Wait!" Cyrus leapt over to Conrad's side. "Listen, thanks for your help and hospitality," he said, scuffing the sand with a bare foot. He belatedly realized he must have lost his boots sometime during their shipwreck. "You know, you could come with us. There's lots of people around who'd enjoy your company. People who talk more than your pet birds do."

Conrad half-smiled. "Do not tempt me, young man. I stay here to wait for the words of the Creator. Begone, for I have fasting and prayer to attend to."

Cyrus sighed. "All right, you stubborn old man. Good luck on this godforsaken island," he said with a chuckle.

"Farewell, insubordinate brat," Conrad replied with a smile. "And this island is hardly godforsaken, since He speaks to me all the time here. Try not to break the universe too much without me around to show you what you're doing wrong."

The two clasped each other's hands heartily, then Conrad plodded down the beach, and Cyrus returned to the boat.

• • •

"So how exactly does this work?" Kris asked as Cyrus returned. "There's instructions on the panel here in front of the seat, but they don't give us anything to do."

Cyrus looked at the seats. They were strange contrivances that tilted back and had straps to cross the chest and handles beneath the seat, which looked like they should be steering apparatuses, but were solid and immobile. A thick woven cushion headrest decked each of the two chairs, but aside from that, the boat was without decoration.

Cyrus scratched his head. "Not sure. Conrad didn't say anything. Maybe it explains itself?" He looked at the small sheet of engraved brass on the front console of the boat. It was the only thing on the console, and hard to miss. "Step one," Cyrus read, "sit in the seat provided."

Kris took a seat. "Now what?"

Cyrus sat down on the other seat. "Step two: please strap on the safety harness," he read, reaching for the leather straps. "Wow, that's pretty polite for a plaque."

"Politeness never hurts," Kris said, buckling her harness on and folding her paws primly in her lap.

"Unless you're complimenting an Orc," Cyrus said. "Reg once got his nose broken for complimenting an Orc and his wife on how well she fought, for a woman."

Kris winced. "The Orc punched him?"

"Only if you mean the female one," Cyrus said with a chuckle. "Apparently their women are fiercer warriors than the men are. Step three: say the name of your destination to your pilot. Pilot?" He looked behind him.

Magnus the phoenix sat perched atop the tapered box at the stern of the craft, and another, larger phoenix was awkwardly climbing inside it. Magnus chirruped.

Cyrus chuckled. "All right, pilot, take us to Starspeak Island. Um, please."

Magnus chirped twice and bobbed his head. Then he stuck it inside the box and squawked and trilled at the larger bird.

Kris watched them in fascination. "They're talking to each other..."

"Phoenixes are smart birds," Cyrus said. "I just hope they know where Starspeak is. Step four: take hold of the underseat handles, then say 'Ignis avis.' *Waugh!*"

The moment the foreign words left Cyrus's mouth, the boat leapt forward at a speed reserved for lightning bolts, Inter-Continental Blast Magics, and critics fleeing an Orcish Opera. Water flew up the sides of the boat in a shower of stinging spray as the boat shot from the shaded harbor and practically skimmed the surface of the ocean.

Kris screamed in terror for a moment, but her scream soon dissolved into exhilarated laughter as the rushing of wind and spray continued, along with some high-speed turns. The rapidity of their movement never slacked.

Cyrus hadn't managed to get hold of the handles beneath his seat, and the sudden acceleration of the boat threw him back into his seat, knocking his head against the cushion. It stunned him for a second or two, but when he realized the rate at which they traveled, he looked behind him.

A narrow jet of white fire shot from the tapered nozzle on the boat's stern, and Magnus held on to the front of the box, head forward and wings back, flames rolling off him in a blazing contrail. Every time the small phoenix shifted his wings right or left, the boat shifted as well. Apparently the larger phoenix was using its innate fire magic to produce a jet of focused force, while Magnus steered.

Cyrus looked forward just in time to see the boat vault over a large wave, and he received a blast of spray in the face. Well, since he wasn't part of the process of getting home, he decided to simply enjoy the ride. He lifted a hand up to Kris, who paused in her giggling long enough to take it, and onward they sped into the darkening sky.

Chapter 4

RELATIVELY FEW PROBLEMS

In which a Former Villain begins Machinations on his (half) Brother
And the Reader gets a Crash Course in otherworldy Theology

THE DARKNESS OF a calm Landeralt night did not typically contain any noises other than the clanking of an occasional golem treading its metallic way down the paved roads, the crash of surf against the seaside cliffs, or the shrieks of harpies as they descended on hapless prey. In fact, the Hereditary Evil Empire was a remarkably quiet place considering just how many of the world's great troublemakers claimed it as home.

Especially quiet were the seaside mansions of some of the great and notable Villains, most of which were empty because the more successful a Villain was, the more Heroes tried to stop him or her. By the time he or she had committed enough foul deeds to merit a land endowment grant from the Empire, it was usually awarded posthumously.

Not so for one particular castle, at least on this night. On the southwestern coast of Landeralt, bordering the Black Reef and the Straits of the Dead, protruding from the sheer black cliffs, was a particularly noisy castle. Sounds of swearing and breaking furniture resounded through the windows, scaring off crows and seabirds perched on the black marble railings of a seafront balcony.

"*Kharestin! Ibne yarrak kafali!*" shouted a man in black, kicking over a marble column in a fit of rage. "That *orsobu pitchi!* What in the Nine Torments was he thinking? Killing off all the Heroes at once? Is he *trying* to bring the world down around our ears in flames?"

The man cast *Limited Matter Annihilation* at a nearby wall (a nonstructural one, luckily). A spray of marble chips and dust spattered across the once richly decorated room, which now resembled something one would see if one released a storm elemental and a berserked steel golem into a king's private quarters. Shattered masonry and statues littered the torn carpets. Shredded draperies and tapestries hung haphazardly off the windows and walls, and piles of coal sat unattended, glowing on the floor, spilled from overturned braziers.

The man swore some more, his epithets growing darker and more vulgar the more he shouted. Finally, he slumped down into a heavily damaged armchair. It collapsed beneath him, provoking yet another outburst of swearing.

A dark-haired Elven woman in a flowing black gown entered the room. She surveyed the destruction and sighed. "*Mend Masonry. Fix Furniture. Repair Rug.*" After the collapsed chair under the man had fixed itself, she walked to him. "Serimal, must you always take your anger out on our nice things?" she asked with a smile and a sad shake of her head.

Serimal rose from the mended armchair, picked up a newly repaired statuette, and threw it out the window. "*Dassak*, Nieva! Do you honestly expect me to be calm at a time like this? When Voshtyr has just killed the only thing keeping the world stable?" He brushed stone dust from his raven-black hair.

"No," Nieva replied, "but I do expect you to channel that energy in a more productive direction." She stepped up to Serimal and straightened his black silk tunic. "I know fits of rage run in your family. Voshtyr has murdered a score of men while angry, and your father was renowned for being the most destructive berserker since the reign of Alethor McBeardhammer the Berserker King. But you cannot allow your anger to get the better of your judgment. Or furniture."

Serimal sighed. He placed his hands on Nieva's shoulders and looked into her eyes. "Oh, this isn't like my father," he said. "Father would have spontaneously combusted or started murdering people the moment he found out about this *iki ucu boklu degnek*. I am prone to rage, but . . ."

"But nothing," Nieva said, shaking a finger at Serimal. "Instead of breaking our furniture, perhaps you might tell me what is going on?"

"Voshtyr's killed the Heroes," Serimal said, turning away from Nieva to touch a column he had recently shattered. "All of the Heroes. And now he's tracking down the rest and slaughtering them as they flee."

Nieva gasped, clapping a hand to her mouth.

"Now you see why I am upset," Serimal said, leaning on the column. "You know I don't like the Heroes any more than Voshtyr does. And I certainly don't want them overrunning the entire world. But they have their place in the Balance. Now Voshtyr is either going to break the Balance or Heroes are going to make a devastating return to power. Neither of which are desirable outcomes."

"What can we do?" Nieva said, sitting down on a settee. "We cannot confront your brother directly. He would crush us without a thought."

"Half-brother," Serimal said irritably. "I don't know, but we must stop him somehow." He shook his head. "He's my half-brother, but honestly, he's got more in common with that demon mother of his, and I've more in common with . . . Wait a moment, that's perfect!" Serimal stood straight up and pointed a finger up in the air. "Jaratyr!"

Nieva looked puzzled. "Who?"

"Voshtyr's *other* half-brother," Serimal said, grinning wickedly. "A pure demon from *Another Place*, the son of Voshtyr's mother. He hates Voshtyr with a passion. Perhaps we can work together!"

Nieva was clearly alarmed. "But you gave up demon summoning a long time ago. Please do not slide back into that foul sorcery, my love, I beg you."

Serimal knelt down next to the settee and looked into her face until her chill silver eyes met his. "Oh, my beloved, you rescued me from that life. I'll not fall into it easily again. But speak with Jaratyr I must, for no one understands Voshtyr's demonic powers better than he would. He would be the perfect ally to stop Voshtyr and begin rebuilding Balance. As the saying goes, what is it you fight fire with?"

"Not demons, certainly. But who will do this foul deed for you?" Nieva asked. She leaned against the wall and looked at the ceiling, which had escaped damage from Serimal's rage. "I would rather you not commit the act yourself."

"I wonder if that unspeakable rat Goras is still around," Serimal said, stroking his chin. It was beginning to sprout a bit of stubble. He had toyed with the idea of growing a beard before, and at this moment he abruptly decided to do so. Anything to make him look less like Voshtyr was desirable, and Nieva had said something about it once. Perhaps now was the time . . .

• • •

Chime.

A man in robes of a confusing purple rolled over on his low mattress, dislodging a heavy black book and two pots of ink. The pots smashed on the hewn-stone floor, spattering the ink everywhere and startling a two-headed crow perched in a cage near the reinforced oaken door. It shrieked and squawked from both beaks as the man cursed and snatched the book from the spilled ink to ensure that none of the pages were damaged.

Chime.

"Just a blasted minute," he grumbled, setting the book down. He arranged his robes, then walked over to a short table in the center of the cavernous room. Stacks of books, a Human skull, two open scrolls, a severed hand, and a crystal ball cluttered the surface.

"This is Goras Gatekeeper," the man said, passing his hand over the ball's surface. "Who is this, and what do you want?"

"Hello, Goras," replied a voice from the ball. A wavy image of a man swam into the crystal. He was in his early thirties, with black hair and a fashionable trenchcoat, one of Villanic Fashion Designer Marita Kaz's "Dashing Highwayman Series," in this summer's popular color "Ravens in a Coal Mine." Which, Goras knew, was subtly different from this spring's "Ink at Midnight" and more trendy than last winter's "Burnt Obsidian."

The young man in the crystal ball smiled. "This is Serimal von Steinadler. I believe we've met."

Goras jumped. "Y-yes we did, at the Second Circle Annual Summoning Contest perhaps ten years ago." He snatched a crumpled purple hat off the chair behind him and pulled the chair up to sit comfortably in front of the ball. "I've also worked with your brother and your father, gods have mercy on his soul."

"Half-brother, and I doubt they will," Serimal said. "Listen, Goras, I need to summon a greater demon but I no longer have the proper equipment and incantations to do so properly. I've prepared a summoning circle and the proper sacrifice, but I'm in need of assistance."

Goras rubbed his hands together in glee. Finally, the brat who had embarrassed him at that contest so long ago was in need of help. Time to extract sweet revenge. "Well," Goras said, looking at his fingernails, "I've many pressing concerns going at the moment, but if you made it worth my time—perhaps two thousand gold—I could see if I could squeeze you in next month . . ."

"Come now, Goras," Serimal said, sounding disappointed. "You and I both know that you are running short of funds to continue that silly Zombie Squirrel Army project you're working on."

"But—"

"And don't try and pull the *busy* card on me either," Serimal said. "Your efforts are stuck because you've encountered Berigir's Law of Soul Conservation, and you've been stuck there for two years, three months, and twelve days. Come and help me for a mere half-hour, and I will give you five hundred gold pieces and the tome that Berigir wrote on his deathbed."

Goras practically jumped out of his chair in anticipation. "He finally overcame energy to flesh ratio problem?"

"No, but he did write a corollary on how to apply Zei'sthaan'i's Principle to creatures smaller than the Nine Races," Serimal said. "It's not something I have the time or resources to use myself, but it may help you overcome your quantity-versus-quality problem. Can I count on your assistance, or shall I see if Rish'tak Plainscale is interested in the book instead?"

"*No!* I mean, ah, ahem," Goras said, sitting down in his chair. He'd involuntarily shown his interest too quickly. Now that accursed brat had the upper hand again. Oh, well, if it would help him overcome Berigir's Law, a little help for the von Steinadler boy would not be too harmful to his dignity. "By all means. I shall be there on the morrow. But I am doing you a favor, Serimal. Do not forget that."

"I will not forget what you are owed," Serimal said. "Tomorrow, at Banecliff Castle, at the eleventh hour."

"Done." Goras cut the communication, then sat back in the chair and chuckled evilly to himself. That fool boy Serimal would be giving him the secret to destroying the world in exchange for a simple summonning. After all, if all the disgustingly cute and helpful forest creatures that so often helped Heroes became miniature, ravening undead monstrosities, no one would be able to stand against Goras Gatekeeper.

Goras slung on a cloak and began gathering his bags and apparatuses for summoning evil creatures, laughing to himself all the while.

Architecture is an important art, even in a world where one is more likely to find dragon poop than pigeon poop on the roof. And in the aforementioned world, both Heroes and Villains require special edifices to plan and execute their plans grand and nefarious, respectively.

Thus the Flying Buttress, a decorative strut perfect for brooding on top of, as the Black Bat often did before leaping off into the night sky in pursuit of criminals. Thus the Mirror Room, wherein an unsuspecting Hero could be lost for precious minutes, giving the Villain time to complete his scheme. And thus the Summoning Chamber, with a pentagram etched into the floor to hold the blood of dark sacrifices to unholy creatures, pulling their twisted minds and bodies from between the ethers.

Such Summoning Chambers often had a small Chamber of Coffee adjoining, as having one's body pulled from between the ethers often causes headache and nausea, and a good cup of Joe covereth a multitude of transdimensional sins.

Banecliff Castle was the ancestral home of the Von Steinadler family. Buried deep beneath the dungeon, the torture chamber, the Endless Labyrinth, and the Haberdashery of Doom, lay the family's Summoning Chamber. The architect, whose name was lost, was also physically missing, probably due to a combination of time and the age-old kill-the-creator-so-his-creation-will-be-unique-and-I-will-have-the-only-one gambit.

So while architecture is indeed an important art, it is occasionally dangerous to the creator.

The Summoning Chamber in Banecliff Castle was relatively small and homey, as far as rooms used for summoning ancient evils go. The blood-red candles ringing the room lent a warm glow to the arches of the roof and the rough texture of the granite walls. Circular grooves and obscure runes carved in the floor added an air of antique authenticity. And just outside the circle itself was a steel spike driven into the stone, with a ring at the top, perfect for affixing those late-night sacrifices to.

Serimal opened the door leading down into the chamber. "Thank you again for being available on such short notice," he said as he held the door open for Goras. "Can I offer you some coffee?"

Goras snorted. "You were always a traditionalist, boy. I think demons don't even *like* coffee. They just use it as an excuse to drink cream and sugar." Goras practically flounced into the room, his gaudy puffed pantaloons and ridiculous gold and purple overcoat billowing gracefully despite the absence of wind in the Summoning Chamber. "Now, where's the sacrifice?"

Nieva came in behind the two of them, leading a white calf. She tied the animal to the stake and put it to sleep with a spell, then nodded to Serimal.

Serimal turned to Goras. "All is ready. Begin the ritual."

And so Goras did. Serimal watched as the sorcerer cut the calf's throat, then placed the knife on the floor beside the circle. The calf's blood flowed across the floor, filling the small grooves that formed the pentagram within the circle. Softly, Goras began incanting choppy phrases in an ancient tongue. Dimly at first, but growing in intensity, a red flickering light began to spread across the center of the circle.

No one really knows much about the summoning of demons. Few have tried, and fewer have survived it. Demons are powerful creatures, not bound by the laws that govern mortals. More than one wizard has summoned a demon, only to be unable to contain or control it, and died horribly, soul stolen and damned forever. The few who dare traffic with demons are either extremely powerful, despicably evil, or entirely mad. Most likely, they are a combination of the three.

The summoning itself is straightforward, possibly because demons like it that way. It was once more difficult, but the rules were revised just before the Twenty-Minute War. If any idiot weakling can summon a demon, it was discovered, more souls could be collected quickly. Where once the blood of a virgin was required to be sacrificed during a total eclipse, all it requires now is a blood sacrifice, a summoning circle, and some geometric shape inscribed within it.

Any shape will do, but five-sided and pointed shapes are more reliable, with pentagrams being the most effective. Pentameters are too full of poetry to summon demons, Pentateuchs are too holy, and Pentagons tend to cost more and fill up with high ranking military types. Scholars and priests have argued about why this is, but to no avail. The truth is that demons simply like the number five and all shapes associated with it.

"Jaratyr, stand forth, *I SUMMON THEE!*" Goras shouted.

A keening filled the room, like a wailing ghost trying desperately to learn how to play the flute. Fire erupted from the center of the circle, and a black shape rose and stood, bathed in the flickering light. Horns sprouted from its head, the only adornment to an otherwise bald cranium. The horns swept back into sharp points. Black leathery wings dominated its back, and its eyes were red and glowing with a fierce, uncanny light.

"*I AM SUMMONED,*" the demon bellowed in an ancient and terrible tongue. "*WHAT IS IT THAT YOU REQUIRE*

OF ME, SORCERER? DO YOU WISH TO SELL ME YOUR SOUL? OR IS IT THAT . . . Wait a minute, aren't you Serimal?"

"Hello, Jaratyr," Serimal said, grinning and pushing Goras aside, who looked like he'd had the proverbial Ton of Bricks dropped on his head. "Long time no summon."

The fire surrounding the demon went out, and he quickly changed his appearance. His wings melted away, his horns shrank, and oily black hair sprouted from his deep red scalp. "Serimal! My word, it has been a long time!" the demon said. "What are you up to these days? I heard that you had stopped summoning demons!"

"Oh, I have," Serimal said. "My fiancée doesn't care for the activity, and I've come to agree with her. But I did need to talk to you, and since you live in *Another Space*, I can't exactly send you a letter. Just wait one moment while I pay the sorcerer."

Serimal turned to Goras. "Here. Both of your payments," he said, handing the sorcerer a yellowed tome with a skull on the cover, and simultaneously plunging a dagger into the man's stomach. "For your service and your crime. Rest in peace, summoner, if you can."

"Wh-why?" Goras sputtered, blood issuing from his mouth.

"You committed a crime against the Creator, against Nature, and against Jaratyr. Hush, just lie down and sleep," Serimal said, lowering the whimpering sorcerer to the ground. "The pain will soon fade away."

When the sorcerer finally closed his eyes, Serimal turned back to the summoned demon. "It's about our half-brother."

Jaratyr's glowing red eyes narrowed. "Voshtyr. What has he done now?"

"Oh, nothing much," Serimal said, shrugging his shoulders. "He's just slain almost every known Hero."

Jaratyr scowled. "Oh, that. Well, that wasn't much of a big deal where I'm from. Most Heroic souls are good people, so we never see them at all. They tend to go . . ." He swirled one of his claws in an upward spiral toward the ceiling. "I would normally say good riddance to them all, but the Balance . . ."

"Not to mention the horrors of war. All those innocents getting caught up in that mess?" Serimal sighed. "Wait, disregard that. You'd probably just find that amusing."

Jaratyr chuckled. "Me? Find the suffering of others amusing? Never. But you do have a point." The demon shuffled his feet around the inside edge of the summoning circle, as the talons on his feet shrank and receded into black toenails. "Those horrors of war will drive people to seek help from the gods, and we can't have all the peasants seeking after a higher power to save them and their pathetic souls, now can we?" He looked at Nieva.

Nieva scowled. "I have no words for you, creature," she said. "Coffee?"

"Coffee is a word," Jaratyr said, looking amused. "Yes, if you please, half coffee, half cream, with three lumps of sugar. Now, where was I?" he asked as Nieva left for the adjoining room. He had finished his transformation. Now resembled a handsome, dark-haired man with glowing eyes and terribly dark sunburn. "Right, Voshtyr breaking the world. What's he working on these days? He's always up to some diabolical project or other."

Serimal frowned. "I'm not entirely certain. All I know is that it involves all five continents and the Essence Stones. He's even attacked the Hereditary Evil Empire to get the Heart of Flames."

"Wait, a Villain attacking the Hereditary Evil Empire?" Jaratyr raised his eyebrows. "That makes no sense! What in the Nine Torments could that idiot be trying to do?" the demon stormed.

"That's just my problem, Jaratyr: I don't know." Serimal turned his back on the demon and began pacing. "I am going to resurrect Fifth Column and see how many members of our former organization are still alive. I already have some contacts within his dark army. We can find out what he's doing. But I know that not even Voshtyr's most Heroic foes could stop him as he is. And if his power grows further, all will fall before him."

"And?" Jaratyr asked, attempting to step out of the circle but bumping into an invisible wall. "You expect me to do what?"

"I am a Villain," Serimal said, "from a long line of Villains. I use no holy magic, nor am I yet worthy to ask the Creator for His help. But I do have a demon here to help me, and who knows the strengths and weaknesses of a demon better than another demon? Half-demon, anyway."

"Well you'd . . . Wait a minute . . ." Jaratyr smiled, revealing wickedly pointed teeth. "Are you suggesting that I would finally get my revenge on that mewling pink raisin my mother spent so much time with?"

"Of course," Serimal replied. "When it finally comes down to thwarting him, you would be most useful, because you already have motivation to inflict harm on our mutual half-brother."

"Oh, would I. Mother always did like little Voshtyr better," Jaratyr said, crossing his arms and slouching in a most undignified pout. "He was always so weak, always needed her attention and help to carry out his pathetic evil schemes. I never got the attention I needed, and look how I turned out! Well-adjusted and almost friendly!" The demon spat on the floor, his spittle catching fire and eating a hole through the flagstones.

"Oh, I know how you dislike him," Serimal said, "but my grievance is worse. I would have been the firstborn of the Von Steinadler family. I was, in fact, conceived before Voshtyr. But Father had to go and dally with that Demoness after getting Mother pregnant . . ."

Jaratyr leveled a disapproving scowl at Serimal. "Watch it, Serimal—you're talking about my mother."

Serimal sighed. "Yes, I know. But since demons bear children in a shorter time-span . . ."

"You were born after Voshtyr was, making *him* firstborn," Jaratyr said, frowning. "You never told me that. I always just assumed you were the younger brother."

Two minions came in the door, gawking at the blood on the floor and the demon standing in it. Serimal waved at them to remove Goras's body, which they quickly did, scuttling off to drag it away to the Body Disposal Room.

Nieva returned with Jaratyr's coffee, which she politely handed to him. She then leaned close to Serimal's ear. "I cannot abide another moment in the presence of this abomination. If you need me, I shall be upstairs."

Serimal nodded, and kissed her on the cheek. She departed without another word.

"Abomination?" Jaratryr said after a moment of awkward silence. "That's no way to speak to your future brother-in-law."

"You're not *my* half-brother—you're Voshtyr's," Serimal said with minor annoyance. "That makes you and her no relation at all."

"Step-brother-in-law?" Jaratyr said, and grinned.

"No. Anyway, inheritance disputes aside, Voshtyr has always been more evil than I. I'm afraid that I've been a bit of a disappointment to Father." He looked back toward the staircase Nieva had just left through. "And to add insult to injury, he just put a price on my fiancée's head," he said. "So, now that we've established our mutual hatred of our half-brother, do you agree to my plan?"

Jaratyr nodded. "As long as you let me out of this uncomfortable summoning circle. It *is* rather constricting, you know."

Serimal shook his head and grinned wryly. "You ought to know better than to try pulling that one on me, Jaratyr. Of all people, I certainly know better than to trust a demon. Now, to business."

After another half-hour of plotting and planning, Serimal trudged wearily back to his private chamber and slumped into a deep chair.

Nieva rose from her seat on the settee and walked to Serimal. "How did it go, my love?" She sat next to him and rubbed his shoulders.

"As well as can be expected, considering with whom I was dealing. Ack! Ah, down a little lower, that's better." Nieva's strong and gentle fingers were always the perfect remedy for stiff shoulders and a tired mind.

"I did warn you not to traffic with demons," Nieva said, running her fingers through Serimal's thick, black hair. "They are beings of pure evil. Even my departed father did not do such things."

Serimal tilted his head and looked up at his beloved Elven princess. "Your father obeyed Elven rules of conduct, Nieva. Even demons, in their own evil way, have a code of conduct. But Voshtyr has none, and I will use any means necessary to destroy him. You do understand, don't you?"

"I suppose I do. But please do not fall back into your old ways. That path is slippery and hard to return from once you have started down it again."

"Not to mention that the Synod of Outer Darkness would be all over my back about it," Serimal said, reaching over to an end table and retrieving a tall glass decanter of wine.

Nieva blinked. "The church of Villains would be against demon summoning? How so?"

"Oh, they're not against it," Serimal said. "Both the Synod and the 'True Church' forbid it, though their motivations are different. The Synod simply wants the monopoly on demon-summoning."

It is important that the reader not become confused when dealing with theology in Serimal's world. It is important, but also impossible. Unlike in our own, Serimal's world has multiple deities, a single Creator, and many otherworldly "demons."

The "gods" are twelve immensely powerful entities that rule over various parts of the world. Each deity has a domain under its control. Each has a patron Race. And each has other duties drawn from a Divine Hat, duties that are usually delegated to their underlings and demigods.

For example, Vertis is the god of the Sky. His domain is that of the air and all things that pertain to it. Therefore, he is also the god of Air magic, the sun, breathing, and the destroyer of the unclean, such as undead and creatures that cannot stand the sunlight. He refuses to lend his power to undead creatures that would use it to merely sparkle instead of burst into flames.

Vertis's patron Race is the reclusive Avierie, the bird-folk found only in the highest mountain peaks. Vertis's underlings, such as Carius the Charioteer, do some of Vertis's work. Carius drives the blazing chariot of the sun across the sky each day, or so the legends say.

Melis controls the waters and all things in and on them. The Araquellae worship Melis for keeping the oceans clean and livable. She is also the goddess of prophets and prophecy, hence the plethora of "water seers" who claim to know the future by looking into calm water.

Infernis, as his name implies, controls Fire, and has a jolly good time doing so. But, sadly for him, none of the Nine Races still reveres him. He is instead greatly respected by Dragons, who believe Infernis is directly responsible for their creation.

Teranis, god of the earth and stone, patriarch of patriarchs to the Dwarves, is also responsible for the training of domesticated animals, hence the popularity of the "pet rock" among some of his more confused followers.

Keriman is the god of luck and travelers. A sad event many thousand years ago robbed him of his patron Race, the Gnomes. Instead, he now watches out for children of all Races, and often inspires good bedtime stories.

Marava and Wanona, gods of Katheni and Istaka, respectively, both care for the wilderness. Marava watches over hunters, while Wanona protects families. Wanona is also the Keeper of Memories, so it is especially funny to Marava, the god of

Mishaps, to ensure that some of the mishaps involve the victims ending up with amnesia. This accounts for many Heroes not knowing where they came from or who they really are, and thus ensures startling and unexpected Plot Twists later on in their lives once Wanona manages to restore their memories.

To create a break from the list of deities, the author wishes to yell at you to *stay awake* as the list is already more than half over. He also promises to hurry up.

Strife, god of Orcs and War, also has the lesser duty of inspiring potters. This explains the many vases depicting epic battles and the Orcish tendency to create durable and beautiful storage containers. It is also helpful to note that the plethora of pottery available for Orcs to smash in fits of anger spares a good number of in-use skulls the same fate.

Sharet, goddess of Elves, is the goddess of laughter and comedy as well. This is often made much easier since she is also the goddess of Mixed Drinks. The latter duty tends to aid the former.

The Ransha are worshippers of their ancestors, but their myths tell of one Ancestor who ascended to the stars. Karista, who is revered as the all-mother by the lizard-folk, supersedes the patriarchal elders and provides female Ransha with rights within the tribe. She is the goddess of revenge, often sending her servants to personally deal with cases where an unjustly slain person's friends and family cannot avenge him. Karista also watches over sailors, after losing an argument with Melis about ocean travel. As a rule, Karista gets the surface of the waters, while Melis wards the deeps.

Yven is the goddess who once protected the Centaurs, as well as the Minotaurs, Cheetaurs, Gryphons, and all manner of other creatures that appear to be two different animals jammed together. She warded them for many years until the Centaurs unlocked a forbidden magic that temporarily sealed her power. While it was sealed, the Centaurs inadvertently wiped themselves out. The remaining "Demis," as they are called, regrouped, but too few of them survived to be called a Race any longer, so they retreated to the status of Greater Mythological Beasts. Yven still watches them as part of nature, when she's not attending to her other duties as goddess of fertility, death, and recycling.

Then there is Brian. Brian is the god of beauty. He watches over Humans and is the special patron of singers and crafters of perfumes and colognes. Brian hates his job and wishes heartily that he had never slain the original god of beauty.

"As I was saying before before that annoying wall of text came crashing down on us," Serimal said, "The Synod—"

"Look out!" Jaratyr said, backing up. "Here it comes again!"

Serimal rolled his eyes. "Oh, good grief. Will this never end?"

All the gods are ageless, but not immortal. Brian's case proves this: they can be slain, though with great difficulty. These "gods" flit back and forth between the mortal realm and *Another Space*, a place accessible only by those of strong magic, and only a small percentage of those. The "True Church" recognizes the gods as divine, but of a lesser divinity than the Creator.

The Creator Himself is shrouded in mystery. It is widely believed that, after having created the world, He disappeared and now stays out of world affairs. Some, such as the followers of the Way of Yasu, believe that the Creator still visits His creations from time to time, relieving suffering and spreading peace.

The slightly misnamed "demons" are the natural inhabitants of *Another Space*. They are venerated by the church known as the Synod of Outer Darkness. They do age and reproduce, but at a different rate than any of the Nine Races do.

In their own space, they have no unnatural powers, but when they are summoned into the natural world by magic, they gain uncanny abilities. Some say this is because of the natural magic inherent in the ley-lines, and some say that it is because of the power of the world's yellow sun (which is not to be confused with the Hero named the Yellow Sun, who gets his considerable power from the Creator instead). The demons' naturally fearsome appearance is mediated by their shape-changing abilities.

And unlike the Nine Races, crossbreeding is possible between demons and the inhabitants of the natural world. However, this is *never* a good idea. Since the natural disposition of most demons is psychotic evil, the offspring of such unions almost invariably have a bent toward Evil. The children will have some of the powers of their otherworldly parent, and only the best attributes of the other. For example, Voshtyr's father, Benjamin von Steinadler, was a very handsome and athletic man. Voshtyr inherited both of these traits, but also glowing eyes of his mother—and also the tendency to steal the occasional soul.

This said, the story may continue, hopefully free of theological impediments.

Chapter Five

HOME

In which Cyrus and Kris reach Starspeak
and Construct a New Life

SOMETHING BIT CYRUS on the ear.
"Ouch! What the—" Cyrus said, jumping in his harness.
The little phoenix Magnus flapped over to the gunwale of the boat and chirruped at him.
Cyrus touched his ear. Well, at least he wasn't bleeding. He looked around, and after a moment, smiled broadly. "Kris, wake up. We're here."

"Mrr?" Kris stirred sleepily in her seat. "We're where?"

It was early morning, and the sun was just beginning to crest the eastern horizon. Their boat had run aground on a sandy yellow beach with palm trees farther up the shore. Some green hills in the distance blended down into fruit orchards, and there was a town of sandstone buildings just a few minutes' walk away. The air smelled of sea salt and ripe oranges.

"Starspeak!" Cyrus unbuckled the harness and leaned over to undo Kris's as well. They were soaking wet from all the spray the boat had generated on their way from the Phoenix Islands. Apparently the boat hadn't been quite fast enough to dry them out as well. "We're home! Conrad wasn't joking when he said the phoenixes would get us here fast. Come on." He pulled the sleepy Kath out of her chair. "It's almost dawn, and Uncle Jacob will be heading out to sea to fish soon if we don't catch him now."

Kris rubbed the sleep from her eyes, then patted Magnus on the head. "Thank you, little bird. You can go home now."

Magnus whistled and hopped back up onto the stern of the vehicle, where he commenced to give the "engine phoenix" some chirped instructions. As soon as Kris and Cyrus were standing on the sand, the boat sped away. And in a matter of moments, it was almost out of sight.

Cyrus took Kris's paw, and together the two of them walked up the beach toward the cluster of sandstone buildings that made up Starspeak's only town.

"Here, don't forget your oilskin," Catherine said to her husband. "In case it rains."

Catherine watched Jacob tie his sandals. His face was weatherbeaten now and looked sunburned even in the shade of the house as he sat at the kitchen table. He scoffed. "It's not going to rain today, Catherine. The Forecasting Stone would have said something about it."

Catherine handed Jacob a cup of a steaming brownish beverage. "That stone is right in about one of four forecasts. I don't know why you trust it."

"It was kind of preoccupied about something today," Jacob said, putting down his sandal and accepting the cup. "I had to kick the thing to get it to answer, and when it did, it said 'Partly cloudy with a seventy percent chance of surprises.'"

"Hmph," Catherine said with a half-smile. "Well, rain is a surprise. Take your oilskin."

Jacob grumbled but slung the oilskin over his shoulder and resumed tying his sandal.

Catherine smiled as she walked back into the kitchen. That husband of hers was an interesting fellow. She'd seen him go from this kind of absent routine to frenetic activity when another fisherman needed help, or if there were a celebration to prepare for down in town. He was just lucky he had her to keep track of things so he didn't get hypothermia.

Catherine wiped her hands on her apron, and turned back to the bread dough she'd been kneading on the stone slab that made up her kitchen counter. It was a recipe for something called Artisan's Bread. She'd picked up the recipe from some coastal Ranshan traders who had passed through Starspeak a few weeks ago. It was simple enough to mix up, and one batch of the dough would make several small loaves. But the best part of it was that the batch of raw dough could be stored in a cool place, and a single batch of dough would make a half-dozen loaves. It could even be kept for more than a week before being baked.

Someone knocked on the door.

"Can you get that, Jacob? I'm up to my elbows in dough." Catherine heard him get up from his chair and open the door. Then there was silence for a moment. "Jacob? Who is it?"

"You'd best come out here, Catherine," Jacob said in a strange tone of voice.

Catherine frowned, but rinsed her hands in the basin next to the counter and walked out to the living room.

In the doorway stood a lanky, red-haired young man of twenty years or so, and a leopard-spotted Katheni girl, both of whom looked soaking wet and tired. Catherine put a hand to her mouth. "Cyrus?"

"Hi, Aunt Catherine," Cyrus said with a tired smile. "Can I borrow a towel or two?"

Needless to say, Jacob did not immediately leave to go fishing. Instead, Cyrus, Kris, and Cyrus's family sat around the driftwood table that Cyrus remembered from years ago and ate an impromptu hot meal. Catherine procured towels and dry clothes for both of them, all the while demanding to know what had been happening since his last letter. She scolded him heartily and repeatedly about not having sent another letter in more than a year. She also wanted to know how Sir Reginald Ogleby was doing and, more importantly, who this young woman was.

Kris, Cyrus noticed, looked distinctly uncomfortable and ill-at-ease. She was more than polite and courteous to his aunt and uncle, but she looked as if she were going to either bite someone or flee the room. Cyrus took Kris's paw and interlaced his fingers with hers.

With her hand firmly in his, Cyrus explained everything. The events of the last year, the Vale Massacre, his falling out with Reginald, his marriage to Kris, and their meeting with the Phoenix Prophet.

Uncle Jacob took the news well, with the exception of the massacre of the Heroes. This news disturbed him greatly, and he sat silently for a long time after Cyrus had finished.

Catherine, however, took the news of Kris and Cyrus as a couple with all the calm collection of a dog chasing its own tail.

At first mention of the fact, she looked shocked, causing Kris to cringe, but within moments, Catherine leapt up and smothered Kris in a motherly hug. "Congratulations, my dear!" she said, holding Kris at arm's length to look at her. "You know, I had Cyrus placed as a terminal bachelor like Sir Ogleby, always wandering around adventuring and never settling down."

"Gee, thanks Aunt Catherine," Cyrus said. "See if you can dig up some more backhanded compliments for me."

Catherine ignored Cyrus. "Now, I wouldn't have guessed Katheni," she said to Kris, who looked even more uncomfortable now, but also somewhat pleased. "Cyrus always liked short girls, though."

"Aunt Catherine!" Cyrus protested.

"What? Don't you remember Connie Faust? Five foot two. And Rebecca Anderson, the cliff diver? Not an inch over five feet. You said you liked her because she made a good chin rest."

"Aunt Cathernie—"

"And Maggie Hunt! Adorable girl, why'd you break it off with a girl who was only four foot ten?"

"Because her name was Magenta. Like the color. Seriously, Aunt Catherine . . ."

"And how could you forget Lydia Weatherblade? Captain of the swim team, Starspeak Archery Champion three years running, and almost six inches shorter than you!"

Cyrus clapped his palm to his forehead. "Because I didn't like being out-athletic'd. Besides, she was the one who broke up with me! Aunt Catherine, please!"

Catherine laughed. "Ah, my little boy wonder. Ever the easily embarrassed one. Anyway, don't you have something to help Jacob with?" she said. "I want to learn all about my new niece, and I can't do that with you interrupting me every thirty seconds." Cyrus sighed. "I guess we can find something to do. You okay with that, Kris?"

Kris nodded hesitantly. "Any chance to meet your family is a good thing," she said with a smile.

"All right. I'll go see if Uncle Jacob wants to go fishing with me after so long." Cyrus kissed Kris on the cheek, then ducked out the door, leaving the two women to talk about . . . well, whatever it was that women talked about when men weren't around.

It didn't take much convincing to get Jacob to take him fishing. Within the hour, the two of them were in Jacob's boat on the sparkling ocean just outside Starspeak's large harbor, their poles loaded with the high-tension line used to catch very large or dangerous fish. Cyrus was hoping for a Pyrradorsal to show Kris.

The water glimmered cerulean in the afternoon sun, fading into a deeper blue further out where it got deeper. The cries of seagulls punctuated the otherwise gentle sounds of the breeze and waves. The salt breeze, though, brought back more memories than Cyrus could handle, along with a wave of nostalgia. To think that only five years ago this was what he had been doing. It was what he would have been doing between then and now if the Heroes Guild hadn't found him. And it was what he was probably going to end up doing now that the bulk of Heroes had been wiped off the face of the planet. Cyrus the fisherman. That had once seemed a high calling.

"What are you thinking about, boy?" Jacob asked as he cast his line out into the deep.

Cyrus sighed. "The future. If Heroes are done and over with, and if Voshtyr's still hunting me, I'm going to have to find something innocuous to do to support Kris and I here."

"Well," Jacob began, "your aunt and I could—"

"Don't even go there, Uncle Jacob. I'm not going to sponge anything off of you. And no, before you ask, I don't want to join the fishing business." He made a wry face. "I've honestly had more than enough fish in my lifetime."

"Ah, but you were so good at it as a boy," Jacob said. "Why, the days you and I hauled in fish by the ton are some of the fondest memories of my life."

"Hauling fish in by the ton are some of the *only* memories of your life," Cyrus said. "No offense, but it wasn't exactly the most stimulating thing I've ever done."

Jacob chuckled. "Well, boy, then you'll have to find a way to get paid for doing something else you're good at. Like sleeping or forgetting to do chores."

"Gee, thanks," Cyrus said with a grimace. "I mean, I could work at the docks or something as a longshoreman, but I can do so much more than just lift heavy crates."

"But anything you do using your Heroic Powers will call attention to you," Jacob said. "You didn't bring anything back with you that you could use to make a living?"

Cyrus shook his head. "No, being shipwrecked will lose you lots of stuff. All I have now is abundant strength, an ability to use magic without rules, a beautiful wife, and a bunch of friends who may or may not still be alive." Cyrus stopped. "Wait, I did think of something a while back, just as a joke, but . . ."

"But what?"

"Well, it was a conversation I had with a dragon that Reg and I bumped into. Something about helping dragons invest their hoards instead of just sleeping on them." Cyrus cast his line out into the water, the weights and hook flying out much, much farther than his uncle's had. "Maybe I could contact Keeth and ask him if he wouldn't mind helping me get started on that."

"You met a dragon named Keith?" Jacob asked in amusement.

"Keeth. Two E's," Cyrus said. "Don't ask. It's a dragon thing."

Jacob began reeling in his line, slowly and in a zigzag pattern to better attract fish. "So you would be in charge of investing money belonging to dragons? What, into industries and merchant vessels and businesses that sell funny hats? That sounds like a highly dangerous proposition, boy."

"How so?"

"Think how angry a normal investor is when you lose his money. Now make him ten times your size and give him teeth the size of swords and the ability to breathe fire," Jacob said. "How's that for an occupational hazard? I'd take a pack of sharks over that any day."

Cyrus chuckled. "I doubt Keeth would incinerate me unless I did something deliberately dishonest. He can tell the difference between fraud and inexperience. Besides, it's something no one's ever done before."

"An untapped market," Jacob said, nodding thoughtfully. "That would be a good way to make money, even without unreasonable charges. Check your line, boy," he added, pointing to Cyrus's pole.

Cyrus glanced up at his fishing pole. The tip bounced and flexed, signaling the nibbling or movement of a fish on the end of the line. Cyrus straightened up and gave the pole a yank to set the hook.

Then the pole gave Cyrus a yank, almost pulling him out of the boat.

"Whoa! Uncle Jacob! We got a big one!" He braced his feet against the cross-braces of the boat. The yank became a steady inexorable pull that started dragging the boat across the water.

"Steady," Jacob said, stepping back to take the tiller and follow the fish. "If it's that big, we don't want it wrecking the boat."

"Psh, I can take it," Cyrus said. "I'm a Hero, remember?"

"Yes, but my boat isn't! If you and that fish break my boat, I can't earn a living."

Cyrus chuckled and began reeling the fish in. "All right, Uncle Jacob, I'll be careful," he said in a childish tone.

The fish, needless to say, resisted Cyrus's pull with all its might. But all its might was less than all of Cyrus's might. Cyrus cranked on the reel for a few moments, then gave the line a mighty tug.

The fish was indeed huge. The long blue fish leapt out of the water, and the sun glistened off the dual ridges of sword-like fins lining its back. Cyrus had snagged a Pyrradorsal.

"Woohoo! We're eating Dorsal steak tonight!" Cyrus shouted, reefing on the line, yanking the big fish in toward the boat against its will.

"Careful, boy!" Jacob shouted. "Mind the boat!"

Cyrus grimaced. This fish was giving him more trouble than he'd expected. "Well, get the bludgeon, and knock it out as soon as I get it in. I can keep it from cutting the hull out from under us. You just keep it from capsizing us."

Jacob retrieved the bludgeon from his tackle box. It was a large wooden club capped with steel. Starspeak fishermen used such weapons to stun or kill the larger fish they caught, fish that would otherwise prove problematic getting aboard.

Cyrus gave another incredible pull on the line, practically dragging the Pyrradorsal alongside the boat. Jacob swung the bludgeon, striking the pointy fish just behind its red-gold eye. It thrashed, but Jacob struck it again before it could damage the boat, and again when the fish continued moving. After the third blow, it struggled no more.

"Whoooee!" Cyrus exclaimed. "Now *that's* fishing!"

Jacob sat back in the boat, breathing heavily. "Let's not do that again."

"Oh, come on," Cyrus said. "Now you've got three hundred pounds of Pyrradorsal to sell at market tomorrow. That ought to help pay for some stuff, eh?" He hefted the enormous fish out of the water and into the boat. The tiny craft almost sank under the fish's weight, and water crept up to the gunwales. "I'll need some of the money, since Kris and I are going to need a place to live, and I don't want to live in your house."

"This amount would more than pay for a small house for the two of you," Jacob said. "Prices on Pyrradorsal have only gone up since you left. And I certainly don't mind helping you get a house of your own, since I don't want you taking up my couch."

Despite Jacob's protests, Cyrus did in fact spend that night on the couch, as the tiny bed he'd used before he'd left was barely large enough for Kris. But the next day, a merchant in search of exotic delicacies happened to be visiting the island, and he paid Jacob the handsome price of five hundred gold pieces for the usable meat of the Pyrradorsal.

This sale did not include the blade ridges. Those, Cyrus claimed for himself. He pulled and sharpened each of the ridges. The spines themselves were naturally sharp, strong as iron, and much lighter. He then took them to market, and he got almost another hundred for the spines. He even kept a few to attempt making a sword for himself.

In less than a month, Cyrus had the money, the property, and the unreasonably-difficult-to-obtain permits to allow him to build himself and Kris a home on Starspeak. And build he did. Near the eastern end of the island, bordered on one side by beach and one by a sheer cliff, he and Kris, along with some well-wishing friends of the Solburg family, built a three-room house made of sandstone, palm thatch, and driftwood struts.

On the day it was complete, Cyrus sent a letter via postal bird to the Mountains of the Morning, addressed to Keeth, Son of Barinol. Hopefully he would hear from his draconic friend soon. That night, he carried Kris across the threshold of their new home, where they would try to begin a new life as ordinary people.

Try being the operative word, since the next few days would prove that extraordinary people cannot live ordinary lives.

Chapter Six

A Gathering of Traitors

*In which the Heroes Guild regroups to Flee
and Serimal begins collecting the Fifth Column*

FAR ABOVE THE ground, the broken ground, the smoking and trampled ground of Centra Mundi, an enormous bird with a passenger coasted out of the range of siege engines and flew over the wall of Bryath Castle. The passenger patted the giant bird on the side of its neck, and leapt from the creature's back. He tumbled through the air, his green clothing flapping wildly in the wind until he managed to straighten his fall into a directional plummet.

Blasts of magic and a storm of arrows shot up at him, but he fell too fast to be a viable target for the horde of black-armored men and foul creatures outside the damaged walls of the capital city. He began to worry that he was falling too fast for even his allies to catch.

This fear turned out to be ungrounded, as was he, as his fall halted ten feet above the ground and turned into a gentle hover before setting him down in the center of the courtyard. Several buildings were on fire. People ran about in a state of panic, being herded in various directions by surviving Heroes. Wounded Heroes and members of the town guard lay in the streets, propped up against walls and carts. It seemed to be the beginning of an evacuation. And the evacuation was exactly what Green had come to report on.

Voshtyr's army had caught up with them mere days after their mass retreat to Bryath and had laid siege to the castle. The first thing they had done was cut all form of communication. Hence his mission.

"Whew," he said, taking off his jaunty hat and wiping his brow with it. "That was a close one. Did you see those *pitchin* shooting at me? I should get hazard pay!"

"Can it, Green," said a man in purple platemail as he walked up to the man in green. He was tall, just over seven and a half feet, counting the boots, and broad as an ox at the shoulders. A shock of somewhat bedraggled blond hair hung through the back of his helmet. A symbol of a sword laid across an open book bedecked the front of the dented armor, and an ornate Damascene sword larger than even Sir Reginald's hung from a catch on the back of the armor. His helmet visor was open, showing off his noble features, his blue eyes, high cheekbones and strikingly white eyebrows. "If this wasn't a *kharestin* war, I'm sure you would. But it is, so you're not."

"We are glad to see you unharmed," said a priest in white and gold, finishing off and shutting down the spell that had stopped Green's fall. He was far shorter than the armored man, with silver hair and an air of authority about him. One might guess looking at him that he was in his late forties. His garments were that of clergy, though some parts of it were subtly reinforced with woven Mithril and leather padding. An array of scroll cases hung at his belt, along with a tome bearing on its cover a symbol of a cup overlayed on a shining sun. "But Purple is right. We have no time for complaints. Tell us, what did Rubic say?"

Green scowled at his compatriots while brushing off his shirt. "Rubic says that if we can get to the Academy, we can use it as a staging ground. But he says we can't stay there forever."

The priest, known as the Yellow Sun despite his white garb, nodded. "I understand. We cannot ask him to put his students in danger to protect us. And what did Baron von Kamish say?"

"Baron von Kamish died this morning," Green said, taking off his hat. The three Heroes stood in silence for a moment before Green continued. "He was shot by a poisoned arrow when the fighting began in Salvinsel. The Solid Wall says the Baron was doing just fine until two days ago, when he lapsed into a fever. He never pulled out of it."

"Nine Torments," Purple said, resting his head in a gauntleted hand. "Did he get the permission to move in on Clawstrike Island?"

Green smiled wryly. "Yeah, he got someone to 'misplace' the passwords and guard shifts. We should have them by tomorrow. So we're just going to snatch Clawstrike Island out from under the Hereditary Evil Empire and use it as a base?"

"Yes," Yellow said. "They are so busy with their own problems that they will not have the time or resources to try taking it back from us. Besides," he added, turning around to administer a healing spell to a wounded guardsman behind him, "the island is mostly a den of pirates and other similar ne'er-do-wells. The world will not miss it."

Purple scowled. "I still don't understand why we can't stay here. We have fortified walls, we have siege engines, and we have supplies to last months. Couldn't we just outlast them here?"

Yellow shook his head. "Our capabilities to fight here are hampered by the risk of getting the civilian population involved. Add to that the diplomatic troubles . . ."

"Diplomatic troubles?" Green said. "Don't tell me Voshtyr's sent an emissary to King Bryath."

"I'm afraid so." Yellow looked up at the castle keep at the center of the city. "We just got word that we need to clear out of the city, and take anything and everything with us that could cause the Villains to attack the city. Our Guild Property, our families, pets, and, of course, the Cookware Heroic."

"What? Those cowards!" Purple slammed one gauntlet into the other, then struggled to pull it out. "They would abandon us to the cold cruelty of Voshtyr and his ilk?"

Green elbowed Purple. "Listen, I don't think it's Bryath's fault, you know?"

"How so?" Purple rasied an eyebrow. "Do you think he is under duress?"

"Sort of, but not really. That's a big scary army Voshtyr's got out there, and given what he did to the castle with a much, much smaller force five years ago, I'd be scared too."

Yellow nodded. "Not to mention that their strongest defense—us—has been almost entirely destroyed. A year ago, no one could have taken Bryath in a siege. Now? We don't even have enough Heroes left to man the walls. Speaking of which . . ." He turned to shout up at the parapets. "Howling Fang! How are you and Frozen Steel doing?"

A burly man clad in wolf pelts paused in his punching of a black-and-purple-clad Villain, who had apparently tried to jump over the wall. "Sorry," he said to the Villain. "Yellow wants something, do you mind?"

The Villain shrugged feebly. "No, not at all, go right ahead."

"Thanks." He leaned over to shout down to Yellow. "I think we're doing all right, but we're going to need someone to replace Steel here in a bit. He took a pair of javelins in the leg, and he can't run between scaling ladders quite as quick."

Yellow waved to him. "All right, we'll get someone up there as soon as possible."

"Is that all?" the Villain asked.

"I think so," the Howling Fang said. "Now, where were we?"

"Facepunching," the Villain replied. "Not so hard this time, okay? I have a date tonight who doesn't approve of men wearing makeup, even to cover bruises."

"If you say so," Fang said, and resumed the drubbing.

Yellow turned back to face Green and Purple. "We are facing a manpower crisis. If we don't get out and to a location without a civilian population before this army encircles the city, we are doomed."

Purple grimaced. "Clawstrike is defensible, but if we went there I would mislike the idea of being less than a dozen leagues from the Empire at all times."

"Beggars can't be gourmets," Green said, "unless they're beggars who are also theives . . . and unless they're really good at stealing food. And I'd say that Clawstrike is a peach, as far as retreat locations go. And a peach is pretty gourmet, as far as fruit goes. And—"

"Thank you, Green," Yellow said, cutting the thief off. "He is right, though. We were lucky enough to find this place on such short notice. Now, let's begin the evacuation. Purple?" He cast an Amplify spell on Purple's helmet. "Announce departure.

Green, get the convoy ready to go, then see if you can find Blue. He's supposed to be protecting Guardian's family. Go."

The three Spectrum Heroes broke off in different directions as Purple donned his now voice-amplifying helmet and announced to the population of Bryath that the convoy would depart in ten minutes time.

"But I can take them!" the blond boy protested, battering his fists against the blue-tinted breastplate of the Hero holding him. "Let me go! My father must be avenged!"

The Hero shook his head. "Let it be, Trigger. I do not doubt your bravery, but you cannot take on that many Villains all at once. Even the Spectrum Heroes all together can't, which is why we are retreating."

"You can't?" Trigger looked up at the Hero's face. "I thought you guys could do anything, Blue."

Blue chuckled. "Anything within the realm of possibility, and some things just outside it. But this many Villains, plus that flying city and all those nasty mythologicals?" He shook his head again. "We could do a good deal of damage, but we would lose. And then I wouldn't be here to make sure that you and your mother got away safely." He set Trigger back down and looked about the room. "Anything else you need in here?"

There wasn't really much in the room to begin with, and what there was had been packed into two small wooden crates. The walls of the stone room was bare except for a cheap painting of the Spectrum Heroes as idealized by bards, another painting of the Solid Wall done in the same style, and a map of the world with pins stuck in it in places where Hero/Villain conflicts were happening. Or had been, Blue thought. Right now, all the pins were stuck in Bryath City.

"Just my posters," Trigger said. The boy pulled the paintings off the wall and carefully rolled them up.

Blue walked over to the room's one window and looked out. From the house's vantage point atop one of the three hills Bryath rested on, he could see the western wall, which had taken the brunt of the attack so far. One of the guardhouses was on fire again, and two more of the siege ballistae had been smashed since he last checked. At least the wall was still holding.

It was a good thing, too, as the seemingly endless horde of Minions, Henchmen, Toadies, Lesser Basilisks, Tax Collectors, and other monstrosities would otherwise waltz right in. Especially the Waltzing Golems, who had already sashayed their way up to pound on the front gate.

Far off in the distance, as if observing the conflict, floated a city in the air, suspended by nothing but clouds. It sent shivers down his spine just to look at it.

"All set," Trigger said, trying to pick up the two crates. He was too young yet to show signs of Heroic strength, but he still managed to pick one of them almost all the way up.

"Then let us depart," Blue said, lifting the second crate with one arm and scooping Trigger and his crate up with the other.

The Hero made his way down the hallway, avoiding the strained bustle of other Heroes and commoners rushing about to collect the necessities and evacuate the Guildmaster's home. Most ran about with stacks of books and scrolls, though a few carried weapon and flag cases.

Over three thousand years' worth of personnel records and some important artifacts had been under the direct care of Richard Guardian. These would now pass to the next Guildmaster when the Guild managed to reassemble and choose one. Which, Blue reflected, was probably not going to be for a while.

"Good, you've got the boy," Green said as he ducked into the house and spotted his friend. "Hiya, Trig," he said to the boy over Blue's shoulder. "Guess what I found you?"

Trigger straightened up as best he could in Blue's grasp. "What, Green?"

Green handed the boy a small, unpainted silver figurine. "HeroCo was just starting work on this one and never got a chance to release it," he said, closing Trigger's hand around the figurine and looking away. "I . . . borrowed the prototype from the office. I figured you should have it."

The boy opened his hand, and gasped. "Green . . . this is . . ."

Green nodded. "It's your dad, Trig. They had the Swift Justice models set to come out this Midwinter. But if the workshop's going to get overrun by Villains . . ." He shrugged. "Better you have it than them."

Trigger's face clouded.

"Hey, none of that," Green said, tilting Trigger's head up and wiping away an errant tear from the boy's eye. "You can make sure they finish production when you lead the Heroes back in here and kick the Villains out." He swung a fist into his own palm and grinned. "Now, if you'll 'scuse me, I have a couple more things I need to 'ensure the safety of' so they don't fall into Villainous hands. See ya!" And with that, he ducked back out the door.

Blue snorted. For all the happy-go-lucky demeanor Green wore most of the time, he could see that his friend was hurting.

He'd been closer to Guardian than most of the other Heroes, ostensibly because the Guildmaster had to keep an eye on the rogue's sticky fingers. But also because Guardian had treated Green like a second son, an older brother to Trigger.

Guardian's death, an explosive self-sacrifice to destroy a dozen Villains and a score of incredibly dangerous Darkmatter Golems, was Heroic to the full extent of Epic Poetry. But it had disorganized the Guild and depressed its members at a time when they could afford neither. And now it fell to Blue to get Guardian's son—the living symbol of the youth and future of the Guild—to safety.

While Trigger still clutched the silver figurine, Blue exited the building. It was time to join the caravan.

Purple sat brooding on a northern parapet overlooking the dark army massed against the walls of Bryath City. It was strange to him that this day had come. To Purple, Heroes embodied invulnerability. The world had prospered under their reign. So how—and why—had it come to this? He sighed and turned away. Philosophy on why evil could triumph over good was the realm of... well, philosophers. Now there was fighting to be done, though it was a retreat. He leapt down from his perch and landed with a loud *clang* in the courtyard, then trudged his way to the south gate.

Green and Yellow were there waiting for him.

"Everything ready?" Purple asked as Green and Yellow met him back at the south gate. The caravan was prepared. Hundreds of peasants had been loaded into the covered wagons. They waited there now, clutching their children and belongings.

Merchants sat with the best of their wares, which they had snatched before abandoning their shops. Livestock was aboard too, terrified by the periodic discharges of siege engines over or into the walls. The sounds of sheep bleating, children crying, and shouted orders blended together into a wash of grey noise. The stink of fear hung heavily in the air, mingled with sharp tang of burning buildings near the west gate, and the smell of blood from the wounded.

Yellow nodded. "I have *Epic Invisibility of the Legion* prepared. It won't last more than a half-hour with this many people, but that should give us enough time to get the caravan away. If they hurry."

"I checked up with what remains of the Salvinsel Salamanders," Green said, twirling *Universality of Insanity*, one of his twin daggers, around his right hand. "They're ready for a hit-and-run to draw off pursuit, but they can't handle a drawn-out engagement. Even with Hero support."

"As if we had much of that to begin with," Purple said with a sigh. "Very well. I shall give the order to move out. Has anyone seen Red?"

Yellow shook his head.

"Not since yesterday," Green said. "He said something about fighting fire with fire, and skedaddled to go get something. He didn't say what."

Purple snorted. "Curse that coward, disappearing just when we need him. Well, we shall have to move on without him. Yellow, whenever you're ready. Oh, and Green?"

"Hmm?"

"Keep your hands off the merchants' goods." Purple pointed a finger at Green. "They're losing enough as it is."

Green chuckled. "Psh, you're no fun at all. Well, gotta go. I'll let Rubic know we're coming." The thief stepped away from the group and knelt down. A wash of neon green energy surrounded him as he looked to the sky and leapt up with a shout of his Heroic name. "*Greeeeeen FALCON!*"

Purple watched the green contrail meet up with a giant bird in the sky, then disappear entirely. "Come on, Yellow," he said, sounding far more tired than he'd meant to. "Let's get these people to safety."

Serimal looked out the window and received a pleasant surprise. "Nieva!" he said over his shoulder, "tell the Minions to light the signal on the roof. Slashback is coming in! Hmm, and have them ready crossbows. I wasn't expecting a rider."

Indeed, the silhouette of a gryphon on the wing, bearing a rider, drew closer in the night, backlit by the half-moon in the northwestern sky. Within moments, the signal fire in the castle's second-tallest tower sprang to life, along with the glowing landing pad bearing a large capital letter "G."

Serimal rushed up two flights of stairs and pushed open the heavy oak door leading to the landing pad. A rush of cold salt wind assaulted his face as he stepped outside to greet his guest. The stars shone brightly, perhaps too brightly for night flying, but Slahback seemed to have made it safely.

The gryphon, or gryphoness, as it happened, shook her head violently to rid it of the black hood she had been wearing. "Hate nightwear," she spat, clicking her beak. "Folds down ears. Uncomfortable." Her feather-tufted, pointed ears sprang free of the restrictive fabric, and she looked much more at ease.

She saluted Serimal with a wingtip. "Slashback is pliss to report for duties."

"A warm welcome to you, Slashback," Serimal said, striding up and offering the scarred gryphon his hand. "It is good to see you unharmed. And who is your passenger?"

The rider slid down from the gryphon's back, then pulled off a black leather facemask, revealing a youthful feminine face framed by straight blond hair. She snapped to attention and saluted Serimal. "Captain Emily Cartwright, Salvinsel Salamanders, at your service, sir. And friend of Slashback's— Wait a minute." She gave Serimal a hard look. "Slashback! What is the meaning of this?" she demanded, reaching for the rapier at her side.

Slashback elbowed the woman, who lost both her balance and her grip on her rapier. "Shut, Emli. Is Koshtyr's brother, not Koshtyr," the gryphon said. "Is friend of mine. And friend of mine . . ."

" . . . is a friend of mine," Emily said, getting up with a scowl. "My apologies, sir. Thought you were Voshtyr. I don't normally draw on people unprovoked, but ol' Captain Demonpants's been doin' an awful lot of provokin' me these days."

Serimal waved a hand dismissively. "It is a common mistake, Captain Cartwright. The only major difference in our appearances is the eyes." Serimal pointed to his. "Mine don't glow, and don't turn funny colors when I'm about to murder someone. And," he said, stroking his chin, "I have a beard."

Emily grinned. "You call that little wispy stubble a beard?"

"Rude wench," Serimal said. "It just doesn't want to come in properly. I've not tried to grow one before."

Nieva stepped out of the door as well, the wind blowing her black dress wildly about her. "Yes, love, it's a very fine beard.

Now come in, all of you, before this wind freezes the lot of you," she said with a smile. "You must be chilled from all that flying. Can I get you something hot to drink?"

"Rum," Emily said with a grin. "If you've any available."

"Milk," Slashback said. "Gallon, pliss."

Serimal chuckled and began herding his guests toward the door. "Ah, Slashback. Ever the dairy hound."

"Not hound. Gryphon," Slashback said emphatically, and stalked inside.

"Dairy hound?" Emily asked as she and Serimal followed in Slashback's feathered wake.

Serimal closed the door behind him, shutting off the frigid wind. "Most gryphons have a fondness for milk. Probably something to do with being half large cat," he said as the continued walking. "But being birds as well, they don't nurse as hatchlings. I suppose that craving carries over their entire life. Slashback, though . . ."

"What about her?"

"She goes far beyond fondness into the realm of obsession," Serimal said. "Any dairy product, you name it: cheese, curds, milk, iced cream, butter, anything of that sort, she devours it by the ton. It's a wonder Voshtyr managed to feed her so long in that dismal swamp."

The broad stone stairway wound down for quite some time before meeting another that proceeded at a much gentler slope. It terminated in a dining room brightly lit by torches in wall sconces and a radiant crystal protruding from the ceiling. The room was not large. It would seat perhaps ten people, with a proportionately sized table made of obsidian. The carpet was a rich green, flecked throughout with silver threads. More light came from a cheerful fire blazing in a fireplace at one end of the room. It was a good thing, too, as the castle was otherwise quite damp and drafty, as Villainic architecture is wont to be.

An enormous painted woodcarving hung on the far wall between two tall windows overlooking the sea. It bore the von Steinadler coat of arms: a pair of black basilisks flanking a shield divided into quarters. Two of the quarters bore a spread-winged bat, while the other two bore a lidless reptilian eye. Atop the shield rested a helmet of simple, swept-back visor design, crested by a crescent. Behind them all were a pair of crossed longswords.

Emily shuddered visibly. "So you're a Villain too," she said softly.

"Yes, Captain," Serimal replied. "The von Steinadlers are and have been Villains for thousands of years. The coat of arms is . . . was . . . my father's. Voshtyr's made his own now, but I'll keep up the family name. Now, where's that drink you were promised?"

Nieva arrived in moments, bearing a silver tray of beverages. There was a mug of hot buttered rum for Emily, a mug of mulled wine for Serimal, and a basin of steaming milk for Slashback, along with an assortment of napkins. The gryphon sat down on a sofa at one end of the table and immediately began greedily sucking down the beverage. Nieva sat down at Serimal's right hand and sipped daintily from a glass of what looked like ice water with lemon.

"So, Captain . . ." Serimal began.

"Please," Emily said. "My name's Emily. I'm hardly Captain of anything after what your brother did to my outfit."

"Half-brother," Serimal said, taking a sip of his wine. "My deepest and most sincere apologies for his actions. They go far beyond the limits of Villainy, into the realm of despicable Evil." He set the glass down on the table and turned to face

Emily directly. "Now, Emily. I know that Slashback trusts you, because of your relation to her former rider, Gavin Cartwright. You two met during the conflagration surrounding the Vale of Dreams, I understand."

"Yeah, had our share of differences with the Heroes, 'specially considering that the Crimson Slash accidentally killed my uncle—her rider. But we didn't want 'em all dead. They're the good guys."

Serimal held up his hand. "Wait. I am not yet finished. Be that as it may, I cannot trust you simply because Slashback does. You understand. So I will tell you this much, and then you can decide if you will stay for what is about to occur or whether you would prefer to be escorted to the location of your choice." Serimal took a much deeper draft of his wine this time and wiped his mouth on a cloth napkin. "You are a mercenary, I believe, and will thus have heard of the Fifth Column."

"The Fifth Column Corporate Espionage Conglomerate?" Emily set her mug down with a muted *clunk*. "The defunct rent-a-spy organization?"

"Not defunct so much as retired," Serimal said, looking into the heart of the fire. It blazed away, crackling every now and then as logs shifted and pockets of pitch flared up.

"I used to run it," Serimal said after a time, "and I'm about to bring it out of retirement to fight Voshtyr."

Emily leaned forward in her chair. "Really? How many people do you have?"

"To protect them, I cannot say," Serimal said. "You'll find out if you stay. I can say only that I have men and women from the Fifth Column who even now are close enough to Voshtyr to stab him in that shriveled thing he calls a heart, should the need arise."

He spun the wine in his glass. "So, what is your wish? You have two options. One, I send you away from here, and you forget everything you heard and saw. Or, two, you can coordinate messages for me and gather the remainder of your Salamanders to help us strike when the moment is right. I believe we could use a few score of righteously angry mercenaries out to avenge their fallen comrades. What say you?"

Emily sat silently for several moments. "You know what," she said, "I'm game. A chance to take down that *yarrak kafali* sounds like just the kind of job I need right now."

Serimal nodded. "Then you shall meet the others. Nieva, my love, would you bring the rest in?" he asked.

Nieva smiled. "Of course, beloved. Let our plotting begin." She rose from the chair and left the room by the large double doors at the south end of the room.

It was time to betray the traitor. Ironically, Serimal realized, had he still been an active member of the Brotherhood of the Black Hand, such traitorous betrayal, combined with conspiracy to commit fratricide and usurp a hereditary title, would have boosted him up several ranks in their dark hierarchy.

Nieva returned momentarily, followed by a tattooed man with strange, black, mechanical arms and legs; a very pale man with a horrid-looking bow strapped across his back, a being that looked like a shuffling black robe with a beak sticking out the front, and an Eastern Islander in a grey silk kimono decorated with embroidered fish.

Emily started as the latter entered the room. "Koshiro!" she exclaimed. "What are you doing here?"

The man looked almost as surprised as Emily. "Greetings to you, Emily-san. I would ask the same of you, but . . ." he glanced over to Serimal, who nodded . . . "but I believe it would be obvious that I am here to cause harm to Voshtyr-dono."

"Please," Nieva said, "all of you take your seats."

The strange group did so, ignored by Slashback, who had fallen asleep with a belly full of warm milk.

"It seems to me," Serimal began, rising from his chair, "it wasn't long ago that I sat in a council very similar to this one executing the plans of my half-brother Voshtyr. It was shortly after he locked me into an Iron Maiden that I began to question the benefits of that arrangement."

Emily winced. The beaked robe sat silent. The pale man and metal-limbed man chuckled grimly. Koshiro frowned. Nieva sipped her ice water. Slashback snored.

"All of you know what he has done now," Serimal continued. "He has wiped out most known Heroes and taken full or partial control of many world governments. He has even dared attack the glorious Empire. If this is not proof of his madness, I know not what would be.

"So now I have asked that you, my friends, my compatriots from my youth, remnants of my faithful Fifth Column, stand up with me against my half-brother's madness. But first," Serimal said, walking around the table, "some of you do not know each other. Allow me to make introductions."

"As long as you are hurry," the beaked robe said, pulling back its hood. Beneath the hood was an Avierie, most of his feathers golden brown, save for around his eyes, where a creeping blackness glowered. "Voshtyr is expect me back soonly."

• • •

The Avierie are the Race with the fewest members. These strange, reclusive bird-folk are known for being excessively territorial, and for being dabblers in dark, shamanistic magics.

The average Avierie stands no taller than five feet, with taloned feet, curved predatory beaks, and feathered wings where a Human would have arms. These wings are unique in that they have three prehensile claws at the end of the wing bone, like two fingers and a thumb, just before the pinfeathers start, allowing them a measure of manual dexterity, at least enough to grasp objects and use tools and weapons.

Avierie are light, incredibly so. An adult male Avierie can weigh as little as forty or fifty pounds, thanks to their hollow bones and streamlined form. This also makes them weaker and more fragile than other Races.

Coloration varies from shades of brown to shades of grey and white. Leaders are born, not elected, as an Avierie hatchling with golden feathers amongst its others is a natural leader and more intelligent than its peers. Avierie with black feathers do exist, but only among the eldest and most powerful of the shaman caste that serve as advisors to the leader caste.

Their society is based on varying levels of rank, or castes. At the bottom are the worker caste, who maintain all Avierie structures and do whatever other menial labor required by the clan. Next are the hunter caste, who, as the name suggests, hunt for the clan. Then come the warriors, who are stronger and faster than the lower castes and receive training in weaponry and aerial fighting. Last are the leadership caste, who guide the clan in time of war and rule in time of peace.

It is a patriarchal society as well. Females are treated as second-class citizens, though a female of a higher caste still holds higher status in society than males of a lower caste. There are some voices in the leadership caste that argue against this discrimination, but they are few and far between.

The shaman class broods above them all, not as part of the caste system, but outside it. They practice magic akin to sorcery, dealing with souls and other things best left alone. It gradually corrupts them, turning their feathers blacker as they progress further in it, until eventually their frail bodies can take no more abuse, and they die.

Of course the Avier would be in a hurry, Serimal realized. He could probably just barely spare the time for this meeting in between his sinister tasks for Voshtyr.

Serimal nodded. "Very well, Skri'ki. I shall make this as brief as possible." He turned to face the rest of the people at the table. "This is Skri'ki, whose last name is not pronounceable in Central. He was once High Shaman of the Silvervale Clan. He now works for Voshtyr, trafficking soul gems and dark-matter and all manner of things no untrained merchant would handle. Not even Lord Roger Farella dares touch such things. Speaking of which," he said, turning back to Skri'ki, "why is Roger not here?"

Skri'ki glowered at Serimal through his black-rimmed eyes. "Lord Farella, he say this: to not contact him again or you are making the risk with your life and his life. He is not to come to meet you here or any place that is not here."

Serimal sighed. "Thank you for delivering the message, Skri'ki. I suppose he is in too deep to help us after all." Serimal moved on to the next chair. "This is Jolan Foster, called the Ebon Lance. He was once a Hero, but has now joined our cause."

The metal-limbed man raised a black metal hand and waved. The whirring of gears and arcane motors was just barely audible with his every movement. The artificial limbs started at the joint sockets for each, the arms sprouting directly from the shoulder, and the legs from the pelvis. It was as if the limbs were not artificial at all but were actually a part of him. His scalp was shaved bald and bedecked with a tattoo, and his green eyes were narrow and full of hate. Unusual for a Hero, perhaps, but that was why Serimal found him so useful.

Serimal moved on. "Some of you already know Koshiro Sakana, the Silver Fish, of the Salvinsel Salamanders," he said, stopping at Koshiro's chair. "Koshiro was one of the founding members of Fifth Column, back before I went to the Villain Academy."

Koshiro rose and bowed politely to each person in the chamber, then sat again. He was short for a Hero, not much taller than five feet. His hair was black and protruded from his head in wavy spikes common to his native land. His eyes were grey, as was his robe, which had embroidered fish all over it. At his side hung a katana with decorative silver scrollwork on the sheath.

"He may perhaps talk too much," Serimal said, chuckling, "but when you get him to cease there is not a stealthier man alive. This over here," he added, ruffling the feathers of the sleeping gryphon, "is Slashback Ricor. She was in Voshtyr's pocket for years, and for all he knows, she's still there. It can't hurt to acquire another airborne ally.

"Some of you I have not seen for years, so you may not know that I am engaged to this lovely young woman," Serimal continued, moving to Nieva's chair. "This is Nievalarai Seriasthani, Princess of Eal'reas, the Chillwind peninsula, on Lorimar."

Nieva rose and curtseyed politely before sitting back down.

"And last but not least," Serimal said, gesturing to the pale man with the strange and horrific bow strapped to his back, "is Zaccheus, a relatively new addition to our outfit, but far more experienced than he will let me say." The young Villain nodded to Zaccheus, who nodded back.

"So who is girl?" Skri'ki asked, pointing a prehensile talon at Emily.

"Emily Cartwright, formerly captain in the Salvinsel Salamanders," Serimal answered. "She's the niece of Slashback's former rider. She may be joining us."

"Or maybe she is tell Voshtyr of what we do," the Avierie said, glowering across the table at Emily.

"Oh, right," Emily said with a sneer. "Because Voshtyr was completely civil and kind to me and didn't even try to kill me a little bit."

Serimal slapped a hand down on the table with a bang that resounded in the small room. "That's very much enough of that," he said flatly. "We are here to address a threat to the entire world, not bicker amongst ourselves. However, if you consider bickering a worthwhile pastime, I encourage you to join Voshtyr's forces. Your infighting will only help us if you're on the opposite side."

Skri'ki snapped his beak shut and scooted back into his chair without another word. Emily glared at the bird-man for a few moments before slouching back in her chair and looking back at Serimal.

"Now," Serimal said, taking his place at the head of the table, "for our first order of business. We must find Cyrus Solburg before Voshtyr does."

"Why?" Jolan asked, leaning his elbows on the table and putting two divots in the wood. "Between the people you have assembled here we have enough firepower, bladepower, and stealth to take on a small army. What do we need some traitor apprentice for?"

"My sources tell me that Voshtyr is dangerously close to completing the P.L.O.T. Device," Serimal said.

"The what?" Jolan said.

"It's a complicated device made of multiple artifacts, designed to enhance and boost the physical, mental, and magical abilities of the user." Serimal snapped his fingers, and a shimmering image appeared in midair. It was a strange machine with turbines, control panels, a pendulum, wires, and a coffin sized just right to fit a person.

Serimal pointed at the image. "This machine, once fully assembled and fueled, can make someone immortal, and depending upon their capabilities before entering, almost omnipotent. Should Voshtyr be able to complete this machine, he will be able to crush all resistance, and there will be nothing we can do to stop him."

Emily leaned over to scratch Slashback behind the ears. "Sounds like a good thing to stop." Slashback emitted a noise somewhere between a cluck and a purr. "But that looks like it's complete already."

Nieva rose from her chair. "It is complete, but it is not yet fueled," she said. "In order to complete its transformation, it needs four incredibly powerful magic gems. The Heartstones of the Elements. Along with one more thing."

"And that is?" Jolan asked.

"Cyrus Solburg," Serimal said. "In order to channel that much elemental energy into one person, the soul of a person incredibly in tune with the elements is needed as a conduit. We've seen Solburg in action, and he's the perfect choice, not to mention that Voshtyr has been out for Cyrus's blood for some time, as well as that of his mentor, Sir Reginald Ogleby."

"The Crimson Slash?" Skri'ki said, fluttering out of his chair. "I am not to work with this man! He iss Hero who has done many breakings of my business!"

Nieva put a hand on Skri'ki's shoulder. "Yes, but difficult times and dangerous opponents make strange alliances."

Skri'ki glowered. "Iss not to my taste. I will not do this."

"What's the big deal here?" Emily asked. "What happens if we don't stop Voshtyr?"

"If he finishes this device and transforms himself in it, he won't need that dark army to take over the world," Serimal said. "He'll become an invincible, indestructible, indefatigable, inconceivable, incorrigible opponent with no morals and no conscience, and other 'in-' words I can't even think of right now. If he transforms, even the full military might of the Hereditary Evil Empire would not be able to stop him."

"And Cyrus?" Jolan asked. "The traitor apprentice?"

"His soul will be consumed," Nieva said, "and all will be lost."

Serimal extinguished the image and planted his hands on the table. "Now, we must do what we as the Fifth Column do best. Recon. Evaluate. Theive. We need to get those Heartstones before Voshtyr does, and we need to get them to Cyrus Solburg."

Skri'ki almost fluttered out of his chair again. "What? Give these things to a Hero?"

"Enemy of my enemy, you know," Serimal said. "He can channel the Elements in an extraordinary way. If the signs are correct, then he can channel entire ley-lines perfectly, given the opportunity. And the Heartsones would hone his ability to perfect himself and his use of the Elements."

"Exchanging one possible tyrant for another." Jolan crossed his arms, and they clanked. "How is he any better?"

"Better a powerful known quanitity, even if good, than an invulnerable one with no moral compass," Nieva said.

Serimal stood up straight. "Now let's get to it. You all know what to do."

Chapter Seven

Too Conspicuous

In which Cyrus finds that he cannot Escape Notice
and an Araquellus analyzes Heroics

SOMEONE WAS SHAKING Cyrus by the shoulders.

"Cyrus," that someone said, "you may want to come out here and see this."

"'S early," Cyrus groaned, throwing his arm across his eyes.

Kris threw open the blue curtains, letting sun in and provoking another groan from her mate. "It's almost noon, Cyrus. That hardly counts as early."

"Is it?" Cyrus sat up and reached for the homespun shirt that usually hung on a post of their bed.

Kris already had it in her paw. She handed it to him with a smile. "Yes, sleepy, it is. And you'd better get out here before I tell your guest that you're sleeping through his visit."

Cyrus grumbled, but slung his legs out of bed as he pulled on the shirt. It was fairly comfortable, if a bit of a strange fit. Kris had made it for him, and it was a fine shirt, but her weaving skills had been in the Katheni style, and the shoulders of said shirt were built for a Katheni, not a Human. It fit a bit tightly, especially considering that all the physical labor he'd been doing since he'd gotten back, in addition to his Heroic Exercises, had built up a good chunk of muscle mass in him.

He stuck his legs into a pair of sailcloth pants and slung the bit of rope he'd been using as a belt around his waist, including the homemade sword fashioned from the Pyrradorsal's fin ridges. His Heroic garb was still in the drawers where they now dry-rotted away. His blue apprentice's tunic simply lay there forlornly, abandoned in the bottom of the drawer. Cyrus still looked at it from time to time and sighed. He always tried to close it before Kris noticed, but she did sometimes anyway.

Cyrus stepped out into the sunlight, blinking and shading his eyes with his arm. "Where is he, Kris?" Cyrus asked, looking about. "I can't see anything with this giant green dragon in the way." Wait a minute, giant green dragon? "Keeth!" Cyrus shouted, and ran toward the great scaled beast relaxing on the sun-baked sand.

Keeth rose and stretched, shaking the sand from his deep green scales. "Ah, Cyrus," the dragon rumbled, "it is good to see you alive and in good health."

The gigantic green dragon was an interesting contrast to the yellow-white of the sand on the beach. The late morning sun had already begun heating up the island, turning the surface of the sea cerulean. Fishing boats were already out at sea, visible from the doorway, and the shouts of children playing on the beach carried down the length of the island. There were snakelike scale marks on the beach from where Keeth had walked, his tail likely dragging in the warm sand. It was a beautiful day.

Keeth extended a massive talon to Cyrus. "Tell me, how does life as a peasant find you?"

Cyrus took and shook the claw, a wry grin on his face. "I've never been so bored in my entire existence. There's only a couple things here that keep me from going absolutely stir crazy."

"Not too stir crazy," Kris said, walking up behind him and wrapping her arms around his waist. "No stirring. You have to *blend* in, after all."

"And here's one of them right now," Cyrus told Keeth, rolling his eyes as he turned back to rub his nose against Kris's. "You get me so *mix*ed up, sometimes, Kris."

Keeth snorted. "You should both be *whip*ped for those puns." The dragon sat back on his haunches and reached behind himself, producing a bag as large as Cyrus, of what sounded like heavy metal objects. "I did not come for your spectacularly poor sense of humor, but to do business."

Cyrus started. "Holy— Keeth, please tell me that isn't money in that bag."

"It is not money in this bag," Keeth said with a toothy smile.

Kris leapt on top of the bag and pulled open the drawstring. She promptly fell off again, a dazed expression on her feline face. "You are a poor liar, Keeth."

Cyrus pulled the lip of the bag toward himself and received a shower of small gemstones in the face. Rubies, emeralds, diamonds, garnets, and other assorted cut and polished stones bounced off his skull. He covered his face with his arm. "Keeth! What . . . How . . . Why . . . ?"

The dragon shrugged. "You said you were in need of funding for your business, and I found myself with a few more gemstones than I am actually in need of. The hoard's a good deal more comfortable with them out, to boot. Spiky nuisances, they are."

Cyrus chuckled. "Yeah, I'd bet, but with the economy the way it's headed, I think it might be a better investment just to keep the gems as gems."

"Bosh," Keeth said. "I trust your judgment, young Solburg. And if this tiny bit of my hoard will help make a difference in the markets of the world, and for you and your family, I consider it worth my while." The dragon smiled, baring his tremendous fangs.

It was almost as disconcerting to have Keeth smile as scowl, Cyrus noted. "Well, welcome to Dragon Investing," Cyrus said, offering a hand to the dragon, "or something like that. Hmm, guess we're going to need a sign . . ."

Keeth lay a talon across Cyrus's hand and shook it gently. "You mean *you* will need a sign, Cyrus. I'll have no part in this mucking about with your human economy. Just ask when you need more capital, and I shall provide it." He shifted his bulk in the sand, piling up a dozen pounds or so of it near the line where sand met grass and dislodging a tiny crab that had been ineffectively trying to pinch through the dragon's scales.

"Agreed. And I shall keep adding gold to your hoard when the investments prove good," Cyrus said. "Sounds like a plan. But you don't want to stick around?"

Keeth shook his head. "I fear not, Cyrus. First, because there is insufficient livestock on this tiny island to sustain a creature of my size, and second, because I have heard troubling rumors of what Voshtyr is beginning to do in the foothills of the Mountains of the Morning. In the absence of my uncle Nivonis and brother Ses, my family has requested my presence."

Kris put a paw on Keeth's flank. "Is he dead too?" she asked softly.

"Who, Ses?" Keeth said, bending his neck to look down at the Katheni woman. "No, of course not. He's just been at odds with the family for some time. I would call him our black sheep, but he's neither a sheep nor black, and he's a good deal less edible. And since I am the next eldest, I must attend family meetings in his stead."

"What is that *kopek* Voshtyr up to now?" Cyrus asked, reflexively putting a hand on the hilt of his homemade sword.

The dragon shifted uncomfortably and tilted his head sideways. "He has driven the Heroes from Bryath, and now he is setting himself up as ruler of all of Centra Mundi. Not only that, but we fear he has begun mining Darkmatter in the lower reaches of the Knife's Edge mine."

Cyrus scowled. "Well, he's a Villain. Er, Arch-Villain. They do that kind of thing."

"Do you think your family might need Cyrus's help?" Kris asked.

Keeth shrugged and looked out at the sparkling cerulean water off Starspeak's coast. "It takes a Hero to defeat a Villain. I could not even defeat Sir Anthony the Mace when he attacked me by Rex Aqui. I doubt that any member of my family would fare better against Voshtyr himself."

"I can't help you," Cyrus said.

"Cyrus?" Kris said. She nudged Cyrus's ribs with her elbow. "You've faced him before. We both have."

"And we both lost, and I got ninety percent of the Heroes Guild killed—what's your point?" Cyrus said. "My 'help' gets people killed. And I don't want to be responsible for the extinction of Dragons too."

Keeth bent his neck so his head was level with Cyrus's, and he snorted smoke into Cyrus's face. "That is enough of that, Cyrus," he said. "You hold yourself responsible for events beyond your control."

"Don't make Keeth knock you on the head too, Cyrus," Kris said, giving him another hug. "I'd prefer you keep your head intact."

"Yeah, it's not my fault, sure. But if I hadn't done what I did, things wouldn't be as bad as they are," Cyrus said, turning away. "You'd do better to go find Reg. He's faced Voshtyr and won before."

"But not the last time he tried," Kris reminded him. She sat down on the edge of the grass and trailed her toes in the sand. "Last time, he needed your help."

"Reginald is hardly likely to want my help for anything," Cyrus said, "or were you not listening at the docks when we left Voyage? Even if none of this is my fault, I doubt Reg sees it that way."

Kris took hold of Cyrus's arm and pulled him down to face her. "Reginald was angry, Cyrus, and had just lost many of his friends. He said things he did not mean."

"And you are drowning in self-pity," Keeth said sardonically. "Stop feeling sorry for yourself. Stop feeling guilty for an atrocity you played but a minor part in. And even if you do bear some responsibility for what happened, why are you just sitting here? Why not do something to redeem yourself?"

"What in the Nine Torments is that supposed to mean?" Cyrus demanded.

"I mean get off that pink posterior of yours and do what you were trained for. There are fewer Heroes now, but the need for them has hardly diminished." Keeth shifted himself and unfurled his wings. "Now, I must go off to my family. They will most likely send me to 'deal with' this Voshtyr problem.

I am therefore off to my doom." He turned his head back to look mournfully at Cyrus. "If you do not hear from me in three months' time, use my investment money to pay for my funeral."

"All right, all right," Cyrus said, "I'll help. You don't have to inflict a guilt trip on me."

"I knew you would," Kris said, wrapping her arms around Cyrus and hugging him tightly. "You have too much good-guy in you not to."

Cyrus gave his mate a wry smile, then turned back to Keeth. "You can't just take me there now? I mean, you can fly and all . . ."

Keeth shrugged. "True, but I cannot fly as quickly while carrying a load, and my family has demanded my presence as soon as possible. You can arrive in your own time. But do hurry."

"All right, you oversized lizard," Cyrus said. "I'll get over to Knife's Edge as soon as I can get a boat, and we'll see what's up. You want me to invest the money before I go or save it for both our funerals?"

Keeth chuckled. "Invest it, Cyrus. I have a feeling that, with your help, we shall both come home alive." The dragon turned to face the ocean and looked back over his shoulder. "Farewell, Cyrus. Join me on Blade Peak in two weeks, and we shall see what our erstwhile foe is up to."

"All right, Keeth," Cyrus said. "Good luck with your family."

The dragon nodded, then crouched and launched himself into the air with a tremendous flap of his membranous wings. Sand sprayed back into the faces of Cyrus and Kris as they shielded their eyes.

"Well, I guess I'm taking a trip, then," Cyrus said. "Just as soon as I find something to invest in." He scratched his hair, shaking some of the sand out of it. "I wonder if Captain Tom is still running that rum import business . . ."

"The questionably legal merchant you told me about? You would trust that scaly pirate with Keeth's money?" Kris said, scowling. He looked out over the ocean. "He would spend it on a treasure map. You know he would."

Cyrus nodded, grinning. "If Tom buys a treasure map, he finds the treasure. It's a good investment. Now let's go see if we can get hold of the Phoenix Carrier Service. It's the only way to reach him on that old boat of his."

Two goblins sat on the edge of an enormous gulch dug into the low foothills of Blade Ridge, dangling their legs over the edge and eating a lunch consisting of rye bread and boiled rats.

"I don't get it," said Gorb. "I've spent time at Villain digs before this, but never one so dangerous. I'm not sure I wanna work at a place called Knife's Edge. Just makes it sound like ye're gonna die if you work there, you know?"

"Chief'll get mad at you if ye don't," Kako said. "Besides, it's not so bad. I've worked nastier."

"Real?" Gorb said. "What about all that darkmatter you been finding?"

Kako shrugged. "It's not the dangerousest stuff we been finding. The whole mine almost collapsed on us when we hit the Fell Tunnels."

Gorb shuddered. "Yeah, that does sound dangerous."

"You'd think you'd name a tunnel something like the Stays Up No Matter What Tunnels, or the Absolutely Zero Problems Tunnels, not somethin' that implies collapse." Kako shrugged. "Anyways, it's not that bad. Chief renamed 'em the Happy Shiny Rainbow Tunnels instead."

"Oh, that doesn't sound so bad," Gorb said.

"Are you kidding?" Kako took a bite of Gorb's rat sandwich. "The name change upset the critter of darkness and flame livin' down there. Turns out he *liked* them tunnels havin' a creepy name, and he comes out all bellows an' scorches an' stuff. I think the least dangerous thing we found down there was raw sulphur."

"Oh, that's bad," Gorb said, looking mournfully at his half-eaten sandwich.

"Not really," Kako said. "We got the Chief watching out for us, an' that 'Frella 'Quellus guy's not too bad." He pointed down at a small stone house a short distance from the mine site. "He's down there, all counting his numbers, makin' sure we get paid right. An' he's doin' hazard an' death pay on this job too. Thank the ugly stars for the Union, right?"

"Yeah, it really doesn't sound too bad that way," Gorb said.

"Of course it is," Kako said. "Cuz you're givin' me your sammich."

"So have you found it yet?" a voice said from a small glowing orb of crystal on a pedestal that rested on a thick oaken table in what had once been the surveyor's office.

The voice echoed somewhat in the small stone chamber, as there were no furnishings aside from the table, a single chair, and a large marble basin of briny water in the corner. The last orange rays of the setting sun trickled in the square hole in the wall that served as a window, casting more shadows than illumination.

"No," said a blue scaled man sitting at the table, "and at the current rate of excavation, it appears that we'll not find it any time this month. We've already lost thirty goblins this week, and your Darkmatter golems keep fusing into the raw ore when they touch it. They are useless for excavation, and I have no idea why you thought they would be anything but an irritant!" He rose to hover about an inch off the chair. Sometimes the hovering mastery that Araquellan nobility possessed was more trouble than boon.

"Calm down, my dear fish," the voice said. "Roger, I want the Shard as soon as possible. If you have to sacrifice more goblins, so be it. They breed unreasonably quickly anyway."

Lord Roger Farella was an Araquellus, and Voshtyr's accountant. He was also Lord of the Deep Keep—and third in line to the throne of the Neptarch, thanks to an unfortunate fishing accident—put a palm to his face and gently floated back to the chair's surface. "Voshtyr, I already have them on double shifts. Grikbik is going to start arguing with me about health and safety if more of his tribe succumb to this operation." Roger massaged his forehead with his fingers. "Is this Shard really worth all the trouble?"

"I don't know, Roger. Is a metal denser than adamant, more magical than Mithril, and rarer than Orichalc worth doing a little digging for?" Voshtyr asked from the crystal ball. "With the Shard, I can forge a weapon that no Hero could hope to stand against. Is that worth a few Goblins?" Voshtyr paused a moment, removing his black left glove and flexing the metal fingers beneath. "Besides, if Grikbik gives you any lip, decapitate him. Goblins understand strength, nothing more. Grikbik is probably looking down on you because you have brains in your head instead of muscles."

Roger sighed. This had been a long day, and he didn't need to borrow any trouble from tomorrow. "As you say," he said. "I shall deal with him on the morrow. My eyes tire easily in this dry air, and I must rest."

Voshtyr nodded. "Have a good salty nap, my scaled compatriot. But I want definite progress by tomorrow. Tell the goblins they can have the weekend off if they mine six tons by the end of the last shift tomorrow."

"Will you actually give them the weekend off?"

"Of course not. But they will work all the harder looking forward to it. Good night, Roger."

"Good night, milord." Roger picked up the scrying ball and dropped it into a magically appearing black and red checkered bowling ball bag. It slipped in next to his bowling ball, abacus, and hand sanitizer. He chuckled as he remembered the time he'd accidentally used the scrying ball for bowling. Voshtyr had attempted to contact him through it at the wrong moment and had been motion sick for a week.

The bag disappeared, and Roger rubbed his eyes. He slid off the chair, taking a book off the table as he went, and stepped into the saltwater bathtub. The book was a magically waterproofed copy of the condensed *Complete Guide to Heroics* by Melvin Darkstar, edition three-point-five, which was far superior to the newly-released fourth edition.

Roger leaned back into the deep tub with a sigh that turned into a stream of bubbles as he submerged and expelled the air from his lungs. The next breath he took was through the gills on his neck, quenching the dryness that had been building up in his system all day from the parched and dusty air of the mine and its environs. He reached into his eyes and pulled two transparent objects that looked like scales from his eyes, and slipped them into a clamshell on the bottom of the tub. Good fresh saltwater always felt so much better on his optics than the Lenses of Corneal Contact he had to wear when out of water for too long.

He touched a small pearl embedded in the tub's side. The spheroid began to glow softly, providing enough light to easily read under the water, but not enough to further tire the Araquellus's eyes. Roger opened the abridged *Guide* and began reading at his bookmark.

> Even when your most dire foe is at the tip of your sword, do not forget that this Dastardly Person is still a Person, and Persons—or People—are capable of a Change of Heart. While it is not the most intelligent thing to do, one must always Offer one's foe a Second Chance. This has more than once brought a Hero down, as Villains often Take Advantage of Kindness and Repay it with Calumny or an Unsporting Trap (see II, 4, vi for more on Unsporting Traps), but it has also yielded positive results. Those turned from Villainy by the Kindness of a Hero often become the most Puissant and Effective Heroes, exemplified by Heroes such as the Scarlet Knife, formerly Melissa Ninthcircle, the Blind Hammer, formerly Nathan Blindfight, and the failed novelist formerly known as Melvin Darkstar.

Roger snorted, releasing a small stream of bubbles through his nose-slits. The naïveté of Darkstar to think that any Villain would change sides so readily, especially when presented with the chance to strike at a Hero who had left himself off-guard. Still, it seemed only fair to give a worthy opponent a chance rather than slaying him outright.

Roger shook his head. What was he thinking? He was supposed to be doing research to better help Voshtyr destroy the remaining Heroes. He must be tired indeed to think that any of this drivel made sense.

He closed the book and shoved it to the far end of the tub. He did admire the courage of Heroes, but their stupidity truly outweighed the sheer tenacity they were capable of. He grabbed the cluster of sea sponges he used as a pillow, laid his crested head on it, and drifted, literally, off to sleep.

Chapter Eight

NIGHT FLIGHT AND FIGHT

In which the Fifth Column Depart,
have Internal Personnel Issues,
and come to an Important Realization

SERIMAL HELD OUT his left arm, and Nieva began tightening the lacings on his silenced platemail. The suit of half-plate had strips of leather between each of the overlapping steel plates to keep them from clanking together when he moved, and the entire piece of armor was painted a mottled greyish black to blend with shadows. It also had the Draconic rune for *Hush* etched in the right shoulder plate, magically silencing any noise made by his clothing, equipment, breathing, or footsteps.

The group stood on the Gryphon landing pad atop the south tower of the Von Steinadler castle, looking over the sea far below them. A large black Pegasus with glowing red eyes stood behind Nieva and Serimal, anxiously stamping its hooves and snorting fire. Emily and Slashback had already bundled up in their stealthy night flying gear. Jolan stood a distance away looking out over the ocean. Skri'ki huddled on one of the parapets, staring at the moon as if it held some secret message for him. Zaccheus had disappeared as mysteriously as he'd arrived, probably for the remainder of the book.

The wind whistled through the rocks and the parapets of the castle and whipped Nieva's tresses haphazardly into her face. The chill night air raised goose-prickles on her skin as she helped Serimal strap down the last few pieces of his stealth armor. She smiled faintly as she recalled the last time she had seen him wearing it. It had been the first time she'd seen him, in fact.

"Agh, not so tight," Serimal scolded.

"My apologies, milord," Nieva said, loosening the strap slightly. "My mind was elsewhere. You did say you wanted it tight . . ."

"Tight as in not falling off, not tight as in cannot move." Serimal turned and faced his fiancée. "I'm sorry, my love. I'm just . . . anxious about this mission. I haven't worked with the Fifth Column in years."

Nieva smiled and stroked the side of Serimal's face with her fingers. "Last time you did, you evacuated the entire city of Kashvan before the Empire razed it. You saved thousands of lives." She looked out at the whitecaps on the ocean to their west. "If this mission is only half as successful, it will be a welcome good day for this troubled world."

Serimal turned and put his arms around Nieva. "You're ever the comforting one, my love. Whatever did I do to deserve you?"

"Naught," she replied. "I chose you because you had principles and held tightly to them in spite of storms of criticism from your family and peers." Nieva laid her head on Serimal's breastplate. "I believed that if you would hold on to me with even a fraction of that fidelity and tenacity, I would be truly happy."

Serimal chuckled. "And have I done well by that so far?"

"You abandon nothing once you have set your mind to it and never falter once you do." She looked up at him. "And I consider myself truly happy. Now, go and uphold those principles we both hold dear, and I will await your return."

"Very well, my lady," Serimal replied. He kissed her for a long moment, then let her go and stepped back. "Tonight the Fifth Column goes to find out what Villainy my half-brother is up to, and how we are to stop him. Farewell."

"Farewell, milord. *Raeshan, rehais*," Nieva said, raising her hand in the Elven farewell gesture. "Go well. Return safe."

She watched Serimal walk over to the rest of the group and mount the black Pegasus that served him as a mount. The winged horse was blacker than the night, with silver feathers in its spreading wings. Its muscled flanks twitched in the cold, and it stamped the castle flagstones impatiently as if it longed for the freedom of the sky. The majestic creature whinnied as Serimal pulled its head around so he faced his contingent of spies.

"Easy, now, Mr. Sunshine," he said, patting the creature's flank. "We'll be going soon enough."

Nieva began praying. From the moment Serimal took off to the moment he returned, she wouldn't stop. She never did when he was doing something dangerous.

"Just look at those two," Emily said as she checked Slashback's saddle one last time. Emily and the gryphon stood a distance away from Serimal and Nieva awaiting departure. "I've seen an Entmoot with less sap than them two."

The gryphon shook herself, her feathers fluffing out to block more of the cold wind. "Is good thing, I think." Slashback tilted her head to the side curiously. "They have trust. When you trust, you can do things you cannot otherwys. How you tink your uncle and I accomplish so much?"

Emily snorted. "I just think it's corny, 's all. The way Nieva defers to him all the time, even though she's the princess."

"Love wants what best for the other, before what best for self," Slashback said, preening one of her dusty white wings. "She hold same beliefs as Serimal, and Elf culture teaches mix of obedience and equality in marriage."

"They're not married," Emily said. She adjusted the thick black leather flying gear she'd worn to get to the castle. It was stealthy enough on its own and protective enough to turn a dagger, if nothing else. Multiple layers of cloth under the leather kept her warm despite high altitude and wind without restricting movement too much. It bore on one shoulder the emblem of the now destroyed Salvinsel Salamanders, her former mercenary organization. "They're just engaged. By any law, that means Jacques *bok*."

The gryphon shrugged her wings. "Not look at me, Emli. Am not gut at relationships. But it work for them, ne? Let it be."

"You're smarter than some Humans I know." Emily wrapped her arms around the gryphon's thick, feathered neck. "And you have better insight into people than I do. What's your insight on Voshtyr, eh?"

Slashback looked up at the dark and brooding parapets of Serimal's fortress. "Koshtyr is scary man. When he haf two option, he choose the one that hurt more people, break more things, is more bad. When we want same things, I help. But how he do things, I not like."

"Do you know why?"

"No. Koshtyr keeps secrets. Sometimes, he is gone for a day or two, and come back . . . pointy."

Emily blinked. "Oi, what? Pointy?"

Slashback looked back down at Emily. "Pointy. Ears pointy, fingers pointy, teeth pointy. It calm down next day, but he look scary. His eyes red too."

"Demonkin," Emily muttered to herself. "So it's not just a Villain name . . ."

"Not say bad tings about Koshtyr, Emli," Slashback said, laying her tufted ears flat on her skull and giving Emily a death glare. "He save life of me and help get revenge on Crimson Slatch."

"So you like that *pic*, then?" Emily said incredulously. "After all that—"

"Not like," Slashback corrected. "Respect. Can respect one you not like. He has power, he help me, I respect. Now I help you fight him because he threat others."

"Threaten."

"Is same word." The gryphon looked at Serimal's castle. "Serimal kind to most, but strong too. I help him, help you. Then I both pay Koshtyr back for help, and make sure he not hurt others." Slashback sighed and lowered her wingtips to brush the stone of the castle's top. "Is complicate some times."

Emily reached up and stroked Slashback's feathered head. "Hey, hon, don't worry about it." She smiled. "You may know people better than I do, but I know gryphons pretty well since I used to work with 'em a lot in the Salamanders. You're loyal, but you can't figure what to do when your loyalties conflict."

Slashback sighed, and her wingtips touched the stone. "I am confuse by two-legs at times. I will help who I tink is best for now. That is all."

"As long as that's us," Emily said with a smile, "I think we'll do all right. You ready to go, hon?"

Slashback saluted Emily with a wingtip. "Yes, Captin Catrite. Ricor iss ready for action."

"Took you dawdlers long enough," said the pale man Serimal had called the Ebon Lance, as he walked up to the pair. "Between you two and those two infatuated airhats, I thought we were never going to get off the *mina koyiim* ground." He was almost eight feet tall, but most of that was the mechanical limbs of black metal attached to his hips and shoulders. His head was entirely bald and had a jagged black tattoo running across it. A neatly-trimmed and rather diabolical goatee decked his chin. In fact, had Emily not known better, she would have immediately placed him as a Villain.

Emily scowled. "Let 'em have their moment." She looked over at Serimal and Nieva, who were standing so close to one another that it looked like Emily might need a prybar to separate them. "What they have is real. You got a problem with it, Captain Clanky?"

The man balled one of his black metal hands into a fist. "Oh, aren't you the little comedienne?" he said with a smirk. "My problem is that I am ready to depart, while you all are wasting my time. There is much slaying to be done."

"We're not going for slaying, Jolan." Emily looked at him askance. "We're spying. Recon only, remember?"

"I do what I want," Jolan snapped. "I'm here to kill Villains, not pussyfoot around."

"Hey, you obey orders just like everyone else," Emily said. "Who do you think you are?"

"I, my *amjik*, am the Ebon Lance," he said. "My friends call me Jolan. You may call me Mr. Foster."

Slashback squawked and stomped a forefoot. "Not call Emli names, Koster."

"Oh, and a delightfully rural gryphon adds to the fun," Jolan said, sneering at Slashback. "Is it just you that cannot pronounce things properly, or does your whole backwater family share your peach inspediment?"

Slashback snapped at Jolan, but he interposed his arm. The sharp beak clamped onto the metal of his forearm with a metallic ringing.

Jolan chuckled. "Oh, I quake in terror before your might." He clamped his other hand onto the top of her beak and forced it open, releasing his arm from her mouth. Slashback writhed, squawking in protest as Jolan bent her neck over sideways, almost forcing the gryphoness to the ground.

Emily lunged for Jolan's neck, but he caught her by the front of her armor and lifted her off her feet with unreasonable ease. "How pathetic," he said. "And I am supposed to work with this material?"

A heavy silver blade made a quiet *clink* as it came to rest on Jolan's shoulder from behind. "Yes, you are," Serimal said coldly. "Put those two down right now."

Jolan released Slashback's beak and unceremoniously dropped Emily, who collapsed, holding her throat. "Kindly remove your blade," he said, his green eyes full of hatred.

Serimal did not move his blade an inch. "Jolan," he said calmly, "I brought you back because I thought you deserved a chance. I brought you back because I needed to prove something to myself. My half-brother . . . he was never the same after he lost his arm. His Villainy became darker and darker, and I need to see that it's just him being evil, not a side effect of magical limbs. Your behavior is not helping. I brought you back here because I needed an expert in slaying Villains, not assaulting my allies. Don't, on pain of very much pain, make me regret my decision."

"Feh," Jolan said. He scowled at Emily. "This is not finished, girl."

Emily stood up and looked Jolan square, round, and hexagonally in the eyes, which seemed to disturb him somewhat. "You mess with me, fine," she said. "But you so much as bend one of Slashback's feathers again, and I'll kill you. Got me?"

"I'll not have this infighting," Serimal said, sheathing his blade. "We have much to do. Let's be about it, shall we?" He strode back to the rest of the group and mounted his black Pegasus.

Emily swung up onto Slashback. "Let's not let that *pic* bother us, eh?" she said to the gryphoness.

Slashback nodded. "Let us find Koshtyr and stop him. Then all will be more gut."

"Keep thinking that," Emily said with a chuckle. "The world could use more optimists in this day and age."

Serimal's motley company lifted from the roof and flew southwest. Emily rode Slashback, both in their night leather, a shadowy harness used to stay concealed as well as possible in the night sky. Serimal rode his own winged steed, while Skri'ki traveled under his own wing power. The Avierie veered north after travelling with them for some distance, returning to Voshtyr's territories and his duties among Voshtyr's host. This time, they included spying on the Arch-Villain.

Koshiro merely rode around, standing on a magically appearing white-gold cloud, which seemed to have no trouble at all keeping up with the group. When Emily asked him about where he'd gotten it, he muttered something about his ancestors and changed the subject.

Zaccheus had mysteriously disappeared moments before takeoff, and Emily had not seen him since. Unfortunately for her and Slashback, this left her only option for a wingman as the Ebon Lance, who hovered alongside her with a stoic scowl on his face. Jets of flame periodically spouted from the soles of his feet and his palms, propelling him in the same direction they travelled. Emily got the distinct impression that this was nowhere near Jolan's maximum speed and that someone would probably be sued for copyright infringement if he attempted to make any likeness of the flying Jolan in a magic lantern show or picture storybook.

They traveled over open ocean for several hours, the salt breeze providing a helpful tailwind, and finally landed on a remote island at the far eastern end of a chain of islands Emily didn't recognize. Palm trees dotted the white sand shore, and the sand reflected the last of the moonlight. It gradually turned pink as Dawn, freshly manicured, spread her rosy fingers across the eastern sky.

Serimal dismounted from his flying steed and stretched his arms. "We'll go to ground here for the day." He looked around.

The island was smallish and sandy, with a single cluster of trees on it and some boulders near the south end. A few curious birds had landed in the branches of the trees on the beach and now chirped and squawked as the Fifth Column moved about. The air smelled of salt and overripe citrus.

"We should be able to find some fresh fruit and water about. Jolan, scout a perimeter. I don't want to be caught off guard." Serimal turned to Emily and Slashback. "Cartwright, you and Koshiro see if you can find us and our mounts some fresh water. Slashback, I need to speak to you privately."

Emily nodded and grabbed Koshiro Sakana by the sleeve of his kimono. "Come on, Silver Fish. If we're where I think we are, we should be able to find some fresh citrus on this island."

The Eastern-Island man glanced over his shoulder at Serimal and Slashback. "Emily-san," he said apprehensively, "are you most certain that you wish to be involved in such activities? The penalty for espionage in most countries is death."

"Only if we get caught," Emily said with a wink. "C'mon, Fish. Whoever finds water first gets to throw the other one in it!"

". . . and they're using Goblins to mine it," Serimal finished.

Slashback looked uncomfortable. The feathers on her head and neck ruffled, and her tufted ears lay back on her head. "Is Darkmatter, yis?"

"Afraid so," Serimal said. "But the odd thing is that they're not processing it on-site as I would expect. In fact, they let almost a ton of raw ore merely evaporate into the sun the other day." He scratched his raven-black hair with his black and silver gauntlet. "I can only assume that they're excavating something more important than the Darkmatter itself. But what could it be . . . ?"

The Fifth Column sat on the boulders on the small island they'd landed on a few hours ago. It was getting dark. The sun sank below the horizon, tinting the ocean gold and orange. Seabirds were coming in to roost in the trees, making it a little difficult to hear the discussion.

"Iss possible they look for source of Darkmatter, yis?" Slashback asked. The gryphoness dug her foreclaws into the white sand. "What is make Darkmatter? Maybe Koshtyr will want make more?"

Serimal gasped and then slapped his hand to his skull, almost knocking himself out. He removed the gauntlet and rubbed his forehead. "The Shard," he said breathlessly. "Why didn't I think of that? If he's after the Shard, we need to stop him as soon as possible! A blade made of one of the Shards could, when combined with Darkmatter, cleave a Thunder Runner in two with a single stroke!"

"Is right," Slashback said, rolling her eyes. "No want invincible immortal for to be armed with unstoppable superweapon. Is smart."

"Right. Now, here's what we must do . . ." Serimal paused dramatically.

The pause extended.

Slashback waited a few moments, regarding Serimal skeptically. "What you do, Serimal? You stop saying things for why?"

"I was waiting for the chapter break," he said, looking around. "It's more dramatic if it cuts me off before I outline our plan."

"Oh," Slashback replied. "Well, tell plan, then."

"Very well, here's what we must do . . ."

Chapter 9

OVERPOWERED

In which Another Actor Enters the Stage
and Meets his Fate

THE HERO SLOWLY regained consciousness. The dust from the decimated city walls was still settling, creating a golden haze in the morning light. He rolled over to scan the sky, groaning as he felt stabbing pain in his ribs. He could barely hear. All the sounds were wrapped up in a hollow ringing in his ears. It was like sound itself were blurry to his ears, much like his vision was. There was rubble all around him, and the walls of the courtyard he lay in were more than half crushed.

"—ut how did they know the boats were going to come here?" said a voice.

"I don't know," said a second. "Had anyone come through here before we were going to set up the evacuation route?"

"Agghhh," the Hero said, trying to join the conversation. By the Twelve, his throat felt like he'd swallowed an entire bag of chalk dust. "Ghhhuuuahg?"

"Crimson's awake!" said the first voice. A short man in his early twenties, wearing wizard's robes and a swept-back helmet walked over to the Hero's side. "Crimson Slash! You're all right, what a relief."

Sir Reginald Ogleby, known far but not wide as the Crimson Slash, propped himself up on one elbow. "What happened?"

"That last blast must have knocked something onto your head pretty hard," said the second voice, which Reginald could now see belonged to an older man with darker skin who was clad in burlap trousers and a rope belt. He wore a ring on each finger, and waves of heat seemed to shimmer off his fists. "Can you not remember what has happened to this fine city?"

Reginald rubbed his head. "I suppose so. Where has my helmet gotten to?"

"You mean this?" the first man said, holding up a battered silver helm with a massive dent in the top. "I think this explains your problem."

"And I will explain away your problem," the second man said. "I am the Chartreuse Star. My friend," he gestured at the first man, "is the Blazing Tree. We two and six others met you here to—"

"Secure the evacuation route for the evacuation of Bryath," Reginald said. "That's right. I arrived here not a week ago. I found out about the mass evacuation of Bryath a few days ago. Are you the two who were supposed to coordinate the retreat with me?"

"We already did that," the Burning Tree said. "That's why we got creamed."

"The city in the sky came down and broke down the walls with magic," the Chartreuse Star said. "They are working with Voshtyr. How they knew that the evacuation route from Bryath would pass through here, I do not know."

Reginald pushed himself up off the ground. He brushed dust and small chunks of sandstone from his once-polished, now badly damaged breastplate. "Where is my sword?"

"Over there," Tree said. "We thought it was a metal end-table at first, it was so big, but most people don't put sharp edges on an end table on purpose."

Reginald retrieved his sword from where it was propped against the wall and slid it into the clips that held it to the back of his armor. "Is the flying city still here?"

"It is probable," Star said. "Many Heroes and their families fled here before the official evacuation order was given, and we are all in danger if we stay. I would not like to speculate upon our chances of surviving another such attack. We must make it to Clawstrike Island, which I am told is warded against that city."

"So Rondheim—this city we're in—is being evacuated as well?" Reginald asked. "Has someone warned the Guild that this is no longer a safe staging ground or supply point?"

The Burning Tree nodded. "The Draconic Descryer sent some messages out earlier, though they may not have gotten through. But at the very least, we have to get the Heroes and all who are already here out before that flying city turns us to red mist."

"They let us get to it." Reginald drew himself up to his full Heroic six foot four inches, not counting the boots. "I will do whatever I can to ensure their safe departure. As a Hero of the Guild, I can do no less. Now, what can I do?"

Star and Tree looked at one another, then back to Reginald.

Star quirked an eyebrow. "Can you drive a boat?"

"The coastal road from the once-mighty port city of Rondheim ran south and west into a dense forest that would hopefully shelter the refugees from the mysterious flying city that had rained death down upon them.

"The brave Hero stood proudly on the deck of the city's sole surviving gunship, cruising to attain a vantage point at which to open fire on the mystical city, should it appear again." The wind whipped Reginald's hair into his eyes, reminding him that his hair was far out of regulation for melee-style Heroes, and that he would need to get it trimmed if he survived the day.

"The Hero placed a firm hand on the tiller and steered it out into the bay toward the shore where the coastal road ran. There were but a few leagues between the town and the forest, and he could easily protect them while they crossed that distance. But first, he would have to prepare his weaponry."

Sweat beaded up on Reginald's brow and on the palms of his hands as he steered the small but powerful boat to hug the coast. The little warship was unmanned but for Reginald. He locked the tiller and began preparing the ballistae and the silver tube mounted on the front of the vessel.

The tube was perhaps as thick around as Reginald's bicep and was capable of generating an intense blast of magical force in the form of a coherent lance. The Constructionist mage who had built the three prototypes had shown Reginald and a few others how to operate the cannons before some unstable rubble crashed down on his head, thus ending the tutorial early. He had called the tubes High Energy Retaliatory Onslaught Emitters, or HEROEs for short.

Reginald looked up, and what he saw made him drop the stack of ballista bolts he had been carrying. The floating city had reappeared on the horizon and was bearing down on the ruins of the city at an unreasonable velocity. He hastily picked up the bolts and loaded the last few ballistae as he began praying to every god he could think of. He uttered an ancient Hero's prayer for hopeless battles:

> Strife, guide my arms in the battles I fight
> >   Infernis, please guide me with fiery light
> Teranis, make solid a path for my feet
> >   Sharet, make my laughter not bitter but sweet
>
> Melis, please show me the future unclear
> >   Wanona, please guard all the ones I hold dear
> Karista, avenge me, if others cannot
> >   Brian, teach bards to sing of my sad lot
>
> Keriman, make my end worthy of tales
> >   Marava, ensure that my enemy fails
> Vertis, make sweet the air of my last breath
> >   Yven, I will see you soon. On to my death.

Reginald wasn't the only one worried. Over on the coastal road he could see the fleeing Heroes and their ward of peasants as they broke into a run, closing the gap between them and the forest cover. Reginald gritted his teeth. There were fifteen Heroes or so, and more than twice that many noncombatant family members there, and they were not going to make it before the flying city closed within striking range.

The Citadel was nearly a third as large as Bryath City. The city itself seemed to be made of white marble streaked with silver tracings. Though it floated, it nevertheless carried with it a thick underlying layer of dirt and turf. Reginald could even see trees and other plants growing on it as the city drew inexorably closer. But it was the base of the city that disturbed him most. Aside from the large slabs of bedrock in its base, the bottom of the citadel also contained what appeared to be large veins of Darkmatter interspersed with some blue translucent mineral. The blue, crystalline mineral glowed with fell beauty, even though no sunlight touched it. Reginald shivered. This was magic he disliked even more than regular magic.

The Kinetics—and their Citadel, which bore down on the fleeing Heroes—were working with Voshtyr. Why, Reginald didn't know. All he knew was that they seemed to want the Heroes dead just as much as Voshtyr did, and that was reason enough for Reginald to shoot down the floating monstrosity.

Blasts of dust and gravel blasted into the air, taking chunks out of the road closer and closer to the fleeing men and women. The air quivered and shimmered in a cone that flashed out of a smaller building on what Reginald assumed was the north end of the city, destroying everything in its path. He could delay no longer.

"The Hero tilted the magical tube toward the approaching city, taking aim at a small conical building that seemed to be the source of the destructive blasts. With resolve in his mind and courage in his heart, the Hero pulled the trigger!"

A lance of brilliant green energy leapt from the front of the tube and streaked across the sky. It smashed into the building emitting the destructive cone, splashing it with incandescent fury and scattering marble into the sky.

"Ha *ha!*" Reginald crowed. "You have just been HEROE'*d!*"

"The Hero's fleeing compatriots and their charges disappeared into the forest, unhindered by further attack from the sky. The Hero tacked south away from the coast, but danger loomed on the horizon. The damaged city had rotated about, and begun following him, the building destroyed by the Hero slowly knitting itself together from its scattered parts!"

Reginald heaved on a line and tied it off on one of the rails. He would have to make a run for it, and bravely running away did not call for narration.

Keeping the wind at his back, Reginald set a course for open sea, hoping to outdistance the flying city. The massive floating edifice blocked the sun, casting a shadow over the bay as Reginald fled.

A huge tremor rocked Reginald's light boat. He grasped the tiller and looked around. His boat had abruptly stopped, despite the full sails. Strangely, the air about him seemed to shift and shimmer as if superheated. Reginald looked at his arm. The considerable amount of hair on his burly forearm stood straight up like it did when he occasionally failed to dodge a magical bolt of lightning.

Then the ship was lifted out of the water and floated into the air. Reginald found his feet losing contact with the deck. "By the Twelve!" he sputtered. He looked up at the Citadel. It indeed had hold of him and his ship with the quivering beam that stemmed from the conical tower. "Put me down, you miserable miscreants!"

The ship floating beneath Reginald shattered. Or no, on second thought, Reginald realized that it had been instantly reduced to its individual pieces. Nails floated free of the boards they had held down, the bolts holding the mast in place unscrewed themselves, and the mast and planks separated to float inches apart from each other. Ropes unraveled, pitch and tar drained away and dripped into the sea, and the HEROE disassembled into its components.

Even his own armor came apart: the leather straps and hinges of his breastplate disintegrated and floated away from him. His sword floated off his back and split into blade, crossguard, and the leather wrappings from the handle. For some reason, possibly the sake of keeping the book clean, Reginald's clothes remained intact.

Reginald goggled at the sight around him. This was certainly the most detailed exploded diagram of a ship he had ever seen. He would have been more interested, but was somewhat preoccupied with his possible imminent demise.

All the pieces suddenly lost bouyancy and fell to the surface of the ocean, creating a chaotic mosaic of ship parts across the water. Reginald continued to gradually rise, until he floated free, a hundred feet above the sea.

Then, his mind was wrested from him. Reginald gasped as he felt another presence—no, dozens, or even a hundred other presences—invade his thoughts and begin systematically searching through his memories and most private feelings. It was distinctly uncomfortable, but very precise, like the exacting detail of a surgeon's scalpel, or in this case, a hundred scalpels simultaneously. The analogy broke down as Reginald attempted to resist the prying minds, sweat beading up on his face as his clamped his eyes shut and tried not to think of anything important.

Ultimately, it proved useless. Reginald was overwhelmed. He found himself in a stupor, recalling things he didn't even remember being told and thinking of secrets that could not, must not, fall into enemy hands, and yet were, through him. The secret escape route the Heroes were taking through Blackwood, the existence and protection of Guardian's son, Trigger, and the unknown location of Cyrus.

Cyrus.

In his mind's eye, Reginald stood on the docks in Voyage, looking at the youthful but weary face of his former protégé. The salt breeze rustled the blue tunic and hat the boy wore.

"I did everything I could to help the Heroes get away," Cyrus said. "I tried to tell you, but you wouldn't get it."

"What?" Reginald demanded. "Don't you start this again, lad! I already said—"

"Where am I, Reg?" Cyrus interrupted. "Where was I supposed to go when you sent me away? Where would our enemies not find me?"

Reginald stopped, puzzled. "What? Well, I . . . I thought you were going home, lad. Weren't you—"

"Where is home, Reg?" Cyrus asked, interrupting again. "Have you forgotten where I live?"

"No, you live on Starspeak," Reginald said irritably. "Though why should I care where a traitor lives?"

"Traitor." Cyrus smiled uncannily. "Don't you dare pin this on me."

Something was wrong here, and Reginald knew it. "Hold one moment," he said. "Why would you ask *me* where you live? You should know that, unless . . ." He trailed off. "You aren't Cyrus, are you?"

Cyrus shook his head, and without warning it was no longer Cyrus who stood on the dock but a pale man in grey robes bearing a symbol of an eye with an hourglass for a pupil embroidered on its left breast. "Thank you, Sir Ogleby, for telling us in your anger what your mind would not yield willingly."

Reginald reached for his sword, but found it missing, even in this memory-vision-dream episode. "What do you mean?" he demanded. "Who are you?"

"We are the past and the future," the man said, slowly blinking his colorless eyes. Everything about him was pale and lacking color, from his almost clear hair to his eerily white skin. "We are the bastion of Reason and Balance. We are the Citadel, and your apprentice is a threat to what we hold dear."

"How is the lad a threat?" Reginald edged closer to the dock on which the man stood. "The boy is not even a full Hero yet."

Abruptly, the man was Cyrus again. "You can't blame me for your failure. Traitor."

Reginald leapt at the man on the dock, but the man disappeared. Reginald spun to reacquire his target, and he gasped in horror.

The city of Bryath, not Voyage, was behind him, in flames. The mighty castle stood above the blaze still but had huge holes in its walls. Above it all floated the city Reginald had just perforated with his ship's cannon, floating in sinister magnificence through the smoke of the smoldering city.

"Some small part of your mind refused to tell us where Cyrus Solburg was," the man said. He stood with his back to Reginald, admiring the smoking ruins. "Even though you believe he betrayed you, you subconsciously held on to one piece of loyalty to him. Well," he said with a sad smile, "you *were* holding onto it, until you told us. Now you have betrayed him as you think he betrayed you."

"You keep saying that I *think* Cyrus betrayed the Guild," Reginald said, advancing on the man again. "But I know he did. Are you saying he was—"

"Not at fault." The pale man approached Reginald until he stood within the Hero's reach. "So you have become the traitor now." Abruptly, he was Cyrus again. "Traitor." Cyrus faded away, replaced with the musclebound, armor-plated Purple Paladin. "Traitor."

"Stop calling me traitor!" Reginald grabbed the Purple Paladin by the brooch that held his purple cloak on. "I have betrayed no one!"

The Purple Paladin clasped metal-clad fingers around Reginald's neck, and was suddenly Reginald's friend no longer. He was Voshtyr, and Reginald felt the awful, terrifying, and familiar spread of black magic from around the metal fingers.

Voshtyr leaned close and whispered in Reginald's ear. "Traitor."

Reginald gurgled and struggled against the iron grasp he remembered, panicking at the resurgence of the terrifying memory.

Memory.

Reginald blinked. That was what this was. It wasn't happening again—it was his memory, and he was reliving it, probably thanks to this strange pale man and his flying city. Reginald stopped struggling and emitted a strangled laugh.

Voshtyr looked puzzled, then furious. Without warning, the vision dissipated, and Reginald once more floated over open ocean, staring up at the flying city.

You should not have resisted us, Hero, a voice said in Reginald's mind. *Now you know how we operate, and we cannot have you tell others. Sleep deeply in the deeps.*

Reginald's arms flung themselves forward, as did his legs, as he rocketed backward toward the ocean. He barely had time to take in a gasp of air as the force of a dozen battering rams smashed into his chest and drove him deep beneath the waves.

Down he went until he could no longer see the bits of his erstwhile boat in the water, until he could no longer see the sun as even a bright dot far above. The pressure around him increased tenfold, and Reginald's eardrums screamed in pain. (They didn't have to scream very loud to be heard, since they were inside his ear after all, and it sounded more like a high-pitched ringing than a scream anyway.)

He realized, belatedly, that he would never be able to discover the truth behind what had happened to Cyrus, and that he would never be able to apologize to the lad for his anger. He struggled against the pressure for a few moments, the thought driving him upward, but not enough.

Reginald's last thought was a fleeting irritation that he had not been able to deliver an Epic Speech as the Last Stand of the Crimson Slash. Then the deep took him, and he thought no more.

Chapter 10

Wet News Travels Fast

In which Cyrus Trades a Weapon for Information

CYRUS WOKE UP to the sound of vomiting. He groaned. That was never a pleasant sound first thing in the morning. Or any time, really. He sat up and rubbed his eyes.

Kris was bent over the other side of their bed, depositing remnants of last night's dinner into the chamberpot.

"Hey," Cyrus said, rubbing Kris's back. "You all right?"

Kris looked up at him and smiled weakly. "Better now. It must have been something I ate."

"Hmm." Cyrus slung his legs over the side of the bed and reached for his dresser.

The only furniture in the room were the two dressers, the bed, and a table. Given that the bedroom took up half of the house, the other half being reserved for the kitchen and dining table, this gave the casual observer the quite correct impression of a very small house. But it was enough for the two of them, and had worked quite nicely for the last month or so.

"Looks like I have an excuse to get the old adventuring gear out again," he said with a smile. "Are you sure I should go? If you're not feeling well . . ."

"No, you should go." Kris stood up and draped a green silk robe over her shoulders. "If your choice is between staying here to coddle me and my upset stomach or going and saving the world, which do you think I would prefer?"

Cyrus smiled. He had bought that robe for her with the leftover coin from the first Pyrradorsal they had caught after arriving back on Starspeak. The deep green of the robe and the light green embroidery on the sleeves offset the tawny yellow of her fur and the dark spots that speckled her body. Her hair—or "head-fur," as she called it—was somewhat disheveled this morning, but the grace with which she moved, even when feeling sick, was still remarkable.

Kris poured a drink of water from the pitcher into a clay cup on the table beside the bed. She drained it, swishing the water about in her mouth.

"I don't know, Kris," Cyrus said. "This could be one of those 'the Hero departs for a Quest, but his Lover falls mysteriously ill in his Absence and dies while he is Away' Subplots."

"Or it could just be a stomach ache," Kris said, giving Cyrus a playful swat on the shoulder. "You think about these Hero things too much. I will be here when you get back." She kissed him, then pushed him away with a finger. "Now, you must go soon or you will miss the boat."

Cyrus chuckled. "All right, all right. When did you get so bossy?"

"When you signed up for having me around forever." Kris handed Cyrus his belt. "My progative."

"Your what?"

"Progative? My right as your mate?"

Cyrus snorted. "*Prerogative.* Yeah, I guess it is. Here, one more for the road, and I'll go." He hugged Kris, holding her close to himself. She smelled of almonds and dried hay, and now, just a bit of sea salt from her constant exposure to the ocean.

Kris nuzzled his neck. "Come back safe, Oh Kay?"

"Hey, no worries," Cyrus said, tilting her chin up so their eyes met. "Not only do I have Keeth watching my back, I'm also kind of the best Hero ever."

Kris giggled. "Well, hopefully a massive dragon is enough to protect you from your own ego. Go well, Cyrus. Return safe."

"Bye, love," Cyrus said. They broke apart, and Cyrus slung his Pyrradorsal sword over one shoulder and a knapsack over the other. "I'll send you a postcard from the sunny, demon-controlled wasteland that used to be Bryath."

"Cyrus!" Kris said, frowning.

Cyrus chuckled, and ducked out the door.

The ship ride was almost entirely uneventful. Except for two near misses with pirates, one collision with a mysteriously drifting block of ice, and a visit by a group of Araquellan merchants.

The latter of these events managed to drag Cyrus from his cabin as he smelled the sweet and spicy scent of amras seeds wafting down to his bunk. The young Hero slung his sword-belt about his waist and ventured up on deck.

The sun coasted across the clear sky unhindered by clouds. Not a breath of wind stirred the sails high above Cyrus's head, and the heat was withering. However, despite the blistering sun and the dead air, the deck hosted a veritable hive of activity. Six

Araquellan merchants stood by crates and barrels of their wares, peddling them to the sailors and passengers of the ship. Three of the Araquellae bore the single fin crest of a common male, two had the female double crest, and one, slightly taller than the others, bore the distinctive triple-crest of Araquellan royalty.

The Royal was a good four inches taller than the next largest male, but even so he stood only five and a half feet tall. All of them had pale blue skin that faded into deeper blue scales at their extremities and near their hips and shoulders. Their deep black eyes took in the faces of their customers and blinked slowly as they smiled.

Their clothing covered very little by human standards. As Araquellae were cold-blooded sea-creatures as well as cold-blooded capitalists, their females looked very much the same as the males, though slimmer and more gracefully built, not having anything above the waist that needed covering for the sake of decency. One of the females wore a sash of a vibrant green about her hips, while the other wore a strange red wrap that appeared to be made of a single long strip of cloth.

The three common males wore what amounted to loincloths made of some kind of rough, grey skin, while the Royal had a very form-fitting pair of short, slick, black trousers bedecked with red beads and pink seashells.

All were armed, and Cyrus could understand why. The sea was, after all, a treacherous place even for those who made their living travelling it. Two of the males had curved tridents held on their backs by sharkskin bandoliers, while the other had a belt bearing a number of vicious-looking black iron barbed hooks, each the size of a man's hand.

The females each had a short silver tube tucked into the waists of their respective garments. Cyrus assumed this was a blowgun of some sort. The Royal bore no obvious weapons, but his organic blades, normally below the surface of the skin of the Araquellan arm, were fully extended and glinted dangerously in the sun.

It could be a trap, or they could be spies for Voshtyr. Lord Roger Farella, Araquellan nobility, was an ally of Voshtyr's, which Cyrus knew from personal—and painful—experience. Given the economic chaos caused by Voshtyr's war machinations, the Araquellae were taking advantage of disrupted supply lines and forming their own black market. Cyrus chuckled at the thought. If it was in the ocean, did that make it a blue market? Or perhaps a blue ocean strategy?

Regardless of their marine market machinations and modifications, Farella was a definite link between Voshtyr and the Araquellae. He would have to be cautious.

Cyrus approached the Araquellan Royal. One of the other males stepped in his way, reaching back behind him for the trident, but the Royal waved him away. "Hmm," the Royal said, looking Cyrus up and down, "you are not the same as others on this ship."

"Well, no," Cyrus said, glancing at the Royal's extended blades. "I'm not a merchant."

"You are a warrior, then?" The Royal sat down on a barrel that one of his companions had brought on board. "It is a great pity. A moon or two ago, we could always find a Hero on a ship such as this one to tell us tales." The blue-skinned man sighed and wrapped a finger up in one of the strings of beads on his trousers. "Tales themselves are a trade good, and we find ourselves lacking in glad tidings these days."

Cyrus shrugged. "I can't help you there, friend. I'm no Hero, and I've been more or less shut off from the world for over a month. I was hoping to ask you for information on what's been going on on Bryath."

"Oh, I can tell you some," the Royal said. "But I will require something in exchange. Nothing in this world is free. Please, sit." He indicated another barrel. "My name is Na'tan."

"Cyrus." Cyrus shook Na'tan's scaled blue hand and sat down. "Afraid I don't have much of value to trade with, though."

Na'tan chuckled, a sound like a laugh through a mouthful of water. "Everyone has stories, my friend. I will trade a story for a story. From where do you hail?"

"Starspeak," Cyrus said, and immediately regretted it. What was he doing telling a complete stranger where he was from?

"Then you can tell me stories of Starspeak. It is a fishing village, correct?"

Cyrus nodded. "I can't say it's the most interesting place, though."

Na'tan pointed at the blade hanging at Cyrus's hip. "That blade is from a Pyrradorsal, correct? It must have been an interesting time slaying such a monstrous fish."

"Well, not really," Cyrus said, rubbing the back of his neck and grinning. "My mate helped me bring it in, and it didn't put up too much of a fight. Not like the first one I ever caught. *That* one was a challenge."

"Oh?" Na'tan leaned forward. "Please, tell me of the first one. In return, I will tell you of the efforts to reconstruct Bryath."

Cyrus cringed. "Was it destroyed?"

Na'tan knocked twice on the barrel and frowned. "Your story first."

The other Araquellae wrapped up their sales and came to stand around Cyrus and their leader.

Cyrus cleared his throat and tried to remember the Heroic Oratory Techniques from the second volume of Melvin Darkstar's *Complete Guide to Heroics*.

"I was twelve years old," Cyrus began, "and I loved to go fishing. Not with the net and boat like my uncle, but with a pole from the docks. It was more of a challenge to bring in a single fish, to fight it from sea to shore, than it was to trap a bunch of them in a mesh of ropes."

"Ah, a hunter, then," Na'tan said with a nod to Cyrus. "Many of my people have been injured or killed by Human fishermen who would reap the sea as if it were merely a field, and not another world. But you play the role of deceiver and hunter. Excellent."

"Um, thanks?" Cyrus said. "It's just the way we do things around Starspeak. Some old agreement with the Araquellae I never understood before, but now that makes a lot more sense. Anyway." He leaned back on the railing.

"So one day, my cousin Marco and I went out to the docks with the intent of catching some smaller fish for supper. We sought Pora, a tasty little whitefish that's pretty common but small enough that it often slips through nets. We sat together on the docks, our feet in the water and our lines slack.

"We were joking around about some talent scouts from the Heroes Guild that had arrived that week and were looking for talent. My cousin was of the firm opinion that I was a weakling and unfit for tasks Heroic. I attempted to dissuade him from that opinion through judicious application of vigorous physical encouragement."

"Did the scouts find you?" asked one of the female Araquellae.

"Issi!" Na'tan said curtly. "*Shen kek ssvan!*"

"Hey!" Cyrus said. "What are you telling her to shut up for?"

"Females speak when spoken to," said one of the males, crossing his arms across his blue-skinned chest.

"I did not know you knew our language," Na'tan said. "Where did you learn it?"

"Places," Cyrus said shortly. "Merchants and sailors. I don't mind the interruption, really. So, no, miss," he said to the female who had asked the question, "I was about three years away from being old enough to catch their interest." He turned and looked at the Royal. "Now, if you are done being rude, may I continue my story?"

Na'tan nodded. "My apologies. I shall not diminish the value of your story again. None of us will," he said, shooting a piercing glance at the assembled Araquellae. "Nor will we speak in our own language of private matters while you are here."

"Anyway, as I was saying, we were talking instead of watching our fishing poles," Cyrus said. "Now, as lazy kids relaxing on the docks, we had developed the technique of tying a bit of string to the tip of our poles and running it down to our big toes. That way we can lay back and look at the clouds but still know if we're getting a nibble. So Marco, he sits up and looks at his pole and tells me he thinks he's got something.

"Just as soon as he gets his hands on the pole, he pretty much dives off the dock. Apparently he had hooked something really big, and it dragged him into the water!" Cyrus made a diving motion with his hands. "I leapt forward and caught him by the ankle, then pulled him back onto the dock and took his pole. Now, keep in mind that this was one of my uncle's deep-sea fishing poles, and it could drag in a shark if someone was strong enough to do it.

"So this big . . . whatever it is, is pulling on the pole, so I pull back. When I do, the fish jumps out of the water on the far end of the line, and guess what fish it is?"

"A Pyrradorsal?" one of the younger males said, and received a sharp glance from Na'tan.

Cyrus nodded. He placed his arms behind his head and leaned back against the ship's railing. "Yep. Big shiny fellow he was too. You should have seen those scales glinting in the sun, those blades on his back whistling through the air."

He sighed. "And then it tried to drag *me* into the water with it. I wasn't going to have any of that, so I yelled at Marco to go get a big rock or something for me while I reeled it in. It was pulling so hard that when I pulled back, my feet splintered some of the planks I was standing on. I was just a dumb kid, so I didn't really know what I was getting into, but he ran off, and I started bringing it to the dock.

"'Bout ten minutes of struggle later, I pull the thing up halfway onto the dock. It almost got me with its nose and dorsal blades as it thrashed around." To illustrate the point, Cyrus drew his home-made Pyrradorsal blade and slashed the air in front of his scaled audience. They tensed, going for their own weapons as well. Cyrus stopped and sheepishly put his blade away.

"About that time, Marco comes back with a rock the size of my head. I throw the pole around one of the dock pylons and tie it off. Now, the 'Dorsal's struggling like mad, and would have cut the line with its blades, but the last five feet or so of line are coated with woven steel to prevent larger fish biting the line off.

"So I take the rock from Marco and start bashing the fish's skull with it. I hit it as hard as I could probably a dozen times or so before it stopped moving. Marco and I sat down and just looked at the thing for a long time. And then this shadow comes over us. I look up, and it's the talent scout from the Heroes Guild. Apparently he had seen us bring the thing in. He asks about it, gets this weird expression on his face, then leaves.

"So that was the *first* time I caught a Pyrradorsal," Cyrus said. "Much more interesting than the most recent one."

"So," Na'tan said, "how many have you caught total?"

"Six," Cyrus said proudly. "Though I did have help with two of them."

"And you were never found by the Heroes' Guild?" Na'tan asked.

Cyrus glanced to the side. The wind had picked up slightly, and the sails above flapped as they caught bits of breeze. "Hey, nothing is free," Cyrus reminded the Araquellus. "You said you had news of Bryath."

Na'tan smiled slyly, and the group of Araquellae chuckled. "Yes, indeed I do," he said. "It is hardly such an interesting tale, though."

"Anything you think might be of interest would help," Cyrus said. "I haven't been there since the . . . Well, for a month or so."

"I see," Na'tan said. "So you know nothing of the reconstruction or change in government, then?"

"They took Bryath?" Cyrus instinctively went for his sword hilt, but stopped himself as he saw the male Araquellae reach for their weapons as well. "I would have thought the Heroes Guild would have held on until there weren't two bricks stuck together."

Na'tan waved his hand dismissively. "Oh, they fought quite bravely against Voshtyr and his Black Guard for nearly two weeks." The Araquellus plucked a string of beads from his trousers and began weaving it between his scaled fingers. "Then they fled, and Voshtyr took the city. The way I hear it, not a single noncombatant was harmed, and Heroes who surrendered were treated with fairness and generosity."

"Bah," Cyrus said. "You heard this from who?"

"Camoran Yrongard, the Lord of Veracity," Na'tan replied, inclining his head. "He is the mouthpiece of Voshtyr's army and quite the Public Relations expert."

Cyrus scowled. "Some accurate source of information *that* is."

Na'tan chuckled. "Neither you nor I specified that our tales must be accurate. Accurate information is worth more than a mere fishing story."

"Oh? And what would you suggest in trade?" Cyrus asked. "For *accurate* information?" He put a hand on the hilt of his sword.

Na'tan eyed the Pyrradorsal blade, looking up and down its sharp, serrated, silvery shaft. "I would trade you a weapon for a weapon. Information in advance is often more effective than a blade, eh?"

"Done," Cyrus said. He drew a dagger from his belt. The dagger he had made as an experiment before attempting work on a sword, to see if he could work the Pyrradorsal's organic blades as well as he could metal. Reginald had taught him the basics of sword maintenance and repair, but not how to make one from scratch. The dagger was not of stellar quality, but held quite the edge. "A weapon for a weapon," he said, and extended it to the Araquellan Royal.

"No, not that one," Na'tan said. "Your sword."

"Ah," Cyrus replied, "you didn't say which weapon, now, did you?"

Na'tan's face contorted for a moment. "You knew what I— Ah, you learn our ways quickly," he said, and he and the group chuckled again. "Very well, I do not deny that this dagger is a weapon, and I will gladly trade for the truth of Bryath." He took the dagger from Cyrus's palm and stuck it point-first into the barrel on which he sat.

They stood in silence for a moment, Cyrus sizing Na'tan up, and the Araquellus apparently doing the same to him. The deck rolled gently back and forth. The silence was broken only by the cries of seagulls and the creaking of the planks until Na'tan spoke again.

"This thing I know from a cousin of mine who works for Voshtyr, and my family does not lie. The sack of Bryath was quick and bloody. Voshtyr let loose his magical beasts as soon as his army had breached the outer walls. In their killing, the creatures did not discriminate between men or women, soldiers or commoners. The slaughter was horrible.

"My cousin advised against this tactic, though it was most convenient at the time, but Voshtyr ignored him. It was best to commit his atrocities all at once, he said, and then dole out his blessings gradually, so people would remember him as being more good than evil."

"A sound theory for a dark Prince," Cyrus muttered. "So he slew all of Bryath, then?"

"Not entirely," Na'tan said. "After the first wave, he pulled his creatures back and cleaned out all remaining resistance more carefully. The populace was left alone after that. He pursued the fleeing Heroes instead. After he'd caught most of them, he left much of the rest of that work to his allies, and he set about rebuilding Bryath."

"So he is there now?" Cyrus asked, looking across the sea to the north, where Bryath lay. The deep blue water held no answers for him, neither did the shallows around a hidden reef a few leagues distant.

Na'tan looked out across the waters to the north. "I will need more in trade to tell you that."

Cyrus stood up with a growl. "I haven't anything but my sword, and if you think you are getting that, you can go to the Torments."

Na'tan held up his. "Please, sir, control your temper. I mean only that revealing Voshtyr's location was not part of our bargain. I will tell you about the reconstruction, if you wish."

"Please." Cyrus sat back down, this time on one of the barrels. Sailors on the deck had begun clustering around the group, apparently hungry for news as well. One had even climbed partially down the rigging and hung by his knees to be closer to the conversation.

"Voshtyr has set up several Lords to watch over parts of his current empire while he expands its frontiers," Na'tan said. "Camoran Yrongard, as I mentioned before, is the Lord of Veracity, a minister of information both true and false. Tara Lastbreath has become the Lord of Order. It is she who wields the horrible might of Voshtyr's army to enforce his new regime. And finally, Igor DeVastian is the Lord of Corpulence. He is in charge of supplying and withholding food and necessities from the territory under control of Voshtyr.

"Together these three have repaired the damage done to the city, and it is once more a hub of activity. The difference lies in the fact that the entire populace is now directly reliant on Voshtyr for their very survival, and most, if not all, are loyal to him." Na'tan wrapped his string of beads around his right fist. "It is why I have moved my business to the open sea, where it started. My cousin warned me that my sense of free enterprise was no longer welcome in the mighty city of Bryath."

Cyrus rose and walked to the ship's railing. "Then it's all over. He's won."

"Were you among the Heroes at the Vale?" Na'tan asked, following Cyrus. He placed a hand on the young Hero's shoulder. "Do you feel your sacrifices were in vain?"

Cyrus shrugged the hand off. "I don't think we agreed on me telling you anything about myself."

"True enough," Na'tan said, mischief in his eye. "Ouch!" He shook his head, then rubbed his eye, finally managing to dislodge the mischief, and held it up to the light. It was a greenish buglike thing, half mosquito, half hamster. "These things get in there every time I make a business deal," Na'tan said in annoyance. "I bought prescription eye drops for it too but that seems to have done me but little good." He threw the squeaking mischief off the boat, and returned to his seat. "Well, we have a little more business to attend to aboard ship, and then we must depart." He offered his hand to Cyrus. "Fare well in Bryath, Cyrus Solburg."

"And you as well, Maras Na'tan," Cyrus replied, using the official Araquellan title for nobility. The two shook hands, then Cyrus retired belowdecks.

Bryath destroyed and rebuilt in Voshtyr's image, Cyrus thought. *Where is all this going to end? What evil have I allowed to prevail?* He sighed.

That evil that isn't your fault? Keeth's voice echoed in Cyrus's head. *If you still believe yourself at fault, get off your pink posterior and do something about it.*

Cyrus smiled. *Ever the voice of reason, Keeth. I made the mess, I'll clean it up. As soon as I help the dragons, I'll see what I can do about Voshtyr and company.*

Cyrus walked over to his bunk to lie down, and then he abruptly stopped.

Na'tan had used his last name during their polite farewell. The last name Cyrus had never told him. How would he know, unless Farella . . . ? Cyrus rushed up onto the deck, almost bowling over a sailor and another passenger on his way up.

When he got there, not a trace of the visiting Araquellae remained. Aside from some water left from where the aquatic folk had stood, there was no sign that they had been there at all.

Chapter 11

Discoveries Good and Bad

In which the Fifth Column Discover the Hiding Place of the Solburgs

SLASHBACK WHEELED IN the sky, coming about for a landing on the small island on the far east of the Citrus Island chain. It was indeed the Citrus chain. Slashback knew this from the Aerial Cartography training she had received while part of Silverwing Mercenaries. All the major features were there, including the permanent settlement on the island of Starspeak.

In fact, it was this particular island she had returned to report about. There was something odd about the island that the gryphoness could not quite place. It could have been the fact that the shoreline was much higher than she remembered, as if the island were sinking. It could have been the massive, black-sailed galleon only a few miles away. Or it could have been that a house on the southern end of the island had several phoenixes perched on the roof.

All of these things bore reporting, so Slashback landed on the tiny island that the Fifth Column had chosen as a base, and stalked over to the voluminous tent Serimal and company had set up as an overnight shelter.

"Well, so far we have come up with a stunningly bountiful cornucopia of . . . nothing," Serimal said, crushing a piece of parchment in his hand. He, Emily Cartwright, and the man with the metal limbs—the man Slashback knew as Jolan Foster—sat around a collapsible table, poring over a map of what looked like the northeastern corner of the Mountains of the Morning. There was little else in the tent, and Slashback took up the entire entryway.

"Ah, Slashback," Serimal said, looking up from his crumpled paper. "I hope you have brought some new information to this pooling of ignorance we have going here."

"I am bring some information, yes." Slashback sat down on her haunches and looked at the map on the table. "That is place we are go, yes?"

Serimal nodded. "Indeed. It is called Knife's Edge Mine, and Voshtyr is digging things up there that he shouldn't." He traced a line between the mine, which was on northern Centra Mundi, and the small island they currently occupied, labeled on the map as Tiko island. "This is only a two-day flight if we push it and make one stop on the mainland."

"I am make it," Slashback said. "If metal-limbs Jolan can keep up, we are need only one stop." She glared at Jolan, who returned the look with equal venom. "Is safe for to land on Bryat?"

Serimal shook his head. "Not entirely, though one of my contacts assures me that two of my old safehouses are still undiscovered and functional. We should be able to use the southern one as a waypoint for at least one night.

"Now, I believe you had a report for us?" he asked.

Slashback dipped her beak and saluted with a wingtip. "I am find several interest," she said. "One, there are many phoenix guarding a house that look innocent on Starspeak. Two, coast is not as expect, and I am think that island is sink.

Last, I am see what appear as pirate ship on approach from northeast."

"Pirates?" Serimal said. "Describe the ship, Slashback."

"Yes, sir," Slashback replied. "It is large galleon, having black sails and a figurehead of large lizard. Flag bears skull and three red scratch marks."

Serimal stood up. "Red Fang? Impossible. I thought Vesuvius died in that 'accident' a month or so ago . . ."

"Apparently not." Jolan clamped a hand on the back of a camp chair, unintentionally putting a crack in it. "So who's this pirate? Someone we should be afraid of?"

Emily gave Jolan a sideways glance. "Yeah, 'less you want your legs melted down and turned into nails, you best stay away from 'im."

"That's enough, Emily," Serimal said. "Vesuvius the Violent commands a small fleet of corsair vessels. He was never more than a passing threat, as every seafaring Hero almost inevitably sank one of his ships each time they went on a Quest that involved oceanic travel. More of one of those random things one might encounter on a long journey.

"Now with fewer Heroes about, and with backing from a mysterious third party who I have come to believe is Voshtyr, his petty piratical playground has expanded and he has become quite the danger to maritime interests." Serimal pointed at the map to a cove on the southern shore of Landeralt. "His base is rumored to be here. Last I heard, he supposedly died during an accident a week's journey south of Voyage.

"Of course," he added, looking back up at his compatriots, "that 'accident' was an attack on an unarmed merchant vessel that was carrying fleeing Heroes, including the one my half-brother currently seeks: Cyrus Solburg." Serimal sighed. "There were no survivors reported from either ship, so I have but little hope we shall see young Solburg again."

"Well, can't we look for 'im?" Emily asked. "I mean, if we're going to stop Voshtyr from gettin' all invulnerable and stuff, we need to find him, right? Surely your intelligence network's better than your brother's?"

"Half-brother," Serimal corrected. "And no, it isn't. Well, it is better, but not as widespread. I started it as a school project at the Academy and never really finished it before my father died. It's more like a hobby than a true intelligence agency."

Emily quirked an eyebrow. "You built a secret spy network as a school project?"

Serimal chuckled. "That's the Villain Academy for you. If you failed that project, you pretty much had the career options of Minion Trainer or Janitor of Doom."

Jolan stood and pushed back his chair. "Well, enough of that *bok*. I say we do something about this pirate."

"Indeed." Serimal twisted the ring on his finger, a ring studded with black gems. It was part of the Dashing Highwayman #7 outfit. "We shall deal with it shortly. Cartwright, I'm sending you, Slashback, and Sakana to deal with the pirates. Get rid of them. Permanently. We don't need them hanging around on our flank, and we can't let pirates run around hurting people unopposed just because my half-brother doesn't see fit to keep the peace now that the Heroes are gone. Jolan, I need you to go ahead of us and secure the safehouse."

"What?" Jolan slammed a metal hand down on the table, knocking the legs out from under the collapsible table and sending it crashing to the ground. Maps and markers scattered. "You send me on an errand a Stormcrow could do, when there's fighting to be done? And you send a foreigner and a *woman* to do the fighting instead?"

Emily stood up, and Slashback bugled a gryphonic challenge at Jolan's words.

Serimal held up his hands. "Peace, friends. I only send Emily as a lookout for Sakana since he cannot be everywhere at once. And why would I not send Sakana?" Serimal gave Jolan a wry half-smile. "Who better to deal with a ship of pirates than a ninja?"

"Good point," Jolan said reluctantly. "I suppose you're going to sit here with your thumb up your—"

"No," Serimal said, "I'm going to investigate the house with the phoenixes on Starspeak. It could be nothing, but wild phoenixes are seldom seen outside the Phoenix Isles. Something is drawing them there, and I want to know what it is."

Slashback nodded. "Is gut plan, Serimal. We go now?"

"No." Serimal picked the table back up to its usual height and snapped the leg back in place. "Jolan and I go now. We need to see what those pirates are up to before we waste any manpower on attacking them. Hence the need for stealth and sharp eyes." He looked at Emily and Slashback. "First sign of anything going wrong, you contact me."

Slashback saluted with a wingtip, and Emily saluted as well, though with her hand instead, as she lacked feathered appendages. They left the tent together.

The two ended up on the west end of the small island. It was dark now, with the moonlight shattering across the surface of the ocean into myriad slivers of luminescence. The birds in the trees were quiet, and the wind from the ocean blew Emily's hair around her face.

"So, looks like you get to work with two different Cartwrights," Emily said with a smile. "Taking on a boatload o' pirates, skulking about and committin' sabotage . . . Sounds like the life, eh, Slashback?"

Slashback reached into the feathers around her neck and pulled out a locket. She looked inside at, on one side, the picture of the young man and grifflet, and, on the other side, the same man with a full-grown gryphon. "Yes," she said after a pause. "It is gut that we do this. Gaffin would be proud of us boat."

"Boat?" Emily chuckled. "Both, Slashback, *both*."

"Is what I say," Slashback said. "Boat of us!"

"Whatever you say," Emily replied, ruffling the gryphoness's ears. "Let's find Koshiro and start planning."

Kris took her footpaw off the pedal and allowed her potter's wheel to slow to a stop. She dipped her paws in a basin of water next to her workstation and scrubbed the clay from them while admiring her handiwork.

She sat in the center of her and Cyrus's house enjoying the hobby and pastime she had learned from an Orcish tradeswoman: crafting pottery. This particular piece was a red clay vase that she had shaped tall and thin. She had been making them for a few weeks now, and this one was to be a birthday gift for the dock manager's wife.

Kris looked about the small house and sighed. It felt so empty without Cyrus there to hold her, without his laughter filling up the two rooms. Not that it had been easy to get him to laugh during the last month. She knew that what had happened at the Vale of Dreams still weighed heavily on his mind. It made her feel almost lonely at times, as she missed the younger, jovial, free-spirited Hero-in-training she had fallen in love with.

She picked up a thin glass rod from her workbench and began tracing the design of a flower on the outer surface of the vase. She hoped that when Cyrus returned from his bout of Heroics, he would recover some of his former good spirits.

A high-pitched melody interrupted her work. She put the rod down next to the wheel and rose from the three-legged stool on which she'd been sitting. The domesticated Pandaemoniums she and Cyrus had planted outside were pleasant to listen to, but were also handy because they provided warning of approaching visitors. She wiped her speckled paws on the front of the grey smock she wore, then took it off and donned the green robe Cyrus had given her.

Someone knocked on the door. Kris walked over and opened it. Before her stood a young man, perhaps a year or two older than Cyrus, with waist-length shimmering blond hair so fair it looked almost white. A charming smile hung on the young man's mouth, and his storm-blue eyes held a sparkle of mirth. He wore fisherman's clothing of the type common to Starspeak. This consisted of a plain white tunic, a pair of worn sailcloth trousers, and a pair of oil-treated leather boots. A length of rope looped about the man's waist, and from it hung a bag of clams. There was a phoenix perched on the bag, and another on the young man's head. Neither of them looked pleased.

"Good even', miss," the young man said. "Can you call off the birds, please? I like warm, but these guys are *too* warm."

"Who are you and what do you want?" Kris asked.

"Selling clams!" the young man said. "Today's clams are fresh and juicy! Care to buy a couple?" He held up the clam bag. The phoenix on the bag squawked and flared up with licks of fire. A stream of seawater trickled from the bag and dampened the earth outside the door.

Kris smiled. "Actually, a few clams sound delicious. Off, you two."

The phoenixes chirped and fluttered off.

"Maybe the clams would be good with some Amras seeds." She absently put an index claw between her teeth as she thought. "And a pickle. And some chocolate."

The young man gave Kris a distinctly odd look. "Er, right, miss. Anyway, they're a dozen for a silver. How many you want?"

"Oh, I'm sorry," Kris said. "I'll get it right away. Come on in." She stepped back inside the house and gestured for him to follow. "I don't think I've seen you around. What's your name?"

"Emmet, miss," the young man said. "I don't come around Starspeak much. My dad and I are clam divers on another island. Say, is that a sword?"

Kris picked up her coin purse and looked back at Emmet. He was examining another of Cyrus's prototype Pyrradorsal blades, the one that hung above the doorway.

"Yes, my mate made it," Kris said proudly. She drew two silver coins from her coin pouch and padded over to where Emmet stood looking up. "He's gotten very good at working those fish blades."

"Oh, is he a blacksmith?" Emmet asked.

Kris handed the young man the coins. "No, he's . . . Well, he was a . . ." She stopped. This was just a young lad from a neighboring island. There was no harm in telling him Cyrus was a former Hero, was there? Still, better to be cautious. "He was a professional hunter." Her conscience pricked at her for the lie, but technically all that Questing counted as hunting, if the thing being hunted is Villains and the rewards obtained therewith paid for life's necessities.

Emmet nodded as he took the coins. "That makes sense. Though you have to be crazy good at hunting and fishing to take down a Pyrradorsal."

"Oh, he's very good," Kris said. "He's more than good. Watching him in motion is like seeing the old legends brought to life again." She chuckled. "I'm his biggest fan."

"So he's like a Hero or something?" Emmet asked.

"Yes. Ah, no. I mean, kind of," Kris stammered. "He's my hero."

Emmet shuffled his feet. "Ah, heh heh, yeah. Why would a real Hero live way out here? I mean, the only thing we've had to do with Heroes around here even halfway recently was when I was still little, and that was just some Hero taking one of the village kids for training. His name was . . . um, Cyprus or something."

"Cyrus," Kris blurted, and immediately regretted it.

"Yeah, that was it," Emmet said. "Well, enjoy your clams, miss. See you later!" He stepped out the door. "They're really good with butter and garlic!"

"Mhmm," Kris said, and closed the door.

"It's Cyrus Solburg's house," Serimal said as he shucked the blond wig off his head. His hair beneath it glistened with sweat from the tropical heat. "And I've finally met the Katheni girl he mated."

"Ech." Emily leaned back against Slashback's flank, fanning herself and the gryphon with a fish-patterned folding fan she'd borrowed from Koshiro. "With all that fur, I can't imagine she's very comfy in this heat."

"You are speak true," Slashback said morosely. She flapped her wings halfheartedly to generate a bit of breeze. "Iss not gut climate for Gryphons or anything else with fur."

Emily waved the fan directly at Slashback's beak. "You poor girl. Anyway, Serimal, what do we do now that we've accidentally found him? If Voshtyr wants him, why don't we get him ourselves?"

Serimal began pacing back and forth in front of the tent entrance, still wearing most of his disguise. "No, my dear. We need to protect him. With the way Voshtyr's been hunting him, Cyrus must be instrumental to Voshtyr's downfall. If only I knew why he—" He stopped and held up an index finger. "Wait, if his mate is here alone, where is he? I didn't see him anywhere on the island when I scouted it."

"Which means . . . ?" Emily said. "Is he on a boat anywhere near?"

"Possible. But he could also have gone to do something important. There's Hero blood in that boy. It would be surprising if he *wasn't* out to do something about the Voshtyr mess."

"And he left phoenixes to guard his mate," Slashback added. "Iss gut choice. Phoenix fight almost as gut as Gryphon. And not fight fair. Fire iss not fair."

Emily chuckled. "Weird kid, that Solburg. Maybe he's regretting his . . . unusual bride choice and has left her to find a Human girl instead."

"No." Serimal turned to face Emily and the gryphon. "Solburg's shown loyalty before, and Kris has been with him in several tough and dangerous situations. He'd not abandon her."

"Unless marriage is scarier than Voshtyr," Emily said, nudging Slashback with her elbow.

"I wouldn't know," Serimal said. "But I hope to find out soon enough. In the meantime, how did your talk with Koshiro go?"

Emily sat up. "Well, Slashback got herself another look at the ship, and we figure if there's something that distracts them for long enough for Koshiro to get on board, he can take anything on there."

"Provided he doesn't announce himself by describing his sword style again." Serimal put his palm to his face. "I swear, that man needs a gag."

Chapter 12

An Epic of Disastrous Proportions

In which Cyrus Wreaks Havoc among those not at fault

CYRUS LEANED AGAINST the cool black rock behind him and basked in the shade of Blade Ridge Mountain. The respite from the sun was refreshing, even though the heat of the day had already passed. He looked out over the quarry, or mining site as the case was, to get an idea of what he was up against.

From here, he could see an entire tribe—no, several tribes—of goblins pushing and pulling mine carts, bags, and the occasional wheelbarrow full of chunks of what Cyrus assumed was Darkmatter. Larger mine carts and pallets of bundled bags were being hefted about by cave trolls. The gigantic creatures were almost half the size of a dragon, with wrinkled grey skin and milky, beady eyes.

From here, he couldn't see the Darkmatter's distinctive purple tint or the way the mineral tended to absorb light, but he did see a goblin accidentally spill a bag of it on a co-worker, who spontaneously combusted and ran around shrieking, wreathed in black flame until a cave troll crushed the unfortunate creature.

The entire area lay desolate. Not a single tree or patch of grass dotted the bleak brown landscape for miles around, another sure sign of the taint of Darkmatter. Wooden watchtowers dotted the rim of the quarry, which was itself lined with archery platforms. Whatever this operation was, it was well-guarded.

Cyrus pulled a strip of jerky from his knapsack and sat down to chew on it as he mulled things over. He didn't manage to mull much, as the sound of large wings beating the air soon met his ears.

"Hey, Keeth," Cyrus said without turning around. "What took you so long?"

A long forked tongue darted past Cyrus's shoulder and wrapped itself around his stick of jerky. It forcefully yanked it from Cyrus's hand and retracted.

"Hey!" Cyrus turned around to face his green draconic friend, who happily munched the remnants of Cyrus's snack. "What's the deal, Keeth?"

"Chmhra jrky," Keeth mumbled around the bit of dried meat. "'S my fvrit."

Cyrus chuckled. "Yeah, you hopeless carnivore. You're quite the jerky junkie." He turned and looked at the goblins in the valley. "So this is the mining operation your family is worried about?"

Keeth folded his wings and sat down on his haunches next to Cyrus. "It is not the goblins that worry us so much as what is being mined, and who is doing it," he said. "My half-sister, Adrii, says that this operation is definitely run by Voshtyr. She has even seen his accountant, Lord Roger Farella, at this site."

"Farella," Cyrus said. "There's a bit of bad blood between he and I anyway. "Anything particularly dangerous I need to be aware of besides the cave trolls?"

"Between that, the Villains that may be about, and the large creature of fire and darkness that Skyvar spotted the other day?" Keeth asked. "It is hardly a playground. This entire operation is a hazard to the surrounding area in general, and my family in particular. It requires a Hero to deal with such a troublesome situation. You will need to end the mining operation, and end whoever is supervising it."

"Oh?" Cyrus quirked an eyebrow. "I have a sword made out of fish. A fishy stick, if you will. It's not that great. What the heck am I supposed to fight these guys with?"

"I hear rumors that you are displaying some talent for magic." Keeth bent his neck down to Cyrus's level. "You could use that instead of stalling for time. I shall provide air support. Now, are you going?"

Cyrus pushed Keeth's snout aside. "Yeah, yeah. I guess I'll start with the goblins as a warmup. But . . . I don't want to be recognized, just in case there's a Villain there that knows me. Any ideas?"

"Perhaps something to cover your face?" Keeth suggested. "Do you have a mask?"

"No, but I have . . ." Cyrus smiled. He pulled his old adventurer's tunic from his knapsack. It was torn and somewhat dirty, as he hadn't worn it since his and Kris's escape from the pirate vessel, but it would still serve one more purpose.

Cyrus drew his sword and cut a single long strip from the bottom of the tunic. He stashed the rest of the cloth, then carefully cut two holes in the strip of fabric. Finally, he placed it around his eyes, the holes lining up *almost* perfectly with his eyes. Cyrus chuckled. "And now I have a Secret Identity. Too bad I don't have a Heroic Name, eh?" he said.

Keeth smirked. "I am certain that disguise will fool no one," the dragon said. "Your hair is part of what the wanted and bounty notices identify you by. I thought you were going to cover your entire head with the cloth, not just wrap it around your eyes. But if it makes you feel better, by all means, use it."

"Lot of help you are," Cyrus said, rolling his eyes. "I'm going in. You stay out of sight until it looks like I need help. A secret weapon is always a good idea."

Keeth smirked. "Especially when your secret weapon is a dragon."

Cyrus bounded down the hill, sliding across the slick slopes and patches of gravel. He was almost three-quarters of the way down when the goblin sentry spotted him.

The goblin had just enough time to sound the alarm on a ram's horn before Cyrus leapt from the hillside and bisected the creature as he landed. The crunch of wicked bones beneath his blade brought back a wave of nostalgia and a spray of blood.

He spun around in time to snatch a javelin from the air and return it, point-first, into its owner.

Six shrieking goblins rushed Cyrus at once, but he dispatched them all with a *Thompson's Tornado* attack. He leapt over the corpses and landed blade-first on the head of a cave troll that had been pulling a chain of mine carts. The beast groaned, but reached up and plucked Cyrus from its head.

Cyrus struggled to escape its grasp, but the beast flung him across the quarry into an empty mine cart, where he landed with a resounding *thud*. The cart, now imbued with the inertia of suddenly containing a young Hero at high velocity, began rolling.

Cyrus stood with a ringing in his ears, feeling dazed from the impact. It took him a moment to realize that the scenery was, in fact, moving. The yelling of goblins, the resounding call of another alarm horn, and the sharp *zip* of an arrow flying past his head brought him back to a cogent state. He crouched in the rolling cart.

The motion soon became an advantage, as Cyrus popped up, decapitated a goblin, and retreated inside the cart when the goblins began firing projectiles at him. He did this several times before the goblins learned to stay away from the deadly rolling Jack-in-the-box. Instead, another troll caught the cart, picked it up, and hurled it at the mountainside.

Keeth caught the cart before it could have an unfortunate intersection with the rock wall. "I told you to use your magic!" the dragon scolded Cyrus as they wheeled and made another pass over the goblins. "Why are you not using it?"

"This zany phoenix guy told me not to make a scene!" Cyrus said. "It's pretty flashy, and I don't want to attract too much attention to myself."

"And I do not wish to return to Starspeak and tell Kris that you were killed because you refused to use all the weaponry at your command." Keeth opened his mouth again, but this time he spit fire instead of reprimands. The gout of flame crisped one of the troublesome cave trolls, creating quite an offensive smell that was a cross between mold, burnt hair, and strawberry jam.

Cyrus felt the heat even through the bottom of the mine cart Keeth was carrying him in. "Fine," he said. "Put me down, and I'll see what I can do."

While still high in the air, Cyrus began focusing on what Conrad the Phoenix Prophet had told him about drawing the elemental energy from ley-lines into himself instead of breaking them off and throwing them at his foes. He set his mind on pulling a Fire line. He wished he could see the raging slashes of color Conrad had shown him earlier, but this would have to do. Suddenly, Cyrus's skin felt like he had a sunburn, then his innards felt like he had a fever. He began sweating, but the sweat immediately evaporated.

Black and red flames shot out from Cyrus's body and spread across the mine cart Keeth was carrying.

He began to panic. "What . . . what is this? This isn't what Conrad—"

"Argh!" Fire wreathed Keeth in superheated air, and he dropped the mine cart. It fell thirty feet and shattered against the ground.

Cyrus performed a Finnigan's Fiery Frontflip and landed in a battle-ready crouch beside the wreckage of the cart. In that selfsame instant, a shockwave of black and red fire flared out of the impact site, incinerating several goblins.

"Sorry, Cyrus!" Keeth shouted as he made a protective pass overhead. "I am fire resistant—not fireproof!"

Cyrus was about to tell Keeth he was fine when he realized he was still flaming all over. He remembered what Conrad had said about him being able to take the form of an Elemental.

A group of goblins converged on him, but quailed back when Cyrus rose to his full height. He took a step toward them "Hi." His voice sounded distorted in his own ears, as if he were speaking across a bonfire. "Let's, ahem, *heat* things up a bit, shall we?"

He turned and threw a strand of fire at a stack of bags nearby. The bags exploded and began burning, belching black smoke when the Darkmatter in them combusted.

Curiously, though, as the black smoke increased, the amount of black in the fire surrounding Cyrus decreased.

The goblins backed off even more. Some fled to the dubious protection of a dilapidated shack a few yards from the mine's entrance.

While they retreated, Cyrus fireblasted another stack of bags, two more mine carts, and a piece of mining apparatus that seemed to be a cross between a crane and a waterwheel. So much for not making a scene.

Not that Keeth was helping maintain a low profile, either. He flapped from one watchtower to the next, breathing blasts of flame into—and through—the flammable structures. Within a minute of the attack, a dozen giant torches burned where the watchtowers had been. This, of course, attracted the attention of the anti-air defenses, crewed by goblins. Two batteries of repeating ballistae opened up on the dragon, forcing him to gain more altitude and stay more or less out of the fight.

The first cave troll tackled Cyrus as he was distracted, and punched the young Hero in the chest with a fist the size of an ox. Cyrus cried out in pain, and then flared out in fire.

The troll reared back, and Cyrus thrust his Pyrradorsal sword straight up into its gut. Fire blasted down the length of the blade with a searing crackle. The troll roared, then wheezed smoke, as it burned from the inside out.

Cyrus rose from the ground and turned to face the few quaking goblins that had not hidden in the shack. "All right, you're done," he said, and took another step toward them.

"Nawp," said a cranky voice from Cyrus's left. "Yer dun, Heero."

Cyrus spun to face the new threat.

The new threat was four feet tall, dirty brown, and wore chainmail and an eyepatch. It also held a pole-axe, smelled of pickles, dirt, and body odor, and was the tallest goblin Cyrus had ever seen. Most of the goblins in this camp, and indeed, that he had seen in his years serving with Reginald, were not much taller than three feet. Most wore patched leather garments, loincloths, dirty cotton shirts and the like. This one had a decently-woven green tunic and pants, armor, and had an air of command about him.

If there had ever been a lord and master of all goblins, it would be this one.

"Git out me camp!" the goblin ordered. "You kill too many! Union not stand for this!"

The flames around Cyrus flickered. "Wait, what?" he said, confused.

The goblin poked Cyrus with the top of the pole-axe. "Union rules sez a job kill twenny, mebbe thirdy gobs a week. Tops. This too many! Back off, Heero!"

"Union rules . . . ?" Cyrus stepped back. "Wait, so who are you working for?"

"F'rella. Sum 'Quellus," the goblin said. "You want ta kill gobs, you talk ta him. He ain't payin' enough for da union to let ya off dis many."

Cyrus lowered his sword, and the fire around him began dying out. "Wait, so you guys aren't just being evil henchmen?"

"Torments, no!" the goblin said. "Pay's great doin' hazardous labor for Villains. Ye get two silver piece a day, 'orrible food, and death benefits. Plus," he stopped and looked out at the carnage Cyrus had caused, "the pay's on a per-job basis, so the more gobs get killed, the more gold each gob gets. But if we can't get da job done, *nobody* gets paid, and we still needs our workers to finish, get me?"

Cyrus scratched his head. It was still warm. A last bit of flame flickered atop his hair. He licked his fingers and pinched the tenacious flame out. "So you're not just inherently evil creatures?"

"Naw," the goblin said. "We's just inherently 'eartless capitalists. Name's crew chief Grikbik," he said, extending a hand to Cyrus.

Cyrus shook Grikbik's hand. "Sorry about the mess, Grikbik. All of you I killed, and all. I mean, I didn't even think you were just hired to do this."

"Don't sweat it," Grikbik said, reaching up to slap Cyrus heartily on the back. "Like I said, we gets us death benefits on this job. Their families is prob'ly okay wit' it."

"Yeah . . ." Cyrus scratched the back of his neck. There was still a lot about being a Hero that he hadn't learned yet. "So, um, now what?" he said. "Do I fight you to the death or something? I kind of lost my momentum . . ."

"*Bok*, no!" Grikbik said. "I likes my skin in one piece, thankies. If yor beef's not wit us, take it up wi' management." He jerked a warty thumb toward a stone building on the far side of the quarry. "See if 'Frella's in. He's a talker, that one. Talk wit' him. Use yor sword if ye likes. He's mighty 'ard to convince otherways."

"Hmph." Cyrus sheathed his smoking blade. "He wasn't easy to convince that way either, last time I checked. Anyway, I'll head up there. Thanks for the tip."

"Whatever gets you off our backs," Grikbik said with a scowl. "We's got a job ta do, an' you're slowin' us down."

Cyrus looked about at the wreckage of the mining operation. "Uh, yeah, about that," he said. "You're going to have to stop mining. It's upsetting the dragons, and all. And it's evil material you're mining."

"So?" Grikbik leaned on his poleaxe. "Yer point?"

"So you need to . . . stop . . ." Cyrus looked around himself. The goblins that had fled into the shack came out and formed a circle around him and their crew chief. They all stared at Cyrus. It was making him uncomfortable. Their beady black eyes bored into him, and he briefly felt like a cornered rabbit.

Until he remembered that he was a Hero, that was.

Cyrus drew his sword again and took a slash at arm's length around the circle. "Back off! You're going to stop digging up this Darkmatter. The more of it you dig for, the stronger Voshtyr is going to get. The stronger he gets, the worse things are going to be for everyone, you guys included. And if that's not enough to convince you, keep in mind that if you keep this up, the dragons who live on this mountain are going to come down here and burn you and your workers to stinky green crisps." Cyrus pointed his fishy stick at Grikbik's nose. "So you're going to cease your operation right now, understand?"

Grikbik chuckled. "Ye got the wrong idea, Heero. We's not digging fer the black *bok*, we was lookin fer a shiny."

"Shiny?" Cyrus lowered his sword-point just a hair. "What do you mean?"

Grikbik motioned to his crew, and they pulled back. "This shiny." The goblin chief produced a bundle wrapped in a moldy tarpaulin. He pulled back one corner of it. A sliver of shimmering blue caught and refracted the fading sun.

Cyrus gasped. The shard of crystal was incredibly beautiful. Unaccountably, he instantly felt as if it would be worth everything he possessed just to own it. And he wanted it.

"We found it on the second day of diggin'," Grikbik said. "But I figured 'they's payin' us until we finds it, yeah? So if we never says we found it . . ." The goblin chief chuckled. "Plus, from how 'Frella talks about it, it might be worth a good chunk of coin for somethin' so small. Could be worth a few fortunes, ne?"

"Give that to me," Cyrus said. His voice sounded flat and tinny, even to his own ears.

Grikbik yanked the bundle back and covered the mysterious shard up. "No, you twit, it's ours. You wants it, you's buying it."

"You are going to give me that Shard right now, or I will slay you where you stand." Cyrus pointed his sword directly at Grikbik's remaining eye.

Grikbik jerked his head at his workers. They stepped in and menaced Cyrus with mining implements, cutlasses, and a slew of other pointy objects that would probably hurt quite a bit if inserted between Cyrus's ribs. "Right," Grikbik said. "Aside from the threats, you got a real reason I should be handin' this over?" The goblin chief sneered.

At that moment, the ground behind them shook heavily as Keeth slammed down to earth, raising a dust cloud. The grit got in Cyrus's eyes but he shook it off and smiled. "Actually, I do," Cyrus said. "Keeth, meet Grikbik. Grikbik, meet The Reason You Should Give Me That Shard."

"Speak softly and carry a large dragon," Keeth said, and snorted a bit of intimidating fire from his nostrils.

Cyrus flared up again. Elemental fire sheathed his body, and he took a step toward Grikbik. "So, give me tha—"

The goblins mobbed him.

Cyrus slashed at Grikbik as the goblins closed in, and their chief backed off. The blow failed to connect with goblin skull, but successfully knocked the Shard out of his hands.

"Mine!" Cyrus shouted, leaping after it.

Keeth roared and spouted a funnel of flames across the goblins trying to bear Cyrus to the ground. They shrieked as white-hot dragonfire seared their pickled greenish hides.

"No!" Grikbik shouted as he tried to swat Cyrus's hand away. "Don't tetch it with yer bare—"

Cyrus stopped. His hand rested on the pulsing blue mineral. "Oh?" he said after a moment. "And whyever not?"

"It'll get ye," Grikbik said, slowly getting up. "I had to kill me own uncle after he picked that blighted piece o' shiny *bok* up. And now it's got ye."

Cyrus felt a surge of anger rising in him as he held the Shard aloft. It was pure and cold, a controlled and focused rage. His pulse quickened and throbbed in rhythm with the sliver of blue crystal in his hand. "Nothing has me," Cyrus said. "I have this Shard now. And you, goblin, will die!" Cyrus swung his Pyrradorsal blade, and noted offhandedly that a strange crackly blue and black mist wreathed it.

Then he passed out.

" . . . rus? Cyrus? Wake up, young one."

Cyrus could hear someone's voice. It was familiar. It belonged to a large person. Or . . . thing. Oh, right, it belonged to Keeth. What was Keeth doing here?

"Heroes do not fall so easily, not even to ancient and tainted magics," Keeth said. "Get up, or I shall tell your mate you were asleep on the job."

"M' ehd feelshfny," Cyrus said. By the Twelve, what was wrong with his head? And why couldn't he see?

"You are lucky you did not have the Shard for long," Keeth said. "It could have stolen your mind entirely. 'Feeling funny' is much better than what could have been."

"I cand shee." Cyrus felt the ground beneath his hands. Grit and rock. From the quarry. Goblins. Why was thinking so difficult?

Hot breath on his face. "Hmm. Give it a few moments, young one. It was, after all, an impressive shock."

"Wahappn?" Cyrus asked. Bright blurriness crept in around the edges of his vision, replacing the stolid blackness.

"You took the Shard from Grikbik and became as a man insane," Keeth said. "I have only ever seen such fury once, when I confronted the vengeful brother of a man who had foolishly assaulted my lair."

"Shard . . . 'swhere?" Cyrus's tongue felt thick and useless, but gradually loosened up. His vision cleared to the point where he could see an enormous green blur he assumed was Keeth.

Keeth looked across the quarry. "I had to remove it from your grasp. After pinning you, I flicked it somewhere over there."

Cyrus could see. The first thing he saw was almost a dozen bleeding sword wounds across Keeth's chest and forelimbs. "Nine Torments . . . Are you all right, Keeth?" The numbness was gone from his tongue as well.

The dragon shrugged. "I shall heal, as always. I must compliment you on your craftsmanship, Cyrus. Your sword held out for many more blows than those of other adventurers who have sought to test theirs on my scales over the years."

"Wait, what?" Cyrus said. "I . . . I did that?"

"Yes."

Cyrus put a hand to his forehead in disbelief. "But . . . I wouldn't . . . By the Twelve, Keeth, I'm—"

"Not at fault." Keeth craned his neck down to look at his gashed chest. "That Shard is more dangerous than even the Pax Draconia anticipated."

"But . . ." Cyrus shakily stood. "I almost killed a friend, just for a bit of rock?" He looked around.

Carnage.

Of the hundreds of goblins who had been crawling about the quarry, not one remained on its feet. Their bodies littered the ground in all directions. The sun was setting behind the mountains. Cyrus had been unconscious for . . . hours, perhaps? Everything that had been flammable in the valley—, the canvas bags, the watchtowers, even the anti-air battery—was in ashes or still in flames.

"I . . ." Cyrus said. "I . . . I . . ."

Keeth stuck out a foreclaw as thick as a man's torso and flicked Cyrus onto his posterior. "Enough of that, young one," the dragon said. "It was the energy of the Shard, not you, that was in control. It was that 'bit of rock' that attacked me, using you as its instrument much as you would attack someone with a sword. Now, are you going to continue sitting there feeling sorry for yourself, or are you going to help me solve this problem?"

Cyrus mustered a half-hearted chuckle. "Help, I guess. Where did you say the Shard was?"

"Over here." The voice came from across the mining pit.

Both Keeth and Cyrus jumped to look for the source of the sound.

It was an Araquellus. To be specific, it was one Cyrus had encountered before.

"Roger Farella," Cyrus said.

The five-foot-tall, blue-scaled man smirked. "Greetings, Hero, I see you've taken umbrage with our mining operation."

The pale yellow of his robe blended with the fading of the setting sun behind him. One bit of his attire Cyrus had not seen before now caught his eye. A pair of thick black gloves decked the Araquellan merchant's hands.

In those hands rested the bit of blue crystal.

"Give that back, Farella." Cyrus took a step forward.

"Or you'll what?" Roger replied innocently. "Cut me up with that sword of yours?"

Cyrus reached for his sword. Several choice Orcish epithets bounced around in his skull as he realized that he had yet again broken his weapon. This time on a friend rather than a foe, but that did not lessen the annoyance factor.

The Araquellus chuckled. "And you, Keeth, son of Barinol, I see you are in good health."

"No thanks to you, you boot-licking coward," Keeth said with a snarl. "Where were your prized Araquellan business ethics when they were draining my blood and plucking my scales?"

Roger sighed. "Sitting in a dark and lonely corner of my mind crying bitter tears of shame. It's always been bullied about by my sense of profitable enterprises and self-preservation."

"That thing's dangerous," Cyrus said, looking at the Shard. "Just give it to us, and the dragons will make sure it doesn't hurt anyone."

"Oh, but hurting people is exactly what Voshtyr wants to do with it." Roger looked into the heart of the Shard. "I can see why. With a weapon forged from this, even an alloy, he would be fearsome in his wrath."

"Keeth," Cyrus whispered. "I'm going to rush him. Get the Shard."

Keeth nodded. "On three," he rumbled. "One, two, th—"

"Aha!" Roger leapt into the air and shot upward a hundred spans. "I think not," he called from high above. "Keeth, son of Barinol, I hope we sometime meet in circumstances that allow us to resolve our differences . . . reasonably."

"Get back down here!" Cyrus shouted. "We can still work this out!"

"And you, young Hero," Roger said. "What do you call yourself?"

Cyrus blinked. Could Farella really not have recognized him? The pathetic strip of cloth serving as a mask was just that: a strip of cloth. No magic, no clever crafting. Well, perhaps it was best to play along.

"Uh, I'm the . . . uh . . ." Cyrus stammered.

"He is nameless," Keeth said. The dragon placed a heavy foot next to Cyrus, as if bracing himself for an onslaught. "He is a Hero who stands for all the Heroes fallen."

Cyrus felt something welling up inside him at Keeth's words. Pride? A sense of responsibility? This morning's fish sandwich? Maybe, but it was mainly a growing conviction that what he did mattered.

"I am nameless," Cyrus said. He took a step forward, and looked up at the flying Araquellus. "I am the Nameless Hero. Friend to the fallen, Faceless to my foes. You tell Voshtyr that his past is going to catch up with him, become the present, and make sure he doesn't have a future."

Roger snorted. "Well, that was certainly a better response than I had expected. But no matter. I suppose I shall see you again the next time you try to foil one of my carefully planned operations."

"Whether tin or aluminium," Cyrus said, "I will certainly foil you soon enough."

Roger nodded. "I shall put it on my calendar." With that, he shot into the sky and banked west toward the setting sun.

Cyrus soon lost sight of the flying fishy financial fellow. "Well," he said to Keeth, "I guess we failed to foil, huh?"

"No, we stopped the mining of the Darkmatter," Keeth said. "And we learned the true nature of that Shard."

"So you knew about that beforehand?" Cyrus asked. He sat down on the quarry floor and leaned against the steep, suntinted shale wall. "Why didn't you tell me?"

Keeth sighed, and the blast of warm air ruffled Cyrus's hair. "The *Princeps Draconum* himself ordered me not to tell anyone what we were truly concerned about. It was the Shard, not the Darkmatter, all along. I apologize for my deception."

Cyrus punched Keeth's scaled leg. "Hey, it turned out okay. And you didn't lie. You just didn't tell me about the Shard. And," he said, looking at the sword cuts on Keeth's chest, "I think you pretty much got your comeuppance for not warning me about it."

"True enough," Keeth said. "Now, I suggest we vacate this place before the goblins still inside the mine decide to come up and see what has happened."

"Good idea. I've already killed far too many of them." Cyrus walked over to the mine cart tracks across the quarry floor and looked down them. "There's another cart I didn't break, if you don't mind carrying me in that."

Keeth nodded and plodded over to acquire the cart. "He recognized you, you know."

"Yeah, I know," Cyrus said. "I could tell he recognized me. I mean, he might be evil and all, but he's not stupid. But why would he pretend not to? There was no one else around to try and fool. Is he going to tell Voshtyr where I am? Are Kris and

I going to have to move again?" He wiped his face. "Or do you think he's up to something?"

"He is an Araquellus," Keeth said. "They are always up to something."

Cyrus sighed. "I just don't want to spend my entire life on the run."

"You will not have to, if you choose to stand and fight." Keeth dropped the wooden cart on the ground next to Cyrus. "You are not alone in this, you know."

Cyrus chuckled. "Yeah, I keep forgetting that. Thanks for reminding me. Are you sure I can't bandage your . . . uh . . . scales? Find some salve or something?"

"No. I will heal on my own. The blood of dragons is strongly magical, as I may have pointed out a time or two."

"All right. Then let's get home, shall we?"

"My home, yes," Keeth said. "It is too late to fly to yours and too far for one day's travel."

"No time to waste, then. Let us be off."

Cyrus climbed into the empty mine cart. Keeth scooped it up and leapt skyward, leaving a splash of rock dust in his wake. Back toward the Mountains of the Morning they went.

Keeth craned his neck down to look inside the cart. "By the by," the Dragon said, "what became of those gems I had you invest?"

"Huh? Oh, those," Cyrus said. "I think they're going to do all right. I kind of hate myself a little bit for what I invested in, but it should turn out all right."

Keeth banked east. "I don't want my funds in anything morally objectionable, Cyrus—"

"Oh, nonononono," Cyrus said. "Nothing like that. Just...I invested it mostly in war-related things. I had originally wanted to do this to help people, like farmers and such. I didn't want to be a war profiteer."

"Neither do I," Keeth said. "But peaceful uses for money are scarce right now, and the sooner this war with the Villains is over, the sooner we can find more constructive uses for my funds."

"Yeah, well, at least I found one fun and interesting thing to invest in."

"Oh?"

Cyrus chuckled. "I financed a treasure hunting expedition."

"Oh, with that shape-shiting pirate?" Keeth chuckled. "The one who pulled that stunt with the—"

"Ha ha, yeah, that one, and how it ended up with—"

"Yes, and the cottage cheese!"

"Man, the Istaka were so mad," Cyrus said. "I think it took their chieftain a week to get it out of his fur."

The Dragon caught a thermal and glided upward. "I can't think of a more hilarious use for my funds," he said. "Captain Tom has a seemingly endless supply of dumb luck. It will no doubt find him the treasure, but even if it doesn't, the stories will still be worth the price." He leveled off. "Now, it is some distance to the mountains. You had best get some sleep."

Cyrus pulled the cover onto the mine cart and settled down in the back of it. Lulled by the rush of wind and steady beating of the dragon's wings, Cyrus soon drifted into a restless sleep. The thought of what would become of the fragile piece of stability he had back on Starspeak if Voshtyr found him still nagged at his mind. But he had friends still. That had to count for something.

Chapter 13

Pirates, Kinetics, and Spies, Oh, My!

*In which Tranquility Shatters,
Something Sinister happens to Kris,
and Koshiro shows why Ninjas are Better than Pirates*

THE FIRST INDICATION that something was wrong was the complete lack of seagulls on the beach. Or possibly the lead sphere that ripped a hole the size of a carriage in the center of Starspeak's only town square. That, at least, was the first sign that the general populace understood.

Either way, Kris had noticed the former before she'd heard the latter, and slept lightly that night on account of it. The bed felt empty and cold without Cyrus in it anyway.

When the sound of an explosion echoed across the water and the island, she immediately leapt up and threw open the trunk at the foot of the bed. She tossed out a quilt and a pair of wading boots, then seized what she was looking for: the short sword and the copper-colored buckler Cyrus had given her on their wedding day. It still shone like it had on the day Cyrus had handed it to her under the Mir sun. The seal of the Heroes

Guild and the rising sun of the Mir Katheni tribe blended together, reminding her of her mate.

Kris threw on one of Cyrus's shirts and one of her shorter homespun skirts, one with the traditional Katheni slit sides for ease of movement. Out into the noise she went, noticing that the shirt still smelled like Cyrus.

And noise there was. More projectiles ripped through the night air, preceded by the sound of an explosion and followed by first a single scream, then more, and the deep and booming bass alarm call of a conch-shell. She ran toward the sounds of trouble.

By the time Kris arrived in the town square, thatch-roofed buildings blazed and hapless townsfolk rushed through the shattered sandstone streets calling out for loved ones and fleeing.

"Kris!"

Kris's ears pivoted to where the sound had come from. Jacob and Catherine Solburg were headed down the street toward her. "Catherine! Jacob!" she shouted. "What happened?"

"Pirates," Jacob said as they met in the shadow of the building that served as town hall, library, and Nature Club meeting place. "They fired the first volley just a few minutes ago, and the raiding boats are already on their way to the island."

"I don't know what they're using," Catherine said. "It's not ballistae. It sounds like something explodes before the projectile gets here."

Kris scowled. "It sounds as if they have made another Kanon. Cyrus told me about it. It is like a ballista but with more range and fueled by foul-smelling powder instead of cables and winches."

"The Kanon," Jacob said. "How in the world would mere pirates acquire such a thing?"

"They're not normally this organized," Catherine said, wringing her hands. She was unsuccessful at getting any water out of them, however.

"This has happened before?" Kris asked.

Jacob nodded. "Usually closer to harvest, when they think they can pick off a few dozen crates of fruit. But right now?" He looked toward the waterfront. "They must be after something else."

"Or nothing, and they're doing this for some twisted sense of fun," Catherine said.

Kris growled. "Senseless. Where are they coming from?"

Jacob put a hand on Kris's shoulder. "Easy, Kris. Cyrus said you'd get a bit territorial about what you consider home, and while I'm glad you took to the old Isle so quick-like, you need to think for a minute. Where will you do the most good?"

"On the front line of defense?" Kris said, puzzled. "I do not understand . . ."

"Help us get the women and children further inland," Jacob said. "Catherine, show Kris where Rebecca and the children are."

Catherine took Kris's arm. "Come, they need your help more than the men do."

"I disagree," Kris said.

Nevertheless, she let Catherine lead her to the community well, where they found a cluster of frightened women and children. The frightened whimpers of the children mixed with the screams from farther away, making an unhappy and unpleasant blend of sound for Kris's sensitive ears.

The well stood inside a ring of cut sandstone blocks that formed the pavement. Houses ringed the well on three sides. The fourth side opened to a road leading to the shops and waterfront. Kris glanced about nervously. It was a dead end, not a defensible place, should something happen. It was the city equivalent of a box canyon. Perhaps she could make use of some of the sandstone houses and the narrow alleys between them.

"Is this all of them?" Kris asked looking at the women and children of the village gathered about the well.

Catherine nodded. "Nobody from the houses closer to the waterfront made it. The pirates keep grabbing them and carting them down to the beach. Pastor Cline said they have them all tied up down there, like they're taking them back to their ship."

Kris growled. These pirates reminded her uncomfortably of the slavers that periodically plagued the Katheni of her home and of the Mir desert.

"Mrs. Kris?" said one of the little girls at the well, tugging on the hem of Kris's skirt. "Are the scary men coming here?"

Kris reached down and placed a comforting paw on the girl's head. "Not if I can help it, Natalie. If they try, they will see the strength of a warrior of the Kath Sul." She stepped away from the children and closed her eyes.

She heard, rather than saw, the crackling of flames from the burning of palm-thatch roofs. She heard, as her ears pivoted to take in sound, the footsteps of men in heavy boots. Her fierce green eyes snapped open as she heard the sound of a drawn sword. It was time to do something about this mess.

Not thirty seconds later, the first pirate came around the corner peering into the fire-shadowed darkness for another house to loot or villager to kidnap. He was a thickly built Dwarf resembling a barrel stacked atop some smaller barrels, with mini-kegs for arms and an angry red beard. What he found instead of plunder was the sharp end of a shortsword, and he realized just how uncomfortable the perforation of his skin was.

Kris pulled her shortsword free of the pirate, who let out a strangled yelp. She dropped to the ground as the pirate swung a short-hafted axe at her head. As the blade whizzed over her head, she kicked out and swept the Dwarf's legs out from under him. Before the Dwarf had even hit the ground, Kris leapt from the ground in a pounce and landed sword-first on his chest.

Another pirate, this time a young Human, came around the corner, saw the coup de grace, and backed up a step. "Jobie!" he yelled. "Some crazy cat just dropped Hammerforge!"

"Silence!" Kris hissed, slashing at the newcomer.

He parried the blow with a cutlass, driving Kris's shortsword into the wall, where it scratched a white gouge in the sandstone.

Kris swung her buckler up from her waist, catching the pirate under the chin with it. He lost his footing and fell backward.

Again, with fluid precision and feline grace, she leapt on the fallen man, this time bringing the buckler down hard on the bridge of his nose.

"Oi!"

A shout resounded down the street. Two more pirates, one another Human male with a gaudy purple sash and a headscarf, the other an Araquellan female with a patch over her left eye and blood dripping from her arm-blades, stood in the middle of the street, backlit by the flames of the village.

Kris snarled. "Back, you!" she spat. "Or you'll end up no better than these two!"

The Human pirate chuckled. "It's just a Kath girl. Here, kitty, kitty. Jobie's got a present for ya."

"Just kill her," the Araquellus said. "Katheni warriors are not to be trifled with."

"Heh, right. I'm terrified of little miss housecat," the man said with a smirk. "But hey, I've never fought a Kath before. If she's that good, mebbe she's worth fighting." He turned to Kris. "Tell you what, kitty, you fight me. You lose, you're dead. You win, I make sure Ed and Bilge back there don't make a mess of those ladies and kids." He gestured over Kris's shoulder.

Kris whipped around to see where the women and children were. They were exactly where she'd left them, and there were no pirates close to threatening them.

It was a trick.

Kris instinctively leapt backward as she spun to face the deceitful pirate. His initial cutlass strike still caught her a glancing blow just below her right armpit, staining her tawny fur with blood. She screamed a feral, wounded predator scream.

The children screamed as well, and their mothers herded them farther into the dead-end corner.

The pirate Jobie stepped back, a glinting cutlass in his left hand. "Heh. Quicker than I thought. But not quick enough." He stepped forward and threw another cut at Kris's lower torso.

Kris blocked it with her buckler and threw a counter-cut at Jobie. He ducked under it and swiped at Kris's feet. She leapt over it, kicked off the wall of the house next to her, and slashed downward at Jobie's shoulder.

She caught the pirate off guard. Her shortsword laid open the side of Jobie's left arm.

"Augh!" Jobie stepped back again. He clutched his wounded arm, then smiled again. It was a disturbing, hungry smile. "Heh, nice one, kitty. Too bad I'm not left-handed, eh?" He tossed his cutlass from his left hand to his right and lunged again.

Kris parried with the shield again. "Better swordsmen than you have delivered that line, murderer."

Jobie snickered and pressed his attack. This time the blows came quicker, more accurately. Kris was on the retreat now, waiting for an opening that seemed would never come. Her footpaws scraped backward as she lost ground. She was being herded back toward the well.

Her sensitive ears picked up the whimpering of the scared children behind her and the frightened breathlessness of the women sheltering them. Kris gritted her fangs. She would not lose to this pirate—no, to this slaver.

"Back!" Kris shouted. She leapt forward, striking at the pirate's heart, or more correctly, where it should be if in fact he'd had one.

Jobie scoffed as he turned her blade aside, but his scorn caught in his throat as Kris took a step inside his guard and swung her unsheathed claws at his throat.

She didn't miss.

Jobie staggered back, clutching his free hand to his neck to staunch the flow of blood. *"Anani sikerim, te orsobu!"* he shouted in Orcish, and spat blood onto the sandstone pavement. "That's it. Maala, kill her."

The Araquellan woman nodded, a slight smile on her pale blue lips. "I told you not to underestimate her."

"Just shut up and finish her," Jobie said, choking.

The Araquellus turned to Kris. "I am sorry it has come to this, brave warrior," she said. "I will make your death as swift as I can."

One of the women Kris was defending began sobbing as well.

"Words," Kris said, a growl in the back of her throat. "Your skill and speed would speak louder, Araquellus. Use them."

The woman nodded and curled both her hands into crescent moon shapes. The bloodstained silverblue blade ridges extending from her arms glinted in the firelight briefly, then she stepped forward to fight.

This time it was all Kris could do to keep up. The Araquellus fought like a dancer, twirling and spinning to deliver attack after attack, never stopping. Her feet shifted from offense to defense, skirting obstacles and matching Kris's own movements so she was never off balance. Kris would have thought it beautiful if the woman hadn't seemed so intent on using it to end her life.

The children watched in mute horror as the dance of blades went on for some time. Then Kris's heels bumped against the cold, rough stone of the well. Her eyes widened as she realized what was about to happen, and as sure as dragons breathe fire, it did.

In one fluid motion, the Araquellan woman knocked Kris's shield aside, and on the return gave Kris the gentlest of pushes on the chest.

Kris yowled as she tipped backward and toppled into the well. She managed to grab the side as she fell, and she slammed into the interior wall rather than fall to the bottom of the well.

"Good, good," the Araquellus said, looking down into the well. "You fought well. Honor and peace to you," she said, and made a gesture with one hand down her face, covering her free eye.

"Peace this," Kris snarled, and leapt out of the well as best she could, bracing her feet on the interior wall and using her arms to propel herself upward. As she leapt, she lashed out and kicked the hanging bucket toward the Araquellus. She landed next to her opponent and whirled to attack.

Kris was too slow. She'd been feeling slow all evening, which, being a Kath, was not a feeling she was accustomed to. As Kris landed and stood, the Araquellan woman split the bucket in half with a fluid stroke, and on the return she brought both of her blades down across Kris's back, laying open fur and flesh.

Kris staggered forward with a gasp. The pain was blinding, too much to handle. She saw something like the blackness of the night sky, with all the stars rushing at her at once as if to bombard her. She sank to her knees, dropping her sword and whimpering quietly as she felt the blood run down her back.

"*Nahisaii*, Kath," the Araquellus said. "I should have known better than to think you would graciously accept defeat."

"What's the matter with you, Maala?" Jobie said, walking up from behind the two. The wound on his neck had healed, as had his arm, leaving nasty scars in their place. One of the pirates must have known healing magic. Jobie stepped closer and put his blade to Kris's neck. "Took you way too long, heh."

"She fought as a warrior. I gave her a fair fight," Maala said. "I could do no less."

"Well, I can do more." Jobie leaned down so his face was level with Kris's. "I wonder how much a Kath pelt will fetch me on the black market?"

Kris didn't have the energy to rise to the jibe, whether he was serious or not. Her body cried out for her not to move and to get away from here at the same time, while her ears still heard the sobs and pleading of the women and children as the pirates approached.

As a tie-breaking vote, her weariness let her move only her head, tilting tear-stained eyes up to look at her tormentor. "Why?"

"What, the pelt?" Jobie said. "Because I'm sure somebody'd pay handsomely for a Kath-skin rug. Heh. And I think I'll enjoy skinning you alive after what you did to my arm and neck, that's why."

"I think she wants to know why we came," Maala said. She ripped a chunk of awning loose from one of the buildings in the courtyard and began wiping the blood from her blade ridges. "We came because you were weak. The strong prey on the weak. It is the way of nature, and it is the way of man."

Kris was too weary, and now too lightheaded, to form complete sentences. "Conscience?" she managed. "You have . . . no . . ."

"Turns out," Maala said, "that the more one silences it, the quieter its cries."

"Never had one," Jobie said with a malicious grin. "Now hold still, rug, and I'll make this hurt slightly less. Heh, nah, it's just gonna hurt."

Jobie roughly grabbed one of her ears and yanked her head back. She felt the tip of Jobie's cutlass prick her chin. Kris closed her eyes.

Then the point of the sword moved away from her, and Jobie made a strangled noise. Another came from Maala.

Kris opened her eyes.

Jobie's eyes were wide with what looked like fear. A small trickle of blood ran from his nose onto his lip and into his mouth.

Kris glanced at Maala. The Araquellus stood stiffly, looking toward the archway they'd come in.

"Ghhhhk!" Jobie said and staggered forward.

Kris gaped. The pirate's bloody nose had gotten worse, and to add to it, his ears and eyes had begun bleeding too. Within seconds, Maala had the same symptoms. Kris turned her head toward the archway.

Three figures stood beneath the sandstone arch. All three were of average height, none taller than six feet, nor shorter than five and a half. One was a woman, the other two were men, one younger than the other. All three were dressed entirely in white, and had white hair and pale skin. The younger man and the woman had colorless grey eyes, while the older man wore a full black face mask, which, strangely, had no eye holes.

The young man held a strange silver stick with a glass sphere floating above it that glowed in a myriad of colors. The woman had her hands folded in front of her. The blindfolded man held one hand out, with fingers curled like the gnarled branches of a long-dead tree, as if he were holding or crushing something.

Then Jobie and Maala dissolved into clouds of fine red mist. A wet breeze passed over Kris, coating her fur.

Coating her fur. In blood. Kris gagged.

The older man turned his head to the younger. Without a word, the younger man stepped toward the cluster of frightened women and children and waved a hand. In unison, they slumped to the ground with hardly a noise.

"Wh—" Kris started to say.

"Hush," said the woman. "Do not speak. Save your energy for healing. They merely sleep." Her voice was soft and comforting, like the mother Kris could barely remember.

"Stand," the older man said. His voice was not so pleasant, and it bore the tone of one used to being obeyed.

And obey Kris did. Her mind said no, but her body moved on its own. She felt pinned, trapped in her mind as she realized they had some sort of magical control over her. But it was not kind and warm like her brother's magic, nor hateful and cold like the frost mage she had once fought. This felt blank, colorless, emotionless.

She floated off the ground, ever so slowly, and came to rest across the young man's shoulder. Without a word between them, the three strangers turned and walked away from the courtyard, Kris with them.

The air about them seemed to shimmer and waver as they walked. The last thought Kris had as she slipped into unconsciousness was that she had heard the strangers's voices, but not with her ears. They hadn't said a word.

"It looks like they've regrouped back on the ship," Emily said. She sat atop Slashback, who was prepped for a night mission. Both gryphon and rider wore black clothing, and Emily's chainmail was muffled with strips of leather interspersed between the metal rings.

"It is a great shame that we could not help the village earlier," Koshiro said. The Eastern Islander was dressed in a nearly skin-tight black suit of clothing that fit him like a glove. True, his gloves fit like gloves, as well, because it would have been bad had they fit like boots. Even his boots, which were more like slippers, as they were of very soft and stealthy material, fit like gloves. They were the ninja equivalent of a toe-sock.

Atop that he wore a simple black tunic with embroidered silver fish and waves on it. To top it off, he wore a facemask that covered his mouth, nose, and the top of his head, leaving only his eyes and a lock of hair exposed. A pair of ornate silver swords crossed his back, a bandolier of tiny throwing-knives ran across his shoulder and chest, and a silver sash rode around his waist.

The three of them stood on a spit of ground across the bay from the burning town on Starspeak. Emily could see the dark, looming silhouette of the pirate ship with its black sails and draconic figurehead lit by the flicker of flames. Every now and then, a scream, shout, or small explosion echoed across the otherwise calm bay. The salt wind, normally clean, smelled of smoke.

Emily looked at Koshiro and sighed. "I'm sorry, Koshiro. We had to wait until they were off their guard or we couldn't take 'em with just the three of us."

"If we act quickly, we may still be able to stop the pirates before they take their hostages on board," Koshiro said, turning and looking across the black water. "Tonight, my sword avenges the souls lost to greed and hate and protects the weak and innocent. Tonight, the heartless creatures that prey upon those who have done them no harm shall feel the pain and fear they so carelessly inflict upon others. These pirates shall feel the wrath of the *Jikan ga Kakaru* style."

Emily quirked an eyebrow. "I'm not sure whether to tell you to get the talking out o' your system now or to save it 'til after the battle, Koshiro."

Slashback cocked her head. "It is sound like you are not liking pirates much, Fish," the gryphoness said. "Are you having something against dem?"

"An age-old feud," Koshiro replied. He turned back to face Emily and Slashback. "Pirates, with their lawlessness and chaotic free spirits, think themselves above discipline and the fine points of the martial arts. They consider themselves better because of this." He shook his head, then began tying a silver headband on. "It is a shame, but many agree that pirates are indeed better than we."

Emily put a hand on her friend's shoulder. "I don't think they're better than you, Koshiro," she said, then chuckled. "You could take that whole boatload yourself if you'd just keep your gob shut."

"For Emily-san, I will be the soul of silence," Koshiro said. "I shall repeat the sacred phrases of the Jikan ga Kakaru to myself only, without the slightest sound."

"If you can," Slashback said with a snort. "I hear you did not so well last time you fight."

Koshiro scowled and looked back out at the water. "We will depart soon, yes?" he asked Emily.

She nodded. "Let's stop this before they hurt anyone else. And Koshiro?"

"Yes, Emily-san?"

"Chew on this." Emily produced from her pocket a small brown cube wrapped in beeswax paper. She handed it to Koshiro. "A special caramel Serimal gave me for you. He said you were fond of sweets."

"*Hi,*" he replied with a crisp bow. He pulled down his mask to pop the candy into his mouth. "Did Serimal-dono say what was special about it?" He began chewing the sweet, and Emily could see the smile in his eyes.

"Something about it having some magic for you." Emily looked at him. "You feel any different?"

Koshiro looked like he was trying to speak. In fact, Emily could see his mouth moving beneath the cloth of his mask, but no sound came out.

Emily chuckled at Koshiro's startled expression. "Looks like the perfect magic for ya," she said. "Let's get you on that ship before its effect wears off."

Emily and Slashback dropped Koshiro onto the pirate deck from a low altitude flyover. He landed without a sound on two feet and a hand, his other hand reaching over his back for one of the silver swords. He straightened up, waved to Emily, and literally disappeared in a puff of smoke.

Emily blinked. "Come around again," she told Slashback.

Slashback nodded and banked for a return pass. Sure enough, Koshiro was nowhere to be seen.

"I hope that candy lasts long enough for him to do some damage," Emily said. "Let's come back in a bit and see what he's done."

Over the burning village they flew. Slashback tilted her dusty white wings to catch the smoky thermals produced by the fires, keeping them aloft long enough for Emily to see the extent of the damage.

Every structure burned. Even the roofs of some of the sandstone buildings smoldered as the fires spread. People rushed about trying to douse the flames or tending the wounded. From her vantage point in the sky, Emily couldn't see any pirates left. They seemed to have retreated to the ship to enjoy their spoils.

"Slashback!" Emily leaned over to speak into the gryphoness's pointed ears. "Take us low over the water. I want to try something."

"Try vat?" Slashback asked, already diving toward the ocean.

"I think I finally found a use for that S.A.C.K. General Allyn gave me," Emily said with a grin.

The reader should note that the S.A.C.K. is in fact a bag of the sort usually carried by the practical and somewhat wealthy Hero.

The acronym stands for a Sack of Alarming Carrying Kapacity. Each S.A.C.K. can hold a great deal more than it should by any rational estimation of mass or physics. They weigh less than ten pounds, but can hold multiple larger and heavier objects without any discernable increase in weight or dimensions.

A typical S.A.C.K. is no larger than a rucksack one would use to carry one's lunch, but can hold a spare sword and shield, two weeks' worth of trail rations, half of one's personal library, a manservant, a carriage complete with two horses, a crowbar, a lantern, a battering ram, and a standard-issue ten foot pole, all with room to spare.

The original S.A.C.K. was invented by an Orcish mage for the purpose of sneaking a few days' worth of food out of all-you-can-eat buffets. But the design was soon adapted to carrying the gear Heroic. This saved Heroes the trouble and expense of hiring a retinue to carry their gear, or the inconvenience of fighting while wearing a cumbersome backpack.

S.A.C.K.s are expensive, often tipping the merchants' scales at a thousand gold pieces or so, but they look much more dashing than a backpack the size of a pregnant dragon and are thus much sought after.

They reputedly work by opening a small hole to *Somewhere Else*, a place between worlds, and storing the required gear there. This has yet to be confirmed by denizens of Emily's dimension or the demons of *Another Place*.

Sadly, the inventor of the S.A.C.K. disappeared while in the process of inventing a more powerful version of the item. Rumor has it he got lost in one of his own bags.

Emily hooked her left foot into Slashback's saddle girth and leaned over as the two skimmed the surface of the ocean. Emily dipped the small grey S.A.C.K. in the water. It began immediately filling, sucking in a great deal more than it should hold.

After a few moments, Emily pulled herself back up. "All right, Slashback. Let's put out them fires!"

Slashback squawked her approval and beat the air with her wings, climbing back to her previous altitude. Once there, Emily opened her S.A.C.K. and tipped it over on the smoldering village.

A torrent, a cascade, a veritable deluge spouted from the opening of the bag, dousing every fire the two passed over.

"Score one for the Silverwings!" Emily crowed. "Er, uh, or the Fifth Column, right?"

"Yiss," Slashback said, the skin at the corners of her beak pulling up into a smile. "You are remind me greatly of your uncle Gaffin, Emli."

"Huh?" Emily said. "Uncle Gavin? Whaddaya mean?"

Slashback veered away as the bag regurgitated a confused shark, which fell into where the fish market had been. "I mean he did such tings for to save people, as you do. Your mind sharp like his. Your heart gut too."

Emily chuckled. "I'm glad you think so, Slashback. "That looks like all the fires though. We should probably check on Koshiro."

Slashback dove again, this time coming to a graceful landing on the docks next to the pirate ship.

Emily dismounted and took a step forward. "Koshiro?" she said, looking about for any sign of the swordsman. "Koshiro?"

With an almost imperceptible rush of wind, a black-clad man vaulted from the deck, performed a quintuple flip, and landed in front of Emily, silver swords extended.

Three seconds later, the boat exploded.

The deafening concussion echoed over the still bay. Emily covered her head as bits of blazing wood rained down on the docks. Slashback sheltered the both of them under her wings. The pirate ship immediately began sinking. Not a soul appeared to jump overboard. In fact, after the initial explosion, the scene was eerily quiet, save for the hissing and crackling of the flames meeting ocean.

"What in the Nine . . . ?" Emily said. "Koshiro! Was that absolutely necessary?"

"You are success!" Slashback said with obvious glee. "Now the village will be safe."

Koshiro pulled off his mask. He looked surprised.

"Oh, here," Emily said. "Serimal gave me this too." She handed a second caramel to Koshiro.

Koshiro took and ate the caramel. After a few seconds, he looked back at the sinking burning boat, then back to Emily. "And that," Koshiro said, "is why Ninjas are better than Pirates."

Chapter 14

BROTHERLY LOVE

*In which Voshtyr Encounters Relatives best left Forgotten,
Reginald gets a Quest Update,
And the Real Fun Begins*

VOSHTYR SLAMMED his goblet down on the feast table in front of him. "*Who* is here?"

The Arch-Villain Voshtyr Demonkin sat at the head of a long black-lacquered table decked with roast pigs, venison, stacks of potatoes, loaves of bread, and the finest fruits and wines from around the world. A dozen other people sat about the table. They cringed as Voshtyr slammed his hand down.

A messenger stood beside Voshtyr, wishing his black and red livery was somewhat more sword-resistant. "If you please, Lord Voshtyr, he called himself your brother. Said his name was Jaratyr."

The richly decorated hall that Voshtyr, the table, the food, the guests, and the startled messenger occupied was lit by open flames in a half-dozen glowing braziers supported by squatting brass demon sculptures with their forked tongues sticking out, and rubies for eyes. Tapestries depicting Deeds Most Foul, Dark Deeds, and Deeds Best Left Undepicted covered the dark grey of the hall's stone walls. An oval-shaped black carpet trimmed in gold covered the center of the floor.

"Jaratyr," Voshtyr said darkly. "You kill one brother and the next one crops up," he muttered to himself. "Very well, send him in."

The messenger bowed and darted off to let in the strange guest, probably considering himself lucky Voshtyr was distracted. The turnover rate of messengers in this castle was quite high.

Voshtyr turned back to his guests, brushing imaginary lint from the front of his black silk shirt. "My apologies, ladies and gentlemen. I was not expecting relatives of mine to still draw breath, much less crash one of my banquets."

One of the guests, an Elven woman in the mess dress uniform of the Army of Darkness™, with a complexion that would have been perfect if not for a network of crisscrossed scars on her face and neck, spoke up. "I thought you'd slain your brother at the Keep of Falling Stars."

"Wrong brother," Voshtyr said. He sat back down in his high-backed chair. "That was Serimal, the pathetic Human one. This one's Jaratyr. He's much more difficult to kill. Trust me, Tara, I know." He snatched his goblet, drained the wine, and slammed the cup back on the table. "If you kill a Demon, it just goes back to *Another Place*. And apparently it can feel free to keep coming back to irritate you as many times as it has the attention span for. And Jaratyr has a very long attention span indeed."

"What in the Green Fields of the Blessed does he want?" asked another of the guests. This one was Human, a man with wavy brown hair, a charming smile, and a poisoned dagger concealed in his sleeve. He wore a blue and white tunic with gold trim and puffed sleeves and a pair of deep blue tights.

"If he wantsh food, itsh too bad," said another guest, a morbidly obese brown-furred Katheni male. He sat at the far end of the long table surrounded by the wreckage of almost a third of the food that had been on the table at the outset of the feast. The Katheni swallowed his mouthful of pork and wiped grease from the yellowing white tufts of fur around his mouth. "I provide sustenance for the people of *this* world, not others."

"Thank you, Igor," Voshtyr snapped. "Your input is, as always, invaluable. Now silence, I need to think about what to do about Jaratyr."

"You could greet me warmly, shake my hand, and offer me a cup of coffee," said a warm and mellow bass voice.

Voshtyr and his guests turned in unison to face the newcomer.

He was almost a foot taller than Voshtyr, and had a skin tone like a cross between a near-lethal sunburn and a brick. Greasy-looking hair covered his head, which was framed by a pair of twisted ebon horns sweeping back from his forehead, over his ears, and into points behind his ears at the back of his skull. Thin black claws sprouted from his hands where fingernails should have been, and a barbed serpentine tail trailed out from beneath the fine black suit and the shimmering white cape he wore over one shoulder. As he smiled, Voshtyr could see the irritatingly familiar pointed smile he occasionally shared.

"Jaratyr," Voshtyr said darkly again.

"Voshtyr," Jaratyr said brightly, to even out the lighting conditions.

"What do you want?"

"World peace. Or perhaps a piece of the world," Jaratyr said. "I hear you lay claim to a good portion of your world these days."

Voshtyr rose from his chair and attempted to stand face to face with Jaratyr, and came up a foot too short, settling for face to chest instead. "Listen here, Jaratyr—"

"You rhymed," Jaratyr observed.

"Nine Torments! Will you just shut up for one *nihaila mavrashk* minute!" Voshtyr shouted, some of his words in a language normally not uttered by mortals. "I have stolen this world fair and square from the Heroes and their ilk. If you think for one moment that I'm going to hand the singular most annoying demon ever one square span of it—"

"Calm down, little brother," Jaratyr said with a smirk. "I don't want any of your little empire. I just want to feed off the pain and suffering you're generating."

"How so?" Voshtyr leaned forward. "How do you feed off such things?"

"Simple," Jaratyr said. "Everywhere you've gone recently, you've done nothing but cause mayhem and madness, death and destruction, sadness and sorrow. And unless I miss my guess, you've been collecting it all. In little gems. It's win-win, really. Was someone going to get me coffee or not?"

The woman, Tara, who had stood earlier, drew her blade, an ornate shortsword with a blade slightly wider than that of a gladius. "This thing is, Lord Voshtyr, your brother has—"

"*Half*-brother." Voshtyr grabbed the front of Jaratyr's fine black shirt and yanked the demon's head down to face level. His concealed arm-blade snapped out of his magical metal left arm, and he held it to Jaratyr's throat. "Now you listen well, Jaratyr. I don't know what you're up to or who you're serving, but you stay out of my affairs."

Jaratyr *tsked*. "Or you'll do what? Tattle on me to our mother? I'm sure that will work out well for you." He examined his claws. "Always has in the past."

Voshtyr, his face a deadly calm, lowered the blade, released Jaratyr's shirt and turned back to his other guests. "I am sorry, ladies and gentlemen, but I must attend to this . . . disturbance. I offer you all accommodations for the night, and I shall see you in the morning."

Most of the other guests got up and began to leave, muttering apprehensively among themselves.

"Tara, Igor, Camoran—you three please stay," Voshtyr said. "Anything you have to say to me, Jaratyr, these three can hear as well."

Jaratyr chuckled. "Even if I tell them about the time you thought a 'fire diaper' would be a good idea for a half-demon to wear, and you ran around the house on fire until—"

"Enough, Jaratyr!" Voshtyr shouted. He slammed his fist into the back of his chair, knocking it across the hallway and splintering the wood backing. "Surely you are not here simply to annoy me, though you are doing admirably well at that. What did you really come for?"

Jaratyr looked first at Voshtyr, then the three lords standing menacingly close to him. Well, two of them stood menacingly. The fat Katheni didn't look like he could menace anything tougher than a seven-layer bean dip.

"Well, since you put it that way," Jaratyr said, "I suppose I'll tell you . . . for a price."

Voshtyr opened his mouth to say something vile, but felt a hand on his shoulder.

Camoran had stepped forward. "Milord, if I may. Perhaps now is the time for diplomacy, since he seems intent on irritating you. I am perhaps slightly less . . . prone to violence than you."

"Bah," Voshtyr said. "Give that demon three minutes, and he'll be under your skin as well." He did take a few steps back, however, and glowered at his demonic half-brother.

"Son of Nephil," Camoran said, bowing at the waist to Jaratyr, "I am Camoran Yronguard of House Darkstar. It is a rare privilege to meet one of your genealogy someplace other than on the battlefield."

Jaratyr smirked again. "Look, Voshtyr, your lapdog has manners. You could learn a thing or two." He looked directly at Camoran. "So, my brother can't speak for himself, eh?"

Camoran adjusted his already perfect glossy brown hair. "Please, Master Jaratyr. Your petty squabbling with Lord Voshtyr, while you may find it enjoyable, accomplishes nothing." He walked around Jaratyr, pulled out a chair, and gestured to it. "If you would enlighten us as to the purpose of your visit, we would be quite grateful."

"Well, it depends," Jaratyr said, taking a seat. He didn't quite *fit* in a chair built for a Human, so he spent several seconds trying to adjust his position to be comfortable. First, he couldn't sit down on his tail, then both of his hips wouldn't fit in the chair at the same time.

Camoran did a most remarkable job of keeping a straight face. Voshtyr, not so much.

"Gah, I give up." Jaratyr shrunk himself down to approximately Human size and sat in the chair. "It depends on what you can offer me."

"In return for annoyance, irritation, and target practice?" Voshtyr said, scowling.

"Now, now, Master Jaratyr," Camoran said, shooting a disapproving look over his shoulder at Voshtyr. "Surely you know that it is poor bargaining to ask for payment without displaying what is for sale."

"Pfeh," Jaratyr said. "You talk like an Araquellus."

"Much can be learned from the marine merchants," Camoran said with a smile. "The fact remains. As Voshtyr said, you have done naught for us but irritate, and I am certain that I can get a bag of itching powder and pour it down my shirt for less cost than whatever it is you ask for."

Jaratyr chuckled. "Indeed, indeed. Touchy, Lord Yronguard."

Voshtyr blinked. "Don't you mean 'Touché?'" he said.

"I've never learned Elven," Jaratyr said, scowling. "Don't expect me to pronounce it properly. And don't go all 'grammar dragon' on me, either. You pronounced *mavrashk* wrong earlier."

"Regardless," Camoran interrupted before things got more hostile. "The fact remains that, before we allow you to access to any . . . souls . . . that Voshtyr may or may not have, we must know what you offer in return."

Jaratyr smiled. "All right, you've made your point. What would you think, little brother, if I told you that your *other* brother is still alive?"

Voshtyr started. "What? Serimal lives? Where is he? What is he doing?"

"That," Jaratyr said with a smirk, "is what will cost you."

"Hmph," Voshtyr said. "I suppose I could part with a few thousand gold pieces . . ."

Jaratyr rose from his chair and turned his back to Voshtyr. "Well, then I suppose my time has been wasted here. I shall tell your brother you said hello."

"Wait!" Voshtyr grabbed Jaratyr's shoulder. "Gold is of little use to demons except when they are in this world. You must have your mind set on something else. What do you want? A weapon? Those love notes you wrote to that priestess?"

"What?" Jaratyr said, eyes widening. "You still have those?"

"Oh, but of course," Voshtyr replied. "You're hardly the only one with blackmail material from our childhood, Jaratyr."

Jaratyr scowled. "No, you can keep the bloody notes. They're not important."

"Then what is?"

"SOULS," Jaratyr said in a booming, sepulchral voice, which by definition is both hard on the voice and on the typesetter, who has to fish more capital letters out whenever someone speaks in the aforementioned voice. "I hear you've quite the collection, and I could honestly use a few to keep up with my quota."

Voshtyr turned away to hide a smile. Finally, now that he knew what his demonic half-brother wanted, he had the upper hand. "I will make you a bargain," Voshtyr said. "You tell me everything you know of Serimal's whereabouts, strengths, and plans, and I shall give you as many common souls as I can spare."

"Counteroffer," Jaratyr said. "I tell you his strengths and what he's up to, and you provide me with Greater Mythological SOULS at the very least."

"Secondary counteroffer," Voshtyr replied. "You tell me his every move, no matter how insignificant, and I will provide you with Daring, Courageous, and Immaculate souls as I collect them."

Jaratyr licked his lips. "Ooh," he said. "What flavor?"

Voshtyr chuckled darkly, and this time Jaratyr did nothing to change the lighting.

"What flavor?" Voshtyr said, turning his head back to look at his half-brother. "I would think that was obvious. Heroic. Now stop shouting every time you say the word 'souls.'"

Black skies
> White sand

Stood the Hero, squinting, upon a blasted land

White birds
> Black clouds

The Hero left no footprints upon the hard-packed sand

Grey trees
> Grey sea

A light approached the Hero across the landscape bland

Grey snow
> Grey stone

And then the light, it spoke aloud, soft, yet bold and grand

"Oh, Hero, you ignored me," the voice it softly said.
> "Oh, Hero, you gave up now, and now you are quite dead."

The Hero stood, and as he did, he looked about in awe.
> The Hero fell upon his knees beholding what he saw.

There He stood, in robes of white, and shining like the sun.
> "Oh, Hero, now you must return and finish what's begun."

"You did not carry out My plan, so now you have another.
    "Become a friend to Races Nine, and to them be a brother."

The Hero scratched his grizzled face and spoke a thought aloud.
    "How am I to do this thing? How shall I make You proud?"

The Shining One began to fly, and flying, spake these words:
    "Just be yourself, dear Reginald, to canines, cats, or birds.

"All your power, steadfast soul, and training it will take
    "To finish well and end this Quest. Now, Reginald, *awake!*"

Reginald opened his eyes. He lay face-down on a beach composed of smooth pebbles of varying hues of brown and grey.

"Awake, human!" said a voice from above Reginald.

Reginald started to say something, but discovered, unpleasantly, that his lungs were full of water. He coughed and vomited the briny water onto the rocks.

"See, Amni, I told you he live," the voice said again. Reginald couldn't place the accent, though it sounded a good deal like a gryphon. "You are owe me two bags of spice."

Reginald groaned and rolled over to see to whom he was talking.

The creature looked about a little less than five feet tall. It was humanoid but with brilliant white feathers tipped with gold and a sharp, hooked beak like a bird of prey. An Avierie. But what was an Avierie doing this far from the mountains?

"Glyss, I am say he is dead because he was not breath!" said a second voice, with much the same accent. "I am not give you spice from this."

"Keh, you are poor sport," said the white Avierie, whom Reginald surmised was named Glyss.

"Where am I?" Reginald said, pushing himself up to a sitting position. He looked about. The shore stretched for a distance in both directions, but terminated in sheer stone cliffs dotted with what looked like caves. It was around midday, though it was difficult to tell from behind the cliffs. The air was still warm, but the waves washing around Reginald's ankles were much colder. The back of his throat still tasted like seawater . . . and vomit. It was hardly pleasant.

Glyss tilted his head almost comically. "You are at ocean, of course!" he said. "Ocean near Bleak Cliffs. You are Hero, yiss?"

"Yes, I am the Crimson Slash." Reginald stood to his full Heroic Height, and immediately sat back down. His legs felt weak and watery, and his stomach churned. Perhaps moments after almost drowning was not the best time to be Heroic. And in retrospect, it was also probably not the best time to announce oneself as a Hero given the current political climate.

"Hmm," the second Avierie, Amni, said, looking Reginald over. "I am hear of you, but . . ."

"But what?" Reginald asked.

"You are not have armor with red bar, and not have sword of very large." Glyss shrugged, the golden feathers intermixed with his white plumage shimmering in the morning sun. "Perhaps you are forget them someplace not here?"

Reginald reached for his sword. Indeed, it was missing. So were his armor and shield. In fact, he looked more like an exceptionally burly, somewhat unkempt, and thoroughly damp peasant than a Hero. "I suppose you have a point," Reginald said. "I cannot ask you to take my word for it, but—"

"Oh, we belief you," said Glyss. "Who would say they are Hero when Heroes are very . . . how you say . . . ghhhkkk?" He drew a line across his feathered throat with one of his talons.

Reginald scowled. "How very tactful of you. Tell me, where is the nearest place I might acquire weapons and armor? I find myself in sore need of them, and I have a Quest I must embark on."

Glyss clapped his wings together. "Oh, I am can make them for you!" he said. "I am powerful mage, and the makings of items is my . . . how you say . . . special sauce?"

Amni poked Glyss with a talon. "Specialty, Glyss. Specialty."

"Special sauce, special tea, what evers! I am make items, not words," Glyss said, ruffling up his feathers. "For a Hero, I am give discount. I once make many items for Guild, you see."

Reginald smiled. "Well, perhaps Fortune has smiled on me then." He looked up at the sky. "Or someone else, perchance."

"Come, come," Glyss said. "Come back to camp. We will get for you dry clothes, and I can see about the armors and weapon."

Reginald stood again. "My gratitude, Avierie. You would help a Hero even in these dire times?"

Glyss shrugged again. "The Guild was friend of Glyss. I will help how I can."

The three of them struck out north, Reginald slowing his pace to keep up with the waddling gait of the two bird-folk, and the bird-folk staying ground-bound to stay with the Hero.

Three hours later, after a bracing climb up a forbidding cliff, Reginald found himself in a small two-tent encampment, warmed, dried, and clothed in what for the Avierie was probably a loose-fitting robe, but that stretched across Reginald's burly frame like a hide across a drying rack. On him it looked more like a short blue tunic than a robe.

It seemed that the two Avierie had found him on the beach as they'd been out collecting samples of various marine plant and animal life. Several bags and crates of various seaweeds, coral, fish, and crustaceans lay stacked about on the plateau, along with some small potted flowers. From the vantage point on the cliff, Reginald could see a vast expanse of ocean with reefs near the base of the cliffs. The setting sun was just beginning to sink into the sea, and the flowers began closing as the light dimmed.

While beginning to find an appropriate replacement weapon for Reginald, Glyss chattered on about news from various places he had seen in the crystal ball he periodically consulted. It was not long before Reginald realized that he had somehow missed almost a month of time since falling into the ocean. But he was alive and would therefore not question it.

Glyss finally approached Reginald bearing a selection of short and long swords. "Here are the swords I am having now." He dropped them at Reginald's feet. "Please to pick the one you are liking best."

Reginald looked at the swords. Several were quite nice, but none were of the size and weight he usually preferred. One of the half-dozen swords caught his eye, however. "You have a Muramune?" Reginald said incredulously. "I thought only six of these were ever made!"

"Oh, is not Muramune," Glyss said, waving a wingtip. "Is cheap knock-off. I buy from sword vendor with 'not a fake' sign on it."

"Merchants," Reginald said, growling. "Well, Eastern Island swords are not my style. What's this?" He picked up another sword. It was plain and grey, a common steel longsword, by all accounts, but it felt heavier in his hands.

And then it reacted.

The blade glinted as a shimmer of light ran up its blade from hilt to tip. Then it began to warp and stretch, widening and lengthening. As it did, it grew heavier. Reginald felt his muscles tense to hold the additional weight.

"Whaaat?" Glyss said, his beak hanging open. "What are you do? Pliss to not cast magic on Glyss swords!"

"I did nothing!" Reginald said. "I know almost naught of magic, and I like it less!"

The blade continued to shape itself into a titanic version of its original shape. It was now a straight-edged blade as tall as Reginald himself, and wider than his previous sword had been. The hilt had a simple leather wrap about it, and the guard sloped just slightly, finishing as a quarter circle between the blade and grip.

"Sharp," Glyss said breathlessly.

Reginald felt the blade, and winced as it bit deep into his thumb upon his merely touching it. "It is indeed," he said. "I've not felt an edge its like."

"No, the sword is Sharp," Glyss said.

"Exactly," Reginald said. "I would wager it could cleave through steel like butter."

Glyss flapped his wings. "No, no, *no!* The sword, it is Sharp! Not edge, not blade. Its name is Sharp! It is made of sharp!"

"What in the Nine Torments are you on about?" Reginald said, giving the somewhat crazed bird-folk an odd look. "This is obviously a magical sword.

Glyss hid his beak in his wings. "Is Weapon of Legend," he said. "Is Sharp. Is not made of steel, but made of sharpness."

Reginald blinked. "Steel does not hold such an edge. It could be Orichalc, but what do you mean, 'made of sharpness?'"

"Pliss to listen," Glyss said, scooping up his other swords. "You know that some swords are some sharp, yiss? Each sword has little bit of sharpness in it. As trait of swords."

"Yes, and . . . ?" Reginald said.

"Not to interrupt, Hero," said Amni, who had crawled inside his tent and had a rush mat wrapped about his head to block out the Hero's loud bass voice. "Listen to Glyss. And please to talk less loud."

Glyss rested his right talons on the flat of the newly-enlarged blade. "Now, pliss to imagine a sword that does not have that bit of sharpness, but is *made* of it instead."

Reginald thought for a moment. Then his rugged face broke out in a massive grin. "Then you are saying that this is the sharpest sword in the world?"

"You are dense, Hero," Glyss said irritably. "It is not just sharpest sword in world, it is sharpest sharp thing whatever sharped sharply!"

"I see," Reginald said, scratching his beard sagely. "So then it could cut almost anything, then?"

Glyss shrugged. "I suppose it could—"

Reginald swung the sword at a cone-shaped outcropping of rock to one side of the plateau. The sword passed right through it. Reginald blinked. It was as if he had missed entirely. Curious, he reached out and touched the stone. It slid, fell off its base, and rolled down the mountain, leaving the cleanest cross-section of stone Reginald had ever seen.

"See!" Glyss crowed. "Is Sharp!"

"Yes, it is," Reginald said, examining the blade. "I felt almost no resistance as I cut it."

"No," Glyss said, "I mean—"

"The Hero knows what you are mean!" Amni said from beneath his mat. "Stop making repeats of yourself!"

"With such a sword," Reginald said, "I can finally undertake this Quest."

"Then pliss to take Sharp," Glyss said. The Avierie deposited the rest of his swords in a bag that seemed too small to hold them. "It is least I am do for friend of Glyss and of Guild."

He took a few steps and looked at the horizon. "A friend," he said. "A friend to the Nine . . . Very well. I shall return to the Keep of Five Flames, I shall break the curse on the Centaurs, and I shall see Demonkin thrown from his own tower."

Reginald hefted Sharp onto his shoulder, careful to not let it slice his arm clean off, and stood again to his Full Heroic Height. "Let the fun begin."

PART 2

Chapter 15

REGRET AND REVENGE

*In which Cyrus Returns to Find Carnage,
Discovers some of his Talents,
And gets a Quest of his Own*

CYRUS PUSHED THE lid off the mine cart and stepped out, blinking against the invasive midday sunlight. Keeth had carried the cart all the way from Centra Mundi. Cyrus still thought it would have been easier to just ride the dragon, but that was taboo in dragon culture. Being carried in a dark, uncomfortable, overly warm metal box on wheels apparently was not, and it was by that mode of transportation he had arrived.

And he arrived to find that his home town was on fire. Or more correctly, that it had been on fire. What was left now was a smoking ruin.

The buildings made of stone were the only ones left, and they were missing their roofs. Blackened patches of ground with bits of charred rubble marked where wooden houses had been. People sat on the ground, blank looks on their faces, stunned by what had happened.

"What . . . ?" Cyrus said.

"I have no idea," Keeth said, his mouth agape as he looked at the wanton destruction. "It looks as if a dragon attacked, but there are far too many footprints about, and most dragons would not stoop to attacking a lone village like Starspeak."

Cyrus approached a man who was sitting amidst the rubble. "Where's Kris?"

"Haven't seen her," the man said without looking up.

Cyrus scowled. "What happened here?"

"Pirates," the man said. "Burned it all. Took a lot of stuff. Killed Sal and Geoffrey." He made a noise that sounded somewhere between a sob and a hiccup. "If those people in black hadn't showed up, we'd all be dead."

People in black? Dread welled up in Cyrus's chest. "Keeth, I have to check on Kris."

"Go," Keeth said. "I shall investigate these pirates—and the black-clothed men this fellow speaks of."

Cyrus nodded, then dashed off at Full Heroic Speed. Trees blurred past in leafy smears of color, grass parted in front of him, and a cloud of dust followed three steps behind him. He was clear across the length of the island and at his house in under a minute.

The house was standing upright. It hadn't been burned. That was something, at least. A pair of distraught phoenixes hopped about on the roof whistling a distressed chirrup, as if looking for something. There were footprints outside the house, though none led to the beach. They were all around, though. He ran inside.

The interior was a catastrophe. Clothes were strung out all over. Kris's pottery wheel lay shattered on the ground. He checked the hiding spots for his weapons. His home-defense sword, Kris's sword, and the buckler he'd given her as a wedding gift were all missing.

"*Bok* in a bucket," Cyrus muttered. "Kris?" he called. "Kris?"

There was no answer.

He stepped back outside, walking onto the beach, dazed. "Kris?" he shouted.

Only the taunting sound of empty waves greeted Cyrus's ears.

"*Kris!*" Cyrus shouted at the top of his lungs. "No, no, *no!* I am *not* losing her again!" He leapt into the sand, anger tearing at his heart and lungs. His breathing grew more ragged. He felt suddenly warm. Warm as he had felt while absorbing the Fire line on the Phoenix Islands.

Cyrus let the heat wash over him, feeling more angry with each passing second. His skin began smoking, then burst into flame. He was a column of fire on the beach.

"Is this part of some plan? Huh?" Cyrus shouted across the ocean. "Well, if it's a plan, this is a stupid plan!" He shook his fist at the empty blue sky. "First my parents, then the Heroes, now Kris? Where's the sense? Where's the justice?"

He sank to his knees, slouching into a molten liquid. Cyrus blinked. He had glassed the portion of sand on which he stood.

"Well," he said after a few seconds of flaming pity-party, "I guess this isn't accomplishing anything." He let the fire die out and watched the glass trickle down the beach into the water. At the same time, he felt calmer, more steady.

And despite how smart Cyrus pretended to be a lot of the time, he just then realized the connection between drawing in Fire energy and his recent fits of rage. He'd already been sheathed in flame when he was fighting the goblins, but it had gotten worse after he'd touched that . . . Shard thing. Had the Shard tainted his use of Fire? And what of how the black smoke from the burning Darkmatter had diminished the dark smoke around him?

The last wisps of fire died out as he watched the glass trickle away from him and harden. Maybe he would have to find a different Element to use. Fire was tricky. What else was around?

Cyrus closed his eyes and focused in on the energies surrounding him. He could feel the Fire, sure enough, and the Water lines in the ocean. But there was another one not too far from here: an Air line. A rushing, playful, capricious zephyr of a line.

Cyrus reached out both mentally and physically for the Air line, as if he wanted it most of anything in the world. It swarmed into his hands and wrapped itself around his arm, then billowed down his sleeve, inflating his tunic.

Cyrus opened his eyes to see sand swirling about him in a miniature tornado. He smiled. He felt lighter, more good-humored. Almost as if not much mattered very much. He felt happy.

And then he remembered why he was wielding magic in the first place. His mate was still missing, and his village was destroyed. How had he forgotten?

Also, he was flying.

As soon as he realized this, he fell to the ground.

"Oof," he said.

"Are you done fooling about?" Keeth asked. The large green dragon lay on the grass near Cyrus's house watching the young Hero. Cyrus had no idea how long he'd been watching.

Cyrus stood up and rubbed his tailbone. Fortunately he had landed in soft, non-glassy sand. "Heh, I guess. Air lines affect me different than Fire lines do."

"One would expect that," Keeth replied. "You as a person are already a mix of the Elements, and overloading yourself with one or the other would bring out and emphasize certain personality traits of yours."

"So Fire makes me . . . angry?" Cyrus looked out over the ocean, feeling the salt breeze ruffle his flame-red hair.

The dragon nodded. "You have a temper at times. Fire brings that out. You have a carefree and spontaneous side too. It seems Air energy brings that to the forefront. For instance, have you forgotten that we must find your mate?"

"No! I mean, no, of course not," Cyrus said hurriedly. "Listen, she's not on the island. When I picked up that line, I could see a bird's eye view of everything for a couple miles. I saw the Citadel."

"The Citadel of the Kinetics?" Keeth's scaly brow lifted. "What could those . . . creatures have wanted with our dear Kris?"

"I don't know," Cyrus said. "What happened to the island? I saw wreckage down by the dock, and everything's burnt."

Keeth nodded. "Indeed. I was speaking to one of your neighbors, and it appears the island was attacked by pirates."

"Seriously?" Cyrus said. "I have had just about enough pirates for one book, thank you very much."

"Yes. But it seems the island was visited by more than just pirates." Keeth looked back at the smoldering village. "It appears there were some mysterious folk who put out the fires and destroyed the pirate vessel."

Cyrus quirked an eyebrow. "Really? Heroes, maybe?"

"It doesn't appear so," Keeth said, "but it is possible. Also, one of the children said something about your mate being taken away by a group of people in white clothing. It's unclear if they were working together or if it was just coincidence."

"Wearing all white?" Cyrus said. "Legends of the Kinetics say they wear no colors but white. Bok. I know I'm not strong enough to assault their Citadel. I . . . I can't do anything, can I?"

"I do not know," Keeth said. "Perhaps there is someone who might know a secret way in or a vulnerability of this . . . Citadel. But one would have to consult the libraries of the Highseekers to find such an obscure thing, and their tower has been buried beneath the earth."

"Or," Cyrus said, looking up, "we could ask a seer." He took a few steps back onto the beach and turned his back to Keeth. "We need to get to the Phoenix Islands. I have an experiment to try, Keeth. I need a crash course in flying."

"Unfortunate word choice," Keeth said with a sigh. "You intend to use pure Air magic to carry you? I advise against that . . ."

Cyrus tuned out Keeth's worries. After all, he was meant to do this, right? Some kind of "chosen one"?

He took hold of the Air line once more, and he felt the rush of giddiness and quickness he had felt moments ago. Then he let it fill him entirely. It was a good time to fly.

"Try to keep up, Keeth!" Cyrus shouted, and he jumped. At the same time, he released some of the stored energy, channeling it through his feet. It blasted him into the sky, his arms flailing. "Oh, nooooooo!" he yelled as he shot up, arced forward, fell for a very long time, and plunged into the sea. Heroic speed allowed him to swim back to his beach in short order. But he did so underwater the entire way.

Keeth chuckled and rose from his seat on the ground. "Stability is what Air magic lacks," he said as Cyrus broke the surface. "Perhaps you should think about what you do before you do it."

Cyrus laughed out loud. "By the Seven Sacred Speaking Stones, that was a rush!" He stepped out of the sea and flopped down on the sand, water dripping from his hair. "I was flying!"

"It looked more like being jettisoned," Keeth said in an amused tone.

"Oh, and on a side note," Cyrus said, looking up at the dragon, "I don't need to breathe when I'm full of Air. I could have stayed underwater forever."

"That makes a certain amount of sense," Keeth said.

"No, I mean, it feels like I'm processing air still, but it's like my lungs are always full of fresh air," Cyrus said. "This is a really useful power!"

Keeth spread his wings. "With a side effect of making you even more scatterbrained than usual," he said. "Now, if you wish me to help you with the basics of flight stability, listen well . . ."

Ten minutes and three sandy faceplants later, Cyrus learned how to keep himself stable in the air. Instead of simply pushing himself around with columns of wind, he learned to wrap a whirlwind around himself and push it. The miniature cyclone held Cyrus in the middle of itself, and the high-velocity jet stream he created pushed him along at an impressive rate.

This was not the original lesson Keeth had meant to teach him. For dragons, the source of stability as well as lift is the wings. Initially, Keeth instructed Cyrus to hold his arms out flat and release small blasts of air from his palms to help him turn and stabilize.

Cyrus replied that that was too complicated, and would almost certainly violate some kind of copyright law. So Keeth coached him as he tried various alternatives.

"All right, Keeth, let's go!" Cyrus said, his voice almost getting lost in the rush of wind. "To the Phoenix Islands!"

"Are you sure the phoenixes won't roast us?" Keeth asked. "Shouldn't we send a message—"

"Come on, old lizard, I'll race you!" Cyrus said, and released a blast of energy, launching himself from the beach, headed northwest.

Magnus chirruped and hopped onto Conrad's head. The small phoenix took a tuft of the old prophet's hair in his beak and pulled it.

"Gah, cursed bird," Conrad said grouchily, swatting at Magnus. He sat up on his palm frond mattress, dislodging the bird. "They won't even be here for ten minutes or so. Let an old man have his rest." He laid back down on the mattress.

Magnus chirruped again, hopped onto Conrad's lower leg, and bit Conrad on the big toe.

"By all that is holy and untaintable by curse words!" Conrad shouted, grabbing at Magnus to throttle the phoenix.

Magnus squawked and flapped his way up to perch atop one of the overhanging beams in Conrad's cave.

"Fine, fine," Conrad said. "I'm up. What is so important that you deprive an old man of his sleep?"

"Um, Conrad?" someone said from the entrance of the cave.

"Cyrus!" Conrad said. "I must have dozed off again. I wasn't expecting you to be here quite so soon."

Cyrus scratched his head. "You were expecting me? How did you—"

"I *am* the Phoenix Prophet, remember?" Conrad said with a chuckle. "Sight beyond time, visions beyond the realms of reality, all that sort of thing. But you aren't here to listen to me ramble. You're here to find out where Kris has gotten off to, aren't you?"

"I . . . How . . ." Cyrus sputtered for a moment before apparently giving up.

"I do believe it was indeed a good idea to visit a seer," Keeth said from the beach. "Much faster than looking through a card catalog."

"Yeah, I heard it was pirates," Cyrus said. "But the Citadel . . . I saw . . . Did they take her?"

"Yes." Conrad picked up a gnarled stick from one corner of his cave and leaned heavily on it. "But if you leave right now to rescue her, you will surely die."

"What, you don't think I'm ready?" Cyrus said. "I just need some help, and—"

Conrad swept Cyrus's legs out from under him with the stick, and while the young Hero fell, Conrad held out a palm. A blast of golden brilliance in the shape of a roaring lion's maw leapt forward and launched Cyrus out the door.

Cyrus coughed as he landed in the sand outside. "Conrad!" he yelled. "What are you—"

The sand heaved under him and exploded skyward, catapulting Cyrus into the air. Columns of sand shot up beside him, arced over, and struck him in the chest, knocking him back to the ground. Cyrus barely had time to wipe the grit from his eyes before Conrad was atop him.

"Pride of the Summerland!" Conrad shouted, bringing his gnarled stick down on Cyrus's chest. The head of the stick shimmered and transmogrified and for a moment resembled a hammer whose head was shaped like a rampant lion.

And nothing happened. The sand settled. The tip of Conrad's staff touched Cyrus's solar plexus.

Cyrus coughed and looked up at Conrad with wide eyes. "Pride of . . . you . . . you're the Golden Hammer, aren't you?"

Conrad looked out at the ocean, his sightless eyes sweeping the surf. "You are not ready to challenge the Citadel, Cyrus. Look at you. And I merely caught you off guard. The Kinetics do far worse. Most of their warriors know what you are going to do before *you* do."

"But . . . you're a Hero from the Age of Legend!" Cyrus said. "I read stories and legends of you when I was a little kid! There's probably not a stronger Hero still alive anywhere on the—"

"Enough!" Conrad shouted. "My strength is not mine. It is a gift that I am even alive centuries after I should have died. After my most trusted friends died. Because of me. Because of my stupid, selfish pride."

"What?" Cyrus rose from the ground and dusted himself off. "But you made it into the Keep of Five Flames! Further than anyone else!"

"And my pride and selfishness killed my friends inside that blessed accursed tower," Conrad said. "I betrayed the trust of men who had just begun to learn how to trust, and disregarded the advice of those I'd heeded for years, all for a chance at fame and wealth. I do not deserve your praise, Cyrus. In fact, I would rather not be reminded of my past.

"I am now able to be the last and only thing I wish to be remembered as: a servant of the Creator. The Phoenix Prophet. He has given me a very long time to think over my downfall, and He's given me a chance to redeem myself."

The Mountains of the Morning comprised the majority of what were referred to as the Barrier Mountains, a mountain range that described a nearly perfect circle around the Keep of Five Flames, a white stone tower of uncertain and terrible legend. Two miles within the interior of the chain lay a forest where magic did not function. All creatures with magic in their blood, such as dragons and gryphons, nymphs and pixies, felt weakened and uncomfortable within this area.

Once inside the walls of the Keep, magic resumed its functioning. That area was referred to as the Circle of No Magic, named so by Lord Colmarian the Headstrong, the man responsible for other creative names such as the Sea of Water and the Tall Mountains. This de-sorcelled zone was a thousand times stronger and more effective than even the most potent magic-suppressant spells in existence, and seemed to be generated by the Keep itself.

The Keep appeared, from an aerial view, to be a normal tower made from white marble streaked with obsidian. It was far from normal, however. At its top, it split into five separate parapets. Each had, at its top, a pipe from which sprang a flame that never went out. Each flame burned a different color. One was brilliant red, another phosphorescent blue, the third a hot white, and the fourth a dark and angry crimson.

The fifth turret rose above the rest, and from it sprang a flame like no other. Those who had flown overhead claimed many things about the tower and the flame atop it, most of which conflicted with each other. Some said that the fifth flame is clear, possessing no color at all, merely flickering with light. Others said that it was of all colors at once, never staying the same for more than a second.

No matter what the truth was, the Keep itself had fascinated Heroes and Villains alike since before the Twenty-Minute War. Legends said that the Keep was built by the Creator Himself, and that at the top He stored the key to ruling all creatures. Thus, on several occasions, parties of either Heroes or Villains—and once, a party comprised of both—had assaulted the Keep seeking this ultimate treasure.

Every single attempt failed. The first party tried and failed just shortly after the end of the Age of Legend. Three Heroes walked up to the main gate and knocked politely on it with a battering ram. One was killed outright by powerful blasts of fire and ice that shot from the battlements of the Keep. The other two took shelter, but unseen opponents attacked and mercilessly slaughtered the survivors.

A group of Villains, determined to not make the same mistakes the Heroes had, came in greater numbers. Five of the strongest Villains in the world made it through the gate and to the tower door. After deflecting much magic and hacking up many invisible assailants, the Villains reached the front entrance. Their leader, Morgana le Flail, placed her hand on the massive stone door to open it. Immediately, tracings of silver appeared on the door and beams of light shot forth, incinerating the Villains. Needless to say, no-one attempted the Keep again until after the Twenty-Minute War.

Then there was the famous Third Assault. A party of three Heroes encountered a group of three Villains just outside the forest surrounding the Circle of No Magic. They nearly fought, but an Eastern Island monk appeared as if from nowhere and defused the situation. Both parties realized, thanks to the monk, that for the purpose of ascending the tower, their differences were unimportant.

With some mildly cryptic poems, the little monk convinced them to work together until they acquired the legendary treasure. Then, with treasure in hand, they could argue about who should have what later at their leisure. The parties agreed, and their leaders, the Golden Hammer and Basil Darkwrayth, shook hands on the deal.

They fought their way into the forest, across the Circle of No Magic, through the barrage of fire and ice, and into the inner courtyard of the Keep. A mage from each party cast powerful magic-suppressant spells as their leaders pushed open the doors to the Keep, and they were inside.

No one knew what happened after that. The party apparently made it up to the third floor, and then disaster struck. Only one member of each group escaped with their lives, their tales too different to reconcile. The only similarity was that in both stories, the leaders disagreed on something and began arguing. Words led to blows, and the parties turned on each other. There the stories diverge. One claimed that a thousand animated skeletons had poured into the Keep. The other said that the cryptic monk became a demon and slaughtered most of the party.

In the three hundred years since that day, only a handful of attempts had been made, all without success. The Guild of Heroes issued an edict that Heroes must not attempt the Keep in parties of fewer than seven. The Brotherhood of the Black Hand declared that any group of fewer than five Villains seen entering the vicinity of the Keep was to be ignored and left to its doom. Of course, these edicts were sometimes ignored.

"Redeem yourself?" Cyrus said. "How does sitting around in the sand with a bunch of birds redeem you, when you could be helping beat the *bok* out of Voshtyr?"

"Because I am here to train you, not to rely on my own strength." Conrad clasped his hand onto Cyrus's shoulder with such force that Cyrus winced.

"Train me?" Cyrus said. "But I'm—"

"A boy about whom there is a prophecy? Yes. A boy with powers unlike any other? Yes. A boy who will get his stupid posterior killed if he tries taking on Voshtyr and his cronies right now? Definitely." Conrad sighed and released Cyrus's shoulder. "You are imbalanced and foolhardy, angry and young. While I can't train the youth out of you, I can teach you balance."

"So I can be a champion or something?" Cyrus asked.

Conrad chuckled. "Of sorts, yes. And if you say one word about being some kind of 'chosen one,' I will kick you into next week."

"Wouldn't kicking me into *last* week be better? So I have more time to train?" Cyrus said with a smirk.

Conrad wiggled his toes in the hot sand outside his cave. He barely felt it through the calluses on his soles anymore. "And that's enough of that thing you use in place of wit," he said. "As Melvin Darkstar once said, 'Beware the chasm of sarcasm, for if there is too much, you might fall in.'"

Cyrus chuckled. "All right, all right. But I don't have much time for training now. My mate's been kidnapped. Catnapped? Anyway, I think the Kinetics have her. I need to go as soon as possible. Who knows what they're doing to her right now . . ."

"You will find out soon enough," Conrad said, his voice soft. "Trust me when I say that they mean her no harm . . . yet. She is alive and well, and they mean to keep her that way until . . ." He trailed off and he gazed toward Cyrus, his white eyes looking through the material world. "Actually, I will not spoil the surprise. Stay here the night, and we shall see if you are ready in the morning."

"Oh, goodie," said Keeth from the beach. More than a dozen phoenixes perched on the dragon's wings, back, and snout. "At least I will sleep nice and warm."

Chapter 16

THE MASTERS OF YOUR MIND

In which Kris finds herself amongst Enemies and Discovers a Friend

KRIS WOKE UP to the feeling of satin and bandages against her fur and the sound of tiny songbirds twittering somewhere above her and off to her left. The sound and smell of sizzling bacon caressed her ears and nose. She opened her eyes.

She lay in a large round bed with green satin sheets and plush pillows. The walls of the room all around were brilliantly white and reflected the sun so it seemed there was not a shadow anywhere in the room. Aside from the bed, decoration was fairly sparse. The white tiled floor had a single dark green throw rug on it in front of a birchwood dresser with gold knobs.

As Kris sat up, she saw two others in the room. She clutched the sheet to herself, but realized she was wearing a traditional Katheni formal gown of the same type she'd made after first meeting Cyrus.

The people across the room from her seemed normal and at the same time very strange. A woman in an entirely white, apparently seamless gown knelt on a pillow near the entrance of the room. Her hair, which was white, hung down to the middle of her back in a complicated double-braid. Her skin was pale to the point of being colorless.

The other in the room was a boy, perhaps no more than sixteen years old. His hair was an unruly shock of golden brown, and his clothing was slightly more complicated. Though it was white as well, his attire consisted of what seemed to be a white leather jacket with a multitude of pockets and a pair of baggy trousers. A stick carved of white ash wood hung askew from a silver loop across his back, and a slim silver circlet rested on his head. Kris couldn't see if anything adorned the front of the circlet, as the boy faced away from her. He hunched over the stove from which the delicious smell of bacon wafted, stirring it with a two-pronged meat fork and humming to himself.

The pale woman stood up and moved toward Kris. Kris looked at her, and felt no fear, despite her situation. She also felt strangely compelled to not break eye contact.

"Welcome to the Citadel, Kris Solburg," the woman said. "I trust that you slept well. Were your accommodations adequate?"

"Who are you?" Kris asked softly. "Where am I?" She felt as if she should be scared that she wasn't scared, but she didn't feel a single negative emotion. It was uncanny.

The woman smiled and sat down on the edge of the bed's green sheets. Aside from Kris's clothing, they were the only thing in the room that wasn't pure, clean white. "You are in the Citadel, home to us all, and now your home as well." She took Kris's paw and stroked it gently. "I hope you feel at home here."

Kris did. She blinked. She felt at home. She had never been here, and yet she felt at home. A frown creased Kris's forehead and smoothed itself out again as the woman closed her eyes.

"Please . . ." The woman's voice sounded not quite so kind now. It was still soft, but cold and deadly, like a sword wrapped in velvet. "You must not disrupt the harmony of this place. It is a good place for all of us and you."

"But this is *not* my home, and whenever I begin to feel otherwise, you—" Kris felt once again the smoothing of her emotions, a forceful calming from outside herself. "Stop that!" she demanded, a growl at the back of her throat.

The woman looked over her shoulder at the boy cooking bacon. He turned, pan still in his hand, and walked over to the bed. The smell of sizzling meat was even stronger now.

Just pretend everything is okay, the boy said. He didn't move his mouth. *Pretend to cooperate with Mel-Shan. I will explain as soon as she leaves.*

Kris still felt tense, or at least tried to, but it was so comforting to just let her worries drain away. She laid back on the pillows and faked a smile. "Oh kay. This is nice. So why am I here?"

"For the safety of the Prophecy," said the woman called Mel-Shan. "We must ward you until it comes to pass."

"What prophecy?" Kris felt no rising apprehension, though she thought she should. "Is it the one about the Huntress?"

Mel-Shan blinked. "Oh, so you do know. Then you know why we must ward you."

"So you don't destroy the world, I suppose," the boy said. "That would kinda ruin everyone's day."

"Destroy the world?" Kris said. "I . . . I don't get it."

The boy chuckled. "All right, I think I can explain it to you." He turned and made eye contact with Mel-Shan. Without a word, she stood and left the room.

As soon as she was gone, the boy sighed. "Whew, glad she's gone. She's really, really nosy."

"Who are you?" Kris asked. "What's going on? What's the prophecy about? Why me?"

"Whoa, there, kitty," the boy said. "Slow down. I am Indikos Nanihai Tarrashan. But that's a mouthful and sounds kind of dumb, so you can call me Indy."

"Indy? But . . . who are you?"

Indy shrugged. "I'm the Tarrashan. Successor to the throne of the Citadel." He puffed out his chest to look impressive, then sighed and let it out. "Yeah. Real shiny, huh . . . ?"

Kris looked around the room. There weren't any weapons readily available, though if she could take the sizzling skillet from the boy's hand, perhaps . . .

"Uh-uh," Indy said, moving the skillet out of Kris's reach. "I'm okay with you wanting out, but not okay with skillet marks on my face."

Kris started. "What? How did you—"

"With my miiiiiiiind," Indy said, wiggling his fingers beside his head. In doing so, he let go of the skillet, which floated mysteriously near the side of the bed. "They don't want to make me the King for nothing."

Kris looked longingly at the skillet, then jerked her attention back to Indy. To her surprise, he was already holding out a forkful of bacon.

"Thought you might like this," Indy said with a smile.

"Because you read my mind?" Kris said.

Indy chuckled. "No, because what carnivore doesn't like bacon?"

Kris gently took the bacon from the tines with her teeth, and she chewed. It was meaty, salty, and delicious. She gobbled down the piece of meat and looked up in time to see the fork floating in front of her with another mouthful on it. She took it as well.

"There we go." Indy's voice was kind, and though it was young, had a sense of sadness to it. "You know, it's nice having someone from the outside around. All I normally get to talk to is the Council, and they're all the same. I mean it, all exactly the same. You, well, you're different. Your mind is . . . I dunno, spicy."

"Stay out of my mind," Kris growled with a mouthful of bacon. It didn't sound intimidating, even to her.

"Right, right, sorry," Indy said. The skillet floated up to his hand, and he took hold of it. "I keep forgetting that outsiders aren't used to that. There's no secrets in the Cidtadel. We all know each others' minds, all the time."

"Sounds awful," Kris muttered.

"Not as much as you'd think," Indy said, picking up a piece of bacon for himself. "It's actually kind of nice to know exactly what everyone thinks about you. Of course, they kind of *have* to be nice to me, but still . . ."

Kris swallowed. "Why's that?"

"The whole 'becoming King' thing, I guess," Indy said, waving an index finger around in a circle in the air. "But I know some of them actually like me. Kind of makes up for it a bit."

"So what makes a King?" Kris asked, and reached for another strip of bacon.

Indy chuckled. "Brainpower, sort of. See, we Kinetics come in three flavors: telekinetics, telepaths, and telempaths. Telekinetics move stuff around with their minds. Like this." The skillet moved away from Kris, and all the individual pieces of remaining bacon lifted out of the pan and drifted about. Kris chomped one from midair.

"Telepaths read minds and send information," Indy continued. "They can see through the eyes of others, pick words and information out of another's mind, or even shut a brain down."

"And the telempaths?" Kris asked, a bit of bacon hanging from her mouth.

"Eh..." Indy rubbed the back of his neck, reminding Kris of Cyrus. "Well, they're scary. They sense, create, and manipulate emotions—fears and stuff. But sometimes they can send good feelings too. What Mel-Shan was doing to you, for example. That, and they can lock your mind in a permanent nightmare of your worst fear. But yeah, pretty much simple stuff like that."

Kris wiped her mouth on a napkin conveniently floating by. "So what makes you the King? Are you better at one of them than everyone else?"

"Oh, I'm not the King, gods forbid," Indy said. "Not yet. Lazik won't let me accede yet. Not that I want to. Too much work, too much responsibility, and too much . . . well, history, I guess."

"So you don't want to be King," Kris whispered.

"Eh, yeah, I do," Indy said. "Just not yet. I'm not done being a kid. But I'm a Tarrashan, which means I don't get a choice."

"So it's a family title?"

"Nope. It's an amalgam. We have suffixes to our names based on our abilities. Teekays are -ras, 'Paths are -tar, and 'Emps are -shan. I'm a Tar-ras-shan."

Kris looked at Indy, her eyes widening in realization. "So . . . that means you can do all three."

Indy bowed. "Awesome as charged."

"So, Tarrashan," Kris said.

"Please, just Indy," Indy said. "I get tired of the title really fast."

"Oh kay. Indy. What am I doing here?"

Indy chuckled. "You're just full of questions, aren't you?"

Kris smiled, her eyes half closed. "And you're full of answers." In a furry blur, she lashed out at Indy, leaving her claws extended less than an inch from Indy's stomach. "If you don't want me to cut the answers out manually, you'll need to start talking."

Indy looked down at her sadly. "I would, except that I drugged the bacon."

"The . . . You what?" Kris said, and felt something fuddling the edges of her mind. "I told you . . . to stay out . . . of . . ."

"Your mind?" Indy got up and retrieved the skillet from the air. "I did. But I didn't keep my influence out of your stomach. Sleep well. And heal up, Huntress. You've got a prophecy to fulfill."

And with that, he left, and Kris slid into a dreamless sleep.

Chapter 17

ALCHEMY AND EVIL

In which Voshtyr constructs his Ultimate Weapon
And Roger Sees the Void

THE ROOM EXPLODED.

"Huh," Voshtyr said, tipping up the visor on his blast helmet. The suit he wore was designed for resisting magical artillery, not exploding rooms, and the pointed fragment of marble jutting through the visor had almost scratched his nose. "That went better than I expected."

"*Better?*" Roger shouted from inside an Orichalc blast shelter, his shout muffled by the foot of indestructible metal. "You just blew up half of my research room! It will take *months* to repair all those leaks!"

"Leaks?" Voshtyr looked about. Now that the dust had settled somewhat, he could indeed see water trickling down the walls. "Oh, sorry about that, old fish. Let me get you out of there."

Roger slammed the door of the cylindrical safe area open and stepped out. It was usually almost impossible to tell Roger's mood, but in this case, Voshtyr felt safe in assuming that the Araquellus was unhappy.

"Voshtyr, this keep is four *thousand* years old," Roger said. "I will *not* have your crackpot 'science' experiments reducing my private slice of history to *rubble!*"

"Easy now, old friend," Voshtyr said, and patted Roger on his shoulder. "Italics aren't good for your blood pressure."

Roger sighed and looked at the ruins of Voshtyr's experiment.

Voshtyr sighed too and looked at his immense success. The marble statue of the Crimson Slash he'd been testing his latest creation on was now nothing but chunks and powder, on fire. The clear yellow liquid he'd just tested was a little more powerful and a little touchier than he'd expected, but still, it had exploded admirably.

The test chamber had fared only slightly better than the statue. The steel plates lining the igneous rock walls had dents in them now, and water trickled through the cracks between some of them. Only the bronze-tinted Orichalc blast shelter in the corner appeared undamaged.

"I tell you, Roger," Voshtyr said, "the spitfires we used against Bryath are *nothing* compared to this stuff. If I can reproduce that blast using more materials, I can take Black Spire in a day."

"And the structural integrity of my ancestral home in mere minutes," Roger said with a scowl.

"Pish tush." Voshtyr took off the helmet and shook his lustrous black hair out. "At least this is less dangerous than my tube experiment."

"*Less* dangerous?" Roger said. "You said the tube project was completely harmless!"

Voshtyr chuckled. "Oh, yes, well, that was a lie to get you to let me use your deepest sub-level."

"Voshtyr! If you break even *one* of the support pylons, this Keep floods completely!" Roger said. "I would survive, of course. But for one thing, I have a lot of perishable goods in this keep. And for another, you can't breathe water."

"Oh," Voshtyr said. "Well, you should come take a look and see if what I've got set up is too dangerous."

"Thank you for inviting me into part of my own home," Roger said. "And what qualifies as too dangerous?"

Voshtyr stripped off the other parts of the armor and stepped over some rubble, headed for the door. "Well, if it's going to destroy everything I've worked on so far, then it's too dangerous."

"And if it would just wreck my home, but leave your projects alone . . . ?"

"Then it's fine." Voshtyr grinned at Roger, and headed farther down the stairs.

Roger shook his head and followed the Arch-Villain. "You need a hobby, Voshtyr. All this is getting to be too much."

"I do have a hobby," Voshtyr protested. "I'm taking pipe organ lessons, and I have that origami club on Thursdays."

"Origami?" Roger stopped on the stairs. "I didn't think you were the type to . . . er . . ."

"To create tiny, fragile objects of beauty that I can hold in the palm of my hand?" Voshtyr chuckled. "Of course. It makes it all that more satisfying when I *crush them without mercy! Mwahahahaha!*"

After a ten-minute walk down spiral stairs and twisted passages, the half-demon and the Araquellan lord entered a long, sloping hall made entirely of volcanic glass. The outside was visible, thanks to luminescent algae and occasional pockets of brightly glowing shards of white rock scattered along the sea floor.

Indeed, they were underwater. Far beneath the surface of the ocean. Roger's ancestral palace, the Deep Keep, had been passed down from royal to royal, father to daughter to son, always remaining in the hands of the one of purest blood, for millennia. It lay in the bottom of an ocean trench, and was guarded by trained predators of the depths and protected from invasion by miles of water. It also provided insulation so that should an experiment go horribly, horribly wrong, it wouldn't magically irradiate the entire world. At least not right away. Unless he did it intentionally, which was "Plan E" for ruling and/or destroying the world. Plan B involved hang-gliding Minions, plan C had exploding squirrels, and D required the release of Anthony the Mace, something Voshtyr was loath to do. And for some reason, the King of the Kinetics was irritated that the use of *his* resources was plan F. Ah well. There was time to deal with megalomaniacal egomaniacs later, after the research was done.

Down they went, beneath the surface of the earth. It began getting warmer as they went, and when Voshtyr rounded the corner, he felt entirely at home.

Because what was in the deepest chamber of the Deep Keep resembled Hell itself.

Lava flowed around jutting columns of volcanic rock, and occasional spouts of water hit the lava and turned to steam to power iron turbines the size of ten men. The turbines drove strange machines with hearts of Darkmatter and crackling energy. A steel walkway suspended from the ceiling wound its way through the hedge of machinery, leading to a larger column where various tables, instruments, and a silver pylon rested.

Also on the column was a barred pen of sorts containing men and women of many races, clad in rags and manacled to the bars. At Voshtyr's approach, one of the women, a bedraggled Mountain Elf, began to weep.

"You neglected to mention that you were using live prisoners, Voshtyr," Roger said through gritted teeth.

"Oh, did I?" Voshtyr asked. "Oops."

The two walked up to the silver pylon. On it rested a simple coppery tube.

Roger looked at the tube quizzically. "This is dangerous?" he said, reaching for it.

For the first time in Roger's life, Voshtyr hit him. The half-demon slapped Roger's hand away from the tube so fast and so hard that it sent the light-bodied Araquellus spinning. He staggered and fell mere inches from the edge of the stone where it dropped into lava.

"*My* immortality!" Voshtyr snarled. His suddenly red eyes crawled with black energy, and his features took on distinctly pointed shapes. "If you so much as touch it, I swear by the void, I'll peel your skin off while you yet live."

Roger cradled his hand and stared up at Voshtyr. "Have you gone mad, Voshtyr?" he asked. "What in the Nine Torments is wrong with you?"

Voshtyr closed his eyes and took a deep breath. When he opened his eyes again, they were the calm glowing green as usual. "Mad?" he said. "On the contrary, dear fish, I am just a few steps from becoming more sane than any mortal creature."

"You just struck me," Roger said, still not quite believing it.

"You almost stole my immortality," Voshtyr said calmly. "And, it very well could have hurt you if you touched it."

Roger frowned. "So I should be thanking you, then?"

"Oh, you're welcome. After all, it's your home."

Roger rose from the stone, unable to keep himself from looking over the edge as he did so, and felt ill. Another handspan, and he would have fried. "Why in the Green Fields of the Blessed would you leave hazardous immortality lying out where anyone can touch it? And what kind of bargain-bin immortality comes in a tube, anyway?"

"Come and see," Voshtyr said. "And by the way: don't touch."

Roger walked over and looked at the tube. It was a simple empty cylinder like a piece of pipe. It shone eerily red in the light from the lava. Runes traced their way down one side, and the same runes, inverted, ran down the other.

Voshtyr reached toward the tube. As his hand got close, the tube almost imperceptibly leapt into his hand, like a lodestone to a metal surface. "I hold life and death in the palm of my hand," Voshtyr said. "It's a weapon and a shield, a perfectly balanced device. Would you care to see how it works?"

Roger nodded. "May as well see what it does before it incinerates my basement."

"Very well," Voshtyr said. "Stab me."

"What?"

"Stab me." Voshtyr withdrew a single silver key from his left breast pocket and walked over to unlock the cell of captives. "I need some sort of wound to show you how this works. Consider it a chance for revenge for that petty slap I gave you a moment ago."

"Well, if you say so," Roger said, extending a blade ridge from his arm. "Just say when."

Voshtyr opened the cell door and smiled in at the occupants. "Hello, beautiful people. I need a volunteer."

"Not happening, demonspawn," said one of the men slouched against the far wall.

"It's Demon*kin*, you ignoramus," Voshtyr said. "Now, if I can't have a volunteer, I'll just pick. Ah, you'll do nicely," he said, pointing at the woman who had been weeping.

Wide-eyed and obviously terrified, the woman shook her head. The man who had been slouching immediately rose and stepped between her and Voshtyr. "You coward," he said. "Can't you just leave us alone? Let us go? We're of no use to one as powerful as you."

"Oh, but you *are*," Voshtyr said. "Someone has to be my Guinea pig, and I'm certainly not using Lord Roger Gill-Neck over there."

"I'm standing right here," Roger muttered.

"Well," Voshtyr said, "since you seem so intent on protecting this woman, I'll take you instead." He motioned the man out of the cage and locked it again. "Oh, and *Sit Still.*"

The man stopped walking as if he had become rooted to the ground. "What foul magic is this?"

Voshtyr ignored him. "Now, Roger, whenever you're ready."

"All right," Roger said. With a rustle, the organic blade ridge in his arm protruded even more. The point glistening wetly. "Any . . . place in particular you want to be stabbed?"

"Just in the chest somewhere," Voshtyr said, waving his hand.

"But what about your heart?" Roger said.

"Oh, don't worry," Voshtyr said. "I'm a Villain. For us, a heart is like an appendix. They're there, but we don't really use them for anything."

Roger screwed up his face and his courage, and poked Voshtyr in the bowels.

"Ouch!" Voshtyr said. "What in the Nine are you doing?"

Roger blinked. "Stabbing you?"

"You call that pansy poke a stab?" Voshtyr said. "Your grandmother stabs harder than that!"

"My grandmother was the War-Queen of the Seven Coral Spires," Roger said huffily. "Of course she'd stab harder."

Voshtyr snorted. "Try again, old fish. Those weak accountant wrists of yours have got to be good for something besides operating an abacus and counting beans."

"Killing clients is bad business," Roger protested. "I don't have a lot of practice with—"

"Just stab me already!"

Roger stabbed Voshtyr.

"*Ouch!*" Voshtyr said. "Curse you, Roger! You stab like a little girl!"

"I could help if you like," said the man Voshtyr had let out. "It'd be no trouble at all."

"Silence, you," Voshtyr said with a snarl.

"I'm sorry, Voshtyr," Roger said. "My heart's just not in it."

Voshtyr shook his head. "How odd. All my enemies and the majority of my allies dream of little else. But you . . . It's no wonder Cyrus and that Kath girl beat you so easily. You can't even harm a stationary opponent. Now I know why you were shunned from the court of the Neptarch. Who would want such a useless— Gack!"

The tip of Roger's blade protruded from Voshtyr's back, right between two ribs.

"That's . . . better," Voshtyr said, coughing blood. "Now . . . keh . . . observe."

Voshtyr turned to face the prisoner and straightened up to his full height. He leveled the copper tube at the man. "Time for a little destruction."

With a grating roar and a flash of blinding green and yellow light, energy lanced from the mouth of the tube. At the same time, a blue-green splash of light washed back out of the base of the tube, enveloping Voshtyr.

Roger rubbed his eyes. "What . . . what was that?"

Voshtyr's body relaxed, and there was no more blood or wound. He chuckled, a chuckle most sinister. "The Destructo-Tube. Perfect healing for me, at the cost of my opponent's body and soul."

All that remained of the prisoner was what looked like a dried husk. His skin was brown and leathery and shriveled like there was no moisture left in his body. His eyes were gone, replaced by empty sockets. A silent scream covered what was left of his face. The dry body clattered to the stone floor like a pile of bony laundry.

The woman in the cell stopped weeping and sat silent, staring blankly at the dead man. Roger turned away from the sight and vomited.

"There, there, old fish," Voshtyr said. "He wasn't anyone important."

"Destructo-Tube?" Roger asked, wiping his mouth.

Voshtyr beamed. "Indeed. Impressive, yes?"

"That's not a very intimidating name . . ."

"Shut up! I came up with it when I was twelve!"

Roger brushed the front of his yellow robes and looked at the lava. "I see. Well, congratulations on a toy well built."

"Thank you," Voshtyr said. "Now, if you'll excuse me: Mwahahahahaaaa!"

"Ha ha," Roger added politely.

Voshtyr stopped his maniacal laugh and looked at his scaled friend. "Oh, that's no kind of Evil Laugh at all, dear friend. How can you be a true Villain with a pathetic laugh such as that?"

"I'm not a Villain," Roger said. "I'm an accountant."

"Same difference. Besides, you work for a Villain. That's close enough. You know what, I should teach you how to laugh properly."

"Oh, dear." Roger put a blue palm to his forehead. "Melis, preserve me."

Voshtyr nudged the desiccated corpse of the peasant with his foot until the husk toppled over the edge of the pylon and plopped into the lava. It went up in flames immediately. "Now," he said, "let's teach you how to laugh. Stand up straight." He pushed Roger's lower back forward with his metal arm.

"I *am* standing up straight," Roger said. "I have impeccable posture."

"Oh, you're just short. I keep forgetting that." Voshtyr tapped the copper tube a few times, and it shrank down into a simple and unassuming copper ring. He slipped it onto his finger. "Anyway, take a deep breath at the bottom of your lungs and let it puff your chest out."

"Ahhhh," Roger breathed. "You do realize I'm just humoring you?"

"Nonsense," Voshtyr said. "You'll make a proper Villain yet. Now, start with a little chuckle. Try it."

"Heh heh," Roger said halfheartedly.

"No, that's not it at all. More gusto. And tack a 'mwa' like a kiss on at the beginning."

"Mweh heh heh."

Voshtyr scowled. "No 'eh' sound. 'Eh' is for philosophers, not megalomaniacs. You're not thinking—you're gleefully reveling in the sheer evil genius of your plan."

"Yes, you're obviously not thinking," Roger muttered.

Voshtyr poked Roger in the chest, right below his collarbone. "Sound comes from right here. Try again."

"Mooahahaha."

"Worst. Laugh. Ever. You sound like a cow."

"An evil cow?"

"No! Just a plain boring, cud-chewing, milk-producing cow!" Voshtyr poked Roger's chest again. "Are you man or cow?"

Roger puffed his chest out and looked offended. "I am neither! I am an Araquellus of the Royal Line, and my time is too valuable to waste with your shenanigans."

"Just one laugh," Voshtyr said. "Just one, then you can go."

"No."

"Come on, dear fish. It's not that hard."

"Mwa ha ha." Roger crossed his arms. "There."

Voshtyr chuckled. "Now one more time, but actually mean it. Think of having balanced the entire Treasury account of Bryath kingdom, and finding that there's just enough surplus to buy yourself a summer home, and no one would notice the money missing."

"Mwahahahahaaaa!" Roger laughed.

• • •

Later that afternoon, Roger and Voshtyr took tea in a converted sitting room elsewhere in Roger's undersea fortress. The room had been changed from a place for recliners and saltwater pools into a ritual room. Sinister arcane circles occupied the center of the room, along with a pentagram and some candles resting on Human skulls. The only bits of mundane furniture were the chairs and table the two occupied.

"Anyway, now that my weapons are almost done, I think I need to pay someone a visit." Voshtyr took a sip of tea. When he put the blue coral cup down, his metal arm clinked against the saucer. "I finally have enough souls to spend on something important."

"Spending souls? Like currency?" Roger asked. "I thought they were power in and of themselves."

"Well, yes and no," Voshtyr said. "They're powerful, but others value them more highly than I, and I can exchange them for things not of this world."

"Such as?"

"Hellsteel," Voshtyr said. "The only metal stable enough to withstand Darkmatter. If I'm going to finish my weapon, I need somewhere between thirty and fifty pounds of it."

"Darkmatter?" Roger stiffened. "What are you building, Voshtyr? I won't have any of that stuff down here—"

"Relax, Roger," Voshtyr said. "I'm not building anything out of Darkmatter. I'm going to build the shell here and then assemble the components elsewhere. It won't contaminate your pretty little fortress."

"You haven't answered my question," Roger said, tapping his foot impatiently.

"How's that mining operation on Blade Ridge going?" Voshtyr asked.

"Not helping," Roger said. "Tell me, Voshtyr, or you don't get to use my basement to test explosives anymore."

"Phooey," Voshtyr said. "You're no fun, old fish. Fine, fine, I'll spill. You know how I'm going to be effectively immortal, yes?"

"You only just almost pushed me into lava on account of it, so yes. But I thought the P.L.O.T. Device was—"

"Only a small portion of my immortality," Voshtyr said. "Technically, all the P.L.O.T. Device does is make me invulnerable and magically unsurpassed, not immortal."

"But I thought the *L* of P.L.O.T. was 'Lifetime.'"

Voshtyr waved his metal hand dismissively. "No truth in advertising these days. That's what I need the Destructo-Tube for. It directly converts soul energy from a target and turns it into years added to my lifespan. It's destructive force for them and life energy for me."

"Oh." Roger felt ill. He drained his teacup and refilled it. "So when you strike someone with the blast, you . . . get younger? You *youthen?*"

"I'm not sure that's a word," Voshtyr said. "But that's the gist of it. As long as I kill someone with the Destructo-Tube every once in a while, I will never age! Genius, no?"

"I plead the one hundred and seventh," Roger said from behind his teacup.

"One hundred and seventh?" Voshtyr said, raising an eyebrow.

"Denial clause," Roger muttered. "By our contract, I have the right to not answer unsafe questions posed by my employer. It's standard in most contracts with Villains."

Voshtyr rolled his eyes. "Bah, hide behind your contract if you must. At any rate, when all parts of my plan come together, I'm going to be an immortal, indestructible, invincible juggernaut of doom with power beyond my wildest dreams."

"Really?" Roger said. "Your wildest dreams."

"That's hyperbole. Of course I dreamed it. I wouldn't be building it now if I hadn't, now would I?"

"Unless you're particularly clairvoyant for a megalomaniac, I would imagine not." Roger took another sip of his tea, then set his cup down on the table. He laced his fingers together and stared at Voshtyr. "So, as I understand it, you are building something *better* than immortality. Something better than invulnerability. You're making yourself weaponry to boot."

Voshtyr clapped his hands, then winced and shook his right hand. "Ow. Right on the money, my dear fish. This antiquated piece of junk," he said, flexing his steel arm, "is a reminder of my worst failure. I will replace it with a devastating upgrade as a symbol of my greatest triumph."

"Wait . . . Your greatest triumph wasn't conquering the known world?"

"My greatest triumph will be conquering death itself, and then everyone else who could possibly be jealous over my good fortune," Voshtyr said. "And my new arm won't just be a new paint job or improved gears. This time I'm building it out of Hellsteel and Darkmatter—don't give me that look. And, as my piece of resistance—"

"That's *pièce de résistance,* Voshtyr."

Voshtyr scowled. "That's what *pièce de résistance* means, you cold-blooded calculator. My central power source and enhancement for the new model . . . will be a Shard of the Star of Anger."

"Oh." Roger said nothing for a few seconds, then recovered his cup of tea and drained it. "So that's the weapon you were talking about when you called me at the mine. A Shard-Hellsteel-Darkmatter contraption would seem . . . hazardous to have attached to your arm. Er, I mean *as* your arm."

"But nigh indestructible and powerful enough to destroy anything that stands in my way." Voshtyr snorted. "I'd like to see the Crimson Slash try and chop *this* one off."

"So let me get this straight." Roger put his teacup down and walked to the center of the pentagram on the floor. "You're going to use the P.L.O.T. Device to make yourself invulnerable to death by outside force. You're going to use that . . . death tube—"

"Destructo-Tube."

"That Destructo-Tube to ensure you can't die from natural causes. And you're going to use your upgraded arm to destroy anything that stands in your way. Am I right?"

Voshtyr leaned back in his chair and smiled. "And no power in the world, in the air, the sky, the sea, or the places beyond mortal reach can stop me."

Roger attempted to abruptly drain his tea again, but found his cup empty. He sighed and put the cup down. "Congratulations. You'll be able to experience centuries of future history long after no one cares about the atrocities you've committed. You'll be able to rule the world . . . forever."

"That's not all." Voshtyr turned away from Roger and placed his metal hand against the wall. "I will kill the Crimson Slash. I will kill the Purple Paladin. I will kill every last Hero involved in my humiliation. And then? Then I will descend like ten thousand furies on that little fortress on Clawstrike Island the Heroes are fleeing to, and kill them, men, women, and children all."

Voshtyr's voice was cold, but not calm. Roger could see the fusion of fury and madness in Voshtyr's eyes as they changed from calm green to blazing red. His volume increased as his Monologue went on. "Not even the Hereditary Evil Empire can stop me. I will crush them as well. The Elves next. And then the Dwarves!"

He slammed his fist into his metal palm as he named each target. "And the Katheni! And the Istaka! Any creature who dares oppose me will fall! Then the world will see Voshtyr Demonkin as they should have five years ago. Then the world will fear me as they rightly should! After I have become the single most powerful entity in the world, and destroyed my only opposition, not only will I rule this world, but I will be in place to challenge *the Twelve themselves!* Mwahahahahahahaha! Muuuuauauahahahahahahaa!"

Roger abandoned his teacup entirely, and sat in mute horror.

Voshtyr sighed and looked at his empty cup. "I'm out of tea." He sat back down in his chair as if nothing had happened and poured himself another cup of tea. "So, on that note, how's the mining operation going? Have you found the Shard yet?"

Roger looked down into the tea leaves at the bottom of his cup, desperately wishing that he had his sister's ability to read fortunes. He avoided Voshtyr's glowing eyes. "Oh, that. Apparently dragons don't take too kindly to goblins mining under their mountains, and they especially dislike mining for Darkmatter."

"I don't care about dragons!" Voshtyr slammed his metal fist down on the table, shattering the coral teapot. "Tell me you at least got the Shard."

Roger paused. This was dangerous. If he helped Voshtyr go through with his plot, were even the Araquellae safe from Voshtyr? Was he himself in danger?

"I did collect the Shard," Roger said, "after an altercation with someone calling himself The Nameless Hero."

"Nameless Hero?" Voshtyr said. "That's a new one. Anyone I know?"

Roger looked away, then shook his head. "No . . . no, I don't think so. He intended to fight me over the Shard."

Voshtyr looked tense. "Were you able to recover it?"

"Of course," Roger said, leaning back in his chair. "It's in a safe that is on the way here. I couldn't risk carrying it myself. And it reacted . . . poorly to teleportation magics."

"How do you mean?" Voshtyr demanded.

"Well, I had handed it to one of your Minions to teleport him back to you with it, but the Shard sparked, and it embedded the Minion in the rock wall. Not to worry, though: I wrote him off as a business expense. But the Shard has to be transported by hand."

"Why didn't you tell me this before now?" Voshtyr said, clutching his head. "That Shard is crucial to my superior power. If something were to happen to it, I would have to spend *months* looking for a replacement!"

"I was . . . waiting for the right time to tell you. And then I was stabbing you and almost stealing your immortality. I guess it just slipped my mind."

Voshtyr tilted his head. "Hmm, fair enough. So, no other complications?"

Roger looked back up. "None at all."

Voshtyr tried to take another sip of his tea, and found he was holding only a shattered handle. "Looks like I've spilt my tea. Time to get to work, then. Skri'ki!"

The far door to the room opened, and a black robe with a beak protruding from the front of it shuffled inside. Skri'ki removed his hood, revealing a greying brown hawklike head, with glossy black feathers spreading from around his eyes and covering most of his face. He looked at Voshtyr. "What is it you are wanting?"

"The souls I have been hoarding." Voshtyr extended his hand. "Give them here."

Skri'ki cocked his head to the side curiously. "And you are to be using them for . . . ?"

Voshtyr wiggled his fingers. "For my own designs! Come, bird, I don't have all day. But I suppose it should interest you. Have you ever looked into the Void?"

Skri'ki crossed his wings. "Never. When one is to stare into Void, then Void is stare into you. One's mind can be lost in such fashion."

"Oh, really," Voshtyr said, sounding as if he didn't care one bit. "Well, you don't have to look then. But give me those soul gems."

Skri'ki ruffled up his feathers, but he produced a small black leather pouch from beneath one of his wings and handed it to Voshtyr.

"If you don't want to see the Void," Voshtyr said, "you'd best leave."

"*Namaais,* Lost One," Skri'ki said with a bow. "In your consorting with monsters, be certain that you are not to become one."

Voshtyr chuckled, a sinister and chilling chuckle. Roger pulled his robe closer about himself. "Oh, don't worry," Voshtyr said. "I'm already there."

• • •

Five minutes after Skri'ki left, Voshtyr had completed the preparations for his ritual. The tiny gemstones containing the living souls of some of his victims occupied shallow depressions in the stone at the points of the pentagram.

"Voshtyr," Roger said, "why did Skri'ki call you 'Lost One'?"

Voshtyr chuckled again. "I thought you'd know more of Avierie culture, dear fish."

Roger shook his head. "No, I could tell you how to interpret the songs of traveling whales, but not of the bird-folk. I know of all beneath the sea, but naught of things above the clouds."

"Fair enough." Voshtyr drew a bag of powdered silver from his cloak and began sprinkling it around the outside edges. "When an Avierie mage dabbles in the darker side of magic or practices sorcery, it turns his feathers black. The blackest of them they call the Ravens, and they are fearsome creatures. Almost as horrific as me, I dare say.

"But what happens when the sorcery takes full hold of them? Well, they either die from the abuse the magic inflicts on them, or they lose their minds. In that case, they become living conduits of dark magic. Any vestige of personality, rationality, or kindness they ever had is stripped away. Many become possessed by Demons. The Avierie call these incredibly powerful conduits the 'Lost Ones' and revere them as your people do ancient oracles."

"So he believes you lost already," Roger mused.

"I'm most obviously not, though," Voshtyr said. "See, I'm sane and rational. I never had much use for kindness, so that doesn't count. Anyway, I think he means it as a sign of respect for being better naturally at something he's struggled for years to understand."

Roger barely concealed a sneer. It wouldn't do to sneer at one's evil overlord. Not if one planned on keeping the lip one sneered with, anyway.

Voshtyr held in his palm a single ruby, ready to drop it in the depression in the center of the pentagram. "Care to travel the Void with me, old fish?"

"I'll pass, thank you."

"Be here when I get back, then," Voshtyr said. He began chanting in a language not of the world. It resonated hypnotically.

Roger's head reeled. He covered his ear-holes and grimaced.

The powdered silver began lighting up, and the gems in their depressions glinted brilliantly, eventually taking on the light themselves. With a flash and bang, the gems and silver disintegrated, and the air inside the pentagram wavered and went dark. Then it turned chaotic.

Roger gasped. What lay inside the circle was grey and ever-changing, and the shapes inside didn't make any sense to his logical mind. Pouches and blotches of color and sound floated around inside the maelstrom. Blackness swept through it like a wind, and he got the distinct impression that he was not wanted there.

In the distance, as if the circle were now a door to somewhere else, or perhaps *Somewhere Else*, another circle opened into a place full of darkness and flames. Roger could see another figure standing and beckoning.

Voshtyr looked back at Roger and laughed as Roger shrank back. Voshtyr had grown fangs, and his fingernails now distinctly resembled claws. His eyes flamed red, and his facial features had grown pointed and distinctly demonic. "What's wrong, dear fish?" Voshtyr's voice sounded like more than one voice at the same time, speaking just slightly off unison. "I'm just off to visit Mum. Hold the fort, will you?" He chuckled once more and stepped through the portal.

Roger couldn't look away. He watched Voshtyr stride through the chaos and meet the figure on the other side. Then the far portal closed, leaving only the grey incomprehensible fog.

Then someone else appeared. He was a distance off, but he appeared to be a giant of a man bearing a titanic sword, a sword even larger than that of the Crimson Slash. He wore black armor and had ridiculously pointy cropped hair. Roger saw the man mouth a single word.

"You."

Roger panicked. He grabbed the table and threw it into the portal. It fell through and chipped the intricate stonework of the summoning circle. Immediately, the portal collapsed with a bang and rush of air. The table, still inside the circle, disappeared as well.

"Oops."

Roger slumped back against the wall and panted. He couldn't shake the feeling of dread the man inspired. He was more terrifying with a single word than Voshtyr had been with years of threats and insults. With the portal collapsed, could Voshtyr return? Would it have shut anyway?

More importantly, had Roger just met an incredibly powerful entity and accidentally given him a tea table?

Chapter 18

THE FLAMING TOWER OF FLAMES AND FIERY FOUNTAIN OF FIRE

In which there are Very Many Hot Things and Cyrus Plays with Fire

THERE WERE FEATHERS on his face.

Cyrus started and sat up. The phoenix that had been perched on his chest took to the air with a squawk.

"Finally up, are you?" Keeth said.

Cyrus chuckled as he noticed that the phoenixes seemed to have taken a liking to the dragon. On each of Keeth's ridges perched a phoenix, and a smaller one perched on his nose, chirruping every few seconds or so. The small bird had some sort of scroll case in its talons.

"Yeah," Cyrus said. "I see you seem to have made some friends."

Keeth groaned. "Apparently birds of a feather do not, in fact, flock together unless there is something warm to sit on. I keep telling them I am cold-blooded, but they seem to have mistaken me for a perch."

"Perch fire on fire, I guess." Cyrus got up from the bed of palm branches and sand, and he dusted himself off. "Anyway, where's Conrad at?"

Keeth looked about. "He left at dawn on his boat with a few of the phoenixes. He told me to tell you when you got up, which is significantly later than I would have hoped, by the way, that you were to go to this location." The dragon snorted, dislodging the bird, whom Cyrus remembered was called Magnus. Odd name for a tiny bird. Perhaps Conrad had named him that out of irony.

Magnus chirruped and fluttered down to drop the scroll case in Cyrus's hands. He then flittered to Cyrus's head.

Cyrus opened the scroll case. Inside was a scrap of weathered vellum with a map in ink on the back. Oddly enough, it was a map of Landeralt, the continent home to the ancient Hereditary Evil Empire, with an X marked in the middle of some mountains in the center.

"The Tower of Fire?" Cyrus said incredulously.

"Apparently so," Keeth said, shifting his green bulk in sand. He stretched out his wings, and two phoenixes took up perches on his wingtips. Keeth rolled his eyes and groaned. "There was some hullabaloo a few years ago surrounding a thief who managed to steal something out of that tower for Voshtyr. But he was caught by the Hereditary Evil Empire. I shudder to think what they must have done to him."

"Great, so Conrad wants me to go to the Tower of Fire? I thought he said I wasn't ready yet."

"He said you weren't ready for the Citadel." Keeth said, wrinkling his nose to dislodge a phoenix that had perched on his nostrils. "He didn't say you weren't ready for a lesser task."

"I don't *want* to do lesser tasks!" Cyrus protested. "I need to rescue Kris!"

"Lesser tasks build to greater ones," Keeth said. "Perhaps your skills need to be taken to a higher level before you can rescue Kris, and this is a stepping stone?"

Cyrus sighed. "Listen, if Conrad thinks it's going to help, I'm not going to question it. I mean, who questions a wise old blind man? He's a seer! I'm not going to question the word of a seer. Especially not one who's already helped me so much. But now I'm supposed to somehow get into Villain territory without getting myself killed, enter a forgotten ruin that's in the center of a volcano, walk through a bunch of tunnels and stuff that are about umpteen bajillion degrees, go where no one else has been able to go, and then . . . do what? Pick up a relic that's made of the hottest fire ever?"

"More or less."

Cyrus wiped his brow. "That's one heck of a training mission."

Keeth shrugged, sending the birds off him, but only momentarily. "Or maybe he just wants you to see the map. You're assuming he's giving you a mission."

"Hmm," Cyrus said, scanning the horizon for a phoenix-powered boat. But he didn't see any. "Still, he told you to tell me to come to his location, right? And this map has an X. Do you suppose he's waiting for me at the Tower of Fire? Is that his location? If he wants me to collect the Heartstones, that wouldn't be a bad place to start."

Keeth watched him curiously. "Well, that's for you to decide. I'd go with you, but I have other matters to attend to. And for the moment, apparently I make too good a perch to be allowed to leave."

Magnus chirruped, apparently in agreement.

"You know, you could just get up and fly around," Cyrus said. "They can always perch somewhere else."

"I know, but I hate to dislodge them," Keeth said. "They look so comfortable."

Cyrus chuckled. "For someone with so many scales, you sure are a big softie."

Keeth nodded sagely. "At least I'm not giving anyone half of my heart. Now, shouldn't you be going somewhere?"

"Right," Cyrus said, rolling his eyes, "off to my death."

Keeth stretched. "Don't forget what I taught you about flying."

"Like 'Don't fall'?"

"Exactly. Now off you go."

After saying his goodbyes to the dragon and the swarm of phoenixes, Cyrus walked to the beach. He grabbed an Air line, absorbed its power, and wrapped himself in swirling winds. They lifted him off his feet and with a downward blast propelled him into the air.

All of a sudden what he really wanted was to go sightseeing. But he had priorities, things to take care of, though it was somehow difficult to concentrate.

He still saw plenty of scenery, but it went by at such a rapid pace Cyrus couldn't get much of an idea of what it was. It was mostly ocean, of course, cerulean ocean that freshened his face and clothing as he swooped close to the surface. He even plunged through one swell, emerging soaked and laughing on the other side.

After some time, he passed over land once more, and assumed that it was the Hereditary Evil Empire, or at least southern Landeralt. The sandy coast gave way to low grasslands, then hills covered in huge, ancient trees, then into spiky and forbidding mountains.

As soon as Cyrus cleared the third peak of the mountains, he felt an immense pull in his chest. He swung his head, and he beheld something incredible.

He hung in the air above the caldera of an active volcano.

Far below him, red molten rock bubbled and splattered the jagged rim of the crater. Pylons of jet-black obsidian jutted from the sheer rock walls and reflected the sinister glow of the lava. It was no wonder Villains preferred lava as a lighting source and decoration. It may have been getting dark, but the glow from the lake of lava in the volcano lit up its entire caldera.

But the most impressive thing of all was the giant obsidian tower in the center. It rested on a tiny island in the middle of the caldera. It jutted up so high that its top cleared the missing peak of the mountain by a hundred spans or more. There was no fire spouting from the single cone on the top of the tower. Strange. If this was the Tower of Fire, shouldn't there be more . . . fire? Even the Keep of Five Flames was supposed to have more fire than this, and it was on a different continent.

Cyrus swooped down into the volcano, skimmed the surface of the lava, and alit on the island. It burned his feet. He immediately grabbed for some Water energy to protect himself. To his surprise, there wasn't any. Or more correctly, it was there, but somehow blocked, or perhaps overpowered by the prevalence of Fire.

Thinking quickly back on what the Highseekers had taught him about counterspelling, Cyrus grabbed some of the plentiful Fire energy and flooded himself with it as he had at the goblin mine site with Keeth. This time, as he let the surge wash over him, Cyrus resisted the rush of anger that came with the power.

As the flames licked around him, Cyrus realized that the fire from the lava no longer burned his feet. As an experiment, he leaned down close to the surface of the roiling lava and put a hand over the surface. It felt warm, certainly, but not scorching hot as it had on his way in. He dipped his hand into the lava.

That *was* too hot. He immediately yanked his hand out. His skin was very red, like a sunburn, but hardly as bad as it should have been.

Fire-resistant, not fireproof, Cyrus thought, remembering Keeth's complaint. He stepped back from the brink of the lava. *So much for the lava-swimming idea.*

He looked up at the tower. The red glow of the lava reflected in a hundred facets in the black volcanic glass the tower was made of. Pyroclastic rock formed the ground beneath the tower. Cyrus could hear the bubbling of the lava and smell the sulfurous scent of brimstone.

He approached the base of the tower. The tower didn't rest on the volcanic rock so much as it seemed to have grown out of it. It towered over him, shimmering in the waves of heat. He could see double doors near the base. They were ornately carved black volcanic glass, just like the rest of the tower. A pair of winged drake statues flanked the entrance. As he neared the surface he saw that there was no visible handle or knob on the door.

Cyrus looked at it for a moment, then placed his hand on the door. It was, strangely, cold to the touch. Traces of red light sprang from his hand and skittered their way along previously unseen grooves in the door, until the whole surface had lit up in an intricate network of glowing crimson. With a creak and a blast of crumbled rock, the door slowly swung open.

Interesting.

The wind rushed around Cyrus as it was sucked into the tower. Once the door was fully open, he realized why. The entire inside of the tower was coated in ice. Freezing air swirled about Cyrus's feet as he stood dumbstruck.

Something's wrong here. Why is there ice in the Fire tower? Shouldn't it be full of magma and stuff? This doesn't make a lick of sense!

He stepped into the tower, careful not to slip on the slick floor. It was supernaturally cold inside. Strangely, the ice did not melt at the inrush of heated air. Only the flickering flames and the Fire energy suffusing Cyrus's body kept him warm. Even so, he could feel the tips of his fingers and toes starting to go numb. He had the feeling that under normal circumstances, he would be frozen solid by now. Nice security system.

And he was soon proven right. As he got further inside the massive tower, he saw what seemed to be intricately carved ice sculptures. One was a Minotaur wielding an enormous warhammer. It had its shaggy arms wrapped about itself as if to ward off the cold. Another was a Human who seemed to be pulling one of a pair of matched swords out of a wall, and had frozen in mid-pull. Other figures were barely visible inside the walls, some with looks of misery on their faces, some with looks of stark terror.

Something grabbed Cyrus's ankle. It pulled him *into* the ice. Cyrus raised his arms out to his sides, which caused him to halt abruptly as the bottoms of his arms smacked the ice. He looked down. A grinning skeleton with glowing blue eyes was reaching up from somewhere near the actual floor, beneath several feet of ice.

"No!" Cyrus shouted. "Leggo, bonehead!" He flared up, and the flames around him vaporized the ice. The grip on his ankle released, and Cyrus climbed out of the hole he'd melted. He looked around for a weapon.

The minotaur had a greathammer.

Cyrus sprinted back to the minotaur statue and attempted to wrest it from the frozen creature's grasp. The right hand broke free, still attached to the hammer. But at least Cyrus had a weapon.

The skeleton that had grabbed Cyrus breached the surface of the ice and grinned at him maliciously.

Cyrus whacked it with the hammer. The weapon was basically a brick of metal on a stick. It crushed the skeleton's skeletonized skull, and a blast of snow exploded from it.

Then another skull rose from the ice, off to Cyrus's left. Its skeleton writhed beneath the surface as if swimming upward. Then another skull rose up on the right, and two more in front of him.

Cyrus began smashing them as they popped up. Sometimes one would duck beneath the ice, and Cyrus missed, cracking the ice instead. It reminded him of a slightly more macabre and chilly version of the Thwhack Ye Goblin game he'd once played at a carnival in Bryath City.

After a minute of frenzied smashing, no more undead monstrosities breached the surface. Cyrus leaned back against the icy wall, for once glad of its chill, and wiped his brow. Something was very strange in this tower, and it certainly wasn't friendly. Where was Conrad, and what was Cyrus supposed to be doing here?

"The first thing about being a Hero," Cyrus said, "is to indulge curiosity when Evil is Afoot."

He walked farther into the tower.

Cyrus climbed two flights of spiral stairs, noting that the tower was dangerous, but probably not as dangerous as it could have been. Ice covered several nozzles in the walls and holes in the floor, and other noticeable signs of traps and wards, thus rendering them ineffective. Tower security had chilled out a little too much to be a threat, but the new hazards made up for it.

He paused at the top to catch his breath. He'd been expecting a few fights with ornery fire creatures and a stray elemental or two, not air so frigid it felt like it would frost the inside of his lungs. His footsteps echoed in the empty corridors. The light wasn't as bright as it should have been. Perhaps it was normally lit by what Cyrus assumed were conduits of lava running through the walls, but the light was obscured and refracted by the foot of ice caked over everything. It felt like being inside a pipe full of ice water.

In front of him at the top of the stairs was a set of double doors. These were, not surprisingly, also crusted over with ice. On the doors were a set of brass handles and a dragon-headed door knocker. Cyrus caught his breath and pushed the doors.

They were frozen shut.

Cyrus flared up again and put both hands to the surface of the door. The ice melted and boiled away, dripping to the floor, where it instantly froze again. Cyrus pushed open the door.

Inside, a giant column of ice dominated the center of the enormous round room. It glowed and flickered with an unsteady internal light. Here he saw the first unfrozen things he'd seen since the skeletons. Two figures in tattered robes stood listlessly near the column, shuffling their rag-wrapped feet and muttering something Cyrus couldn't quite catch. Against the column, slumped to the floor, lay another figure, clad in a deep red cloak.

Cyrus gasped. The red cloak bore a grinning skull wrapped in the intricate gilded ring that was a symbol for the International Brotherhood of Heroes.

The Red Death? What was he doing here? Cyrus hadn't seen him since the Heroes had escaped the Vale of Dreams.

Unfortunately, his gasp caught the notice of the other two figures in the room. They turned to face him. Their faces matched the symbol on Red's robe. Both seemed like grinning skulls wreathed in blue fire. Cold seemed to emanate from them. In unison, they shrieked and ran toward Cyrus, claws outstretched.

"Red!" Cyrus shouted as he sidestepped the first one and tumbled past the second. "Red Death! Get up! There's monsters!"

"I know," said a gravelly voice from the red cloak. "Aren't they just something?"

Red stood up, and the sight of him was shocking. Where his ragged cloak didn't cover, his grey-white pasty skin showed through, and his bones showed through the skin. His face, usually the pointy picture of hearty health, was sallow, and his eye sockets were deeper than Cyrus had ever seen.

But his eyes were the worst. One of them was his normal grey, but the other was a pit of blackness, with no iris or pupil. It was just a solid ball of black, encrusted around the edges by what looked like grains of black sand embedded in his skin.

"It took me six Villains before I finally managed to make these two ghouls." Red's voice was low and sounded raspy. "No better way to beat the darkness than at their own game, eh?"

One of the ghouls swiped at Cyrus again. He hit it full force in the chest with the hammer. It slid backward on the ice, shook itself, and came after him again as if it hadn't just been smacked by fifty pounds of giant hammer.

"What happened to you, Red?" Cyrus asked. "Call these things off, will you?"

Red produced a book from beneath his robe. It was black and wrapped in skin, with jetstones in the cover. Runes in some language Cyrus didn't know were written in what looked like fresh blood. As soon as he saw it, Cyrus's mind clouded with the same dark, overpowering rage he'd felt when he held the Shard.

"Red," Cyrus said, "that book is very dangerous. Put it down, right now."

"Put it down?" Red said. "This Infernal Tome has granted me power beyond my wildest dreams. I *will* use it to kill Voshtyr and all his minions. I *will* avenge my friends, I *will* purge the world, and I *will* take what is rightfully mine. But I will *not* take orders from some half-finished whelp of a Hero who thinks he knows better than I do. Do I make myself inescapably clear?" He pulled a curved grey sword from his belt. "Or do you want to make an issue of it?"

Cyrus swept the legs out from under one of the ghouls, then brought the hammer down with all his might on the undead monstrosity's chest. Bone splintered and ice shattered, and the creature moved no more. "Sure," Cyrus said, panting. "Let's make an issue of it. I challenge you to Heroi— Ack!"

Red leapt forward before Cyrus could finish his sentence. "No Heroics, kid. No rules to get in the way. Survival of the fittest." He stabbed at Cyrus a dozen times in rapid succession. "Just you and me and my ghoul friend." That struck him as hysterical, and he lapsed into laughter.

Cyrus reared back to clobber him, but Red recovered and gave Cyrus two stabs in the shoulders and one cut along his face. Cyrus discovered that a greathammer was an entirely ineffective weapon as far as parrying went. He leapt backward and swung the hammer up, knocking the blade from Red's hand. "Stop it!" he shouted. "I don't want to hurt you!"

"Funny," Red said leaping up to catch his blade before it hit the floor, "I *do* want to hurt *you*." He sprang at Cyrus again, his sword moving as an almost untraceable grey blur.

Cyrus focused on dodging this time, but even then he could barely keep up. The strikes came faster and faster as dark energy began swirling around Red's blade. He seemed to be drawing power directly from the ominous book tucked beneath his arm.

Wicked claws laid open Cyrus's back from shoulder to shoulder, and he cried out in pain. He'd forgotten about the second ghoul.

Red laughed in a sinister fashion. "Bwa ha ha. Forgot to keep an eye on your opponents, didn't you?"

"Nope," Cyrus said, wincing. "I was just watching the important one." He swung the hammer backward over his head, crushing the ghoul to the floor. He leapt with the momentum and vaulted back over the hammer. He landed on his feet and slid away from Red on the ice. "Now that we've got fewer distractions, you want to try that again?"

Red growled. "Do you know how hard it was to make those?" He charged.

Cyrus tried to raise the hammer, but the tainted Hero was too fast. Red leapt atop the head of the hammer, then lunged at

Cyrus's throat. Cyrus leaned away, but before he knew it, Red was behind him. Cyrus spun and brought the hammer around again.

"You're dead," Red said. "You just don't know it yet."

Cyrus felt his throat. It felt rough and tight. There seemed to be flakes of skin coming off it. "You . . . you didn't . . ."

"My signature attack," Red said. "*Crimson Shadow.* You've got about thirty seconds 'til every vein, capillary, and blood vessel in your neck develops an uncomfortable number of perforations. A few seconds less if you stress yourself."

Cyrus coughed. Tears pricked the back of his eyes. He'd been beaten up, had Kris kidnapped, and now he was going to die at the hands of another Hero? It just wasn't fair.

"So, I guess this is it for you," Red said. "If you like, I can put you out of your misery quicker."

"Quicker?" Cyrus said. "Oh, I can do quicker." With all his might, he reached out for Air energy. And he found a lot of it. It filled his body and lungs and swirled through his fingers and toes. He felt the quickening of his limbs and organs. Even if it cut his time to live in half, he would still be able to do something with it.

Cyrus gripped the hammer closer to the head and charged Red, catching the Hero off guard. The metal head slammed into Red's torso and catapulted him away.

Cyrus followed. He released his grip on the hammer so his grip slid to the maximum length of the handle, and he swung it at Red.

Red leapt over the weapon and tumbled to his feet. "Too slow!" he taunted. "You're only going to—"

"Hit you on the backswing?" Cyrus said as he continued the swing. He spun in a full circle, a la *Thompson's Tornado,* and slammed the hammer into Red's back.

The Hero cried out as the impact flung him across the room and into the giant icy pillar at the center, cracking it. His blade and the tainted book fell from his grasp as he writhed on the ground, clutching his spine.

"Sorry," Cyrus said, tasting blood in his mouth. "If I could just hit that book and not you . . ." He looked at the book, then at Red's sword. Cyrus picked up the sword. It felt like it was made of pain. It seared his hand and tensed his tendons and muscles so hard it felt like a seizure. Gritting his teeth against the pain, Cyrus lifted the sword, which he noticed bore the etching on the hilt '*Zandira*,' and plunged it into the pages of the Infernal Tome.

A piercing keen filled the air, and all the ice in the room began to crack and shatter from the walls. Red's skin and eyes began changing back to their healthy Human hue, and sulfurous mist poured from around the sword in the book.

Cyrus slumped to the ground. His breathing was getting more difficult, even though he had plenty of Air energy left.

"Cyrus . . ." Red croaked, pushing himself up from the ground. "I'm so sorry, Cyrus. I . . . I don't know what I was doing. Your neck . . ."

Cyrus shrugged. "Hey, no sweat. I just about killed one of my friends while under the influence of a magic rock the other day. So no hard feelings."

"But I can't reverse it," Red said, looking at his hands. "I hardly ever get to apologize to those I've killed before they've died, but . . . sorry."

Cyrus winced and put his hand to his neck. He could feel blood oozing out between his fingers. "I don't hold it against you, Red," he said. "I'm just glad I could snap you out of it."

"But I don't deserve it," Red said, pounding his fist on the melting ice. "You gave up your life to save me, when all I'd done was try and kill you."

Cyrus shrugged. "Hey, it's what any true Hero would have done, right?" He coughed, and he spat up blood. "I guess I'd better look for some way to fix this before I don't have any more blood to cough up."

"It's hopeless," Red said. "The only things I've seen that are immune to death by *Crimson Shadow* are golems, zombies, and elementals."

"Elementals?" Cyrus turned to look at the column of ice. To his surprise, it was no longer there. Instead, a massive column of fire had taken its place, and now it shed light across the entire room. He stepped toward it.

"What are you doing?" Red said. "Are you insane?"

"Nope," Cyrus said. "I'm either dead by thoat-stabbing or dead by fire. But maybe, just maybe—" He coughed again, and the blood began trickling from between his fingers. "Maybe I can survive this." He looked back at the column. "Here goes nothing."

Cyrus stepped into the column.

A flash of light erupted around the room as the raging red beam of fire flared white. Heat overtook all of Cyrus's senses as he took in all the Fire he could contain. And even more washed over him. It was hotter and more pure than the lava, and he could feel himself crisping. Then he let go of all the other elements that made up his body. Within a second, he was overtaken entirely by Fire. He felt something hard and cool press against his chest and fall into his hands. Then he stepped out of the column.

"Cyrus?" Red said, his jaw slack with amazement.

"What?" Cyrus said. His voice sounded odd to him, like he was speaking as the crackling and rushing of a large fire distorted by a heat haze so it formed words.

Red pointed at Cyrus. "You're... you're made of fire. You're an Elemental!"

Cyrus looked at his hands. They were still his hands, but they were translucent and wreathed in fire and heat. It looked like lava flowed beneath every part of his skin, and tongues of flame had replaced his hair. His skin, his mouth, and perhaps even his bones were made of pyroclastic materials. His throat didn't hurt. In fact, it wasn't even scratchy anymore.

"Whoa," Cyrus said. "Cool."

He held in his hands a ruby the size of his palm. The gem burned furiously with inner fire. He held in his hands the Heartstone of Fire.

Chapter 19

SPY VERSUS SPY

*In which Information is Exchanged
Prisoners are Taken
And Other Things Are Done in Passive Voice*

"ALL RIGHT, SO we know where Kris Solburg is," Serimal said. "She's in that thrice accursed floating city. And there's not a thing we can do about it." Not a thing he could do, and it was a puzzle Serimal had been banging his head against since early in the morning.

Serimal and his Fifth Column sat around a map table on the deck of a sleek black sailing ship. The overcast weather kept most of the warmth out of the air that evening, and even the tropical islands that bore birds that were constantly aflame were not very warm.

The boat floated just outside the territorial waters of the Phoenix Islands and just outside the range where Phoenixes would bother flying out to incinerate the boat. Not that they would have had much luck, as the ship was nigh invulnerable to fire. It was *The Handbasket*, a dangerous corsair vessel that regularly ran trips to and from the Island of the Damned, which reportedly contained the entrance to Hell itself.

"How does she get to go off playing around in castles in the sky?" Emily Cartwright said. She'd stripped down to just a tunic, breeches, and a swordbelt. Serimal guessed she enjoyed the cooler air.

"It is better her than you, Emily-san," Koshiro said. The wandering swordsman leaned against the mast, his back to the conversation, and his black spiky hair waving in the wind. "But do we know where Cyrus-san is?"

"Well, we just got a report from some fishermen off the coast of Landeralt," Serimal said. "One of them spotted a man-sized tornado rocketing toward the center of the continent. We think Solburg's ability to absorb and release unheard-of amounts of Fire energy may have expanded to Air energy as well. If he can fly, and if it was him they spotted, and if he continued in that direction . . ." Serimal traced a blue line on the map before them, leading first from Starspeak to the Phoenix Islands, then to the center of Landeralt at a giant mountain.

"Is Fire tower," Slashback said, peering down at the map. "What does Cyrus do there?"

"I have no idea," Serimal said, looking at the map. "He can't possibly be hiding in there, and he has a vested interest in attacking the Citadel to get his mate back." He moved a small token on the map that looked like a shield bearing the letters T and K. "The Citadel was last seen here heading west after attacking Rondheim Port. So what is Cyrus doing in Landeralt?"

"Taking a volcanic vacation?" Emily said.

Serimal shot Emily a *That's Not Funny* look and looked back at the map. "Not when he has so much at stake. No, he has to be doing something else. Training, perhaps?"

Slashback cocked her head. "Getting fires to use on flying city?"

Serimal slapped his hand down on the map. "That's it! Solburg is after the Elemental Heartstones!"

"The what now?" Emily said.

"Magical gems that stabilize and amplify Cyrus's peculiar magical ability," Serimal said. "If he's going after them, he'll be trying for all four. And we can help him find them."

Koshiro turned around. "Serimal-dono, I hope you do not believe in those fairy tales about the Hearts of the Elements."

"Fairy tales—that's exactly it," Serimal said. "The Fairies of Shiel Glade gave me a tale—er, a report—about elemental imbalances last week. I didn't pay much attention to it at the time. But if the Elements themselves are falling out of balance, then that means that Voshtyr, by disrupting the Good and Evil of the Balance, has somehow knocked the Elemental balance off as well."

"And Cyrus is going to fix that?" Emily asked. "How?"

Serimal put down his pen and looked at her. "Not intentionally. If our information is correct, he's had contact with the Phoenix Prophet, an ancient and powerful seer. If that seer is training him up to ready him for an assault on the Citadel, then there is an ulterior motive. Do you know what will happen if those four Hearts are ever brought to the Keep of Five Flames?"

"Someting bad, I think," Slashback said, flapping her wings and almost blowing the map off the table. "We must stop him."

"On the contrary!" Serimal said excitedly, looking back down at the map. "We need to help him. My great-great-grandfather had an ancient tome, one of the two copies still known to exist of the *Tome of Saint Michael.* Why a Villain had it, I'm not sure, but in that book, it says that the Keep of Five Flames has the power to reset the Balance."

"Reset?" Emily asked. "Like, entirely restart the entire thing? What in the Torments happens to us if the Balance gets reset, then?"

"The book never said," Serimal replied. "At best, it resets the Balance, purging the most evil and restoring the greater good for all, as well as rebalancing all the Elements, and we all live happily ever after. At worst, well, it destroys everything that is imbalanced and starts over from square zero."

"Yes, that sounds bad."

"Not as bad as this," said a voice from above the bow. Jolan floated down on metal limbs and took his place at the table. "Guess what's happened to your precious castle?"

"Which one?" Serimal asked. "The Citadel or the castle I own?"

"Unless you keep all those formerly intact priceless Eastern Island vases in the Citadel, you have very limited options."

Serimal started. "What? What's been done to my family home?"

Jolan slammed a stack of parchment down on the table. "I took some drawings of the thing, but it was basically a giant city that floated through the air above the ocean, dusted some of your battlements, and cracked open the interior. I think they took your lovely fiancée."

"*What?*" Serimal shouted. "We need to get back there immediately! I won't have Nieva put at risk because of my activities!"

"Oh, that's not the half of it," Jolan said. "No sooner were they done with that than the Hereditary Evil Empire swooped in, declared it a disaster area, and cordoned it off. I couldn't get in without making a huge mess..."

"And I told you not to cause any massacres." Serimal put his hands to his head. "The Kinetics have Nieva...?"

Emily rose and put a hand on Serimal's shoulder. "I'm sorry, Serimal. If we'd known, I could have taken another rider on Slashback..."

"Do not worry yourself about it," Serimal said, his voice sounding calmer. The look in his eyes was hard and angry. "We can solve this problem."

"Oh, and here's a notice that they're claiming your home for tax evasion," Jolan said, handing Serimal another slip of parchment. "This is probably more... problematic."

Serimal scowled. "Those heartless bureaucrats. I have paid them every copper they've asked for in land taxes. Voshtyr must be trying to claim what's left of our father's legacy."

"Or it could be that I told him you were still alive," said another voice. Jaratyr the demon appeared on the deck in a puff of brimstone. He was wearing a fine light grey suit and a stylish hat. Probably the "Dapper Gambler #2" suit in last winter's color, "Cloud Ashes." Jaratyr chuckled. "You know. Just to make things more interesting."

Jolan spun and thrust at Jaratyr with a suddenly manifested lance of black energy. "Die, demon!"

Jaratyr parried it with the back of his left hand. "Tsk, Serimal, I thought you would keep a better leash on your dogs." He swatted Jolan away with a lash of his barbed red tail. Jolan crashed into the wheelhouse and slumped to the deck unconscious. "Anyway, I have some disturbing news for you."

"Is it worse than losing my fiancée, my family home, and finding out that I was an idiot for trusting a demon?" Serimal asked, glaring at Jaratyr.

Jaratyr chuckled. "Well, while the last is certainly true, and though my heart bleeds for you over the others, I came to tell you that Voshtyr has built two things you might want to know about."

He sat down at the table and put his feet up on it. "First, he's got an upgrade planned for that metal arm of his. He's got a Shard of the Star of Anger, some Darkmatter, and he's bargaining with our mother for some Hellsteel to keep it all stable."

Serimal scowled. "That sounds like a formidable weapon indeed. I can't think of anything besides a Weapon of Legend that could stand up to something like that."

"That's not even the worst of it," Jaratyr said. "Fancy metal arm aside, he's also cooked up a little metal tube that's more or less an 'I win' button for any fight with a single opponent. I don't know exactly how he made it, but it's pretty fearsome."

"Now we need someone to gief us more gut news," Slashback muttered. "Day can not get worse."

There was an uncomfortable silence at the table for a few seconds. Then Jolan began swearing as he regained consciousness and started dragging himself out of the crater he'd made in the wheelhouse when Jaratyr had flung him across the deck.

"All right, you misbegotten spawn of a thousand years of darkness!" he shouted. "You want to fight, we can fight! If you're here to kill Serimal, kill him! If you're here to doom all of us to capture and torture by Voshtyr, then you're going to need to go through me." He spun his crackling black lance, ionizing the air around him. "Whatever you do, just stop standing there being smug."

Jaratyr cast a spell that Serimal barely identified as the *Fwitz* spell, and the demon appeared behind Jolan.

"Oh, sorry," Jaratyr said into Jolan's ear. "Were you being literal or just showing off with Heroic bravado?"

Jolan coughed blood and slumped to the deck.

"Jolan?" Emily said, leaping up from her chair and running to his side. "Don't die on me, soldier!" She glared at Jaratyr. "What in the Nine Torments did you do to him?"

"Yes, that's exactly right!" Jaratyr said, then looked at Emily. "Confused? It's a little trick one picks up from being a Demon. I simply grabbed his punishment out of the Nine Torments and slapped him with it early. His sin is wrath, you see. Has been for ever so long. The wrathful are to be eternally torn to pieces by one another, you know."

Emily's eyes narrowed. "How could you, you . . . you . . ."

"Monster? Helll-ooooo, Demon . . ." Jaratyr said, pointing at himself. He rolled his eyes. "Anyway, Serimal, I thought those bits of information might come in handy. Also, Voshtyr's offered me souls in exchange for my services."

Serimal scowled. "Of course he has. And . . . ?"

"And souls are tastier than revenge. Revenge is sweet, but kind of has a bitter aftertaste. If you can't come up with a counteroffer, I'm afraid I'm going to have to—"

"Stuff it, Jaratyr." Emily stood up and faced the Demon. "You and Serimal both know we don't traffic in souls. 'S why you answered us in the first place, yeah? You knew that you're too used to being evil, and you know you need a change of pace, so you're helpin' the good guys for a change."

"Is that it?" Jaratyr asked, sounding amused. "Perhaps I was simply bored."

"Or you were bored. Yeah, we believe that one. No, you think you can get more out of the good guys—because get this: we always win."

Jaratyr chuckled. "Oh, she's delightful, Serimal. Are you sure she's not a Hero in disguise?" He leaned to Emily. "Two words, my dear: Vale. Massacre."

"That doesn't count. That was a setback, not a loss," Emily snapped. "You take a look at history. Miles the Conquerer vs. Colmarian the Headstrong? Who won that one?"

"Colmarian," Jaratyr said, "but only because—"

Emily stood square in front of Jaratyr and looked up into his face. "Justinian the Iron Wall vs. Akros Akropolis?"

"Justinian. In fact, he—"

"Saint Michael vs. the wizard Morival in the Twenty-Minute War?"

Jaratyr crossed his arms and scowled. "What do you want me to say, Miss Cartwright? 'Yippee, shucks, Good always wins, so I must become a good guy now'?" He leaned down even farther so that his nose was touching Emily's. "No. You can stuff that in your ear. I'm evil. I *like* being evil. It makes me feel all warm and tingly inside. If you want to make an annoyingly self-righteous speech, do it elsewhere. You're wasting my air."

"You're done, Jaratyr," Serimal said. "If you've nothing else to divulge, get off my ship."

Jaratyr snarled, and everyone on deck cringed back as the Demon lost his veneer of handsome civility. "Fine, then! See if I help you again, you rotten ingrates! You filthy, weak, pathetic *mortals!* This world will burn without my help, and good riddance!"

Jaratyr's spine flexed and twisted horrifically, and Serimal could hear the sickening snap of bones as Jaratyr sprouted wings from his back and tore his fine suit off. He sprang into the air, muttering curses in a language best not heard by mortals, and flew off into the east where the sky was just beginning to darken.

There were a few moments of silence from the crew before Emily spoke. "Wow," she said.

"I think that went pretty well," Serimal said, resting his elbows on the railing.

"What?"

"Oh, he'll help us again." Serimal chuckled. "Jaratyr was born with a horrible defect for a demon."

Slashback cocked her head. "And vat is dat?"

"A conscience."

Chapter 20

CASTLES IN THE SKY

*In which Kris discovers she has a Companion,
Finds the Truth about her Prophecy,
And begin to Plot their Escape*

KRIS ACHED ALL over. She sat up in her green satin bed and rubbed her eyes. She was still in her assigned room in the Citadel of the Kinetics. She swung her legs over the side of the bed, felt nauseated, found the bucket beside her bed, and emptied her stomach.

Within seconds, Indy Tarrashan was at her side with a glass of water and a towel. "Hey, whoa there, kitty. Here, drink this."

Kris tried to growl at him, but instead took the water and drank it. "You drugged me," she said, handing the glass back.

"You tried to claw my poor sensitive stomach out," Indy said. "I think we're even."

"No, I didn't," Kris said. "And we're not even because you aren't sick from the side effects of what I did to you."

Indy chuckled. "Hoo boy, do you have one coming. Kris, you're not sick from the side effects of the drug. You're sick from side effects of something else."

Kris wiped her mouth with the towel. "What do you mean?"

Indy shook his head. "Listen, it's not my place to tell you. If the others didn't tell you, that means Lazik had a reason not to."

"Not wanting her to become panicked, perhaps?" boomed a voice from the entrance.

Kris saw a man who appeared to be in his late forties, with silver hair, a distinctive hawk-like nose, and striking blue eyes. His face was shaved so close it looked as if he'd never had facial hair, and his hair was neatly trimmed and combed back out of his eyes. He wore a white formal suit that was open at the collar and missing its sleeves. Two more of the pale men similar to Mel-Shan flanked him.

"It is not every day that one learns one's true identity or that one must fulfill prophecy, no matter how unlikely that result will be." The man approached the bed and inclined his head slightly. "My lady Huntress, allow me to explain your . . . situation. But first, I must deal with my unruly successor. Indikos!"

Indy bolted straight upright. "Yes, Lazik?"

The older man glared sternly at Indy. "Watch your tongue, Indikos. You are not King yet, and you will address me by my title."

"Yes, Tarrashan," Indy muttered, looking at his feet.

"Good. Now, I must express my displeasure in how much time you have spent with the Huntress. Would you care to explain?"

Indy shuffled his feet. "Eh, she was interesting, and no one else was being nice to her, so—"

"Indikos, is that any reason to jeopardize the results of the prophecy?" Lazik asked. "Mere kindness to one of the lower races? Even one such as the Huntress?"

"There's no reason not to be nice to people," Indy said, looking up. "Even if you think they're less than you. That's what separates good rulers from jerks."

"Enough!" Lazik clapped his hands. The two men who flanked him moved forward and took positions on either side of Indy. "Impertinent scoundrel. You may not speak to the Huntress again until her part in the Prophecy is fulfilled. Now get out."

Indy glanced back at Kris apologetically as the two pale men ushered him out of the room.

After the commotion had settled down, Lazik turned and sat down on the edge of the bed. He smiled. To Kris, it seemed fake, and sent a shiver down her spine. That smile was the one she sometimes got when about to make a kill on particularly unaware prey.

"So, Huntress," Lazik said, "I suppose you would like to know just exactly what is going on, hmm?"

Kris pulled her sheets closer to herself. "Yes, um, Your Majesty?"

Lazik chuckled coldly. "Oh, do not worry yourself about the title. I wouldn't expect one of the lower races to understand our machinations."

"Indy explained some of them to me," Kris said.

Lazik's eyes narrowed. "Oh, did he? I must have further words with that boy, it seems. But this is irrelevant." He stood and walked to one of the windows, then opened it and let the sunlight in. He closed his eyes and let the light wash over him for a few seconds, then turned back to Kris. "You, Kris Solburg, daughter of Marcellus Baravaati, are the Huntress mentioned in the Prophecy of the End of the World." Lazik held out a hand.

Suddenly Kris was floating out of her bed. "Put me down!" She grabbed at the sheets. She felt no trust for this man, not one bit, and she wished she had armor on rather than the elegant but somewhat flimsy green sleeping garments she'd awoken in.

"'He meeteth then the Huntress, though she is not his kind,'" he intoned, and his voice filled the entire room. "'Together in the starlight, their destiny shall find.' Sound familiar, Kath?"

"What? N-no, what do you mean?"

"Do not play stupid, woman." Lazik's voice was deadly calm. "'From them, the two of Balance shall spring, and then shall grow in power and in stature, their fates they do not know.' It is the Prophecy of the End of the World, or part of it. Have you never heard it?"

"I . . . maybe my brother told me of it once," Kris said, losing her grip on the sheet. She now floated three or four feet above the surface of the bed. "I do not know what you mean. Are you saying this Huntress is me like the old woman said?"

"Ah, so you do know," Lazik said. "Think about it, young Kath. Where did you meet your . . . mate?" He rolled his eyes and looked disgusted.

"In the forest. I almost killed his master." Kris stuck her tongue out at Lazik. "So your prophecy is not about me."

Lazik shook his head. "No, that is not where you met him. You encountered him there, perhaps, but where did you really come to know him?"

Kris thought for a moment. "On a roof, under the . . . stars . . . Oh." Her sentence petered out as the thought struck her.

"There, now she understands," Lazik said. "I believe you are the Huntress and that Cyrus is the Light from the Fallen.

Together you will produce the pair that will balance the world. And I will have them balance it in my favor."

"Produce . . . Are you saying that Cyrus and I . . . That we could . . . ? But we can't . . ."

"Produce children?" Lazik said. "Or as your kind would say, cubs? Of course not. That would be impossible. But then again, prophecy is all about making the impossible a reality, is it not?"

Kris whimpered. This didn't make any sense. She'd known when she'd taken Cyrus as her mate that they would never have children. She'd been fine with that. Mostly. But now this man was telling her otherwise? And that he had plans for the children she couldn't possibly have?

Lazik floated up in the air beside her, and with a flick of his wrist, he held her spread-eagle, paws, claws, and tail away from her center mass.

"What— What are you—" Kris stammered.

"Hush, peace," Lazik said. "You will not be harmed. I am merely confirming prophecy. Now speak to me, little ones. Speak to your master." He put his hand to the soft white fur on Kris's belly and closed his eyes.

Kris tried to struggle, but found she couldn't move at all. She had to wait for Lazik to finish whatever it was he was doing.

Eventually he stepped back. "Yes, yes, I was right!" It was the first emotion he'd shown. "You are indeed carrying two minds—and minds of such strength that I can feel them even before their birth. Once I bend them to my will, they will be my perfect champions. They will remake the world as I tell them, without argument, without question, the perfect servants from the cradle to the afterlife."

So it was true. Kris mentally reeled from the information. She was the Huntress. She was carrying twins. Cyrus's children. The impossible was a reality. The prophecy was true. Or was it? If this cruel man was to do what he said—and take her children from her in the process—then the world wouldn't be balanced. It would be tilted irrecoverably to one side: his. That could not be allowed to happen. Not while she still had breath in her body.

Kris snarled. "Monster! You leave my cubs alone!" She felt protective and angry. If he was right, then it was her duty to protect her little ones from such a fate. "I'd see myself dead before you did this thing!"

Lazik sighed. "I knew that you would say something along those lines. You Katheni are a stubborn and rebellious people. I still don't understand why slavers think they can enforce their weak little wills on you."

"Let me go!"

"No." Lazik's voice was shiveringly cold. "You will do as I say. Your misbegotten half-breed children will do as I say. The world will bow to me, because I will it to be so."

Kris's eyes narrowed. "Arrogant. You are arrogant. What makes you think your will is so important?"

Lazik's eyes seemed to swirl and glint as if they contained windstorms. "My will? My will is beyond question. Even the wisest of the kings of old knew that the lords of the Kinetics were to be feared. If I willed it, I could crush a man into fine powder. If I willed it, I could make brothers fight one another to the death. If I so willed it, I could tear apart the sky and draw fire from heaven! *If I willed it, I could drag the moon down from the sky and shatter it against the strongholds of men!*"

He stopped and caught his breath. He relaxed and straightened back up from the crazed pose he'd occupied a moment ago. "Now, since you have no intent of cooperating, I will break your mind. After all, it takes only the body to produce a child." Lazik put both hands on the sides of Kris's head.

Kris's eyes widened as she felt Lazik among her thoughts, prodding her memories, and prying into the innermost of her secret thoughts. "No!" she screamed. "N—"

Her consciousness shattered into black.

Kris awoke on a stone slab atop a black marble column that faded into nothingness in the pit below her. The starless night sky did nothing to illuminate her surroundings. And for some reason, she couldn't muster the energy to get up. A single tear traced its way down her face, trickling through her spots, and dripped onto the slab.

She felt confused and somewhat urgent, but couldn't remember why. It was like having an idea she just barely couldn't remember, or having a joke on the tip of her tongue but finding herself unable to tell it.

"Kris?"

Kris lay still on the slab. "What," she whispered.

"Please get up, Kris."

She couldn't turn her head. "I can't," she said. "He hurt my mind."

"You are stronger than he is, both in heart and in mind. I have seen it. Please get up."

"But he could bring down the moon. My mind can not even learn Central very well." Kris whimpered, and another tear trickled down her face.

"If Lazik Tarrasshan had half the power that he has ego, perhaps he would be a danger. Please, Kris. You must rise so you can free yourself. I will help you if you turn to me."

Kris felt a gentle hand on her head, stroking her head-fur. "Who . . . are you?" She turned her head and saw a beautiful Elven woman with dark hair and silver eyes, wearing a multi-layered robe of flowing white silk fastened with pearls.

"I am Nieva Valcorian," the Elven woman said. "And look, you are already stronger than you thought."

Another voice boomed in from somewhere above them, from the night sky. "Hey, I'd love to listen to you ladies chat some more, but I can't keep your connection up for much longer before ol' King Cranky notices. Hurry up and make an escape plan or something."

"Indy?" Kris said, pushing herself up on one elbow.

Nieva smiled. "He told me Lazik forbade him to talk with you. He said nothing about telepathy or letting me speak to you."

Kris smiled. She felt better already. "So," she said, "when do we escape?"

"Indy tells me my room is next to yours," Nieva said. "I am being held to ensure the good behavior of my beloved fiancé. If we can both escape this place, then my beloved can continue his work, and you can return to Cyrus."

"Wait, how do you know about Cyrus?"

"We know many things, my beloved and I. We wish to help Cyrus topple Voshtyr. And for that, he will need to know that you are safe." Nieva patted Kris's shoulder. "Now, to plan our escape, look around your room when you wake up. You will need a weapon of some sort to defeat the guards. Indy and I will come up with a way to protect your mind against detection as we escape. Will you work with us?"

Kris put a paw on top of Nieva's hand. "Of course. Can we meet in person?"

Nieva shook her head. "Not while we are being observed. But I look forward to our meeting once we are free."

"And that's about time, ladies," Indy's voice said from the sky. "If you hang on about five more seconds, you can watch the Council session begin."

"What will that look like?" Kris asked.

"Watch the sky," Indy said. "One star, one mind. Here goes!"

And with that, the sky lit up in a riot of stars.

Chapter 21

Pack Tactics

In which Reginald Meets a Little Wolf
And Hears a Tale of Ancient Enmity

"So where are we, exactly?" Reginald asked. The sun was almost directly overhead and it was a beautiful day. The gentle breeze kept the heat down to a tolerable level, and even insects refrained from bothering the Hero and his avian travelling companion. The second Avierie, Amni, had parted ways with them at the last crossroads.

"We are between Merope and Mountains of Mornings," Glyss said. "Iss normally nice place, but Voshtyr iss cause many problem for peoples around here."

A red brick road wound its way through the foothills down to the tiered town Reginald had been to during his last altercation with Voshtyr. Wheat farms lined either side of it, and most of the city was surrounded by them as well.

"So I'm back on Centra Mundi," Reginald mused. "I thought I recognized those mountains. I don't suppose there's a way to get faster transportation for us?"

Glyss shook his head. "My spells are for making things, for movings of objects, and for finding of things. If you need me for to find a person or a thing, I am can do that. Or make new armors, I am do that too. But travel? Not so muchly."

"Hmm. Could you summon me a horse? Loath as I am to rely on magic, I really do miss Wraith."

"Is horsey still alife?" Glyss asked. "I am can find horsey for you!"

Reginald scratched his beard. "Mayhaps. I've not seen him in a month, and with this war going on . . ."

"Let Glyss cast spell, and we will see." Glyss sat his feathered posterior down on the edge of the road and began muttering to himself in a language Reginald did not understand. A few minutes later, he sat straight up and looked at Reginald. "Horsey is big black horsey, yiss?"

"Yes, he's a Landeralt Charger with a pedigree three spans long."

"Right, big black horsey. Come to Glyss, horsey, come to Glyss!" Glyss waved his taloned wings in a circle, and with a puff of smoke Wraith appeared on the grass in front of them.

Wraith whinnied in terror and bucked.

Reginald stepped up to the panicked horse and took hold of his bridle. "Easy, boy, easy. Shh, shh, you know me, old friend," he said, calming the horse down. "There we go, there now. Oh, it is good to see you again. Mwah!" He kissed the warhorse on the nose and turned to Glyss. "What an incredible feat this is! You, my good bird, are a true magician."

Glyss bowed. "All my pleasure for a Hero of the Guild. Just wait; I am make you armor that you will want kiss Glyss for."

"Armor?" Reginald grinned. "This day keeps getting better."

"Yiss, but pliss to not kiss Glyss," Glyss said, covering his beak with his wings. "Is awkward and makes marks on beak."

• • •

With a warhorse available, Reginald traveled much faster. Glyss was able to fly without outdistancing the Hero. The two of them continued on for a bit until they hit another crossroads. Glyss announced that he needed raw materials with which to make armor, and he departed, promising to track Reginald down for an armor fitting.

Reginald took the west fork and headed into the forest. If he wanted to avoid the swamp and most of the Mir desert on his way north, he could cut through some of the forest surrounding the Keep of Five Flames. He hoped to reach the edge of the forest before nightfall, and then the Keep by early the next morning. It wasn't until nearly evening that Reginald saw a shape on the horizon, closing fast. Reginald drew Sharp, his sword, and urged Wraith carefully forward. After a while, it became clear that the shape was flying, and was, in fact, a dragon. A green one.

The dragon flew over, did a double-take, and wheeled back around. It landed a few yards away. A reddish bird of prey clung tenaciously to its horns.

"Reginald!" the dragon said. "I had thought you dead!"

"Keeth?" Reginald asked. Now that he got a closer look, it was indeed his friend Keeth. "By the Twelve, it *is* you! How are you, you great reptile?"

The dragon lay on his belly. "I am well, thank you. I almost did not recognize you without your armor. And is that a new sword?"

Reginald nodded. "Indeed, it is Sharp."

"I would imagine," Keeth said. "That is generally a desirable trait of a sword."

"No, the sword, its name—"

"I knew what you meant," Keeth said with an amused smile. "I recognized it by the scrollwork on the hilt. Keep good care of that weapon, Sir Ogleby. It may one day save your life."

"I plan on it," Reginald said. "So, as I have been out of contact, how have you fared over the last . . . what, two months?"

"Well," Keeth said. "I have been helping your erstwhile apprentice on a somewhat inane Quest, though I think it may help save the world."

"Cyrus is alive and well?" Reginald said. He looked away from the Dragon. "I suppose that is cause for celebration."

"Don't sound *too* ecstatic," Keeth said. "Cyrus is a good lad with noble motives, and what happened at the Vale of Dreams was not his fault. He leads the Life Heroic now, despite your abandonment of him and the harsh words you departed with."

Reginald hung his head. "I . . . I know I treated the lad poorly, but if all you say is true, then he is well on his way to making up for his part in what happened in the Vale." He felt himself choking up and cleared his throat. Heroes didn't cry over silly things like this. What would the Purple Paladin say if he'd been there?

"I think that lad learned his stubbornness from you," Keeth said. "He is . . . on a Quest of sorts now, to rescue Kris."

Reginald was taken aback. "Someone kidnapped the girl?"

"Sadly, yes," the Dragon said. "It involves lengthy exposition. But you and I can travel together for a time, and that will give us all the time we need."

Reginald grumbled halfheartedly, and they continued on their way.

• • •

Reginald rode the seldom-used road between Merope and the Keep of Five Flames. The road, which further south and west consisted of solid red bricks, was in disrepair here, and slightly overgrown. Tufts of grass sprouted between many of the fading bricks and rough cracks in the mortar.

The forest that encompassed the Keep was visible on the horizon, as were the mountains that circled the ancient tower. Waves of long grass covered both sides of the road. Much of it had already gone to seed in the late summer sun, making the road seem a mere back-country path. It had been more in ages past: the highway to the most epic and unconquerable challenge in all of Heroic Lore.

Wraith ambled along quite nicely for a horse who had been slain with magic, regenerated by a Ranshan priest of Karista who specialized in healing animals, served as an ignoble pack horse for fleeing Heroes, and then dragged through the ethers back to his former master.

Poor Wraith had been killed by a *Slay Horse* spell in Reginald's conflict with Voshtyr, the same battle in which Lydia Weatherblade the White Tiger had turned traitor. Once the animal cleric had found him, it had been quick work to regenerate the horse and restore life to his body. Such restoration was impossible for Humans and the other Races, for they had souls, but it could be done for animals, though the cost was prohibitively high. Fortunately for Reginald, he'd carried Horse Insurance with the optional Rider rider, so the procedure had cost him only the ten-gold deductable.

Reginald rode for several hours. He was interrupted only twice—once to let his horse take a break, and once to talk to Keeth. Keeth walked beside Reginald and Wraith for a bit, then had said he was hungry and took off again, flying out of sight. For an hour Reginald continued onward to the Keep, enjoying the mid-afternoon sun.

He hoped to get to the Keep of Five Flames and keep the promise he had given to the Centaurs who were cursed to live there, invisible, until someone freed them. Perhaps they didn't count as one of the Nine Races, but they were centuries old. Perhaps they would have some insight into how he could go about uniting all the Races against Voshtyr, as his Blessed Quest would have him do. And even if they did not, it had been more than a month since he had seen the Centaurs. It wouldn't do to have them think he had forgotten his promise.

Then he spotted something moving in the tall grass.

It looked like an animal of some sort, but it was merely lying there, faintly moving its legs. Cautiously, Reginald dismounted. Drawing Sharp from its saddle-sheath, he slowly approached the creature.

It was a wolf. Or, more correctly, it resembled one. It was an Istaka, one of the Races native to Centra Mundi—a race of intelligent, bipedal canines. The Istaka appeared to be hurt. It lay on the ground whimpering.

Humans are always quick to give improper names to things and peoples they do not understand. For example, when Lord Colmarian the Headstrong sailed west in his winged ships and discovered a new land, he mistakenly believed he had landed on the mystical island of Lorimar. Thus, an entire continent was misnamed Lorimar, and the real Lorimar has yet to be discovered.

A similar mistake was made with the Istaka. Humans generally refer to them as "wolf people," but as with the Katheni, there is much variety within the Istak species. Many do resemble bipedal wolves, but some resemble foxes, dingoes, or other varieties of canine. Though, in defense of humanity, wolf Istaka *are* the most common.

Being canines, their muzzles are much longer than human faces. The average Istak male stands five and a half feet tall, with a three-span tail. In body, Istaka are much like Katheni, with nearly the same leg build. However, both Races would be insulted if you were to say so. The two Races do not get along well at all, at times fighting like . . . well, like cats and dogs. In fact, the only race the Istaka dislike more than the Katheni is Orcs. The feeling is easily reciprocated, as Orcs hate everyone.

Even though he subconsciously knew better, Reginald laid his sword down and walked over to the injured Istak. He knelt beside it and cleared his throat. "Friend, are you hurt?"

The Istak raised its head and howled. Five more Istaka jumped from the tall grass and attacked Reginald. One leapt straight onto his back, knocking him off his feet. Another landed on him and snapped at his throat just as he hit the ground.

"'A foul trick!' quoth the Hero, and launched the wolf from him with a powerful kick!" Reginald sprang to his feet in time to counter a pounce from a third wolf with a grievous barefisted blow to the Istak's jaw, sending it sprawling and yelping. "And thus did the deceitful wolves get what they so richly—"

Two Istaka working in concert attacked next, one barreling into the backs of Reginald's knees, the other jumping up and landing on Reginald's back. They almost took him down, but Reginald rolled with the hit, grabbed the two Istaka by the scruff of their necks, and carefully slammed their furred heads together as he came up.

"The Thunderous Thud of Canine Cranial Collision was music to the ears of the Hero, who now turned to seek his weapon."

The weapon in question was, in fact, in the paws of an Istak. The wolf-person was stealing it, or at least trying to. Sharp was taller than the Istak, and currently too long and heavy for even the well-muscled creature to lift. The wolf glanced at Reginald with panic in its eyes.

"Leave that be and stand your ground!" Reginald yelled.

The Istak dropped the sword and backed slowly away from it.

"Stand your own ground, Human," a voice snarled from behind Reginald.

He whirled around just in time to catch a heavy paw in the face. Reginald tumbled backward, barely keeping his balance. His antagonist was very large for an Istak, over five foot ten and muscled like an ox.

The Istak glared at Reginald. "Those are my friends you just injured. All they wanted was your horse."

Reginald dusted himself off, blood beginning to ooze from the claw-gouges on his face. He saw an Istak trying to seize Wraith's reins, but the warhorse was fending the wolf off with vicious kicks whenever the Istak got close enough to grab them.

"Actually, I need that horse," Reginald said. "He's been through enough already, and he's my only mode of transportation."

"That's too bad," the Istak said with a growl. "Since you attacked the hunting party, I will have to make you pay."

"I attacked them? I think not," Reginald said. "I stopped to help one I thought was injured and they attacked me from hiding. Besides, you are hardly the one to make me pay for anything."

The Istak snorted from his canine snout. "We'll see." He adopted a crouched fighting stance. "I am Honovi, hunt leader. You will die here, and we will eat your horse."

Reginald smiled. "I am sir Reginald Ogleby, the Crimson Slash, formerly a Hero in Good Standing with the currently defunct Guild of Heroes. I will teach you that Heroes are not to be tangled with lightly."

A look of shock crossed Honovi's muzzle, but Reginald gave him no chance to react to his last statement. He charged.

Wraith was *not* a happy warhorse.

First, he had been forced to ride in the company of a dragon. Then the indignity had been expanded to include a dragon *and* a pair of large cats. Next, he was temporarily killed—always a bother—only to be dragged back to life by an inept animal cleric. After a somewhat frightening battle—and a humiliating retreat—he had lost Reginald for nearly a month, and in the interim had been forced to carry baggage like a pack mule. That was interrupted rudely by a conjuring spell that tore him through the black nothingness without so much as a carrot or lump of sugar for his trouble.

Now, he was surrounded by bruised and hungry wolves while his rider fought a very large wolf. Snorting, he lashed out with his hooves at a nearby wolf, which dodged out of the way. This was not a good day. Wraith needed some fresh clover, badly.

"Then didst the Hero tackle the leader of the Istaka! Man and Wolf crashed to the ground in a whirl of frenetic fighting!"

"Silence, Human!" Honovi growled and sank his fangs into Reginald's shoulder.

"The Hero ripped the wolf free from his toothy hold and hefted him into the air. The Istak twisted acrobatically in midair so as to land on its paws! But to no avail, for he landed in the path of a mighty unarmed blow from the Hero's legendary fist!"

Honovi tumbled tail-over-ears and landed in a heap of dusty brown fur on the overgrown bricks. He picked himself up and backed away from Reginald. "Listen, we didn't know you were a Hero. We wouldn't have attacked if we'd known. We don't want to fight you."

"Now that you know your opponent can't be taken down by guile or weight of numbers, you're just going to give up? You can't stand to fight someone who may actually be your equal or stronger than you are? Coward!" Reginald yelled, charging again.

Honovi leapt sideways, avoiding Reginald's charge, and attempted to trip him with an extended foot-paw.

Reginald instantly modified his rush. "Seeing the attempted trip, the Hero took hold of the Istak's footpaw and didst drag him bodily across the ground!" He whirled and threw Honovi to the dirt, placing a foot on the Istak's chest. "And there we are. Victory is Mine," Reginald said, pulling back his fist for a final Heroic blow.

"*No!*"

Someone tackled Reginald from behind. It was an adult Istak, but rather small, even by Istakan standards.

"Please, please don't kill him," the attacker whined. "He's my only friend. He doesn't mean it. He's sorry. Just let him go, please!" The Istak clung to Reginald's leather jerkin.

"Well, goodness. I wasn't going to kill him." Reginald pried himself loose. "If it really means that much to you, and if he vows to stop assaulting travelers on this road . . ."

"Oh, thankyouthankyouthankyou!" the small Istak said.

"I vow no such thing." Honovi stood, clutching his side and neck. "I am not your friend, Yazi, and you are out of line, saying what I will or will not do."

The small wolf immediately dropped to the dirt, ears flattened to his head. "I'm sorry, Honovi. I wasn't thinking. Of course, you're right, it wasn't my place, I'm sorry . . ."

Honovi looked at Yazi in disgust. "Stop sniveling, and get up, you pathetic runt. And get away from that Hero. He's dangerous."

"Right, sorry, moving right now." Yazi slunk away from Reginald's side and moved over to where the larger Istaka stood.

"Not next to me, dimwit. Stand somewhere else!" Honovi growled, fur bristling. He kicked Yazi as he walked by.

Yazi slunk farther away, tail between his legs, and sat down in a miserable grey ball.

Reginald scowled. This treatment of the smaller wolf was irritating his sense of fairness. "You, Honovi. What are you going to do, then? I have defeated you in single combat—does that count for nothing?"

"It would if you weren't trespassing," Honovi said brusquely. "You're in our hunting grounds without permission, and that makes your life forfeit."

Reginald gave the Istak an amused smile. "Forfeit, you say. Fascinating. I suppose you'll be the one to take it from me, then?" he said with a chuckle.

Honovi backed a bit farther away, but growled softly. "I hardly seem capable. I have personally never been defeated before, so I dislike you from the start." He looked at the other Istaka, who were circling the apparently inedible Wraith, trying to keep the horse from escaping. Wraith looked more than likely to collapse the skull of the first Istak to touch his bridle.

"I will take you to the Pack Leader," Honovi said grudgingly. "You will ask him for permission to cross our huntinglands. You, Hero, have my pledge that we will not attempt to harm you further."

Reginald stared unflinchingly into the Istak's brown-gold eyes. "I see no reason to go with you anywhere. I have defeated you by force of arms, so my life is hardly forfeit. But," he said, holding up a finger to stifle Honovi's intended interruption, "I will accompany you nonetheless, for the sake of Honor—both yours and mine."

Honovi smiled grudgingly. "My thanks, Hero. I hope the detour will not trouble you overly."

"How far is your village?" Reginald asked.

"Not far at all!" Yazi said cheerfully. "Just a little ways into the for—"

"*Shut up, Yazi!*" Honovi said with a shout that sounded almost like a bark. "Nobody was talking to you!"

Yazi cringed. "Sorry, sorry! I won't do it again, I promise . . ."

"No, it isn't far," Honovi said to Reginald. "Our village is just inside that forest over there." He gestured to the forest in the distance that surrounded the base of the Mountains of the Morning. "We should be there in less than hour."

"All right then," Reginald said, picking up Sharp and attempting to re-sheath it. Sharp cut through the side of the scabbard. Reginald sighed. He'd have to find another one, and ridiculously oversized scabbards were annoyingly rare.

"Let us proceed."

Reginald rode Wraith at the back of the pack of Istaka down the forgotten brick road to the forest. Wraith seemed unhappy with Reginald's choice of company yet again. The midafternoon sun shone right into Reginald's eyes, causing him to squint as he rode toward his forested destination.

This detour was problematic, but in Reginald's mind it also offered opportunity. He was still headed more or less in the right direction, though he certainly was not going to make it to the Keep of Five Flames by tomorrow. Still, here he was, riding in the center of a group of one of the hardest-to-reach Races, who were also the third most xenophobic, second most territorial, and first fuzziest in the world. Perhaps he would have some opportunity to bring them around to his cause and make himself a friend of the Istaka.

After a few minutes, Yazi dropped out of the tail end of the pack and walked next to Reginald. "Hello, Sir Ogleby," the little wolf said. "My name is Yazi. You probably caught that, sorry, didn't mean to be repeating myself. Also sorry if I surprised you earlier. I was just trying to help my friend, Honovi."

Reginald looked down at Yazi. The small Istak's left ear was ragged, as if someone had bitten a chunk out of it, and a set of newly-healed claw marks showed through his fur. "Greetings, Yazi. Mine name is Reginald. I take no offense at your actions. I would do the same to protect a friend, but . . ." He lowered his voice and leaned down from Wraith toward the small Istak . . . "why do you think he is your friend? I heard how he talks to you and have seen how he treats you. I have enemies who treat me better than that!"

Yazi cringed. "It's . . . No, you have it wrong. They do like me. It's just that I do things wrong all the time, and they have to keep me in line."

"And another thing," Reginald whispered, "why do you cringe like that all time? I'm not going to hurt you."

"You won't?" A strange expression passed over Yazi's muzzle.

"Of course not! You are no threat to me, and I never hurt people without reason." A thought occurred to Reginald. "Yazi, would you like to be *my* friend?"

Yazi's eyes lit and his ears pointed straight up. "Yes, please, Sir Ogleby! I would like that very much!"

Reginald smiled, though perhaps his smile was tinged with sorrow. Yazi was a friendly soul trapped in a bad spot. It was painfully obvious to Reginald that Yazi was very low in the Istakan social hierarchy. If there was an Alpha male in this pack, Yazi was probably the pack Omega. "Well, that's settled, then." Reginald took Yazi's grey paw and shook it. "And call me Reginald."

"That makes me so happy!" Yazi wagged his tail at a frantic pace. "Did I tell you that I thought you were fantastic in that fight with Honovi? Not, of course, that I thought Honovi did badly, but you were really fast and tricky like a fox! Honovi was all acting like 'I'm the Alpha here' and you came up and *pow!*" he said, swinging a furry fist, "You showed him what his place was!"

Reginald laughed. "You talk too much, Yazi. Just like my former squire."

Yazi's face fell. "Oh, I'm sorry. I didn't mean to bore you, I'll stop right away . . ."

"No, no," Reginald hastily amended. "I meant that in a good way. He's made his mistakes, but he's a good lad. Now stop apologizing for everything. It makes you seem pathetic."

"Right, sorry, I won't . . . uh . . ." Yazi stopped, confused.

Reginald grinned. "Anyway, you remind me of my squire. My *former* squire, I should say. He says many things, sometimes so quickly that I cannot understand him. You do that as well."

Yazi scratched behind his right ear. "Oh? Where is he? Your squire, I mean."

"I don't know," Reginald said. "He's off trying to save the world in his own fashion." He chuckled. "No doubt he will do so with the same reckless bravado he does most things with. And he has to save the Kath girl as well. His mate, you see. She was kidnapped by Villains."

"Ooh," Yazi said, glancing up at the rest of the Istaka, who were walking ahead of them. "I wouldn't mention Katheni around this pack if I were you."

Reginald looked at them also, then back to Yazi. "Why not? I have heard that Istaka and Katheni often quarrel with each other, but why is it?"

"Well," Yazi said, perking up. "Honovi and Ouray, that's the tall one next to Honovi, have both fought against Katheni, and they really don't like them very much. As for every other Istaka, I don't know. We have this old legend about it, though."

"I like Old Legends. Would you tell it to me, friend?"

Yazi's tail started wagging furiously again. "You're serious? You really want to hear me tell you a story?"

Reginald straightened in his saddle and scanned the grassy horizon. No threats, other than the Istaka. And they were perhaps half an hour from the forest. At least this detour wasn't going to take too terribly long. They were almost in the shadow of the Mountains of the Morning. Reginald wished briefly that he could take to the air as the Avierie did, so that he could see the legendary tower the mountains encircled. "Certainly," he said after a moment's thought. "Get on with it, then!"

"All right, I will." Yazi cleared his throat and began his tale.

"At the Beginning of All Things, the Creator made the first Istaka and Katheni to live together in harmony. Then the Trickster, being full of guile and mischief, took upon himself the body of a dragon and conversed with Marava, the first Katheni. The Trickster told Marava of a miraculous and dazzling treasure that he could find buried beneath an oak tree. The Katheni, innocent as he was, believed the Trickster and dug beneath the oak tree.

"The Trickster then went and told Wanona, the first Istak, that a Katheni was stealing his secretly buried bones. Wanona was confused, for he knew nothing of theft. The Istak went to look at his secret stash of bones, and he discovered a puzzled Katheni, who was expecting treasure, not bones. Wanona was furious and attacked Marava. The two fought until both were near death. The Trickster laughed long and loud as he abandoned the dragon's form and floated away on the southern wind.

"The Creator saw his creations fighting each other, and He stopped the fight. He was saddened by how easily the Trickster had deceived them. In order to prevent further conflict, He took them in His hands. Wanona and his family He took in His right. Marava and his family He took in His left, and He placed them in two different lands where each could live and multiply without quarreling with the other.

"The Creator eventually took Marava and Wanona up to the skies with Him and set them to rule over their respective Races forever and ever. But they never forgot their enmity.

"When we Istaka finally invented ships, we found Katheni in another country. There have been several small wars between individual tribes over the centuries, and we generally don't get along well. I guess it's just something in our blood."

The brick road began fading into thick ferns and lichens as it veered north to enter the forest. As Yazi finished his tale, Honovi walked back to them. "If you're done now . . . We are about to enter the forest. I recommend that you dismount now, Hero. Ouray will take your horse somewhere where he will not be eaten."

"Actually," Reginald said, "wait just a moment. I think I'd like my friend to take care of my horse."

"Huh?" Yazi looked up at Reginald. "Do you mean me?"

"No, I mean Keeth. Look over there." Reginald pointed at the horizon. The shape of a dragon on the wing was growing more distinct by the second.

All the Istaka except for Yazi dove into the forest as Keeth flew in and landed heavily in the clearing.

"Greetings, Keeth," Reginald said. "Did you acquire a good meal?"

Keeth nodded his head. "That I did. I think I need a nap, though. But . . . what have we here?" The dragon looked down at Yazi. "An Istak? Is he friends with the ones hiding in the bushes there?"

Honovi stood up from behind a large bush, irate. "We were not hiding! We were . . . preparing an ambush!"

Keeth's eyes narrowed. "For whom? Not for Reginald, I hope. Only fools would attempt to ambush a Hero, much less a mature dragon."

"Leave them be, Keeth," Reginald said, patting the dragon's scaled shoulder. "I go to see their chieftain to get permission to pass through his hunting grounds on our way to the Keep. Not to mention a small matter to settle with that one, there." He gestured at Honovi. "I was wondering if you might watch Wraith for me while I'm in the forest."

"Of course I will," Keeth said.

"Thank you. Now then," Reginald said, stepping past Honovi and into the woods, "shall we go?"

Chapter 22

ELEMENTAL, MY DEAR HERO

In which Cyrus Deals with Imbalance
And Seeks another Heart

CYRUS, IN FLAMES, sat on the front step of the Keep of Fire. The Red Death stood a respectful distance away staring across the lava in the caldera of the volcano. The sheer rock walls glowed eerily red still, and the smell of sulfur pervaded the air.

"So," Red finally said, "do you think that's permanent?"

Cyrus looked at his hands. They were still made of fire, seemingly solid, but he found that whenever he touched something, he burned it, or—if it weren't flammable—his hand discorporated around it.

"You know," he said, "I'm not sure. I sure hope not. How am I supposed to hold Kris again if all I do is burn things?"

"Bushed if I know. All I know is that I want out of this friggin' volcano."

Cyrus sighed. "And how do you plan on doing that, walking?"

"Aha, I had the foresight to bring along a couple of Scrolls of Teleportation. Here," Red said, handing Cyrus a scroll.

The scroll burned to cinders in Cyrus's hand. Cyrus sighed. "Gee, that worked out wonderfully. Any other especially flammable things you'd like to hand to me?"

"Yeah, my mother's quiche. Why she thought brandy would make a good ingredient for quiche is beyond me," Red said. "Anyway, you'll have to find your own way out now. I only had two scrolls. Anyone you want me to tell about what's going on?"

Cyrus nodded. "Yeah, you can tell them that this Keep was activated by the Nameless Hero."

"That's a dumb name. A name that isn't a name?"

"Oh, shut up. I came up with it on the spot. I was under pressure," Cyrus said. "Just spread that around, will you? And see if you can help me find information on where the other Keeps are. I need more of these Heartstones." He turned a large ruby over in his hands. For some reason it was the only thing he could hold on to at the moment, probably because it was itself from the heart of the Keep of Fire. "Maybe if I get all four, I'll be back to normal."

Red clapped Cyrus on the shoulder. Then he yelped and yanked his hand back. "Sheesh," he said. "You do know that most of the old Elemental Keeps have been raided for whatever treasure they used to hold, right?"

"I . . . I didn't know that, no," Cyrus said. "I guess I'll just go look and hope that the stones are still there. I mean, I don't really have any other options."

"Well, good luck. It's kind of a long walk to any kind of civilization." Red unfurled his other scroll and started reading it. He looked back up for a second. "Oh, and stay away from firefighters." With that, the Red Death disappeared.

Cyrus sat alone for a few moments, then got up and stretched. "Well," he said to no one in particular, "time to get walking. I wonder if lava burns things made of fire?"

"No, it doesn't."

A shimmering image—Cyrus wondered if shimmering was just the 'in' thing for images this year—of Conrad appeared before him, floating a foot off the ground and pointed at a ninety-degree angle away from Cyrus.

"You have done well acquiring the first stone," Conrad said.

"Over here, Conrad," Cyrus said.

The image pivoted to face Cyrus. "It was no mean feat, considering the evil that dwelt within its walls. You certainly do not lack fighting skill. You think on your feet, and you would sacrifice yourself to save others. You may become a true Hero yet."

Cyrus hefted the Heartstone. It felt hot even to his fiery form. "Well, I got this one. Now what? Can I just fly to the next one?"

"No," Conrad said. He looked to the west. "The other is too far for you to fly to before this age begins drawing to a close. You will need to travel in the rivers of fire beneath the earth."

"How do you mean?" Cyrus asked. "You mean lava?"

Conrad's image nodded. "Step into the molten rock, Cyrus. As I said, you are blessed. It can no longer harm you."

"Okay, if you say so," Cyrus said. He took a few steps and stepped into the lava. Into his mind blasted images of a network of channels, tunnels, and floes. He could feel every place the lava was connected to. He could feel himself blending into the lava, dissolving, and . . .

Cyrus stepped out of the lava, breathing heavily. That was a rush. He wasn't sure what to make of it. It wasn't unpleasant. It felt like becoming part of something larger than himself.

"Now you see how all pieces of the world are connected," Conrad said. "Should you wish it, you could travel in an instant to any point in the world that touches the burning lifeblood of the planet."

"It feels like losing myself," Cyrus said. "I don't want to—"

"Fear not," Conrad said. "It is not absorbing you. You are choosing to temporarily join something larger than yourself. As a soldier is but one man, so you are just one bit of flame joining a greater fire. After all, if one holds two candles apart, they both burn, but if held together, they burn brighter."

Cyrus took a deep breath and looked back at the black tower behind him. "Okay," he said. "So where do I go?"

"On an island far to the west, you will find the Tower of Water, and there you will meet your next challenge." Conrad's shimmering image began to fade. "Remember that there are things in this world that require not a sharp blade but a sharp mind."

Cyrus was left alone. He took a deep breath. This was complicated. But he had to do this to help Kris, didn't he? Conrad hadn't said, but it seemed like he was being prepared for something. But what?

He sighed. It wouldn't do him any good to try and puzzle it out now. Maybe once he acquired another Heartstone, the answer would become clearer.

Cyrus stepped into the lava once more. This time he stopped to think the entire network out. It looked like it connected to the very center of the world, and from there to every volcano, lava floe, and artificially imported lava pool in the world. If he mentally moved toward a source of lava, he could feel and see things start to warp and bend around him, much like a teleportation spell.

So he tried it. Cyrus picked a lava vent near the center of the continent of Lorimar and stepped toward it. Everything around him blurred red and gold, and he felt as if he'd traveled an incredible distance with a single step, like he was wearing Seven League Boots. Only if normal Seven League Boots took one seven leagues in a single step, then this mode of transportation was a ten thousand league boot.

And Cyrus emerged from a miniature volcano.

On the bottom of a lake.

The water seared Cyrus like acid. He screamed, feeling the water quenching his skin, his breath, his very life. He leapt up, shooting toward the surface in a bubble of superheated steam. He tried to harness a water line to push himself out, but he found himself completely unable to find one, despite being in a lake. Was it because he was made of fire?

He shot out of the water like a steaming missile, haphazardly grabbing whatever Air energy he could muster. He used it to throw himself at an island with a tower of blue-flecked marble on it.

He smashed into the dirt and lay there, steaming and flickering in front of the edifice. The architecture, Cyrus noted through his rattled brain, looked a great deal like that of the tower Cyrus had just left.

"That was impressive," said a voice from above him. "It isn't every day I see a Fire Elemental foolish enough to try swimming lessons."

Cyrus looked up. Standing over him was a large man in layered plate mail. Aside from the man's face, which was framed by long, straight blond hair, there wasn't an inch of skin showing anywhere through the purple-tinted sheets of metal.

"T-the Purple Paladin?" Cyrus said, pushing himself off the ground. "Wh-what are . . ."

The man looked down, then picked Cyrus off the ground with a gauntleted hand. "You don't look like a normal Elemental. What are you, exactly?" For some reason, the flames around Cyrus, though dim, seemed to have no effect on the Hero.

"C-Cyrus Solburg," Cyrus managed. "Once apprenticed to the Crimson Slash."

Purple dropped Cyrus on the ground in surprise. "By the six shrieking notes of Pandemoniums!" he exclaimed. "It *is* you! I haven't seen you since you were just a lad, but . . ." he looked Cyrus up and down . . . "I don't recall you being made of fire last time I saw you."

"Oh, this old thing?" Cyrus said, getting up and dusting himself off. "Call it a present from the universe. I've got an elemental Heartstone." He held up the ruby, glad he'd held on to it and not left it on the bottom of the lake. Apparently being made of fire made even plain water deadly. Retrieving the gem would have been lethal, or at the very least, exceptionally painful. "My . . . uh . . . current teacher says I need them all to master my magic use."

"Gotta find 'em all, eh?" Purple said with a tired smile. "It's always the Seven Sacred Sage Stones or the Five Fire Flowers of Fa'har, or the Nine Nifty Neo-Negative Nova Nunchaku. What is it with you younger Heroes and your Numeric Collections?"

"Fetch Quest," Cyrus said with a grimace. "Everybody has to do 'em eventually."

The two lapsed into silence for a few moments. The waters of the lake lapped at the pebbled shoreline, and a bird called from somewhere far away. The lake was huge. Cyrus could barely see one side of it, and he couldn't see any of the others, though he thought there might be mountains to the north. It was almost like an ocean. The only reason he could tell that it wasn't was because the water was fresh, not salt. Across the the lake, on the shore he *could* see, he noticed a small village with thatched roofs.

White puffy clouds scudded across the afternoon sky. Apparently Conrad had been right: while it was night when he had left, it was still day here on the western end of the world. It was probably still even the same day.

"Anyway," Cyrus finally said, looking back at the tower. "I guess I'd better go in there and get the Heartstone."

"It's not there," Purple said.

"What?" Cyrus grabbed Purple's arm. "It can't be gone! I need it to rescue Kris!"

The Purple Paladin shrugged. "I was just inside, and there's not a scrap of treasure, not a single useful artifact, not so much as a sheet of parchment to help win this war. I should have expected as much. This is the easiest of the four Elemental Keeps to get into, after all."

"Isn't half of it underwater?"

"Don't half the mages in the world know how to cast *Fishy Lungs*?"

Cyrus chuckled. "Valid point, good sir. I've kind of been tending to my own affairs recently. Can you catch me up on how are things going with the Guild?"

"Poorly," Purple said with a scowl. "We were forced to flee, and our checkpoint in Rondheim was destroyed. Very few Heroes have made it to our retreat location on Clawstrike Island, I'm afraid."

Cyrus winced. "Ouch. Do you know if . . . uh, the Crimson Slash is okay?"

Purple shook his head. "He hasn't been seen since he single-handedly piloted an attack boat and held off that flying city to help some of us escape Rondheim. But he's a stalwart fellow. I have no doubt he'll turn up eventually."

"Yeah," Cyrus said, looking down. "I really hope so."

Purple clapped his gauntlets together. "Well. Guild aside, you are still on fire. How were you planning on fixing that?"

Cyrus examined his flaming hands. "By grabbing the rest of the Heartstones. This one caused my current transformation. Maybe if I get all four, I can get back in balance again."

Purple pointed across the shoreline at a rowboat beached nearby. "Well, if you wouldn't burn a hole in my boat, I would offer you a ride to the far shore." He pointed toward the village. "Perhaps someone there will know where the Heartstone from this tower has gotten to."

Cyrus started to reach for an Air line, but found himself too exhausted from being, ironically, almost burned to death by water. "Yeah," he said weakly, "I could probably use a ride. Is your armor magic?"

Purple knocked his gauntleted hand against the dark purple breastplate. "This suit of armor was forged by Strife himself, enchanted by the mystic hermit Balfour, and blessed by the patron saints of combat themselves: Saint Helm and Saint Greaves."

"Okay . . ." Cyrus said. "But is it magic?"

Purple rolled his eyes. "Yes, yes, it is magic, Cyrus. The breastplate is built to withstand any attack, physical or magical. The gauntlets forever hold any weapon without fear of being disarmed. The boots can tread across caltrops, skim over acid, and even step upon the water. The greaves grant faster movement on the battlefield. And the pauldrons increase my physical might beyond compare." He glared at Cyrus. "So yes, they are magic."

"Would you say your breastplate is immune to fire?"

"Yes, and . . ." Purple stopped and raised his eyebrows. "Oh, no, you are *not* using the Holy Breastplate of Balfour as a seat cushion."

Twenty minutes later, the two of them landed on the far shore near a small fishing village. The buildings seemed to be mostly made of woven grass and thatch, with very few stones to be seen anywhere and no metal whatsoever. An old Elven man sat on a stool near one of the huts, mending a net. He gawked at the knight in purple and the young man on fire as they disembarked.

Cyrus stepped off the purple breastplate onto the sand, which glassed under his feet. "Thanks," he said, handing the armor back to its owner.

Purple grumbled and snatched the breastplate, muttering something about sacrilege and children in this day and age and what was the world coming to.

The two walked into the village toward what looked to be a bazaar at the north end of town. About fifty people, Elves mostly, stood about chatting or griping about some sort of war that was going on and complaining that the prices at the bazaar were too high on account of it. Many stopped their conversations to stare at Cyrus for a moment, but just as quickly returned to their conversations. Apparently the shoppers at the bazaar were used to the bizarre.

The air smelled of fish and spices, smoke and livestock. Cloth shades had been set up over most of the booths, and a short distance away a caravan of traveling merchants rested. The occupants of said caravan had their wares spread out on blankets and under tents near their canvas-covered wagons.

Most of the merchants were Elven, but a few stood out from the rest. One was a Minotaur, a hulking bull-man, selling what looked like ornately painted porcelain plates. He looked like a disaster waiting to happen. Another was an enormous dark-scaled Ransha who was for some reason poking a stick at a fat and uncomfortable looking white goat.

The owner of the goat was an Elf wearing clothes of woven flax, most probably a Hippie Elf or a Grass Elf. He was swearing in Elven at the large Ransha, who seemed not to understand a word of what was being yelled at him.

Cyrus walked up to the Ransha. "Excuse me," he said. "I think he wants you to stop poking his goat."

The Ransha looked down at Cyrus. "Ashraki non narro Central," he said, an innocent and very toothy smile on his face. "Sermo et lepus."

"I've been telling him that for ten minutes now!" the Elf shouted. "This lummox only babbles that Ranshan at me, and he won't leave my poor Buster alone!"

"Ah, excuse me, gentlemen," said a voice from one of the merchant stalls. "Ashrak said, 'I do not speak Central. Please talk to the rabbit.'"

Cyrus looked over to where the voice came from. A large white rabbit sat on top of one of the tables chewing on a tuft of celery. Also on the table were various dangerous looking weapons ranging from barbed chains to broadswords.

"Ashrak speaks Ranshan, Istask, and Avier," the rabbit said. "He's very smart, for a Ransha. Those are complicated and obscure languages."

"But he didn't learn Central?" Cyrus asked, walking up to the table. "You know, the most common language in the world?"

The rabbit shook its head, and its ears flopped about. "I said he was smart. Intelligence does not always equal common sense."

"Talking rabbit," Purple said, pointing at the rabbit.

"Yes, yes, I'm a talking rabbit," said the talking rabbit irritably. "And you're a flabbergasted Human. Stop pointing. It's rude."

Purple kept pointing. "Talking . . . rabbit."

Cyrus lowered Purple's arm and then gestured over his shoulder. "So what's the story with the goat-poking going on over here?"

The rabbit turned to look at the Ransha. "Oh, that goat ate one of our tablecloths while we weren't looking, and with it, one of our magical gemstones. Ashrak got the idea to scare the . . . hrm, to scare the . . . gem . . . out of the goat."

"Oh," Cyrus said. "Clever."

"How is the rabbit talking?" Purple said, lifting the tablecloth and looking under the table. "I see no puppet masters or anything of the like . . ."

The rabbit gave an exasperated sigh. "That is because I am not a puppet. I am a magical aberration. You try getting pulled out of a Hat of Alarming Carrying Kapacity a few hundred times and see if some random magic doesn't wear off on *you*."

"So the magician who owned you was somewhat of a H.A.C.K, then?" Cyrus said with a chuckle.

"Oh, goodie," the rabbit said. "Another comedian. Would you care to buy something, sir? Our weapons are the finest in Lorimar. Hand-forged by that goat-poker over there and enchanted by myself. Perhaps a fireproof one for you, sir?"

"Actually I'm looking for something that may have been scavenged from that tower over there." Cyrus pointed across the lake at the Tower of Water. "A gem, maybe about this big?" He held up the Heartstone of Fire.

"Good gracious!" the rabbit said. "That looks just like the one the goat ate, only red!"

"Of course it does," Purple said with a scowl. "Of all the magic gemstones a goat could accidentally eat, it would have to be that one."

"Oh, dear, oh, dear," the rabbit said, worriedly wiggling his nose. "That must mean you are the Nameless Hero."

"What?" Cyrus took a step back and tried to draw a nonexistent sword. That seemed to be happening to him with annoying frequency lately. "How did you—"

"Well, the man who came here and dropped the gem off paid me five hundred gold pieces to hang onto it until the Nameless Hero came by to pick it up," the rabbit said. "And here you are looking for it."

Cyrus looked over at the goat. "Who did you say dropped it off?"

"Oh, he didn't say his name. He was a tall fellow in a cloak, had his arms all wrapped up like they had been burned or something. Very heavy footprints, though, and I could hear the sound of metal about him, and I mean more than just his armor."

"By the Twelve, I hope that's not Voshtyr," Cyrus said. "But . . . probably not. He would more likely have taken the stone for himself. But what can we do about getting it out of that goat? Can't we just pay the farmer and kill the goat?"

"I heard that!" the Elf shouted. "No one touches my Buster! She's my livelihood, she is!"

"Your girl sheep is named Buster?" Purple asked.

The Elf just gave him a mean look.

"Well," Cyrus said, "if we can't kill the goat, that's . . . problematic. I need that stone." He scratched the back of his head. "So he's just poking it with a stick. Why?"

The rabbit hopped back to his stick of celery. "Trying to scare it. I tried telling it that income taxes were going up by three percent, but that didn't do it. So Ashrak's been following it around for the last ten minutes, poking it."

"Cyrus!" Purple said, nudging him. "The goat has just—"

"Nath!" shouted the Ransha. "Agnus effluvo!"

Purple chuckled. "Indeed, it effluvoed all over the place."

"My gem!" said the rabbit, and scampered off the table and over to where his compatriot stood.

Cyrus followed. The fat white goat, now looking slightly less uncomfortable, was walking away with the Elf, happily munching on the stick it had been poked with. On the ground where it had stood was a large messy pile of excrement, with a barely visible sapphire buried in it.

"Don't goats normally do . . . uh . . . pellets?" Cyrus said with a wry face.

"It *was* a magical gemstone," the rabbit said slowly. "Lots of water properties. Very powerful. Probably a potent laxative."

"Sounds like the Water stone," Cyrus said.

Purple raised an eyebrow. "It very well could be. Pick it up, and let's have a look."

"What?" Cyrus said. "I'm not reaching into a pile of goat effluvo!"

"Don't look at me," the rabbit said. "I don't have opposable thumbs."

"Ashraki non tactus effluvo," the Ransha said. "Yecch."

Cyrus chuckled. "Oh, this is great. Listen, I'm *made of fire*. If I touch that stuff, it'll bake harder than your grandmother's cornbread. You get it out, Purple."

"I am *not* dipping the Holy Gauntlets of Balfour in a pile of goat *bok!*" Purple growled.

"So you'd go after it bare-handed, but not with the gauntlets?" Cyrus said.

"Of course I'd sacrifice my own cleanliness in order to maintain the purity of the Holy Gauntlets of Balfour," Purple said. "They are the most pure, untainted . . . Oh, no, you are *not* getting me to . . ."

One unpleasant moment and half a bar of soap later, Purple chucked the sapphire at Cyrus's head. "There, take the cursed thing," he said. "And good riddance."

"Thanks, Purple," Cyrus said with an impish grin. He held up the two Heartstones and looked at them. "You know, these look practically identical except for the color. Same cut and everything. Say, Nath?" He turned to the rabbit. "That is your name, right? That's what the Ransha called you."

"Nath Quickpaw, merchant extraordinaire," the rabbit said. "What can I do for you?"

"Wait, are you a Villain, then?" Cyrus said. "The name scheme's kind of . . ."

"Descriptive?" Nath said. "I am a Speed Mage, after all. But not a Villain."

"Fair enough," Cyrus said. He leaned on the table, accidentally setting the tablecloth to smolder. "These look like some pretty good weapons you have here. I take it you are doing a lot of business these days?"

The rabbit shrugged, which looked very strange on a quadruped. "Well, I've done better. Ashrak's doing fine since there's a lot of demand for pointy objects these days, but my own part of the business has suffered, because usually only Heroes have enough gold to afford Enchanted Blades and the like. And Heroes have been scarce lately."

"Sounds like you could use an investor," Cyrus said. "Here, take my card." He reached into one of the pouches on his belt and pulled out a card. It burned to ashes instantly. "Oh." Cyrus looked at the ash. "Well, I was going to offer you a hard copy, but it looks like if one of my possessions leaves my person, it's subject to burning."

"Your property is so hot you can't even give it away," Nath said, wiggling his nose. "So whom are you investing for?"

"My name's Cyrus Solburg, co-founder of Dragon Investing, LLC."

"I believe I've heard of Dragon Investing, but LLC?"

"Large Lizard Company. Long story." Cyrus stretched and looked out over the lake. "Anyway, you and Ashrak there make something that's already worth investing in, and is going to be in high demand as soon as I can help get the Heroes Guild back on track to kicking Voshtyr's posterior. Heroes are going to make a comeback, and they will need weapons. I'm willing to invest twenty thousand gold pieces in your business. What do you say?"

Nath almost fell off the table. "Twen . . . twenty thousand . . . My goodness, of course, of course! I could research putting *Hurry Up* on a weapon permanently! The Green Falcon's been asking me about that for years!" The rabbit hopped around in a tight circle of glee. "That, my dear fellow, sounds like an excellent idea. What do you ask in return?"

"Well, I know that the Heroes are going to need weapons—and soon. If you agree to set up a magic armament store on Clawstrike Island, and if you agree to pay Dragon Investing, LLC thirty percent of your net earnings for the next five years, the money is yours."

"Sounds steep," Nath said, hopping up onto the head of a warhammer. "But it would take me years to save that much on my own. I think, if we tweaked the details of the contract a bit, it will be quite acceptable."

"Great. Now all I need is a sword," Cyrus said. "Luckily, you sell those."

"Indeed I do," Nath said. "What would you like?"

"Do you have any that can handle instant, massive changes of temperature and elemental form without weakening?"

"This one might fit that bill." The rabbit hopped along the table until he reached a grey-green sword with a spread-winged dragon on the hilt. "This fine weapon is made of Orichalc, the second rarest and most durable material in the world.

Cyrus tilted his head. "What's the rarest?"

"Oh, Hellsteel, but you'd literally have to take one of Dante's tours to get some. And trust me, it's not worth it." The rabbit shivered. "At any rate, Orichalc can handle abrupt changes in temperature from icy cold to blazing hot without any damage to the integrity of the metal. It is invulnerable to most acids, has a tensile strength a Minotaur couldn't bend, and holds an edge like a tax collector holds his bags of money."

"Sounds perfect," Cyrus said. "Hey, Purple?"

"Yes?" The Purple Paladin turned back to face the two of them. He'd been looking at some Orcish vases on the Minotaur's pottery cart. "What can I do?"

Cyrus grinned sheepishly. "Lend me some cash?"

After a Heroic amount of grumbling, the Purple Paladin paid for Cyrus's new sword.

"Pleasure doing business with you, good sir!" Nath said, putting one fuzzy paw forward.

Cyrus chuckled and waved his flaming hand at the rabbit. "That's probably not a great idea. Unless you're fireproof."

"Hardly," the rabbit said. "Besides, that's my lucky foot, anyway." He went back to munching on his stalk of celery. "Good luck on beating up the bad guys!"

A few minutes later, Cyrus sat on the bank of the lake holding the two gemstones in his palms. "Well, I'm still made of fire. I thought maybe having another Heartstone would change me at least a little." Cyrus sighed. "I guess fire is just my dominant trait?"

"I don't know." Purple sat on a large chunk of driftwood a short distance away. "It's magic. Like your mentor was always saying, I have little to no use for it."

"Except for your super-awesome magic armor of Balfour."

"That doesn't count," Purple said with a scowl.

"And your magical sword."

"Still doesn't count."

"And whatever beneficial or healing spells your friends use on you."

"All right, all right, whelp! I do enjoy the benefits of magic. There, are you happy?" He glowered at Cyrus, then threw Cyrus's new sword at the young Hero's head. "Take your *kharestin* sword and stop bothering me."

Cyrus tossed the two gems into one hand and snatched his sword with the now-free hand. Flames licked around the hilt, but the sword didn't seem damaged. "Ha, you missed. Wha—?" Cyrus felt a rapid change wash over him, and the sword fell through his hand. He felt a chill run up where his spine should be, and all at once, the fire around him went out. Instead of a body of fire, Cyrus now had a body of superheated steam.

Purple fell back off the log. "How strange," he said, brushing himself off. "Now what have you done?"

Cyrus sighed, and it sounded like the hissing of water in a hot skillet. "I think we just made it worse." He looked at the two gems sitting together in the palm of his hand. Except there weren't two gems anymore. The ruby and sapphire were gone. They had been replaced by an amethyst of the exact same size and weight of one of the stones he'd previously held. There was no other stone to be seen.

"Well, good luck on that one," Purple said, flapping the last of the sand from his armor. "I have much to attend to. Just don't go after the Heart of Air next, or you will more than likely discorporate permanently."

"Thanks, Purple," Cyrus said downheartedly. "You saved me a lot of time. Remind me to pay you back one of these days."

Purple put a fist over his heart and bowed slightly. "I depart. Shall I tell Sir Ogleby of your condition?"

Cyrus looked away. "Uh, no. But . . . if you do see him?" He looked back. "Tell him I said sorry, will you?"

Purple smiled. "The bond between a Hero and his Apprentice never truly breaks," he said. "It can be dampened or stretched to the breaking point by the actions of either. Some have even slid into Villainy, and yet the bond remains. I think your apology will be well-received."

"I hope so, Purple, I really hope so."

Chapter 23

From Pansy to Paladin

*In which Yazi gets an Extreme Heroic Makeover
And Reginald Receives News to which
He Does Not Want to Respond*

REGINALD WALKED THROUGH the darkling forest surrounded by Istaka. Most of them had been remarkably silent since their thrashing—save Yazi, who chattered constantly. The little wolf stopped talking only when another Istak threatened him, which was frequently, but even then was silent for a short time only.

Reginald heaved a heavy sigh. The animated little wolf was more interesting than his other traveling companions, to be sure, but at least the surly and defeated Istaka did not talk quite so much.

"Anyway, we're almost there," Yazi said, "so I'd probably better quiet down. Some of the people at the village don't like me as much as my friends here do. Talk to you later!" The small Istak darted to the back of the party.

The narrow path they were following gradually widened into a large forest clearing containing several dozen huts and scattered bonfires. The Istaka village.

The huts turned out to be tents of all shapes and sizes, from small and square to tall and conical. All were decorated with pictures depicting scenes of hunts and battles. Istak cubs darted in and out of the tents wrestling and tripping over themselves, overseen by their watchful mothers and siblings. In a cooking pit near the center of the village roasted an impressively large deer, and the smell of cooking meat mingled with the scent of leather tents and churned-up earth.

The Istaka that noticed Reginald's arrival and presence in their village bristled. In either fear or anger, Reginald couldn't tell. Females herded their pups away from him, and the males stepped in front of their tents as if to deny him entrance. Reginald shrugged. He didn't know what Honovi had told them, but it couldn't have been good. He had been expecting just such a welcome, or the lack thereof, as the Istak were known to be somewhat of a reclusive Race.

Honovi nudged Reginald's arm. "This way," the Istak said, headed for the large hut in the center of the village. Reginald followed.

As soon as they arrived, Honovi ducked inside the hut. Reginald heard muffled voices speaking for several minutes. Finally, Honovi came back out. "The chief will see you now."

Reginald entered.

A small fire on the floor illuminated the sparsely-furnished tent, the smoke rising through a hole in the roof. Two Istak males stood at the back of the room, and a silver-furred wolf sat on a wicker chair between them.

Reginald bowed to the elder Istak. "Greetings. Mine name is Sir Reginald Ogleby. I seek passage through your hunting grounds."

The Istak stood stiffly to his feet and returned Reginald's bow. "I am Helush-Ka, leader of this pack. I understand that you are a Hero and that you defeated Honovi's entire hunting band. I was told you attacked them with no provocation and almost slaughtered them all."

Reginald started to object but the old Istak held up a paw to silence him.

"But I know how Honovi cherishes his image, and I know of his tendency to exaggerate." A smile twitched at the corners of the Istak's silvered muzzle. "Your victory is quite impressive by itself. What is more impressive to me is that despite your superior strength, you still ask my permission to cross our land, when it is painfully obvious that there is no way we could stop you."

"It's common courtesy, Helush-Ka," Reginald replied. "If everyone did whatever they wanted based on how strong they were, it would result in pure anarchy. Someone must obey the rules and set an example for the rest."

Helush-Ka nodded. "You are correct. Based on this alone, I would let you pass. However, you have caused some small disturbance with your defeat of Honovi. Honovi is one of several young males who may soon become Alpha wolves, and this defeat will jeopardize his position."

"I see," Reginald said. "I am on somewhat of a Blessed Quest that involves the friendship of many Races. What does this caste dispute entail? I do not wish to make enemies of anyone." His eyes narrowed. "Well, perhaps enemies of a few, but no one of your tribe. How can I help settle this dispute?"

"Honovi wishes for his brother Mantuka to avenge him," Helush-ka said, laying a paw over his eyes and looking incredibly tired. "Since you are not of this pack, I cannot command you to fight him, but I do request it of you. If you do not, then the top of our pack structure is disrupted. If you will fight him, you will have safe passage, no matter the outcome of the fight."

Reginald thought for a moment. Two days lost, but this was a chance at great diplomacy with the Istaka, a chance he might not have again.

"I accept," he finally said. "But I do have one question for you. That small wolf in Honovi's band—what is his story?"

"Yazi?" Helush-Ka said. "He was the runt of a litter and is now the pack Omega. It is sad, but his small stature and slight build ensure that he will remain there. Why do you ask?"

Reginald's shrugged. "Curiosity. So, when shall I fight this Mantuka?"

"Two nights from tonight. Mantuka is returning tomorrow from a trading journey amongst the Humans, and he will need time to rest before your conflict. For tonight, I invite you to share the hospitality of this village. Honovi will show you to a house. The meal is in an hour. I hope you enjoy wild game. At least one of our hunting bands was successful." The Istakan elder smiled. "We always treat our guests well."

Even if you plan to kill them in a few days, Reginald thought.

"Sir Ogleby? Are you awake?"

Reginald stirred, squinting against the early morning sunlight invading his dim tent. "Who's there?" he asked groggily, reaching for his sword.

"Oh, I'm so sorry! I really didn't mean to wake you. I'll just come back later. Sorry about that!"

Reginald sighed and sat up in his bedroll. "Come in, Yazi. I needed to wake up anyway."

The small Istak padded into the hut and let the flap close behind him. "I really didn't mean to—"

"Yazi, stop apologizing for everything," Reginald said. "Apologizing once for a mistake is fine. In fact, it is good manners, and I do it myself. However, when you apologize three or four times for every insignificant thing, it sounds less like apologizing and more like groveling. If you constantly grovel, you will never rise above pack Omega."

"But I would never—" Yazi winced. "Wait, you know I'm Omega? Is it that obvious?"

"Painfully." Reginald began putting his shirt on. "You take abuse from every Istak in the pack without complaint. Only an Omega would do that."

Yazi sat cross-legged on the dirt floor of the tent. He sighed and stared at Reginald's back for a moment. "You have an amazing amount of scars, Sir Ogleby. How did you get so many?"

"I told you to call me Reginald." He glanced down at his torso. He did have quite the collection of scars, he noted. He hadn't even checked them recently, and he had certainly lost count. He finished donning his shirt and turned to the little Istak. "I fight for a living, Yazi. It's what I do. But no matter how good you are, you will get hit by something or other eventually. For me, the scars are a reminder that I am not invincible. And when you've fought for as long as I have, you've had plenty of time to catch your share of stray arrows and the like."

"I wish I could learn how to fight well." Yazi sighed and began scratching himself behind his right ear. "Maybe if I got a bit better, Taki's father would acknowledge me."

A smile cracked Reginald's lips. "Who, may I ask, is Taki?"

Yazi looked embarrassed. "Her name's Takala, and she's the most beautiful girl in the world." His tail swished back and forth on the hard-packed dirt, launching miniature swirls of dust across the tent.

"And you can't possibly get her attention because you're pack Omega?"

"Right. Well, not really. See, Taki—I call her that—she's the daughter of a Beta, and she's already got a suitor: Pimne. She deserves better than Pimne, though. I don't think it would really matter who she would be mated to, as long as it wasn't him."

Reginald buckled on his large belt. "And why is that?"

Yazi looked away. "He's mean and cruel to everybody. I don't mind when he hurts me. It's my place. But he wounds animals for the fun of it, and he supposedly killed one of his sisters when they were growing up. I don't want anything bad to happen to Taki. Just the thought of Pimne hurting her makes my blood boil."

"As well it should," Reginald said, straightening his attire and brushing it down. "Any man who would not be infuriated by the mistreatment of a lady is no kind of man at all."

"But there's nothing I can do to prevent it," Yazi said, hanging his head. "By pack law, her father has to choose a mate for her within the next two days. Pimne is the only one who's got a chance so far. I'd challenge him, but Pimne fights better than I do. Everybody fights better than I do. If I challenged him, I would be dead, and he would still get Takala."

Reginald placed his right hand on Yazi's head. "How about this, then: I teach you how to defeat this Pimne, and in return you protect Miss Takala from ever being harmed. Do we have an accord?"

Yazi looked up, eyes sparkling with hope. "Are you serious? You'd really help me like that?"

"Of course, lad. In this situation, a Hero could do nothing less."

Reginald spent the rest of the day training Yazi in unarmed combat. Lacking the time for thorough training, he instead focused on basic strategy and a few useful wrestling moves.

It was early afternoon. Reginald sat in the grass beside a sandy fighting pit the Istaka used for training, talking to the small Istak.

"You're very quick, Yazi, and hard to get a hold on. Use your size to your advantage. A small, quick opponent often bests a stronger, slower one." He made a gesture that involved trying to catch one of his meaty hands in the other, and missing. "It occurs to me that I've forgotten to ask you what kind of fight it will be."

Yazi grimaced. "It starts off psychological, with a lot of bluffing and trash talk involved. However, once the actual fight starts, it's a no-holds-barred, fangs-and-claws brawl. It's to the death, unless one of us yields first. If the lower-ranked combatant—that's me—wins, he takes the social place of his opponent. If he loses, the winner chooses what happens to him. The usual choices are either a demotion in status or banishment. In my case, since I'm already an Omega, the third option . . . would be death."

"You cannot afford to lose, then," Reginald said. "No holds barred, eh? Then it sounds as if nothing I teach you would be against the rules."

"That's because there *are* no rules!" Yazi said, grinning.

"Exactly," Reginald said, flexing his shoulder. "So what you must do is fight as little like a wolf as possible."

Yazi's grin disappeared. "What?"

Reginald stood up, brushing grass from the seat of his trousers. "Pimne will be expecting a short fight with a short wolf. So you need to give him something he won't anticipate: a longer fight with a wolf who doesn't fight like one. Combine the things I've been teaching you with how you naturally fight, and it will catch him off-guard. After all, it's unlikely an Istakan fighter who relies on claws and fangs would know how to counter any gambit used by a Heroic Boxer."

"I'm not a boxer, I'm a wolf," Yazi said. "Awooo!"

"Not your pedigree, Yazi—your fighting style," Reginald said. "I think if you're clever and use attacks that aren't common to Istakan fighters, you may attain the advantage you need to beat down a larger opponent."

Yazi shook his head. "No, never. You think I can beat him?"

"I would say yes, if you finished it quick enough, possibly. But from what I've seen of how you act, no. Not a chance—unless you can win the first part," Reginald said, tapping his head. "You're so conditioned to being Omega that when you come up against a higher-ranked wolf, you automatically submit and back down."

"No, I won't. You'll see!"

"*Don't contradict me!*" Reginald bellowed.

Yazi cowered. "Sorry! So sorry, I didn't mean to—"

"See, that's exactly what I mean," Reginald said, lowering his voice. He put his hand on Yazi's head and ruffled the wolf's fuzzy ears. "Every time a higher-ranked wolf snaps at you, you go into groveling mode. I cannot train that out of you in a single day, but begin to heed how you react to others. Subordinancy has been beaten into you, and now you must fight it out of you. Start thinking like an Alpha: nobody barks at you and gets away with it."

Yazi seemed to stand up taller. He took a hearty breath. "Right. I will. If it will keep Pimne from hurting Taki, I can do anything! Not only that, but if I beat him I take his place as a Beta, and then Taki's father will have to accept me as a suitor for his daughter!"

Reginald grabbed Yazi around the neck with his arm. "Excellent. Now, back to your training. This is how you break free from someone who has a lock on your neck . . ."

Reginald slept soundly that night, as he always did after a good workout. He would perhaps be sore in the morning, but not as sore as little Yazi would be. Reginald had given the Istak quite the drubbing. It was in sport, but when training, a teacher could not afford to go easy on his student if the student was to succeed.

His restful sleep was cut short because of a warning from his bladder. Reginald sat up, back stiff from the day's activities, and stepped outside to relieve himself. He was returning to his tent when a flicker of movement caught his eye.

He saw Yazi dart furtively from behind a tent and into the woods.

Intrigued, Reginald followed, treading as softly as he could.

The forest was beautiful at night. Crickets chirruped from hidden homes in the bushes, and he could hear an owl hooting a ways off through the trees. Moonlight filtered down through the tree canopy leaving dappled patches of light scattered across the surfaces of fallen logs, large rocks, and the ground cover. It gave the forest an almost dreamlike quality. There was enough moonlight to see, but just barely.

Reginald trailed the little wolf for a few minutes, until Yazi abruptly crouched and wriggled silently into the bushes, disappearing. Puzzled, Reginald peered through the brush and into a forest glade.

In the midst of the clearing, an Istakan female sat on a fallen log, her pure white coat dazzling even in the filtered moonlight. She sat as if waiting for someone, and she kept glancing down another path. Finally, she heard something, and she stood to greet her awaited. But judging by her expression and the way she recoiled, her visitor was not the person she'd been expecting.

A mottled grey-and-black wolf stepped into the clearing, grinning toothily. "Hello, Takala. What a pleasant surprise to find you here on such a fine night. It must be a sign." He took the white wolf's paw and kissed it.

Takala pulled her paw back, shuddering. "Good . . . good evening, Pimne . . . What . . . what do you want?"

Pimne put a paw over his chest. "Oh, Takala, you wound me. I came to see you. You in all your moonlit splendor," he said, taking Takala by her shoulders and seating her once more firmly on the log. "What male could resist your beauty?"

"Anyone who is not my mate," Takala snapped, writhing free of Pimne's grasp. "You are hardly that."

"Not yet," Pimne smirked, sitting and stroking Takala's tail. "But your father has only two days left to choose your mate, and I am the only worthy one. It is all but certain."

Takala snatched her tail from the mottled wolf's grasp. "You? Worthy? Ha! I think not. You sniff around all females. You steal the prey of the weak. And you kill your own kin. How are you worth—"

A heavy grey paw struck Takala across the muzzle, cutting her sentence short. Pimne shook his head. "I would not say such things, my beloved," he said, eyes narrowing. "They ill become a female of your beauty."

Reginald started forward, only to stop as he saw movement out of the corner of his eye. He saw Yazi crouching beneath a bush on the far side of the clearing, twitching as if trying and failing to find the courage to leap from his concealment.

Takala's eyes burned with feminine wrath. "Does the truth ill become beauty, then?" she growled softly, "or are you incapable of facing that truth?" Takala abruptly swung her own paw at Pimne.

Pimne caught Takala's paw without apparent effort, and twisted. Takala yelped, sinking to her knees. With a brief one-two motion, Pimne slapped the wolf-girl twice more, then dropped her. "You ought to know better. Defying me will bring you nothing but unhappiness," Pimne snarled. "As you will soon find out. Two days. Two days and you are mine!" With that, he disappeared into the woods.

Reginald, feeling his brow creased in his most opprobrious and righteous scowl, glanced at Yazi again. This time the small wolf almost made it from his hiding place, but after a moment, he slunk back down into the brush.

Takala sat quite still for a time, kneeling in the dirt, tears trickling their way down her snow-white muzzle. Abruptly, she rose, dashing off into the woods, her sobs clearly audible.

Yazi and Reginald stood simultaneously, and shock registered on Yazi's muzzle. "R-Reginald? What are you doing here?"

"You just *let* him do that to her?" Reginald said, scowling at his fur-covered protégé. "Why didn't you try to save her?"

"I . . . I'm just a coward," Yazi mumbled, slumping to the ground and putting his head between his grey-furred knees. "I tried to get up, I really did. The training you've given me told me that I could stop him, but the rest of me said no, I couldn't. And then I thought of what would happen if by some freak chance I *did* win. The pack would have killed me or thrown me out to be a lone wolf." He sighed. "But I can't let Pimne treat Taki like that! I just can't stand it!" Fierce tears sprang to the little wolf's eyes. "I'd take the punishment, just to keep her from that . . . that . . ."

"That craven, crook-pated clotpole?" Reginald asked, kneeling and placing an arm across Yazi's shaking shoulders. "He's that and worse. If I hadn't been expecting you to leap to Takala's defense, I would have torn that mottled *pezevenk* limb from limb. However, I do wonder what you were doing out here at such a late hour, my young friend."

Yazi shrugged, a slightly embarrassed grin decking his muzzle. "I was coming out here to talk to Taki. We've done it ever since we were pups. We'd sneak off into the woods at night and play, because her parents wouldn't let us play together in the daytime. I was always her champion, and she my princess, like we'd read about in some Human books."

He looked at the moonlight filtering through the dense foliage. "The last few years have been different, though. We began to see more in each other, in a different way. It was impossible for us to be together officially, though," Yazi added, all trace of grin gone. "I was a runt, an Omega in the making, and she was the daughter of a Beta. Then came the day when she learned that she was to be mated within the year."

"And she had no choice?" Reginald asked.

"None," Yazi gritted. "She met me here the night she found out. I can still hear her weeping, still feel her tears on my shoulder. The only Istak who is of sufficient rank to be her mate is Pimne. That was why she wept. And as the days grew fewer, we saw less of each other. Until tonight. Tonight was to be the last time we ever spoke, the last time she would be able to get away. And tonight, instead of me . . ." Yazi left his sentence unfinished, his paw clenching and unclenching in repressed anger.

"Now I see why you must fight and what you must do," Reginald answered softly. "This settles it. Tomorrow, your training begins in earnest."

Two important events marked the next day: the return of Mantuka to the Istak village, and Reginald falling flat on his face.

The next morning, as Reginald continued Yazi's crash course in fighting, he noticed a large group of Istaka clustered around the southern end of the village. Blocking an ineffective paw-swipe, Reginald picked Yazi up, tucked the small wolf beneath his arm, and walked down to see what the commotion was about. Yazi struggled briefly, but gave up after his best was to no avail against the Hero's massive strength.

A crowd of Istaka had gathered along the dirt path where it entered the village. Parents held their cubs up to see above the crowd, and some of the older Istak young lined the edges of the road as if expecting gifts from the central figure of the crowd. Excited talking and barking filled the air as they clustered around.

An Istak who stood head and shoulders above the rest ruffled the ears of the younger Istaka as he passed through the crowd, and he greeted the rest. He was tall and black-furred and bore a large pack on his brawny shoulders. He and several others had entered the camp from the southern trail, the one leading through the southern pass of the Mountains of the Morning toward Filar and Merope.

Reginald locked eyes with the black Istak in the center of the crowd. Heroic hazel met Istakan gold, and they stared at each other for a long moment until the black wolf turned away to hand his pack to another.

Yazi finally managed to struggle free of Reginald's grasp and drop to the ground. He looked across the clearing. "That's Mantuka," Yazi murmured, tugging gently on Reginald's sleeve. "He's the village Alpha, the one the chief trusts with the most dangerous and difficult tasks for the village. He's very strong. Not an Istak in the village can match him for strength. I wouldn't blame you if you decided not to fight him . . ."

Reginald snapped from his reverie. "Hogwash, lad. I intend to fight this Mantuka, and very few things could dissuade me at this point. It is now a matter of honor rather than my penchant for violence. But," he said, turning around and placing an arm across Yazi's slight grey shoulders, "I think it is now time for you to show me what you've learned."

They returned to the sand-strewn fighting pit where they had been practicing. This particular patch of forest had been cleared of underbrush, and a square shallow hole had been dug in the center. The hole was now full of sand, and the Istaka used it to practice wrestling and fighting. A rope strung along tall stakes in the ground ringed the edges of the pit, delineating the boundaries for any given fight. A squirrel chattered cheekily at the pair as they stood apart in their defensive positions.

Yazi leapt first, bridging the distance between them in a split-second. He twisted in midair to avoid one of Reginald's fists. He attempted to grab onto Reginald's unprotected right shoulder, but Reginald brought his elbow back and gently knocked the little wolf aside into the dirt.

"Come on, lad. You can do better than that."

"You're bigger and stronger than I am!" Yazi protested, springing up and shaking the dirt from his fur.

Reginald scowled. "So is Pimne. Have at you!" He leapt at the small wolf, attempting to catch him with both hands. He missed, and received a furry backhand for his trouble.

Yazi stepped back, looking surprised that he had managed to land a blow on Reginald. "I . . . I'm sorry, Sir Ogleby, I . . ."

"*I told you to call me Reginald, runt!*" Reginald yelled, swiping at Yazi again.

Yazi flinched, but kept his nerve. "Not this time!"

They danced back and forth in a hostile waltz for nigh on two minutes. Reginald kept shouting at Yazi, but Yazi ignored the jibes and taunts.

"*Only one day, runt!*" Reginald bellowed. "*Tomorrow Takala belongs to Pimne!*" He threw a punch just slightly too wide.

Ducking under Reginald's flying fist, Yazi leapt at his legs, catching him around the ankles and holding on with all his might.

Reginald fell flat on his face, wind knocked from him—and abruptly felt four fangs close softly on the back of his neck.

They quickly removed themselves as Yazi stood, sides heaving.

Reginald sat up, wiping the slobber from the back of his neck, and looked at the young Istak. "Where did *that* come from, lad?"

"I just realized," Yazi said, looking up into the forest canopy, "that there's only thing I can do to keep Taki safe."

"And that is?"

Yazi looked back to Reginald, his expression a mystery. "Thanks for the lessons, *Reginald*. You must be tired from all of this. Let's get you back to the village and get some food in you. You'll need your strength if you're to best Mantuka." Yazi offered Reginald his paw.

Reginald took it and pulled himself to his feet. As they walked back to the village, he could not help but wonder what the little wolf was up to. He prayed it was not something foolish.

Reginald spent the day of the fight resting and stretching, performing regulation Heroic Pre-Combat Calisthenics.

When evening fell, two near-identical brown Istak summoned Reginald to the center of the darkening village. A torch-lined ring had been set up there similar to the one he and Yazi had been practicing in, only larger. Seats ringed the sand-filled circle, and a large crowd of Istaka had already begun filling them.

Helush-Ka and his bodyguards approached Reginald. "Greetings, Sir Ogleby," the chieftain said. "I hope you are prepared for your duel?"

"Of course," Reginald said. "A Hero is always prepared for combat."

"Then we shall begin immediately. Mantuka!" Helush-Ka called.

The tall, black-furred wolf stepped out of the crowd and stopped in front of the chieftain. "Yes? Is this the Human who defeated my brother?" He looked Reginald up and down, sizing him up.

"Yes. I am Sir Reginald Ogleby," the Hero answered. "You must be Mantuka. I hope you prove a worthy opponent."

Mantuka smiled, revealing very sharp fangs. "Oh, I will. I may even surprise you, Hero."

Reginald nodded. "Shall we begin, then?"

"Absolutely. Fight with honor, Hero." The black wolf entered the ring.

Reginald and Mantuka stood on opposite sides of the ring, preparing for their duel. They were about to begin, when a commotion started outside the circle.

After a few confusing moments, a red fox Istak wearing a black tabard stepped out of the crowd. "A challenge has been issued. Yazi, son of Kizikoni, has challenged Pimne, son of Nitus for his place as Beta. Pimne, do you accept this challenge?" The messenger wolf turned, scanning the crowd.

Reginald clapped a hand to his forehead. *What is the little fool thinking?*

"I do!" a voice rang out above the crowd noise. The mottled wolf stepped out of the crowd. "I relish the chance to put the runt back in his place!" Pimne said, licking his chops.

"As I do the chance to finally put you in yours," Yazi said, stepping out of the other end of the crowd. "You've been a blemish on the Beta rank for far too long."

"At this time," the messenger continued, "since the primary duel has not yet begun, the combatants of honor have the choice of which fight shall take place first. What is your decision?"

Mantuka glanced back and forth between the two would-be antagonists. "For my part," he said, "I have no grudge against Yazi, and I have never cared for the attitude of Pimne. Were it entirely my decision, I would let them fight now."

"I agree," Reginald said. "This small Istak has endured his low rank for long enough. Let him settle this quarrel now, Mantuka and I shall settle ours after."

The messenger nodded. "It is settled then. Please exit the ring and allow the combatants to enter."

Reginald and Mantuka complied.

On the way out, Reginald placed his hand on Yazi's shoulder. "Think like an Alpha, Yazi, and do not forget what I taught you."

"Thanks, Reginald," Yazi said, looking up at the Hero's kind face. "Even if I don't win this, I think it'll still make a difference to me." He turned and walked into the ring.

Creator, don't let him be killed, Reginald prayed silently.

• • •

Yazi and Pimne squared off in the combat ring. The crowd was silent as the two wolves circled one another.

The larger wolf leered, revealing sharp incisors. "Really, Yazi. I knew you were dumb, but to challenge *me*, of all the Istaka here? Really stupid. I will shred you."

Yazi glared at the mottled Istak. "That's what you think!" he snapped. "You've never seen me fight, have you? I'm like a furry whirlwind." The small Istak's ears pointed straight up, and his grey fur bristled.

"Whirlwinds are full of nothing but air!" Pimne said.

Yazi crouched, ears flattening. "And yet they kill people all the time."

Pimne sneered. "Fine then, runt. Take one step over this line, and I'll separate your limbs from your torso," he drew a line in the dirt with his foot-paw.

Yazi looked at the line, grinned, stepped over it, and leapt at Pimne's throat. The crowd immediately burst into growls, howls, and cheers of support for both parties.

Pimne, caught off guard by the unexpected attack, toppled over backward. He struggled to break the smaller Istak's grip on his neck for a moment, then changed tactics and kicked Yazi in the stomach.

Yazi skidded across the loose sand and rolled back onto his foot-paws. Pimne circled the small wolf, looking for an opening. Spotting one, he darted in for an attack, jaws snapping.

Yazi side-stepped and delivered a blow to Pimne's exposed snout, more as an insult than anything else. Laughter burst from several members of the crowd.

Pimne yelped in pain. "That's cheating! Unfair!" He clapped a paw to his suddenly bleeding nose.

Yazi's eyes narrowed. "You can't cheat in a game with no rules." Whereupon he kicked Pimne in the jaw.

Pimne's teeth rattled together, one puncturing his tongue. But the larger wolf kept his balance and backed up two paces. Blood spattered the arena sand as he sneezed. Then he growled and rushed Yazi again. This time he was more successful.

As Yazi swung his furred fist again, Pimne ducked under it, leaping up and sinking his fangs into the smaller wolf's shoulder while his arms pinned Yazi's to his sides. The crowd gasped, and the white wolf, Takala, covered her eyes.

It was Yazi's turn to yelp as blood flowed from his punctured shoulder. He gritted his fangs, yanked one paw free, and jabbed Pimne in the eye. Pimne's grip slackened as he snarled and tried to remove the blunt claw from his eye socket.

Yazi took advantage of it, pulling his right arm free and clamping his paw onto Pimne's injured nose. Pimne howled in pain and swiped at Yazi with his claws, scoring deep gashes in the grey wolf's hide.

Yazi held on, bashing Pimne repeatedly in the head where his ear met his skull. "That's . . . for touching . . . Taki's . . . tail!" Yazi shouted, punctuating the sentence with blows.

Pimne growled, weakly trying to block the repeated jarring blows. His resistance grew weaker with every strike. The crowd began chanting "Ya-zi! Ya-zi!"

Yazi let go of Pimne's mottled hide. "I'm beating you, Pimne. How does it feel to finally get some of what you constantly do to others?"

Pimne's sides heaved and his tongue lolled from his mouth as he got to his unsteady footpaws. "It's . . . not over . . . yet . . . Omega. I'll . . . show you . . . your place . . ."

"My place?" Yazi snorted. "You're about to take it from me, willing or no." Yazi kicked Pimne in the chest, causing him to double over. While the air was still leaving Pimne's lungs, Yazi tackled him so that the two Istaka hit the ground nearly simultaneously.

Latching his fangs onto his opponent's throat, Yazi struck hammer-like blows on both sides of Pimne's rib cage, splintering bones and rattling the larger wolf nearly senseless. After five seconds of brutal pounding, Yazi stood.

"Pimne," Yazi said, panting, "I don't want to kill you, but I will if I must. Do you submit?"

Pimne was too battered to speak. Instead, he tucked his legs and tail into his body, lay down before Yazi, and whined pathetically. The fight was over. The entire crowd, even the ones who had been egging Pimne on earlier, erupted in cheers.

Yazi walked over to the edge of the ring, searching the crowd. "Takala!" he yelled.

The beautiful white wolf-girl stepped out from the crowd and looked at Yazi. "Yazi! You did it!" she said, smiling.

Yazi smiled back, tail wagging furiously. "Takala. As a gift to you, I will allow you to choose the fate of my opponent. What will be done with him?"

Takala looked across the ring at the dusty grey and black pile of fur. "I think," she said, "that he has been injured enough. Let him take your place as Omega for a time. If he doesn't like living that way, he can always leave the pack."

"As you wish," Yazi said, still smiling.

The assembled istaka clapped and howled their approval.

Reginald jumped as an Istak behind him placed a heavy paw on his shoulder. He turned and faced Mantuka, whose dark fur glistened in the torchlight.

"Well, Hero, it looks as if the time you spent with little Yazi has paid off. Shall we begin our own contest?"

Reginald nodded. "Let's get this over with." He removed his plain cotton shirt, leaving himself clad in only a pair of brown trousers.

The two combatants entered the ring once again and prepared to fight. An expectant hush fell over the assembled wolf pack, broken only by the hungry yipping of a small cub. Then, as if by some unseen signal, man and wolf sprang toward each other.

Expecting little resistance, Reginald put only a fraction of his strength into the charge. Much to Reginald's surprise, Mantuka nearly knocked him off his feet. Reginald staggered backward, bare feet sliding in the sand. "What?" he exclaimed. "You're . . ."

Mantuka grinned, showing his fangs. "Much stronger than I appear," he said, and rushed Reginald again.

Reginald met the rush and brought a full-strength grapple to bear on the black wolf. To his utter astonishment, Mantuka met the grapple with equal force. A grin broke across Reginald's face. Perhaps this would be an interesting contest after all.

The fight lasted nearly twenty-five minutes—near half an hour of furious blows and acrobatic dodges, blocks, counters, and incessant narration. The crowd had roared and howled themselves hoarse, so in the last few minutes of the fight they merely watched in tense anticipation. Reginald was just slightly stronger than Mantuka, but Mantuka was just slightly quicker than

Reginald. For some reason, Mantuka did not attempt to bite Reginald, though they fought with no other weapons.

Finally, Reginald managed to secure a crossbar headlock on Mantuka, and the wolf slowly sagged to the ground. "Thus did the Crimson Slash defeat his noble opponent in the arena of Honor," Reginald said, releasing Mantuka and taking a step backward. "Well then, Mantuka. Is your brother's honor satisfied?"

Mantuka took a moment to catch his breath. "Yes," he managed, "it is. Well fought, Hero."

The crowd of Istaka began dispersing to prepare a small feast, saddened by Mantuka's loss but heartened by Yazi's victory. Soon the smell of roasting venison filled the air again, as well as a heavy, sweet scent Reginald immediately identified as mead.

"Thank you," Reginald said, helping Mantuka up. "But I must ask: why did you not use your natural weapons? The gods gave them to you for a reason, you know."

"It wouldn't have been fair," Mantuka replied, brushing himself off. "You have no such weapons. To fight armed against an unarmed foe is hardly sporting."

Reginald smiled. "We think alike, I see. With your strength, quickness, and sense of Honor, have you ever considered becoming a Hero?"

"Many times," Mantuka replied. "However, such a thing would be selfish. If I left the pack and went on quests for my own glory, who would defend my friends and family? My abilities are better used here than they would be anywhere else, for these are the people I care about. Especially in this dark age. If I made myself known, would Voshtyr and his ilk not hunt me down like prey?"

"I see your point. Still, it seems a shame that a person of your strength . . ."

"Do not worry about it," Mantuka said, smiling. "This is where I want to be."

Reginald smiled also. "Then this is where you should stay. But should the need arise, I will return and ask you once again."

Mantuka nodded. "On that day, perhaps, I will change my mind."

Reginald awoke, and immediately wished he hadn't. He felt *terrible*. Small pieces of dust in the air repeatedly bombarded his skin, each feeling like a small boulder. The throbbing in his head and the fuzziness on his tongue didn't help matters either. He blinked against the invasive sunlight, and realized, despite the splitting headache, that he might have drunk a little too much of the heady mead the Istaka had been passing around at last night's feast.

With a groan, Reginald swung his feet down from the bed he was lying on. He stood up, and immediately sat down. He silently vowed *never* to become intoxicated again. By an act of supreme willpower, he got to his feet once more and opened the curtain that served as a door to his guest hut.

"Greetings, Reginald!" Yazi said, standing in the doorway and grinning like a hyena. Which he wasn't. More like a dingo. "How did you like the party, huh?"

Reginald winced. The small grey wolf was very happy about something and was talking very loudly on account of it. "It was fine," Reginald managed to say, "except for the mead."

"Something was wrong with it?"

"Not the quality—just the quantity." Reginald sighed. "And I have no one but myself to blame for that."

Yazi looked at Reginald. "You look terrible. Here, I have two things that'll fix you up! Stay right here!" Yazi sprinted from the doorway.

That's amusing, Reginald thought. *That's the first time a dog has ever told me to stay.*

Yazi returned in a few moments bearing a large damp cloth, which Reginald gratefully wrapped around his head, and a cup of some thick, odd-smelling drink.

"What's this?" Reginald asked, swirling the reddish liquid around in the cup.

Yazi grinned mischievously. "It's what you might call a hangover cure. Try it. It's very effective."

Reginald eyed the liquid dubiously. "Well, if you say so." He quickly drank the liquid down. For a moment, it tasted vaguely sweet. But then it changed to a sense-enveloping burning. Reginald coughed, and his eyes began watering. All the alcohol in his system rapidly sweated out of him as the fiery liquid blasted his bowels.

"Incendrix berries mixed with honey and water," Yazi said. "Useful for curing hangovers and . . . well . . . tanning hides. Except when we use it for tanning hides, we don't put any honey in it."

"Wonderful," Reginald coughed. "I'll keep this in mind next time I need to tan my innards. At any rate," he said, mustering his senses, "did something good happen? Something besides you no longer being pack Omega? You seem excited."

Yazi's tail began wagging again. "Yes, yes it did!" the little wolf said, his face a toothy grin. "After I beat Pimne, I spoke with Takala's father, and he flat out chose me as her mate!"

"Well, I'm very happy for you, lad!" Reginald said, clapping the Istak on the shoulder. "I knew you had it in you to be something other than the bottom of the pack."

"But I couldn't have done it without your help, Reginald. Thank you so much."

"You're welcome. That's the sort of thing Heroes are supposed to do."

Reginald checked the saddle girth on Wraith, who had finally gotten adjusted to being surrounded by strange canines. As Reginald finished cinching the saddle strap, he felt a light tap on his shoulder. He turned around to see Yazi, Takala, and Mantuka standing behind him.

"Well, then, Hero, I suppose this is good-bye," Mantuka said, extending a paw.

"I suppose it is." Reginald clasped Mantuka's paw and shook it. "You're sure you don't want to join the Guild of Heroes?"

Mantuka smiled. "Yes, I am sure. They are hunted now, and I prefer to be the hunter, not the hunted. Besides, I would rather not pay dues to them. Feel free to come back any time you want to spar with me. I would enjoy the challenge."

Yazi stepped up next, giving Reginald a ferocious hug. "I really can't thank you enough," the little wolf said. "You've given me a real life, something I can be proud of."

"I didn't give it to you," Reginald corrected. "You took it yourself. I just gave you the tools to go and get it."

"I thank you as well," Takala said, curtseying gracefully. Her white tail curled behind Yazi's back as she smiled at him. "I have loved Yazi for years, for he is sweet and caring, not traits you find often among my kind. But because of his status..."

Reginald smiled. "Well, he has solved that problem for himself. I will pray for the best for both of you."

"To Wanona?" Yazi asked. "I thought Humans almost never followed Wanona."

Reginald looked up through the tree branches. "Actually, I think the Creator Himself likes me," he said. "Else I would not have survived mine own stupidity. I will pray to Him and no others." He turned to Yazi. "Let your experiences here be a lesson to you. When you become leader of the pack, make sure that the Omega is still treated as a person."

"Me? Leader of the pack?" Yazi chuckled. "Heh, that'll be the day. Anyway, good luck on your travels."

"Yes, and be careful in these woods," Takala said. "There are places that are very dangerous, even for experienced hunting bands."

"Thank you, all of you," Reginald said. "Farewell. May we meet again!"

"Farewell, Reginald!" Yazi said. "You've made yourself a friend of the Istak, Hero! Goodbye!"

A friend of the Istak. The phrase echoed in Reginald's mind. He nodded. With that, he mounted Wraith and rode off.

Chapter 24

Escape from the Sky

In which Kris Formulates an Escape Plan
And Takes a Leap of Faith

K RIS WOKE UP abruptly. Actually, it wasn't so much waking up as being harshly dragged back to consciousness.

Three men stood beside her bed along with the woman named Mel-Shan. The latter bore a tray with food on it. One of the men was Lazik, who stood scowling with his arms crossed. Apparently his day was going just as poorly as Kris's seemed to be. One of the others carried a stick of white wood, with a crystal sphere floating gently over the top. Kris recognized him as one of the men who had "rescued" her from the pirates. The third was an entirely bald man with a tattoo of a dragon on the side of his head.

"Confusion, recognition, and mild hostility," the bald man said calmly. "She recognizes you, Eri-tar, and has hostile feelings toward the Tarrasshan."

"No kidding," Kris growled. "What did you wake me for? More ego trips?"

"To feed you," Lazik snapped. "We cannot have your offspring dying simply because their mother is an uncooperative idiot."

Kris tried to leap at Lazik, but found herself unable to move. "Wh- what is this?" she said.

"Oh, don't bother trying to move," Lazik said. "I've dissociated your mind from most of your body. You'll find you cannot move from your neck down. That's all you need to eat, isn't it?" He smiled cruelly.

Was her escape thwarted before it had begun? Would they leave her paralyzed until the cubs were born? Tears pricked the back of Kris's eyes. In Katheni culture, the crippled hunter was the most tragic and disgraced figure possible.

"Anger, directed at the Tarrasshan, and also frustration at herself," the bald man said in a monotone. "Turmoil verging on panic."

"I will eat," Kris said. "But only to gain strength to kill you."

"Oh, you won't be doing that," Lazik said, motioning to Mel-Shan.

The woman began feeding Kris a thick soup with various vegetables and much meat in it. It was vaguely spicy, and Kris recognized many spices from her homeland of Sur Palma. So they had been in her mind while she was asleep, and they had seen her memories. This was not a good sign.

Lazik leaned close to Kris and stroked her cheek. "You will not be given a chance to kill me, or even escape," Lazik said. "You see, when you are not eating, you will be locked in a corner of your own shattered and easily controlled mind. You've already been under for nearly a week, did you know that?"

Kris glanced about the room. Nothing seemed to have changed, but it could be true. "And what if I choose to cooperate?"

"Val-shan?" Lazik said.

The bald man looked at Kris. "Deception. Secrecy. More anger."

"*If* you ever choose to cooperate, as you obviously are not right now," Lazik said, "then we will leave you to your own devices, so long as you stay within the confines of this building. Until then, Huntress, you will be lost in your own mind."

Kris's eyes darted about the room looking for a weapon, as Indy had suggested she do. Curtain rod? Too flimsy. Fish tank? Tasty, but hardly practical. Books, papers, footstools . . .

The bald man looked confused. "Seeking, confusion, questions." He turned to Lazik. "Tarrashan, I think she is planning to escape."

The lampstand! Two ornate wrought-iron lampstands sat near the doorway, holding braziers of burning coals. If she were to dump one out, preferably on her enemies, she could then wield it as a somewhat bulky club. Less bulky if the brazier were a separate piece.

The bald man kept narrating her thoughts, or perhaps her emotional state. "Excitement, joy? Tarrasshan!"

Kris thought about Cyrus. His smile, the way his hair waved in the breeze, his silly blue hat. She wondered briefly where the hat had disappeared to in their last adventure.

"Love . . . and hope."

"And we can't have that." Lazik put his hands on the sides of Kris's head again. "Your beloved Human boy won't be able to save you here. And he certainly won't be able to save you from your own mind."

The painful and terrifying presence appeared in her head again. Kris screamed, her world shattered into blackness.

• • •

Kris sat on the black slab in the middle of nothing again. This time it felt even more impossible to move. She sighed.

"Did you find a weapon?"

Kris tilted her head. It felt as if her skull weighed as much as a pair of draft horses plus cart. "Yes. No. Sort of." She rolled her tongue inside her mouth. It felt thick and dry. "What has he done to my head?"

"Brute force attack." Indy sat on a glowing white stone hovering over the pit. Beside Kris sat Nieva, now dressed in black and seated on the same black slab Kris lay on. "You're lucky you're alive. He's more sledgehammer than scalpel, and you really don't want to sledgehammer a brain. It gets sticky really fast."

"They have been more subtle with me," Nieva said. "Two of the empaths have been tasked to ensure that my sleep is always filled with dreams of what horrible things will happen to me should I not cooperate or what will happen to my beloved if I attempt to escape."

"Uh, yeah, about that," Indy said. "That's kind of my fault. He was going to go all sledgehammer on you too until I suggested the dreams."

Nieva looked hurt, but quickly covered it up. "I suppose you do what you must."

"Don't be that way," Indy said. "I don't want your brain ending up like a big pile of mashed potatoes. All the gravy in the world can't make mashed brains work properly again."

"So my brain is going to be mashed?" Kris said. "What if he does it again?"

Indy winced. "Every time he attacks your mind like that, it's going to be harder and harder for him to put it back together. He's much, much better at destroying things than building them. He kind of sucks as a Tarrasshan, actually."

"Wait, what all has he seen in my mind, then?" Kris said. "Does he know you are helping me?"

"I don't think so," Indy said. "Or he'd have had my skinny hide by now. I managed to keep his search team out of anything particularly important, but they got a lot."

"You protected my mind?" Kris asked. She smiled. She had an ally indeed. But then another thought occurred to her. "Wait, that means you saw my mind too . . ."

"Ah, heh heh, yeah, sorta," Indy said. "But just a little bit. Well, some. Well, actually, a lot. Sorry."

Kris grabbed Indy by the collar. "*What did you see?*"

"Hey, hey, look, don't get your tail in a knot," Indy said. "And look! You're moving in your mind again! What a great sign! Put me down, pretty please?"

Kris growled.

"Right, right! Just a few little things, like what happened to your family, and that one cave with the ogre, and how your tail curls when Cyrus—"

"*Oh kay, that's enough!*" Kris said abruptly, dropping Indy. "I am . . . um . . . sorry I yelled. You were only trying to help."

Nieva put a hand on Kris's shoulder. "Please, I need your help to get out of here. Between myself and Indy, we should be able to repair your mind. But Indy will need direct access to you, and he cannot get to you with Lazik watching."

"If I'm real careful," Indy said, "I can tweak his blocks on you so that he thinks he's incapacitated you, but you'll still be able to move. If you can get him really mad at you, he'll let his guard down. Another reason he sucks as a Tarrasshan."

"And?" Kris said. "Won't he just break my mind permanently?"

"Not if I can help it," Indy said. "It'll hurt you, sure, but if he lets his guard down, I can get inside his mind, ever so briefly, and make sure I know exactly what he did, how he did it, and how to fix it. I'll also remove his priority of watching me, so I can sneak into your room without raising any suspicion."

"I will share your pain," Nieva said. "It will make it easier on you."

Kris shook her head. "My mind, my problem. Cyrus would be Heroic and brave right now, so I will too."

"Oh, smokes, here they come again," Indy said. "Good luck."

"What, so soon?" Kris said. But they were just here and fed me!"

Indy shook his head. There was nothing jovial about his expression and tone. "No, Kris. It took me three days to bring you back to where you could talk to us again. They've fed you twice since then, and you didn't so much as twitch a whisker."

Kris drew in a deep breath. "Then let's hope this time goes better."

"I will pray for you," Nieva said, and bowed.

Kris woke up with the same jerking start she'd woken to last time.

"Oh, so she manages to wake." Lazik seemed to be wearing the same clothes she'd seen him in last time, or perhaps it was another identical suit. "It seems you are of stronger mind than I originally thought."

Kris experimentally twitched the tip of her tail beneath the covers. It moved. She looked around. The bald man was not present, but Mel-shan was, and the suffix -shan meant she could read emotions as well. To cover up her pleasure in being able to move, she scowled.

"So what is it you want now, Tarrasshan?" Kris said. "Come to taunt me again? Come to see if you can break my spirit or my resolve?"

"Oh, heavens no," Lazik said. "Just to have a polite conversation. How are you enjoying being trapped in your own mind?"

Kris growled. "Taunts, is it? Well, mister smart guy, you can take those taunts and hang them in your tiny naked ear. I'll have none of it."

"Ooh, such spirit, even when your situation is hopeless." Lazik ran a hand through his silver hair. "A pity you're not more cooperative. We have much in common, you and I. A passion for life, the spirit to do what we will. The sad part is that I have the power, and you do not. A true shame, it is, that both our wills cannot coincide."

"My will may not tear the moon from the sky," Kris said, "but it still matters. Let me go."

"No." Lazik smiled. "A shame it may be, but I am no simpleton. You hold within you my keys to the world." He placed his palms on Kris's belly. "I will not give that up, even if I must destroy your mind for good."

"Then I'll destroy your face!" Kris said. She whipped her hands up out of the sheets, unsheathing her claws as she did so, and clapped them onto Lazik's face. With one swift motion, she dragged the razor claws through the flesh on his face from ear to chin.

Lazik screamed and staggered back. He shouted words in some dark language, and flung his hand out at Kris. She was slammed back into the headboard of the bed, and she floated slowly out of the bed. She felt a noose-like grip tighten around her throat, and she clapped her paws to her neck.

"Vile wench," Lazik said through gritted teeth. Blood poured from the slashes on his face. "I should have known I could not trust you to act like a civilized creature nor accept your fate. You have too much the animal mind left in you." He curled his fingers, then twisted his wrist and pointed his fingers straight up.

Kris felt his presence in her mind again, but this time she also felt another. Indy?

"I cannot take the jungle out of the cat, but I can take the mind out of her," Lazik said. "After all, a feral panther or leopard can bear its cubs just as easily as a Kath bears them. If all you can do in society is claw people, then your mind should match theirs."

Blackness shredded Kris's consciousness, but something was different. As opposed to the hostile rending shatter that had happened last time, this was more wispy, like being smothered in a cloak.

It still hurt. A lot.

Kris woke up on the slab again, this time with Indy and Nieva both hovering over her.

"Yes!" Indy said, seeing her eyes open. "She's alive! I am *so* awesome!"

"Welcome back to the land of the living," Nieva said. "You did remarkably well, even without my help."

Kris sat up. "So did we do it?"

Indy did a little dance. "Oh, we *so* did it! When you wake up again, you should be able to move freely and all kinds of stuff. Also, I've kind of mind-blinded Lazik to me, you, and Nieva. We're golden for an escape plan, just as soon as you get your fuzzy butt up and moving."

Kris grabbed Indy and hugged him. "Thank you so much."

"Hey, what can I say?" Indy said. "I'm a sucker for pretty ladies. Now let's get the two of you out of here."

"Um, how?" Kris said.

"Like this," Indy said, and he poked Kris in the forehead. "Shaboozie!"

Kris snapped awake. It was dark and silent in her spacious room, the only sound the rustling of the breeze through the green silk curtains. Mel-shan sat in a high-backed chair a few feet away, fast asleep.

Kris slipped out of the bed and padded past the sleeping Kinetic. She grabbed the lampstand and considered dumping the burnt-out coals out of the dish and onto Mel-shan's head. But restrained herself. Burning people wasn't exactly the ideal of stealth. Instead, she slipped out the door without a sound.

In contrast to her room, the rest of the building seemed to be sparsely furnished. The only adornments seemed to be decorative marble columns and a few odd white-leafed trees in white stone pots. Lots of white, she noted. Didn't the Kinetics have any taste in colors? The marble was white, the hangings were white, the floor tiling was all white. Not a spot of color anywhere. She'd never seen white as such a sinister color.

"They need an interior decorator," she muttered to herself.

"We'd hire one, but most of the decorators these days have an unhealthy obsession with lava," Lazik said, stepping out of the shadows. The torchlight accentuated the barely-healed slashes down the sides of his face. "It comes of working solely for Villains for the last few months."

Kris bristled. "I thought you were—"

"Mind-blinded to you?" Lazik chuckled sinisterly. "My dear girl, I am the Tarrasshan. *The* Tarrasshan. Indikos thinks he is better and stronger than I, but that whelp is inexperienced. To tamper with the mind of the ruling Tarrasshan is a thing near impossible. Now hold still," he said, stretching out a hand. "I owe you some injuries, but I don't wish to harm the Two of Balance."

Kris threw the lampstand at him.

Lazik swatted it away with invisible force, but that gave Kris the chance to sprint the distance between her and Lazik. She exposed her claws and leapt on the king of the Kinetics.

The two toppled backward. Kris slashed at Lazik with ferocious swipes. Lazik thrust a palm forward and threw her off into the wall behind her.

He picked her up with nothing, and held her in midair. "You," he said, "are becoming more of a nuisance than you are worth."

"Except to some," a woman said from behind him. Kris looked over Lazik's shoulder and saw Nieva, a glistening shard of ice surrounded by whirling snow in her hands. "One man wants her back intact, body and mind."

The ice fragment leapt forward and smashed into Lazik's torso, catapulting him across the room and encasing his body in ice. The Lazik cube slid to a stop against a wall and wobbled as if it might fall. But then it came to rest facing the side wall.

Kris pushed herself up from the wall. "Thank you," she said, holding her ribs.

Nieva rushed to Kris's side. "Are you all right?" She pressed her hands to Kris's sides.

A cool white light spread from around her hands, and Kris could feel the pain draining away from where she'd struck the wall. "Better, thank you," Kris said. "Have we met?"

"Only in your mind," Nieva said, leading Kris down the hall. "Let us depart this place before he breaks free of that spell. It only holds for a short—"

"Graaagh!" Lazik shouted, busting free of his icy prison. "Nieva Frostreach! I knew I had heard the name Nieva before!" He dusted shards of ice from his sleeveless shirt. "I should have known that the son of a Villain would fall so easily for a Villainess as sinister and insidious as you."

"Silence!" Nieva's eyes glowed bright blue. "Unless you enjoy being impaled upon icicles, I suggest you say nary another word."

"Does that simpleton Serimal even know who you are?" Lazik said, advancing on the pair. "Have you told him of the countless victims frozen in your castle? The village crushed beneath the glacier on your front steps? The tribe of frost giants so afraid of your wrath that they cower before you?"

"Enough!" Nieva threw a spattering of icicles at Lazik. "You know nothing!"

Lazik laughed and threw the icicles aside, then thrust a fist toward Nieva. She was flung backward, knocking down a potted white-leafed tree and slamming against a pillar. "I know more than you think, frost witch. I would wager that your 'beloved' doesn't know a thing about you, really. And he never will, because you'll die here."

"Run!" Kris said, grabbing Nieva's wrist and yanking her away from the column. Behind them, the column exploded into dust.

"Hmm, missed again," Lazik said, looking at his fingers. "Run if you like, little rats, but you won't escape. We're in a floating fortress a mile above the ground, you know." He chuckled. "How ironic it is to hunt the Huntress."

Nieva slammed the door behind them. "Where are we going?"

Kris looked at her. "I haven't been out of my room. I thought you knew."

The two stood with their backs to the door in a room that seemed to be a large communal kitchen. The white tiling was the same here, but a quadruple-basin sink, cutting boards, and ovens lined the walls. A dumbwaiter without any obvious pulley system occupied a slot in one wall, and a rack of knives rested not far away.

Kris retrieved a large vegetable knife and a pot lid. She sniffed. These were hardly Kath-crafted weapons, but they would do in a pinch. And this was more than a pinch. It was more like a vice-tight squeeze inflicted on a sensitive portion of one's anatomy by someone without one's comfort foremost in mind.

Nieva held out her palms and ran them along the edges of the door. A thick layer of ice built beneath her palms, sealing the door. "I do not know how long that will hold him," she said. "We need to make a plan. Somehow, we must get out of this castle."

Kris looked around. There wasn't much in the way of an escape route. In fact, they seemed to have boxed themselves in. They were trapped. And Kris didn't like being trapped.

"There is no door," Kris said. "We may have to fight him. You have some more ice magic, yes?"

"Mine is magic—his is not," Nieva said. "His is strength of mind and has nothing to do with the elements. I cannot counter it."

Kris looked puzzled for a moment. "Can you block it, then?"

Nieva stopped. "I . . . I suppose I could try. But he is the king of this city, of this race. I do not think my magic is strong enough, espcially not here." She sat down with her back against one of the cabinets. "We may not be able to escape."

"Don't give up," Kris said. "I mean to see Cyrus again, to let my cubs be born free—free to do what they want, prophecy or notand I need your help to get out." She pointed at the dumbwaiter. "Do you think we would fit in that?"

Nieva ran to the hole in the wall and looked inside. "I think so. It will be close, but we should—"

The ice around the door shattered with a mighty boom, and marble dust rained down around it. Nieva ran back to the door and began icing it again.

"We don't have time for that!" Kris said. "Get in!"

The door blasted back across the room, knocking Nieva down, decimating a cupboard, and knocking flatware about the floor.

Lazik stepped through the doorway and cracked his knuckles. "You are making me destroy bits of my own home," he said. "I do not appreciate it. One of you is going to pay for this." He looked at Nieva as she lay on the ground. "And since I cannot harm the Huntress . . ."

With a gesture, Lazik separated half a dozen knives from their holding block. They twirled about his head like sharp, pointy hornets. "I will take my pound of flesh from you."

Nieva raised her hands, and a wall of ice shot up from the ground between them and Lazik. Immediately, six knife points jutted from the surface inches from her face. "Get in!" she yelled to Kris. "Go!"

Lazik raised his hands and twisted his wrists. The tiles on the floor ripped up and whirled around. He thrust his hands forward. The spinning tiles shot at the wall of ice and shattered it to bits. One tile remained, spinning straight at Nieva's head.

Kris leapt forward and slammed her pot lid down on the spinning tile, shattering it harmlessly to the floor. "Come on!" She dragged Nieva from the floor and ran.

The two dashed for the dumbwaiter. Kris leapt inside and held her paws out to Nieva. Nieva grabbed them and pulled herself in as knives, plates, bowls, cutting boards, vegetables, soup pots, and everything but the kitchen sink spattered the walls around them and the door of the dumbwaiter as it closed.

Then a massive crash shook the dumbwaiter, rattling it loose from its place. It dropped in freefall. Kris and Nieva screamed as it plummeted.

A few floors later, it crashed to a halt.

"W-what was that?" Nieva said, looking up into the darkness.

"The kitchen sink," Kris said. "Come on, let's get out of here."

• • •

Kris and Nieva ducked around another corner. The corridor wasn't very wide, but had a pair of wide bay windows in the outer wall. Kris could see nothing but sky and clouds outside. She could hear Lazik still railing against their "ingratitude and ignorance." He was coming closer with each passing second.

Kris leaned against the wall, breathing heavily. "He found us, three floors down, in less than a minute!" she said, panting. "How do we run from a man who can hear our thoughts? And in his own castle, no less?"

"It is worse than you think," Nieva said, walking to the window. "Look."

Before going to the window, Kris looked back around the corner. Lazik was gone. Or maybe he was playing mind games. Kris sighed inwardly. That was exactly what Cyrus would have said if he were there. She slunk up to the window and looked out.

She groaned. The sky was above and below them. The ground was leagues below. She spotted a city that looked so small it could be a depiction on a map. Kris drew in a breath then let it out through her fangs. "That . . . is a long way down."

"We are in the Citadel, their stronghold, Lazik's center of power," Nieva said. Here the Tarrasshan can not only read our minds, but he also knows all the places we can run to."

"And all the places we can not." Kris frowned. "This is crazy. I'm the Huntress. I should be hunting him, not the other way around."

The masonry at the edge of the window exploded, sending dust into the air and fragments skittering across the floor. "You cannot hide from me, children!" Lazik said from behind them.

"If you cannot run, and you cannot hide, then what can you do?"

Kris looked at Nieva. "We can jump."

Nieva's habitual calm broke. "Jump out the window? We are leagues up in the air!"

"There's a prophecy about me," Kris said. She gave Nieva an odd half-smile. "I can't die until it is fulfilled. If we jump off, we should be fine!"

"But there is no prophecy about me!" Nieva protested. "What if we jump and only I die?"

"You'll die if you stay," Kris said. "You think Lazik will let you live after helping me escape?"

Nieva sighed. "You are right, Huntress. Let us pray, then, and jump. If only there was a god of foolhardy ideas or bad plans to pray to . . ."

"There is Vertis, god of the Sky, if you believe in that sort of thing. We'll be passing through his domain. But as for me, I place my faith in the Creator. He gave life to everything that exists, and it is to Him that everything returns when they die. The timing," she said, "is up to Him. I would suggest y—"

A pillar shattered, spraying chunks of rock across the two.

Nieva shrieked. "He's here!" The Elf flicked at the air with all her fingers simultaneously, and ten icicles spun away from her hands. She thrust her hands forward, and the icicles launched forward, shattering the glass and clearing the widows for escape. "This is it," she said.

"Ready?" Kris said.

"Not at all," Nieva said weakly.

"Good. *Now!*"

They jumped.

Chapter 25

Fairy Tales

*In which Serimal Reveals his Plans,
Emily figures out Fey Politics,
And Jolan Meets his Fate*

"GIVE ME YOUR report on Operation Bo Peep."

Serimal sat with Emily, Jolan Foster, and Slashback in the fading sunlight amidst the ruins of Serimal's family castle, the grand manor fortress of the Von Steinadler family. It was once one of the most defensible castles in all of Landeralt, but now seemed to have been renovated by an enormous sledgehammer. A massive skylight had replaced the proud battlements, and half the gargoyles on the west wall had been reduced to fashionable busts. Or, at least, busts fashionably portraying the lower halves of their subject rather than the tops.

The white marble insides of the east walls, which had never before seen direct sunlight, glowed orange and pink in the last of the setting sun. The west walls would have glowed, but were mostly in fist-sized chunks scattered about the ground, cliffs, and sea bottom along the coast, and were thus not inclined to glow at that exact moment.

Jolan scowled. "Most inane operation name ever," he said. "But it worked. I got in, got the stupid rock, and sold it to a rabbit. Solburg picked it up out of a pile of goat—"

"Right," Serimal said. "That means he has two of them. We need to get him the last two so he can take on Voshtyr. Cyrus will need his own 'I win' button if he's to counteract the 'I win' button Jaratyr told us Voshtyr is creating. Once we get him the last two, all we need to do is point him in Voshtyr's direction, and then sit back and watch the fireworks."

"The Dwarves have the Earth Heartstone, don't they?" Emily said, scratching Slashback behind her pointed feathered ears. "You're not likely getting that from them."

"Brownies," Serimal said, snapping his fingers.

Jolan snorted. "I doubt baking them brownies will make them give you a priceless gem. I'd think a better choice would be one of those illegal liquors that'll put hair on your tongue."

"No, no," Serimal said. "Brownies, as in the Fey. Not brownies, as in the dessert. I have, or had, contacts within both the Day Court and Night Court of the Fey. And the Night Court are notorious for their acts of clandestine thievery."

"So you want to get fairies to steal the Heartstone for you?" Emily asked. "How likely's that?"

Serimal shrugged. "It depends on the court. The Day Court wouldn't, as their mischief is more like causing stray peasants to dance, misleading travelers, stealing people's wine, and that sort of thing. The Night Court are much more malicious. They steal children, drive animals insane, and transmogrify people's heads into donkey heads. Thought the latter's only happened once that I know of."

"So you'd get the Night Court to do it," Jolan said. "What makes you sure they won't double-cross you? They do have that reputation when dealing with mortals."

"They're also terrified of Gryphons," Serimal said, scratching Slashback behind the ears and smiling. "Legend tells that the first King of the Fey quarreled with Yven, goddess of Demis. The ensuing prank war ended with Yven transforming herself into a Gryphon and eating the King."

Slashback licked her beak. "Fey iss tasty. Like marsmellowsh."

"As a precaution against the Fey getting too nasty again, Yven gave Gryphons a taste for the smaller Fey, particularly the Night Court and any fairies who play pranks that are especially likely to cause damage." Serimal patted Slashback. "Especially Brownies."

"Brownies taste like chocolit bar," Slashback said.

Emily giggled. "Now *that* wasn't something I expected. Fey are Gryphon candy, huh?"

"Is like chocolit cover fytamin," Slashback said. "Like . . . like brownies almost. Is gut, and gut for you." She ruffled her feathers and nudged Serimal's hand with her skull. "Keep scratchin. Is gut."

Serimal chuckled. "All right, all right. We'll find the Night Court tonight, and see what we can do with them from there. Emily, I'm tasking you and Slashback with Operation Chicken Little, and Jolan—"

"I am *not* taking another mission named after a stupid children's rhyme," Jolan said, crossing his mechanical arms. "Don't you have something better for me to do? Like Operation Kill Voshtyr?"

Serimal shook his head. "We're spies, Jolan, not assassins—remember?"

"Says you," Jolan said. "I became a Hero so I could kill things without worrying about my conscience bothering me."

Emily rolled her eyes. "By the Nine Torments, you're as bad as a paladin. Except paladins take the whole 'holy war' thing too far, and you just take the 'aren't I just the best anti-Hero ever' thing too far."

Jolan manifested his lance again and pointed it at Emily's head. "One of these days, girl, you will push me too far, and you'll find I've renovated your skull and added skylights like that one." He pointed to the hole in Serimal's roof.

"*Enough!*" Serimal shouted. "Good grief! If I have to hear one more word out of the two of you fighting about some pointless thing, I am skipping to the next chapter!"

"Right," Emily said. "So, are we going to go drop the sky on Cyrus? How'd you suggest I go about doing that, eh?"

"Not the sky," Serimal said. "I'll fill you in on the way. Jolan, you stay here and guard what's left of the keep. I need some things out of the basement, and it doesn't look like they removed the foundation, so they should still be here when I get back."

Jolan grumbled. "Fine. Can I kill anything that comes in here that's not supposed to be?"

Serimal gave Jolan his very best *You know what I mean* look and headed for the door. Or more correctly, the lack thereof, as the door seemed to have gone missing with the other third of the architecture.

• • •

"I guess that makes sense," Emily said as she, Serimal, and Slashback touched down outside Shiel Glade. "I just think Cyrus'll get suspicious if we keep just handing the Hearstones to him, is all. He's not as dumb as most Heroes."

Shiel Glade was a unique place, even among the many magical locales on Centra Mundi and throughout the world. It was a small forest that covered no more than one-thirty-second of Centra Mundi's land surface. It bordered the west face of the Mountains of the Morning. Its single most noteworthy feature was that it boasted the highest concentration of creatures with magic flowing in their blood of any forest in the world, and was home to the Courts of the Fey. Plus, it was creepy.

Serimal shrugged. He removed his black gloves and tucked them into his belt. "Well, you may be right about that, but it isn't as if we have many other choices. It's not like he'll just accept a direct present from the half-brother of his Arch-Nemesis."

Emily frowned. "I don't think Cyrus is Voshtyr's Arch-Nemesis," she said. "I think that'd be Crimson, yeah?"

"The Crimson Slash is near retirement age, hasn't been seen since the evacuation of Rondheim, and anyway has no business picking up an Arch-Nemesis at this point in his career." Serimal patted Slashback's head. "Stay here, girl. I'll call when it's snack time."

Slashback nodded. "Haf gut time in creepy woods."

Serimal and Emily began walking into the tangled growth of the ancient forest. "It's a task for younger Heroes. Gaining Nemeses is a thing best done in one's youth."

"Kind of like running a secret spy organization?" Emily said with a smirk.

"That's not at all the same, for many and varied reasons, none of which occur to me immediately," Serimal said. "And in place of a counter-argument, *shush*. We're almost at Abbot's Wall."

Emily opened her mouth to say something, but Serimal shushed her again. The two continued into a rapidly darkening patch of woods and ducked into the underbrush.

The two Courts of the Fey, the Day Court and the Night Court, split from one another during the Age of Legend, just before the founding of the International Brotherhood of Heroes. Some Old Legends say that the fairy split was caused by a dispute between Oberon and Titania, the King and Queen of the Fairies—half marital dispute and half political gambit.

The nature of the dispute remained a mystery to modern historians, who wouldn't have even the remotest clue as to what was going on without the Old Legends. Some claimed it was the culmination of centuries of debate on the true nature of pranks and mischief, while others maintained it was a true clash of Good and Evil, and that the split was necessary to maintain the Balance.

Regardless of the reason, the split divided the Fey race into disparate halves. The Day court, ruled by Titania, was the sweetness and light of fairy tales, the stuff of love potions, pixie dust, and circles of magic mushrooms and toadstools. Oberon and the Night Court took on a darker role as dispenser of mischief of a more malicious sort, meting out its own brand of justice on the mortal world. Theirs was the realm of changelings, babies stolen from their basinets, magical favors for fell prices, and centuries of life lost to magical slumber.

Shiel Glade was the one remaining place where members of both Courts tolerated each other and, however grudgingly, acknowledged one another's existence. And it was precisely this spark of magical conflict that tainted the entire forest. Plants grew wild and strange, some even taking on carnivorous traits. Circles of mushrooms caused unwary travelers to lose their sense of time and place and, occasionally, never leave the forest again.

Only the truly aware, or those who had a guide from the Fey, knew of Abbot's Wall. It was the one line of law and sanity that ran the entire length of the forest, separating the territories of the Night and Day Courts.

And Emily tripped right over it.

"Ow!" Emily said, staggering forward and clutching her left foot. "Where did that come from?"

Serimal looked down. "Oh, you found Abbott's Wall. Excellent work. Now I know where we are."

A wall made entirely of mortar and what appeared to be mortar-polished brook pebbles lay along the ground near their feet. It was just shorter than knee height, and mostly hidden by the thick bracken that cluttered most of the forest floor.

"And what, pray, is Abbott's Wall?" Emily asked, rubbing her shin.

"Something without which, had your foot not so cleverly found it, we would be lost in this forest probably forever," Serimal said. "Now I can find my contact. *Hey Abbott!*"

A sound like the tinkling of shattering glass trickled up from down near their feet. "I just hate it when people do that," said the sounds of glass.

Emily looked down.

There stood a small old man no taller than her index finger. He sported a tiny top hat, waist-length grey beard, and jaunty clothes of green and black. A pair of wings like that of a dragonfly protruded from his back. He stepped out from beneath the roots of a tree by their feet. "You know how old that joke gets?" the fairy said, rubbing his eyes. "Give me one reason I shouldn't just move the two of you interlopers to the Stand of the Forgotten and leave you there."

"Hello, Abbott," Serimal said. "Remember me?"

"No," the fairy said. "Why should I remember some devilishly handsome young man with raven-black hair, the décor of a noble Villain, and the impudence to insult the Keeper of Secret Ways?" He worked his wings, causing him to flutter up to Serimal's eye level. "Hmm. You do look familiar now that I see you. Wine Handler or something, right?"

"Von Steinadler," Serimal said. "Remember, old bug?"

"Voshtyr?" the fairy said.

Serimal's face twisted in anger. "No, you daft pixie. It's Serimal. The *good* brother!"

The old fairy guffawed, slapping his sides in mirth. "Ha ha ha! Oh, you fell for that one as a child, too, Serimal! Bwa ha ha!"

Serimal rolled his eyes. "Oh, goodie. Are we done making fun now, you arthritic insect?"

Emily giggled. "Oh, isn't this just precious! You two are hilarious. Go on, argue some more!"

"I need to see if his eyes change color," the pixie said, promptly punching Serimal's nose with his tiny fist. "Take that, ye vagabond!"

"Gwah!" Serimal staggered back as a spray of glittering dust spattered his face. He tripped over a root and fell backward into a patch of orchid-like flowers. Immediately, the flowers began a melodic shrieking, and Serimal clapped his hands over his ears. "By the Nine Torments, Abbott! I came to talk to Oberon!"

Abbott stroked his tiny beard. "Well, no glowing redness, so he's either got excellent allergy medicine or it's really Serimal."

"I can vouch for it being Serimal," Emily said. "I'm not on great terms with Voshtyr, so I'd not be very likely t' follow him about."

Abbott looked Emily up and down. "Well," he finally said, "how could I possibly distrust the word of a pretty young thing such as yourself?"

Emily blushed. "Right... So you'll help us get to Oberon?"

"Of course," Abbott said, sweeping off his miniature top hat. "However, the path is mighty dangerous for the Big Folk. Perhaps if you'd care to get a pair of wings, I could show you the better way?" He winked at her.

Emily, confused, looked down at Serimal in the patch of Pandaemoniums.

Serimal frowned, shook his head, and drew his hand across his throat.

"Eh, thank you, I'll pass for now," Emily said, looking back to Abbott.

The fairy scowled. "Fine, then, be that way. When ye're dying of old age, remember that I offered."

• • •

The two walked through the now thoroughly dark forest lit only by the faint, firefly glow of Abbott and a ring on Serimal's finger that shone like a torch.

"So," Emily said, looking over to Serimal, "what was that 'death' gesture all about?"

Serimal raised an eyebrow. "What, this?" he said, repeating the hand across the throat gesture. "Well, I suppose I can answer that with a question. Do you like being tall?"

"I'm not tall," Emily said. "I was the shortest soldier in the Salamanders."

"Let me put it this way. Would you rather be measured in feet or inches?"

Emily stopped. "Oh."

"Exactly," Serimal said. "The only path you'd be walking would be that of becoming Fey yourself if you took old Abbott up on his offer."

"Can't believe I let you stop me," Abbott grumbled. "Spoilsport."

Eventually, the three arrived at a clearing in the heart of the forest. As Emily stepped into the glade, she noticed that each leaf, mushroom, flower petal, and shrub glistened with the shimmering wings and sparkling clothing of the Fey kind.

But there were others here besides just the pretty fairies. Dark, toadlike creatures squatted near some of the mushrooms. Tiny men with scorpion claws for arms and stingers behind clambered about on rocks. And taller, pale men and women who looked almost like Elves but with night-black eyes stared intently at the pair as they entered the clearing.

In the center of it all sat a charismatic middle-aged but full-sized man with a flowing white beard and a wreath of holly about his head. He held a goblet of wine in one hand and a knobbled stick in the other as he sat on a throne of living tree branches.

Before him stood a pair of small men, perhaps knee-high to Serimal and Emily. One wore a dapper blue suit and short pointed hat of the same color with flowing blond hair beneath it and a charming grin on his face as if he hadn't a care in the world. The other, with stubble on his chin and a morose look on his wrinkled face, looked older and more serious. Soot stained his patched trousers, and he seemed to be missing half his pair of suspenders.

"If I have told you once, I have told you ten thousand times," said the white-haired man on the throne, "you cannot thieve from the Royal Treasury of Bryath! The Fey are ever denied passage to it, and every time one of us trespasses there, it drains from our energy until the transgressor dies."

"Unless you keep us alive, eh, father?" the man in blue said. "If you'd just let us go in, we could get all of it! They'd never notice, what with that war and all."

"Urisk Tanglethorne Puck!" the man on the throne said. "You take your mischief too far from the Glade. You are lucky I don't wish the inhabitants of the country ill, or I'd task you to one of their houses."

Urisk, the man in blue, rolled his eyes and gave an exasperated sigh. "What'd I tell you, Hob?" he said to the man next to him. "He's no fun anymore."

The older Fey, Hob, wrung his cloth hat in his hands. "I don't want no trouble, yer Majesty," he said. "We was just funnin', we was. Just tryin' to give the ol' Villains the ol' heave ho."

"Urisk thieves and you lie, Hob," the king said, for such he appeared to be. "Whatever shall I do with the two of you?"

"You could task them with something incredibly dangerous," Serimal said, stepping forward, "which, upon success, would put the fear of the Fey back in the hearts of a Race that has long forgotten them."

"Well, if it isn't Serimal von Steinadler," the king said. "My, boy, you've changed a good deal. Still haven't lost that hippie haircut, though."

Serimal self-consciously touched his neatly kept ponytail. "King Oberon, I have a proposition for you."

"Can't do, I'm afraid," Oberon said. "Already married. What a mistake that was."

Emily giggled.

Serimal sighed. "Your Majesty, I request the assistance of your least trustworthy vagabond and jackanape. One wholly without a moral compass, whose thoughts are nothing but evil continually."

"Sounds like my son," Oberon said, giving Urisk a stern glance. "What is it you're after?"

"Oh, merely the rarest and most powerful gem in all the Dwarven treasury," Serimal said, looking at his fingernails. "Though I doubt even the Night Court of the Fey could get up to such mischief easily."

The clearing buzzed with tiny conversations. Emily could barely make out individual voices. It was as if the forest itself were having ten thousand miniscule arguments with itself.

After a few moments, Oberon waved his knobbly stick, and the arguments died from a dull roar to a barely audible hum. "We know your family's reverse psychology very well, Serimal. Your brother—"

"Half brother," Serimal said.

"Your half-brother," Oberon said, scowling at Serimal for the interruption, "and your father both tried to use it to manipulate the Courts of the Fey."

Serimal chuckled. "Father, as I recall, succeeded."

"Only because Titania has a crippling weakness for barrel-chested men with too much body hair," Oberon said, making a wry face. "I have no such weakness."

Emily smirked. "What, for barrel-chested women with too much body hair?"

Serimal shushed her.

Oberon laughed dryly. "Har har, miss. If only you hadn't described Titania so well. At any rate, you'll get no help out of us. Your family has done naught but cause us and the land harm."

"And if we help you twice?" Serimal said. "What if we not only balanced the land but solved your quarrel with these two here?" He gestured at Oberon's sons.

"You couldn't deal with these two," Oberon said, sounding exasperated. "There's not a punishment in the Nine Torments that could keep these two incorrigibles from their shenanigans."

"Oh, I have one," Serimal said. "*Slashback!*" he shouted to the air. "*Snack time!*"

Slashback crashed through the branches above, crowing gleefully as she pounced upon the pair of small men. Both shrieked in terror as they tried and failed to avoid the gryphoness's sharp talons. She pinned them to the mossy ground and sniffed them, then gave each an experimental lick.

The rest of the Fey cowered back into their trees, bushes, and fungi, watching with wide eyes as Slashback tasted their princes.

"Hmm, iss tasty Brownie," Slashback said, the skin around the corners of her beak turning upward. "But this iss nice Pixie Stick too."

"Please, Father, your Majesty, King of the Fey!" Urisk cried. "I'll do anything you want. Just get me away from this fiend!"

Oberon, himself looking just a little uncomfortable around the gryphon, managed a nervous laugh. "Ah, heh heh, a gryphon. How ingenuous. I didn't think of using horrible monsters to keep my sons in line. What an idea that is."

"And keep them in line I can," Serimal said. "Were I you—and this is just a suggestion, your Majesty—I would give them a choice. Especially the blue one."

Emily noted the strange charismatic confidence in Serimal's voice and body language. She'd seen it before, like when Voshtyr had addressed the mercenary groups in his tower. Apparently the suave Villain motif ran in the family.

"Give your son a choice between working for me as a punishment for . . . whatever it was he did," Serimal continued, "or becoming gryphon chow."

"I am liking sekont option," Slashback said. "Tasty pixie iss tasty."

"Augh!" Urisk shouted. "Please, Father, I beg you!"

Oberon looked back and forth between his son and the gryphon. "I don't know if this deal is to my liking," he said cautiously.

"I can not haff?" Slashback said, sounding disappointed as she looked at the terrified Fey in her claws. She craned her neck forward and sniffed Oberon. "I can haff big marsmallow instead?"

"Ack!" Oberon said, recoiling. "Fine, you fiend! Take Urisk—and take Hob too. Have them steal whatever you want! Just get that beast out of here!"

Serimal bowed politely, the confident smirk not leaving his face. "Thank you, your Majesty. You have been most gracious." He turned to Slashback. "Come on, Feathers, bring our little bags of trouble, and let us begone."

"And good riddance, Villain," Oberon said huffily. "Scram! Before I send you to the Stand."

Serimal bowed again, then led the way back out of the clearing, mercenary girl and gryphon in tow, along with their newfound, albeit unwilling, accomplices.

"Well, you sure got 'im," Emily said as they left the forest. "How'd you know 'e'd go for it?"

The four of them had followed Abbott's Wall back to the outside edge of the forest, and now they stood at the west end enjoying an excellent view of the coast. The late afternoon sun, coming from the opposite direction as it had this morning, made the forest seem much less threatening. They stood on the loam where the trees gave way to grass, and Serimal could smell an odd combination of sea salt and moss.

Serimal flopped down on his back in the grass. "I didn't," he said. "That was the second scariest thing I've ever done."

"What . . . ?" Emily said. "What do you mean?"

Serimal closed his eyes. "If I'd said one wrong thing, shown one moment of weakness, the two of us would be trees in the Stand of the Forgotten, not remembering who or what we were."

Emily shuddered. "Boy, I'm sure glad you didn't tell me that."

"And I'm glad that bit of crossbow diplomacy worked," Serimal said. "I like having functional legs."

Slashback chuckled. "At least you would still haff some *limbs*, Tserimal."

Both Emily and Serimal groaned.

Voshtyr landed on the marble tiles with a bang as the flooring shattered beneath his impact. He twirled a simple copper tube in his left hand. "Ah, it's good to be back at the family mansion," he said, looking around the ruins of the Von Steinadler castle. "Can't say I much like what Lazik's done to the place, though. I told him to retrieve Nieva, not remove the walls and ceiling."

His eyes changed from green to sinister red. "Serimal! Brother dearest! Come out and play!" He spun the tube and flicked it out at arm's length. A marble column a few yards away exploded into dust. "I know you're here," he called. "You can hide until I reduce the castle to rubble, the rubble to dust, and the dust to nothing, but you'll just be wasting both our time!"

"Then waste this, Demonkin!" Jolan hurled one of his black lances at Voshtyr's head. Voshtyr dropped to the ground, and the bolt passed overhead and blasted the single remaining load-bearing column for the only patch of roof left standing on the entire castle. It collapsed into rubble.

Voshtyr pushed himself up, dusting himself off. "Tsk, tsk, Hero," he said, looking at Jolan. "Destroying centuries-old architecture? That should come out of your pay!"

Jolan scowled. "Don't even start with the cute insults. And no, before you start, I don't care what your plans are, what the number of Heroes you've killed today is, or how pathetic you think I am. You keep your *kharestin* Monologue to yourself."

The two sized each other up.

Voshtyr flexed his metal arm, snapping his concealed blade in and out of its chassis.

Jolan took a wide stance and allowed all four of his mechanical limbs to vent pressure. "Looks like you've had some work done too," he said. "Who designed yours?"

"Beelsephaz, Chief Demonic Artifactor," Voshtyr said. "Do you like it?"

"It's not bad . . . for cheap trash," Jolan said. "Mine were designed by Dair Kormari Angelis, master wizard and fine father."

"Cheap trash?" Voshtyr said. "Can yours do this?" His fingers folded and split into knives.

"Something that tawdry?" Jolan said. "Of course not. Mine can do *this!*" A set of glowing claws sprouted from the fingers of one hand, and his other hand transformed into a hammer. "Your little knife fingers are nothing!"

"Oh, really?" Voshtyr twisted his wrist sideways and tapped on the back of his hand. A full projection of the world appeared, hovering above the arm. Little red pinpricks of light floated inside it. "Can you track all your forces around the world with *your* arm?"

"No, but I can call my lawyer with my foot!" Jolan bent down and removed his left foot, which he held it up to his ear. "Hello, Cornwall and Associates?" he said. "Jolan Foster. No, I don't need anything, just making a point. Goodbye." He put his foot back on. "Top that, nancy boy!"

"I can and will!" Voshtyr looked peeved. He tapped his shoulder. "Death ray!"

Jolan slapped his thigh. "Explosive launcher!"

Voshtyr pointed to his elbow. "Grappling hook!"

Jolan pulled a silver screen out of his left arm. "Tanning screen!"

"Blender!"

"Beverage warmer!"

"Sandwich press!"

"Nailgun!"

"Alarm clock!"

"Hang glider!"

"Spork!"

Jolan looked at Voshtyr askance. "You have a spork?"

"Well . . . yes?" Voshtyr said. "You never know when you might need a spork."

"That's the dumbest thing I've heard all day," Jolan said.

"Well," Voshtyr said, his eyes flaring brilliant red, "that's just downright rude."

"And . . . ?" Jolansaid. "Why do I care what you think?"

Voshtyr flicked the small copper tube at the man. "Because . . . rude . . . people . . ." he said, punctuating each word with a blast from the tube . . . "make . . . me . . . *angry!*"

Jolan dodged behind pylons and bits of collapsed stonework, trying furiously to dodge the hideous blasts of crackling energy Voshtyr hurled from the copper tube. Jolan dodged into a stairwell, and Voshtyr aimed at the roof. With a cacophony of crumbling stone, the stairway collapsed in on itself. And on the Hero.

Voshtyr blew a wisp of smoke off the rim of the warm tube. "Heroes," he said to no one in particular. "They just don't make them like they used to."

A black bolt lanced through the air and impaled Voshtyr through the spine. He stiffened and pivoted as if there were a board strapped to his back.

"And these days, Heroes learn to attack before they narrate,"Jolan said, another black lance springing into being in his hands.

Voshtyr chuckled. "Jolan Foster. The Ebon Lance. How fitting it is to find you here," he said. "Aren't you trying to kill my entire family?"

"I started with your father, then slew his brother and his family, and finally tracked down your mother," Jolan said, circling Voshtyr. "Well, your father's wife. Since the beginning of last year, you've had no blood relatives left but Serimal."

"Pity you couldn't have gotten him first," Voshtyr said. "But wait. Are you trying to out-Monologue a Villain, Jolan? You're not going to have much luck."

Jolan pinned Voshtyr to a wall with a second lance through his gut. "You shut up, Demonkin. I've been waiting for this a long time. I used Serimal to lure you here. And now not only do I finally get to wipe out the heir to the von Steinadler line, the world will hail me as its savior for doing so."

"Ah," Voshtyr said, raising a finger. "You do realize that if you kill me, that makes Serimal the heir, you buffoon."

A third lance took Voshtyr in the right shoulder. "Of course. And when he comes back here, after I tell him you are dead," Jolan said, stepping very close to Voshtyr and breathing in his face, "he won't be expecting a lance between the eyes. I even think I can put enough hate into one of these lances to make it look like your black magic killed him. A tragedy, but I was too late to stop his senseless murder at your hands."

Voshtyr was silent a moment. "So is that all, then?"

Jolan balked. "What?"

"Are you done Monologuing?"

"I am a Hero! We don't Monologue."

Voshtyr shrugged. "It sounds like a Monologue to me. There's just one problem."

"Oh, really," Jolan said with a sneer. "And that is?"

Voshtyr's eyes turned black as the Void. "No one kills my brother but me." Voshty lifted both feet off the ground and kicked Jolan in the stomach, catapulting him across what had once been Serimal's dining room.

Voshtyr tore two of the lances out of his chest and crushed the black energy into nonexistence. He tore the third one out and twirled it in his right hand. He twisted his left wrist, and a blade sprang out above it.

Jolan pulled himself out of the rubble and manifested another lance. "How in the Nine Torments are you still alive? You should be dead thrice over!"

Voshtyr chuckled, and the dark sky grew darker as the stars, one by one, winked out. "You'll have to kill me at least three more times, Ebon Lance. I had souls for breakfast. Mother showed me an absolute fantastic way to cook them!"

Voshtyr sprang at Jolan, and the two of them crashed through the ground to the floor below.

Jolan sprang backward and grinned. "Good, so it will be a fight then."

"Hardly," Voshtyr said. "You tell me it was you who killed my cousin Cassius?"

"Yes, and he squealed like a pig as he died," Jolan sneered. "Hardly dignif—Ack!"

Voshtyr pulled the black crackling lance from his shoulder and hurled it back at Jolan, decimating a pillar behind him in the ruins of the great. He followed up the attack with a blast from the copper tube.

It caught Jolan square in the chest, blasting the Hero across the room and into the cold fireplace. He dragged himself out with a shocked expression on his face. And wrinkles. It felt as if the blast had aged him by a half-dozen years or so.

"Interesting," Voshtyr said. "I didn't know what it would do to a Hero. It just kills peasants instantly."

"What is . . . that thing?" Jolan said, trying to catch his breath.

Voshtyr spun the tube. "Oh, this little toy? Well, Roger tells me the name isn't very . . . Well, that it isn't important. What is important is that every time I hit you with it, I gain the years of life you lose."

"Then you're not hitting me again," Jolan said, gritting his teeth. "Have at you!"

The two battled back and forth, up and down, all throughout the castle manor, destroying the ancient edifice even further. Columns fell as the night grew darker, until there was no light at all, only utter blackness.

Jolan crouched in a doorway, breathing heavily. He'd taken two more glancing blows from the copper tube, and now felt old, blind, and arthritic. He could feel his eyesight dimming and his joints aching.

"Are you ready to give up?" Voshtyr's voice seemed to come from all around in the darkness. "Surrender, and I promise to make your death a tiny bit less painful."

"Trust the word of a Villain?" Jolan said, panting. "A von Steinadler at that? Not likely. Not while I still draw breath."

"Oh," Voshtyr said right in Jolan's ear, "if that's the difficulty, we can arrange for that to cease."

"*Ten Thousand Lances!*" Jolan yelled, spinning and hurling a black lance directly at the voice. It split into thousands of miniature lances, each the size of a throwing knife, and shot forward, perforating everything within sixty feet of Jolan.

There was silence for a moment. Then Voshtyr's sinister laugh filled the blackness. "Mwahahahaha. Did you think you could kill me so easily? Now that you've expended your signature attack, you've nothing left."

Another blast from the Destructo-Tube lit up the blackness in a flash of green and gold. Jolan threw a lance as he saw Voshtyr in the flash. He missed. Another shot, another direct hit. Another thrown lance, another miss. Everywhere Jolan swung, the lance failed to connect.

Two shots later, Jolan crumpled to the ground, a withered old man, physically in his late nineties. "C- curse you . . . Voshtyr," he said, his voice rasping. "Curse you and all your family."

Voshtyr's glowing eyes appeared in the darkness, and he stepped into view, somehow visible even in the inky blackness. "Apparently, you *were* the curse on my family. And I just broke you. How does that feel?"

Jolan raised his arm weakly, giving Voshtyr a rude Orcish hand gesture of defiance.

Voshtyr plunged his arm deeply into Jolan's chest. "Give me your soul, Hero. It will make up for the loss of . . . my . . . family?" He looked confused. "Where in the Nine Torments is your soul?" He dug around.

Jolan chuckled. "Heh heh, I get the last laugh, von Steinadler. I used to be a tax collector."

"Then you have—"

"No soul. Heh, heh heh, heh heh ha ha ha!"

"Rrrragh!" Voshtyr yelled and ripped his hand free. Another flash in the darkness, and Jolan laughed no more.

Chapter 26

OF TRANSFORMATIONS AND DANCE MOVES

In which Cyrus Completes his Collection, And some Dwarves get Served

"THIS WAY, CYRUS," Conrad said. His shimmerage appeared over the surface of the lake.

Cyrus got up from where he sat on the driftwood. "I got another Heartstone, Conrad. But this just makes it worse. What am I supposed to do as steam—get wrinkles out of clothes?

"Don't give up yet, young Hero," Conrad said. "You are more than halfway done. Next you must travel through the waters, as you did through the fires. Your goal is south, a lake in an oasis in Salvinsel. There you will meet persons needed for the coming battle."

"More than halfway?" Cyrus said. "I have two of four. That's half, by my math."

"Trust me, Cyrus," Conrad said. "I am, after all, a seer."

"You know, I'm sorry, but I can't help but be a little annoyed that you seem to know everything before it happens," Cyrus said. "Isn't that, like, cheating at life?"

The shimmerage shrugged. "Perhaps. But this is not the time for dallying. Step into the water, and let it take you away to those who can aid you further. We will not speak again until you have passed through your own crucible." Conrad faded into nothing once again.

Cyrus stepped into the lake. His gaseous body blended with the water, making him more a Human-shaped cloud of bubbles than anything else. The addition of Water to his own personal Balance apparently ameliorated the painful effects of water on his composition. He gripped his sword tighter and discovered that if he really tried, his hand would solidify into something like ice. At least he could still hold objects.

He felt the same connection in the water that he had in the lava earlier, like it was a vast and interconnected network. He thought of a lake he and Reginald had once camped by back when Cyrus was still an apprentice. It was just to the east of Baron Von Kamish's kingdom in a remote portion of the badlands west of the Sur Palma desert. He smiled as the thought reminded him both of Kris's former home and of the trout he had put down Reginald's trousers during that trip.

With a rush of water and bubbles, Cyrus sank into the lake. Much like his frenzied rush through the heart of the world, he shot across an incredible distance, only this time, he felt all the connected waterways, tributaries, streams and creeks that could lead to his destination. He chose one of the rivers that ran south then out to the ocean, across the southern sea, and up another river on Salvinsel.

Cyrus burst out of a crystalline lake in the middle of a more or less barren landscape. The only vegetation that marked the crumbling red rocks and channeled scablands were scrub and sage, with a few more varieties clustered around the lake itself.

He stepped out of the lake and checked himself over. He wasn't wet. Well, he was, but it seemed to be only from having an elemental imbalance.

"Hullo," said a man on the opposite side of the lake. He was wearing only pastel green shorts and a necklace that appeared to have a half-dozen claws on it. "I wasn't expecting this lake to contain a spirit." He looked disappointed. "Man, of all the spirit-haunted lakes and springs in this world, why'd I have to pick one that's haunted by some guy instead of a hot chick?"

"Um, I'm not a spirit," Cyrus said.

"Oh, right," the man said. "Because normal people made entirely of swirling mist, bearing awesome swords pop out of lakes all the time. So, do I get the sword and become king or something?"

Cyrus chuckled. "No, you'd have to pull it out of a rock. Hey, don't I know you?" He took a closer look at the man. "No, I probably . . ."

"I wear a lot of green most the time," the man said. "And I might look familiar because I may have slept with your sister. Do you have a sister?"

Cyrus shook his head. "Wh—"

"Shame," the man said. "I like red-heads. Anyway, so, if you're not a spirit, what are you? An Elemental?"

"Just shut up for one minute, sheesh!" Cyrus said. "I'm a Hero, or I was. Was gonna be. But stuff . . . happened."

"Yeah, that kind of sucked," the man said. "I'm the Green Falcon."

Cyrus started. "Oh, so *that's* where I've seen you before! I'm Solburg. Cyrus Solburg, the Crimson Slash's apprentice."

Green got up. "Hey!" he said. "Old Sir Grumpypants, eh? Last I heard, he was cussing you up one side and down the other as a traitor. How'd that turn out?"

Cyrus looked down. "Not so good. We haven't spoken since he left for Landeralt after the Massacre."

"Pity," Green said with a shrug. "He's a good man. And from what he told me whenever we were out drinking, he said you were a pretty good kid too."

Cyrus looked around. He and Green appeared to be the only two people within a Stone's Throw Heroic—which varied between one and three miles depending on the Hero. The red rocks that made up the terrain looked rough, like they'd been crumpled up by giant hands and just left there. The small river that fed into and out of the lake he'd just sprung from trailed off and was lost to sight as it ran down a bend in a canyon. The air was dry, even here by the lake. It certainly felt warm and dry like a desert should be.

"So, Green said, "did you really do it? Betray us, I mean?"

Cyrus shrugged. "Sort of. I sent a false message because I didn't know how to tell Reg I was being forced to. They had my wife hostage. People keep telling me it's not my fault, but it still tears me up."

Green nodded. "It's called a conscience, kid. All Heroes got 'em, and that's what makes us different than the Villains. Sure, we got enough power to beat the heck out of anyone we want to, but the fact that we do what's right with it is what makes us better than your common bully."

"So you don't blame me?" Cyrus said.

"Sure I do," Green said. "You're dumb and ignorant, and as much as I love the ladies, there's no way in the Nine Torments I'm betraying all my bros in the Brotherhood for some skirt."

Cyrus gritted his teeth. "That's completely unfair! I was—"

"Kidding! I was kidding, keep your panties on," Green said. "You know, I wonder if we couldn't get you and Sir Grumpypants back together again. He's got a temper . . . *you* got a temper . . . but you've both had time to cool off since all this *bok* went down."

"Not very likely," Cyrus said. "I'd like to, but he was furious when we parted ways."

"Excuse me, pardon me!" yelled a knee-high man in blue tights as he ran past the pair of them. "Beware of angry Dwarves!"

"Wait, what?" Cyrus said, following the running man with his eyes. "Is that . . . is that an overgrown pixie?"

"Oioi! Big folk!" said another small man, about the same height, though uglier and chubbier than the first. He ran up to Cyrus's knee. "Is one o' you Cyrus Solburg?"

Cyrus looked at Green. Green shrugged.

"Um, I am," Cyrus said. "How did you know? And what's this about angry Dwarves?"

"Oh, goodie. Thank me lucky stars." The little man threw a rock at Cyrus. "Love to stay and chat, I would, but I be likin' me hide in one piece. Toodeloo!" He doffed his somewhat squashed hat and took off at top speed into the rocks and disappeared.

Cyrus and Green sat silent for a moment.

"What in the world was that all about?" Green asked, throwing on his green vest and giving Cyrus a very strange look.

"Not a clue. And what is this . . . ? Oh." Cyrus looked at the rock in his hand. He'd caught it by reflex and was just now noticing it was in fact a gem. A gem of the same size and shape as the ones he'd just collected two of. "Really. I . . . I can't believe my luck. This is—"

"Ours!" bellowed a deep and throaty voice. A squad of six Dwarves encased entirely in suits of full plate armor and wielding halberds and axes pounded around the corner. The leader, a Dwarf with a silvery beard and a red band painted on one of his armored shoulders, pointed at Cyrus. "That stone is property of the People's Republic of the Underground! Give it back or die where you stand."

Before continuing with what at first glance appears to be a violent confrontation between short stocky bearded men with flawed political ideas and a pair of young Heroes, the reader should understand that Dwarves were once some of the most freedom-loving, self-motivated people on the planet.

The change came about under the rule of the last Underking, Alethor McBeardhammer, the Berserker King. Up until the First Armageddon, Dwarves were a highly capitalistic race that relied on a hereditary monarchy supported by a representative body known as the House of Lodes, which was comprised of members of the mining and smelting guilds, the merchants' association, and the like. The House of Lodes advised the Underking on matters of foreign policy and domestic law.

The system worked well for centuries, until the rule of Alethor. The McBeardhammer clan had been in power for three decades when Alethor chose Axebeard McShieldforge as his trusted advisor. Axebeard was a charismatic Dwarf with a large support base among the people. He had come from a humble background as a cobbler's son and had risen to favor in the royal court through his adept handling of the Great Shoe Crisis a decade before.

Using his post as Trusted Advisor, Axebeard gradually replaced all of the key members of the House of Lodes—and eventually members of the Royal Court itself—with his own supporters. When Axebeard finally struck, Alethor and the McBeardhammer clan were ill-prepared and outnumbered. Alethor kept his reputation of the Berserker King to his grave, and took more than his share of Axebeard's forces there with him. But the coup was nevertheless successful.

A bloody purging of the McBeardhammers followed, and when it was all over with, Axebeard set up his own rulership by redistributing the property of his slain enemies to the poorer Dwarves, thereby solidifying their support. And thus was the People's Republic of the Underground born.

Because of the radical shift in economic and political status, the race of Elves distanced themselves from the Dwarves, partially because they did not want to be caught up in the slaughter and partially because Axebeard himself was about as nice a diplomat as a rabid three-headed hellhound.

The system holds to this day, but only because the current ruling class of the People's Republic confiscates all mined materials beneath the world's crust and gradually distributes needed goods and services as it sees fit, thus ensuring the entire Race's dependence on the system.

It should also be noted that Dwarves speak with a brogue. This is a long-standing tradition universally recognized, though the origins of this accent have been lost to the abyss of Time.

• • •

Green stepped in front of Cyrus. "Listen, kid, I don't know what's up with you and the rock, but I'd hate to see your friendship with Sir Grumpypants fall by the wayside. Why don't you just fizzle into the lake or something? I can take care of these angry beer-sodden midgets."

"Oh, and isn't the green one a wee bit of a racist now?" said one of the Dwarves, opening his visor. "That's nae a kind thing to say to a fellow now, is it?"

"Stuff it, shorty," Green said. "We got your magic rock, fair and square. Sort of. Okay, not really *fair*, exactly, and it's more octagonal than square, but the point is, we have it, and how we got it is irrelevant."

"Green," Cyrus said, feeling another uncomfortable change sweeping his body.

"Not now, kid," Green said. "So, you want to fight over it? I'm the Green Falcon. I'll take all of you on."

"Green," Cyrus said again, slouching to the ground.

"What?" Green said, turning his head. He stopped immediately.

Cyrus lay on the ground, his body turning slowly to what looked even to himself like viscous mud complete with bubbles and chunks of rock. "This is . . . really uncomfortable."

The Dwarves looked at him in bemusement. Finally the leader turned back to his men. "He's used the stone! Get him, lads!"

Hilarity ensued. The six Dwarves bowled Green over as he tried to stop them, and they all attacked Cyrus. But as soon as they struck him, their halberds, axes, and even their fists got stuck in the thick mud that comprised Cyrus's entire body.

"Ach, I can't hurt it!" one of the Dwarves yelled, trying to pull his axe free. "It's made of mud!"

"You think you've got something complain about?" Cyrus said slowly. "How would you like to *be* made of mud? It's really depressing. I need a hug." He grabbed one of the Dwarves and gave him a hug.

The Dwarf shrieked as Cyrus accidentally absorbed him.

"Oops," Cyrus said. "I guess I should have known that would happen. Figures."

"Let my man out of there!" the lead Dwarf demanded. "Are ye daft? We can settle this peacefully, without drowning anyone in mud."

Cyrus sighed. "Fine, whatever. I don't care."

"Wow, being made of mud must be depressing," Green said, pulling himself out from under a pile of Dwarves.

"You have no idea." Cyrus wiped away his face, which was most unsettling. He watched his reflection as his face re-formed. "All these elements affect me in one way or another. This one just feels worse than the other ones." He ejected the Dwarf, who coughed and sputtered, dragging the mud out of his beard with his fingers.

"So," Green said, "I'm a Hero. I don't want to kill all of you guys for just some dumb rock."

The lead Dwarf nodded. "Neither do we want slain, boy. An' we've no great love o' Voshtyr an' his designs o' world domination. If-in 'e wants the great People's Republic o' the Underground, 'e'll 'ave quite the fight on 'is 'ands, he will."

"So it looks like there's only one way to settle this," Green said, drawing his knives.

"All right," the Dwarf said, readying his halberd. "What'd that be, then?"

"A dance-off, of course!" Green threw down his knives points first in the dirt on opposite sides. "He who has the smoothest dance moves keeps the stone. Have at ye!"

The Green Falcon leapt into the air and did a backflip, then launched into a series of acrobatic loop-kicks and tumbles.

The Dwarves looked at each other as if stunned. And then, as a squad, began to dance.

It is a little known fact that Dwarves, of all the Races in the world, are the best dancers. It stems from the fact that, over the course of the takeover by Axebeard and his ilk, most forms of political and personal expression were either severely limited or completely banned. No speech was allowed against the government, nor fliers permitted to be printed, and any assembly for any purpose had to have a government monitor present to enforce these laws.

One thing Axebeard overlooked was the art of Dance. Thorbeard Hammerheart, a master of Break Dancing, an ancient art combining the artistic and graceful movement of dance with the destructive power of berserker rage, began teaching local Dwarves his art as a manner of political protest. Over the next few years, handfuls of Dwarves would show up in front of the Polithaus where Axebeard held his meetings, and they would dance in protest. At one point, five hundred Dwarves danced in unison in the Grand Square of Underhall, and then they attacked the building.

Dancing gave the Dwarves their freedom from a tyrant, and thus they practice it to this day.

• • •

The Dwarves opened up with a set of unison squat kicks, followed by some traditional Polka crossed with some sort of violent stomp.

Green countered with an Electric Slide and the Wyrm.

The Dwarves launched into a spinning Break Dance, and pulverized boulders as they spun on their heads, slammed to the ground, and did flips off one another.

It went on for five minutes. Green's lack of teammates severely limited his available options, and at the end of that time, he ran out of impressive dance moves.

The Dwarves finished by running up the side of the valley and jumping onto one another's shoulders, then striking a dramatic pose all at once. They held the ta-da pose for a moment, all breathing heavily and glistening with sweat. And maybe some glitter.

The two tiny men Cyrus had seen earlier stepped out of the shrubbery and clapped. "Well done, well done!" said the little man in blue. "Very impressive, both sides. But the victory goes to the Dwarves."

The Dwarves laughed and clapped Green on the back. "Ye may be a Hero, lad, but you just got served."

"I . . . I . . . Well, *bok*," Green said. "Sorry, Cyrus, I guess you have to give it back."

"I don't think so," Cyrus said, and he began dancing himself.

First he shuffled left, then he shuffled right, then he collapsed in on himself into a puddle, which then grew dozens of muddy feet, the soles of which were reddish rock like the valley around them. They all began tap-dancing.

The Dwarves looked at the gooey Cyrus strangely, but the oddity didn't end there.

Cyrus swirled back up and jumped onto his head, spinning like Green and the Dwarves had, but as he spun, he gradually morphed into a column, which then shaped itself into Cyrus, who once again stood on his feet. Only two of them now.

Green looked like he was about to say something, but Cyrus wasn't done.

Cyrus began one of the leaping, swirling dances he'd learned from the Katheni of Mir. It was a dance for a single male dancer. But then he moved into another dance, this one for two people. Hee split into two slightly smaller versions of himself, and danced . . . with himself.

He did the Wyrm, much as Green had, but with thrice as much wiggle, since it appeared that his backbone was as morphic as the rest of him. For his finale, he broke into six small versions of himself and replicated the Dwarves' last move and pose, complete with hard breathing but sans glitter.

"There," Cyrus said, morphing back into one. "Now *you* got served."

Everyone involved, after a moment of uncomprehending silence, began clapping, the two Fey men the loudest of any.

"Well, game and match, I guess," Green said. "Gem's yours, Cyrus. Fair and square, right guys?" He looked at the Dwarves.

"Aye, lad, fair enough," said the lead Dwarf. "I've nae seen fresher dance moves above the ground, ever. The stone's yours, for now."

The Dwarves saluted Cyrus, then turned around and looked at the pair of Fey. "Now, as for you, thieves . . ."

"Gah! Run, Urisk!, Run!" said the older of the two tiny men.

The pair of Fey ran off again, the Dwarves in hot pursuit.

Cyrus chuckled. "Dance-off?" he said to Green. "That was . . . unexpected."

"Hey, don't look at me," Green said. "How was I supposed to know they could dance? I mean, they're built like barrels! Big bearded barrels of booze!"

"And you got served by 'em."

Green slapped a palm to his face. "Okay, seriously, knock it off. All I heard is they can't do the Wyrm because they just fall over and roll around because they're too stocky."

Cyrus laughed, then sighed. "Sure, Green, sure. But something's really bothering me."

"Oh, besides the fact that you can apparently now become a Mud Golem dance troupe all by yourself??" Green sat down on the edge of the lake and retrieved his fishing pole.

"These Heartstones," Cyrus said. "They were supposed to be stupidly hard to get. That's why they were stored in the Keeps of the Elements, right—to make it hard to get them?"

"Uh, sure, Cyrus," Green said. "Actually, I spent most of my time in my Magical Geography class looking at Sally Ann in the row in front of me. But sure, whatever."

Cyrus sighed. "Right. Well, if they're so powerful and hard to get, why do I keep ending up with them so easily?" He crossed his arms. "I mean, what, is the next one just going to fall out of the sky?"

A shiny object fell out of the sky and whacked Cyrus on the head.

Of course, since he was still comprised of mud, it sunk into his skull.

"Ow, what was thauugh!"

A brilliant yellow canary diamond sank through his head and protruded from his mouth. He pulled it out. It was, yet again, the exact same shape and size as the ones he'd previously collected.

Green pointed at Cyrus. "Um, Cyrus, you just . . ."

"Really?" Cyrus said, looking up at the sky. "*Really?* I mean, seriously, this is ridiculous!"

He held up the stones he'd already collected. The amethyst stone, which was the combination of the first two Heartstones, had already combined with the topaz, which he'd gotten from Dwarves, leaving a nearly black stone alongside the canary diamond.

"It's too weird to believe," Cyrus said. "I mean, I thought I was going to have to go explore all these towers, avoiding traps and defeating Minions and having Epic Battles against Boss Creatures at the top of every tower, all to make myself stronger. And instead, they're showing up in random places and just falling into my hands! Or . . . you know. What's the meaning in that?"

"I dunno," Green said. "Maybe you didn't need to get better with a sword. Maybe you had to get stronger in other ways. Maybe it was the people you met, or the journey itself. As you've collected these stones, have you learned anything useful?"

Cyrus put his hand through his head, then pulled it out and scratched the surface of the mud. "Not really. I kind of helped out another Hero who needed some sense beat into him. Oh, I made another business partner. And I had to bust a move to show you and some Dwarves up. Those are okay, but they're not exactly Life Lessons, you know? And they're not as awesome as getting really good at fighting."

"And the last stone—learn anything with that one?"

"Yeah, I don't get that at all. Well, here goes." Cyrus put the two stones together into one hand, and they merged. With a flash of brilliance, the stones became a single sparkling multifaceted diamond.

And then Cyrus changed. Buffeting winds swirled around him. His skin solidified, his hair became first licks of flame then true hair once more. Then his form became corporeal, once more wearing the garb he had worn as an apprentice Hero: the blue tunic and sparkling silver chain shirt. The only thing he was missing was his floppy old blue hat.

"Oh," Cyrus said. "Hey, I'm back to normal. That was . . . anticlimactic."

"*Bok* in a bucket!" Green said, popping out from behind a rock. "You didn't tell me you were becoming an Everything Elemental!"

"Huh? What's an 'everything elemental'? Is this what real elemental balance looks like? Some dumb kid who thinks he should be a Hero? I already looked like this before!"

Green dug around in the pockets of his trousers. He pulled out an improbably large book entitled *Hero's Guide to Monsters* and flipped it open. "Here," he said, pointing at one of the pages.

Cyrus looked at the book. Green held it open on a page labeled "Periodic Table of Elementals." The table listed all the usual Elementals: Fire elemental, Air Elemental, Sodium Elemental, Titanium Elemental, and the like. But at the very bottom of the table, on the far right, was a box set apart from the other listings. In the box there was a large question mark and a silhouette of a person, along with the words "Everything Elemental?" and "Unknown, but possible."

"Huh," Cyrus said. "So I'm either the most powerful elemental on that table or just some dumb kid with a shiny rock."

"Or you could be a dumb kid with a shiny rock who is also the most powerful elemental on that table," Green said.

"Thanks for that," Cyrus said.

"No problem."

"You're half right." A young woman on a gryphon swooped down over the two Heroes and landed a few feet away.

Cyrus drew his sword. But it felt so extraordinarily light he almost launched it across the lake. He could see a shimmer along its length like a rush of wind surrounding the blade. He also felt his skin harden, like a callous only flexible. He was startled to notice that his skin beginning to become somewhat flinty in appearance.

To top it off, his hair caught fire.

"Whoa," Green said, dropping his book.

"I know," Cyrus said. "Isn't this awesome?"

"Yes, she is," Green said, looking at the woman on the gryphon. "Can I help you, O beauteous creature?"

"Can it, loverboy." The young woman saluted Cyrus. "Captain Emily Cartwright, Salvinsel Salamanders, Aerial division. This is Slashback Ricor, Mount First-Class, same unit." She jerked a finger toward Cyrus. "And you, Cyrus Solburg, have a few things to do." She opened a pocketwatch and pressed something in the middle. Her shadow split apart, and the second shadow shifted, rotating around her ankles until it lay perpendicular to her, then stood up. It solidified into someone Cyrus recognized.

"Voshtyr!" Cyrus said, gripping his sword. "I'll kill y— Oh, wait, you're not Voshtyr. Voshtyr doesn't have a diabolical goatee. You're Serimal, aren't you?"

Serimal stroked his diabolical goatee diabolically. "Finally, someone recognizes me," he said. "Cyrus Solburg, we of the

Fifth Column Corporate Espionage Corporation have been watching you since you defeated Voshtyr and his Ranshan horde at the Keep of Falling Stars."

"Fccec?" Green said, trying to pronounce the name as an acronym. "You guys need a catchier acronym, like S.P.I.E.S. or something cool like that."

"Sinister Purpose Inconspicuous Espionage Service?" Cyrus said.

"Some Peculiar Instance of Extreme Sneakiness?" Green suggested.

"Stealthy People Infiltrating Entrenched Stations?"

"Sexy Persons In Expandable Stockings?"

"Stabbing Peons In Extraordinary Situations?"

"Softly Perpetrating Incognito Exploration . . . I need something that starts with S."

Cyrus looked over his shoulder at Green. "You're really bad at this."

"Stupid Protagonists and their Incredibly Exaggerated Sentences," Emily Cartwright muttered.

"You're both bad at paying attention," Serimal said, taking his hand off his now well-stroked goatee. "Can I get on with being dramatic now?"

Cyrus sheathed his sword and sat down next to Green. "Sure, go for it." His body began to calm down. In a puff of smoke his skin softened back to normal, and his hair changed back to just hair.

"So," Serimal continued, "as you well know, your wife is held captive by a wicked, evil man—"

"So is he wicked *and* evil, or like, really, really evil?" Green asked.

Cyrus smacked him over the head. "Shush, that's my wife he's narrating about."

"She is held captive along with my beloved," Serimal said, giving Green a malicious glance. "And I know that you are quite possibly the only person in the world who can get into that flying castle and stand a chance at rescuing them both."

"Me?"

"Yes," Serimal said. "But you could not face Voshtyr as you were. That is why we have been . . . helping you along in your Quest."

Cyrus and Green exchanged a look. "Helping me . . . how?" Cyrus asked.

Serimal smiled. "How do you like your diamond?"

"Oh, that was you?" Cyrus said. "I wondered about that."

"And now that you have become an Everything Elemental, you are ready to face Voshtyr."

"Yeah, maybe," Cyrus said. "I don't know. I don't know if I can trust you. And I certainly don't know if I've got a handle on how being an Everything Elemental works. But . . ." He looked at Green and then back at Serimal. "But I'll sure give it a try."

Serimal clasped Cyrus's hand and shook it heartily. "Excellent, I knew you would. So here's the plan . . ."

"So, yeah," Green said. "I'll just nip back to Bryath and let them know hope is on the way, shall I?"

Serimal stopped. "Oh. I see you haven't heard then," he said. "The Siege of Bryath is over."

"Oh, good," Green said. "That means I can get back and tell Blue that I won our bet."

"Voshtyr won the siege," Serimal said curtly. "He brought incredibly powerful Spitfires and knocked down half the exterior wall. It took him less than a day to get into the inner keep."

Both Cyrus and Green were silent for a moment.

"Shoot," Green said. "I owe Blue fifty gold pieces."

Cyrus looked back at Serimal. "Wait, does that mean he's in control of the government?"

"He's *been* in control of the government," Emily said. "He set up most of it when he took control of Centra Mundi. His cronies have been running the show almost since the Vale."

"So are we going to take it back?" Cyrus asked.

"I don't think there's more than a handful of Heroes left," Green said. "We couldn't take on an army right now, much less all the Villains in the world. We're kind of an endangered species."

Serimal put a hand on Cyrus's shoulder. "I know this is hard to deal with, but we have to do what we can first. And first, we rescue our respective beloveds, all right?"

Cyrus blinked at him. "You want me, one of the last Heroes around, to team up with you, brother to the most vile Arch-Villain in history?"

"Half-brother. And yes."

Cyrus nodded. "Right. Sure." He turned to Green. "Okay, so I want you to go back and find the rest of the Spectrum Heroes. I'd help, but I'm not sure where they all are, though I have seen Red and Purple recently. Purple I left on Lorimar, near the lake, and I'mn not sure where Red teleported to."

"Yeah, I'm here, and Blue is playing bodyguard for Guardian's son Trigger," Green said. "Yellow was on Clawstrike tending wounded last I checked.". "I can get 'em all together for you. No problemo."

"Good." Cyrus nodded. "Go do that."

"Catch you later, sweet-cheeks," Green said, blowing a kiss at Emily.

Emily rolled her eyes.

Green knelt down, thrust a fist in the air, and then leapt into the sky shouting "Greeeeeen *Falcon!*" He disappeared in a flash of (what else?) green.

"All right," Cyrus said. "Let's get going."

"You're right, we should." Serimal chuckled. "And by the way, I like your first suggestion for S.P.I.E.S. Sinister Purpose Inconspicuous Espionage Service? Not too shabby."

Chapter 27

Reconciliation

*In which an Important Object is Retrieved,
An Old Friendship is Repaired,
And Exactly the Opposite happens to a Castle*

REGINALD LEFT THE northern edge of the Mountains of the Morning sometime around noon. He and Wraith met up with Keeth just outside the forest, and they traveled for several hours.

It was mid-afternoon by the time they reached a hill overlooking some quite trampled plains. Angry grey clouds hung low over the hills, obscuring some of the mountain peaks and swirling malevolently.

The grass was just beginning to grow again where it looked like it had been beaten flat by thousands upon thousands of feet. There were still patches where no plants grew, leaving only dead earth. Only one patch of soil on the plain looked truly healthy, as if someone had purified it and planted grass seeds and a small tree.

"What manner of unholy place be this?" Reginald said, dismounting. He couldn't hear or see any wildlife. In fact, he hadn't heard so much as a hornet since leaving the mountains.

"This must have been where Voshtyr's Dark Army prepared for the Vale Massacre," Keeth said. "Dark deeds were done here, and even Nature itself rebels against it."

Reginald looked up to the horizon. "Shouldn't there be an enormous tower up that way?" he said, pointing north.

"Hmm," Keeth said. "I am almost certain that the Tower of the Highseekers should be around here somewhere, though I have only seen it from the air. The wizards who run it tend to be territorial about their airspace."

"If you could take to the sky," Reginald said, "perhaps you might find it."

"A most excellent idea," Keeth said. "I shall return in a moment." The dragon took to the air, flapping his enormous membranous wings.

Wraith snorted and shied away from the dust cloud raised by Keeth's wings.

"Easy, Wraith," Reginald said, patting the charger's neck. "We'll get you used to that great reptile eventually."

Reginald tromped about the field for awhile looking at the lingering destruction and trying to think of some way to fulfill his current Quest. He still had Elves, Dwarves, Orcs, Ransha, Araquellae, and Katheni to make true friends of, according to the vision he'd gotten while drowning.

Or while not drowning. Or while being suspended from time for a month. Whatever it was that had happened, he still needed to unite people from such different backgrounds. Reginald knew he was no diplomat, and even straightening out the civil war between the Elves would be no easy task.

At least he was already a friend to Humans, he reminded himself. He was a Human, and in his own opinion, which he valued greatly, he was quite good friends with himself.

The toe of his boot caught on something, nearly tripping him, as he walked through the one patch of grass where everything seemed healthy. Reginald stopped and scuffed at whatever it was. It seemed to be a scrap of rough cloth, possibly from a tent. He pulled it up. It was indeed either part of a tent or a scrap of sailcloth.

But there was something beneath it. Reginald stared at it in amazement for a moment, then picked it up.

It was Cyrus's old floppy hat.

Reginald brushed it off. It had quite a bit of dirt on it, but was still obviously blue, and it was in remarkably good shape for how long it had probably been there. If Cyrus had somehow left it there before the Vale, it had been there for nearly two months.

He looked at the hat for a few moments, and he felt tears prick at the back of his eyes. He really did miss Cyrus. The snarky humor, the readiness to help, the easily-goaded conscience. The traits that made a good Hero, Cyrus embodied them all. And, Reginald realized, he'd overreacted a bit when Cyrus "betrayed" the Heroes.

He'd never taught the boy the proper response to being captured, as it hadn't come up during his training. Well, it had, but he had been preoccupied with having his ribs broken at the time, and he'd forgotten to use it as an object lesson later. That was the first thing about being a Hero: never miss an opportunity to make your moments teachable. It was time to track Cyrus down and apologize. It was no good at all in these dark times to have a strong friendship ruined.

A Friend to All Races. The thought niggled at the back of Reginald's mind again. He turned back to Wraith and hung the floppy hat on the saddlehorn.

"Reginald!" Keeth said from the sky, slowing to a hover. "You will not believe what I found!"

Reginald held up Cyrus's hat. "I found my apprentice's hat," he said. "What did you find?"

"The Grand Highseeker," Keeth said. "Come, he may help you win this war of yours."

Reginald clambered over a pile of rocks and sat down. Piles of rubble and shattered stone spikes littered the otherwise flat ground. It looked as if someone had been digging, or blasting, through the top few layers of dirt and stone and had uncovered the top of a white stone tower.

"I fail to see this Highseeker anywhere, Keeth," he said, wiping his brow.

"Oh, he is down here." Keeth perched atop a larger boulder. "He sent me a message with magic. He said he would bring his tower back up, but there are—"

"Bring it back up?" Reginald said, again scanning the crater and shattered rock. "I can see he's buried it somehow. What is he planning to do?"

"He'll use Earth Magic to bring it back up if you agree to help him with a problem. He says there are a distressing number of fortified zombies on the upper floors, and he is not inclined to let them get to him."

"Zombies?" Reginald said. "I laugh at the undead. Come, tell him to raise his tower. I shall ensure that he does not get his pansy magical bottom bitten off."

Keeth cocked his head and waited a moment. "He says you are a meat-headed buffoon, and that these zombies are fortified with enough magic to break steel against."

Reginald chuckled and drew Sharp. "Then it is a good thing that my blade is made of sharpness itself. Tell him to raise his tower, or I shall raze it myself."

Keeth snorted. "Cyrus must have rubbed off on you more than you thought. I shall tell him you are well-equipped to take care of his problem."

A few moments later, the ground rumbled, then shook, then positively leapt about. All of a sudden, the ground beneath Reginald hefted itself into the sky, taking the Hero with it. A tower shot from the bowels of the earth and defiantly pointed itself at the sky once more,

Reginald teetered at the top of it, his hair and tunic billowing heroically in the stiff breeze. "That was exciting."

Keeth flapped up from the surface below and landed on the tower beside him. "I must say, that is one way to hide a tower. Who would look for such a structure underground?"

"Someone would look there," Reginald said, "or else there would be no zombies in it, eh? Where are they, by the way?"

"Right there!" Keeth said, pointing a claw behind Reginald.

"Grrrruuuuuaaaaagggggghhhhh," said a zombie, shuffling toward Reginald from a descending stairwell at the center of the tower roof. It looked like it was encased in stone armor, with only its rotting teeth and dead eyes visible through a stony helmet. Its skin glowed with soft phosphorescence, and its hands had wickedly curved black claws.

Reginald hefted Sharp. "Well, then, time to get to work."

Keeth raised a claw. "Just don't start—"

"The Hero took a mighty stride forward and did lay into the undead abomination with his dangerously sharp sword!" Reginald said, leaping forward and hacking the zombie in half with a single deft stroke.

"Narrating." Keeth put a paw to his face.

"Aha!" Reginald said. "The sword of Sharpness cleft through the enchanted armor like a . . . like . . ."

Keeth mumbled through his talons. "Like a fat man at a dinner buffet?"

"Please," Reginald said, glancing over his shoulder with an offended look on his face. "Something a little more Heroic."

"Perhaps it is a terrible buffet," the dragon suggested, "and even eating it is a Herculean task."

"Cleft through the magic like a judge through lies at a trial," Reginald said, ignoring the dragon. "It passed through them with ease, as if their hardness and resilience mattered not a whit."

Keeth chuckled. "I like the buffet better. Oh, and do watch your flanks, by the way." He snorted a ball of fire out one nostril to barbecue a second zombie that had emerged and was headed for Reginald's left side.

"Aided only by a wisecracking dragon and his mystical blade, the Hero cleft his way through innumerable foes and down the stairs to rescue the beleaguered mage below!"

The sounds of muted groans and shattering stone echoed inside the deserted tower. The portraits of famous mages hung askew on the grey stone walls, and the crystals on the walls gave barely enough dim blue illumination to see the murals of famous magical duels and battles.

An abandoned reception counter occupied the southern side of the tower, and a few scattered and overturned writing desks cluttered the floor. The floor itself bore a mosaic of a man reaching into the clouds and pulling a flame of fire from it, which was supposedly a picture of the Highseekers' founder, one of the first men to truly begin studying Magic.

Reginald cleft through several dozen of the enhanced zombies and descended to what he guessed was the ground floor of the tower. As he stepped into a section of the tower that was better lit, thanks to diamond-shaped windows in the walls, he could see what appeared to be the atrium of the tower. As he looked around, a glowing Human hand appeared and tapped him on the shoulder. Reginald looked at the hand. It gave him a thumbs-up and beckoned him toward one of the reception counters.

Curious, Reginald bisected the last zombie in the room and followed the hand. It slowed, then stopped and pointed at a button beneath the counter.

Shrugging, Reginald pressed it.

A section of wall behind the desk slid away revealing a doorway. Standing in the doorway was a young man of around twenty-five years, or perhaps more, judging from the silver hair and creases in his face. But possibly he wasn't as old as he appeared either, as there was a distinctly youthful energy with which he carried himself and a bounce in his step not present in that of an older person.

"Well, that was easier than I expected," the young man said. "Thank you very much, Hero. Those zombies can be just the life of the party, you know?"

"My pleasure," Reginald said, bowing. "I am Sir Reginald Ogleby, known far but not wide as the Crimson Slash."

"Oh, right," the young man said. "You were Cyrus's mentor, right?"

"You know of Cyrus?" Reginald said, sheathing Sharp.

The young mage nodded. "Yes, I had a few words with him back when he started breaking the conduits of magic I use to pour my breakfast cereal in the morning." He extended his hand to Reginald. "William Weatherblade, Grand Highseeker."

"Well met," Reginald said, shaking his hand. "Though that name sounds familiar. Any relation to Lydia Weatherblade, former Heroine?"

William rolled his eyes. "They always remember her first. What do I have to do to one-up her, explode?" He sighed. "Yes, she's my sister, though I wasn't aware of the 'former' status on her Hero membership. What'd she do, kick a puppy?"

"Joined Voshtyr and his Dark Army," Reginald said with disgust. "Right in the middle of a battle I could've used her help with." He nodded to William. "You, at least, seem to be on less than amicable terms with that cretin."

"Cretin?" William chuckled. "You mean Voshtyr or my sister?"

"The former."

"Well, given that those were *his* zombies trying to eat my tender, tasty flesh, I would say no, I'm not overly fond of him right now." William sat down at the desk. "Clever man, Voshtyr. He knew my traps and such would kill the men and Minions he sent in. And so they did. But what I didn't count on was having their bodies reanimate as completely magic-proof zombies in less than a day. I had no choice but to submerge the tower and hope help would come."

"You are lucky I was here," Reginald said, puffing out his chest. "There are things in this world that only the strength of a man's arm, the courage of his heart—"

"The alcohol tolerance of his liver, and the length of his back hair can overcome," William said. "Yes, yes, you're strong and mighty. Now get over yourself and tell me what's been going on. I sort of lost contact with the outside world a few months ago." He pointed out the window. "I was literally buried alive for a while. How's Cyrus?"

Reginald sighed. "I'm afraid I've been out of touch almost as long as you have. As for Cyrus, we parted ways, and not on the best of terms," he said. "It was in part Cyrus's fault that Voshtyr wiped out most of the known Heroes in the world, you know."

"Ouch," William said. "And so Voshtyr took over?"

"More or less," Reginald said. "We managed to preserve Guardian's heir and a few important things from Guild headquarters. But the survivors had to take refuge on Clawstrike Island, and it is a dark day for the world."

"Sounds like a whole dark week." William swung his feet up and plopped them on the desk. "Anyway, now that I'm back on top of the world, as it were, is there anything I can do to help?"

Reginald nodded. "Yes, if you could—" He stopped mid-sentence as he looked over William's shoulder. "Actually, could you help me destroy a flying city?" He pointed out the window at the Citadel of the Kinetics, which had just crested the top of the mountains.

• • •

"Lazik!" Voshtyr bellowed as he appeared in a puff of black smoke inside the Citadel of the Kinetics. "Tarrasshan! I demand to know just what you are doing with . . ." He trailed off as he looked around and saw wreckage all over the floor and chunks missing from the wall.

He followed the trail of destruction through the castle's great hall, a guest room, two corridors, a thoroughly wrecked kitchen, and another hallway before he found what he was looking for.

Lazik stood on the edge of a windowsill, looking out of the floating citadel and down.

"Lazik!" Voshtyr bellowed again. "I demand to know just what you are doing with Nieva Frostreach!"

Lazik turned his head toward Voshtyr. "Letting her jump out a window, apparently."

Voshtyr took a step back. "By the Infernal Tome, what did you do to your face?"

Lazik snarled. "A trivial matter that doesn't concern you. What might concern you now is that the woman you are looking for—along with a Kath girl who does not concern you in the slightest, so don't ask—just leapt out of this window."

"You let her jump out a window?" Voshtyr said, flabbergasted.

"Yes, wasn't that the first thing I said to you?"

Voshtyr grabbed two handfuls of his own hair. "Curse you, you completely cerebral misanthrope! If I'm to rule the world I'm supposed to marry the Elven princess and live happily ever after, and you've let her jump out a window?" He ran to the window. "You say she jumped just now?"

Lazik nodded. "To her death, I would think. Too bad for you. Your plan is foiled. Boo hoo."

"Aerial units five, seven, eight, and eighteen, converge on me and provide covering fire," Voshtyr said into his wrist. His eyes flared red as he turned back to Lazik. "If you want your soul to remain firmly connected to your body, I suggest you cease the snarking and give me a boost."

"My dear Voshtyr, nothing would please me more than to defenestrate you."

Voshtyr jumped out the window. Lazik sighed and thrust his hand forward.

Kris and Nieva leapt from the window.

It was the first time Kris had fallen for long enough to truly appreciate that falling was not fun. It was terrifying. Sure, the wind rushing through her ears and rippling her fur felt nice, but imminent splattery death often puts a damper on small pleasures.

It seemed like she would fall forever. But it wasn't forever. The two fell twenty or thirty feet before landing on something wooden.

Kris felt she should roll and come up claws bared, but she was so surprised not to be dead that she just lay there. And Nieva landed in a splash of frost and snow that somehow bled off her momentum.

Kris found herself lying on the deck of a small boat. In midair.

The only other occupant of the skiff was a middle-aged man with white hair and colorless eyes. He looked shocked for a moment, a moment just long enough for Kris to finally roll to her feet and bare her claws. He started to draw something out of a belt pouch, but Kris leapt forward, kicked the man hard between his legs, and shoved him off the deck. The man didn't so much as make a sound as he plummeted away.

"Whew," Kris said. "Looks like the prophecy was right."

"Thank the Creator and His Twelve," Nieva said, tucking a lock of her now very disheveled hair behind one of her pointed ears.

"You follow the Creator, or the Twelve?" Kris said.

"Well, it is more appropriate to worship the Creator than His creations." Nieva unceremoniously flopped down on the deck. "He must have thought we were worth saving."

"Why would a Villainess worship the Creator?" Kris said, tilting her head sideways. "Don't you spend most of your time trying to destroy His creations? How many Villains' Doomsday Devices are built to destroy the world?"

Nieva sighed. "Far, far too many. But keep in mind, Huntress, that some Villains do in fact mend their ways."

Kris smiled. "It is good to hear that others believe as I do."

Nieva nodded. "So where are we?"

"On a boat," Kris said. "I think." She walked over to the ship's helm and looked at it. The wheel itself was built over some kind of glowing white crystal that had foot pads near its base. She stepped on one.

The boat lurched forward, then accelerated smoothly through the air.

"Whooooooeeee!" Kris said, a massive grin splitting her face. The wind whipped at her whiskers. "We're flying!"

The boat was indeed airborne. It responded beautifully to the slightest nudge of the wheel as it coasted away from the flying city.

"Perhaps we can escape with this," Nieva said. "I take back my unkind thoughts of you, Huntress."

"That's all right," Kris said, steering right. "Wait, unkind thoughts? Why?"

"Because I thought you were nuts," Nieva said. "Who jumps out of a window in a flying castle? Besides, you're very— *look out!*" she shouted, pointing behind them.

Kris glanced back over her shoulder.

Death flew at them on swift wings.

Around the group appeared the starlit wreckage of what had probably been a grand and mighty castle. As the energies of the teleportation magic faded around them, Cyrus stepped forward and looked around.

He whistled. "Wow, this is a piece of work. What happened here?"

"*Des kharestin orsobu pitchin!*" Serimal roared. "Jolan! Where are you, you black-hearted coward?"

"By the North Star," Emily breathed, looking at the wreckage. "This place was bad when we left, but not *this* bad."

The skin above Slashback's beak wrinkled as she sniffed the air. "It smell like acids. And old men. And deat."

"Deat?" Cyrus said.

"She means death," Emily said, "and she's right. Kind of like scorched flesh. Can't you smell it?"

"Rrraagh!" Serimal yelled and kicked over a pile of rubble. "Voshtyr is behind this. I just know it!"

"Only partially," said a voice from the shadows. Out from behind a shattered slab of stone rose a hulking, winged shape with horns.

Cyrus whipped his sword out and leveled it at the creature. "A demon? Here? Stand back, all. I can take care of it!"

"Wait! Stay your hand," Serimal said. "Jaratyr?"

The demonic form stepped out into the twilight, its form coalescing into that of a tall man with black hair and severely red skin. He bore in his arms the body of an aged man with black metallic limbs and a grievous stab wound in his chest. "Your friend is dead," Jaratyr said.

"Jolan," Serimal said, running to Jaratyr's side. "What . . . what happened to him?"

"Voshtyr happened to him, that's what," Jaratyr said through clenched pointed teeth. "This is what that tube I warned you of does to a Hero. When fired at a normal mortal, it withers him to nothing immediately. It seems that Heroes are more . . . resilient. But multiple strikes even Heroes cannot bear."

"Is that the Ebon Lance?" Cyrus said. "I wouldn't have recognized him, except I'd know those metal arms and legs anywhere."

"Ten thousand curses," Serimal said, slamming the heel of his hand against a shattered column. "Jolan . . . forgive me, I would not speak ill of the dead, but I could not see past my anger." He looked down at Jolan's aged body. "I can't win. My half-brother has beaten me at every turn."

"But I have the Heartstones!" Cyrus said. "You said I could take him on when I had them, right?"

Serimal turned to Cyrus. "Listen, Cyrus. Having the ability to defeat Voshtyr doesn't help us at all if we don't know where he is. If we knew where he was, we could throw you at him, but until then . . ."

"I know where he is," Jaratyr said. "I can show you exactly where he is."

"Now why would you do that?" Serimal said, whirling to face the Demon. "Haven't you been telling Voshtyr everything I've been doing this whole time?"

Jaratyr snorted. "No, you buffoon. I've been telling him only as much as he needed to hear to trust me completely. And by playing both sides, I got this Hero killed." He looked down at Jolan, dead in his arms. "It's time we ended our mutual half brother."

Serimal sat down, suddenly looking very weary. "All right. If we know where he is, we can send you after him, Cyrus. Can we teleport directly there?"

Jaratyr shook his head. "No, he's set up wards against unauthorized teleportation. If you tried to 'port in there right now, you'd end up on your tail with a massive headache, and Voshtyr would know exactly where *you* were."

"How far away, then?" Emily asked. "If it's not too far, Slashback and I can take 'im."

Jaratyr scratched his head. "From here? Well, we're on the wrong continent, for one. It's almost two days nonstop by air, and you mortals can't do that." He looked around the assembled group. "Now, I don't know exactly how far out from that tower the 'no teleporty' field extends, but he hasn't spent a whole lot of time on it." The demon knelt to lay Jolan's body down on a slab of busted stone and stood up again. "I can't imagine it would extend farther than fifteen leagues or so."

"Fifteen leagues," Cyrus said. "That's still a long way on foot, but I'm quicker than that in the air, if I get enough Air lines under control."

"But if you pull on the ley-lines too much, Voshtyr will definitely notice," Serimal said. "My sources report that he's got six or so different kinds of magic detectors running nonstop to make sure no one sneaks up on him. If you come in hot, he'll shoot you down before you can get close."

"How about this," Emily said. "Not every one of us is a Demon or a Hero. I say we 'port in as close as we can safely get, and Slashback and I can fly him in."

Serimal shook his head. "No, I'm not putting you two in danger. Voshtyr would swat you out of the air like pesky fairies. Wait!" He leapt up. "I have a small five-man airship, the *Hellbat*, hidden in one of my old Fifth Column safehouses! The boat runs in a high-performance stealth mode, and it could slip past some of Voshtyr's defenses easily. It wouldn't take us long to get to the safehouse, either. It's a small place in the hills just west of the Vale of Dreams. She's a fast ship, hence the name. We could close fifteen or twenty leagues in no time at all!"

"All right," Cyrus said. "Let's do that then. What are we waiting for?"

"Thank you, Jaratyr," Serimal said. "I knew your good tendencies would win out in the end."

"Pfft," Jaratyr snorted. "Just don't tell Mother. She'd be mortified if she found out. And then she'd mortify me, in a more literal sense."

Slashback banked left, skimming the clouds along the mountain range just south of the Mir desert. She carried Emily and Cyrus, while Koshiro and Serimal rode in a strange contraption that was half balloon, half boat.

The *Hellbat* was a black lacquered ship that resembled a flying coffin with fins on the sides and an enormous oblong balloon where the masts should have been. A pair of propellers at the aft of the vessel cranked out an enormous amount of air, which propelled them rapidly across the sky above the landscape.

They flew north and were now overlooking the blasted plain. Voshtyr's dark army had camped here once. A large cluster of them remained still, farther off to the southwest, surrounding the mountain keep that was reportedly Voshtyr's base of operations. There were still significant ground forces between them and the tower, but if they were lucky, they could fly over them without too much trouble.

To make matters worse, The Citadel of the Kinetics loomed over the coast only a few leagues away. Cyrus hoped the flying city wouldn't shoot the small boat down. Serimal said they were running stealthy, but still . . .

"The Tower of Highseekers is back!" Serimal said as they swooped lower. "What a good sign! And . . . wait, there are people down there. That looks like a Hero. Take us in closer, Koshiro. Slashback! Dive!"

The two groups dropped in altitude and buzzed over the pair of figures. One of them was a younger man with silver hair, the was other an older man built like an enormous stack of bricks.

Cyrus recognized them both. "Put us down," he told Emily. "I've business with those two."

"The kind of business where you gets 'em a fruit basket," Emily asked, "or the kind where you introduce them to the business end o' your sword?"

"Neither," Cyrus said. "The kind where I see whether or not one of them has the latter kind of business with me."

Emily nudged Slashback with a knee, and the gryphoness slowed to a hover, then dropped to the ground.

Cyrus dismounted and began walking toward the figures.

Reginald ducked as something shot over his head. He drew Sharp and spun to see what it was. It was a pair of people on gryphonback. Reginald squinted at the riders. He couldn't make them out, but he did recognize the emblem of the Salvinsel Salamanders on the gryphon's barding. He also saw a strange flying craft carried by a large balloon.

"Allies," he said to William, who seemed to be casting as spell of some sort.

William canceled the spell. "Oh, friends of yours?"

"Possibly," Reginald said. "In this day and age, anyone not trying to slay me is a friend. Maybe they can help us with that flying city." He pointed up at the menacing fortress in the sky.

"I don't know," William said. "The Citadel of the Kinetics? That's a pretty tall order. I might need to get back inside the tower and use the Focused Lens of Focusing to properly boost any attack spell I could shoot at it."

"The Focused Lens of—?"

William scowled. "I know, I know, it's not a very creative name. But think of a magnifying glass, only for magic, and that's what it is. I've always wanted to use it." He looked up at the castle, which was still drawing nearer. "And now might be the last chance I get."

Reginald looked back at the two gryphon riders, who had now dismounted and were walking toward him and the mage. Reginald couldn't believe his eyes. took a step forward. "Cyrus?"

There he was, looking the same as Reginald had last seen him, though he was wearing peasant's clothing. Actually, if anything, he looked better. Stronger. More full of life than he had after the defeat at the Vale.

"Hi, Reg," Cyrus said, a half-smile tugging at one corner of his mouth. "Long time no see."

A thunderous boom interrupted the meeting. Heroes young and old spun to look at what had made the sound.

Two things of note were happening. First, the Citadel seemed to have launched a small airship as well, and then it shot a blast of inky darkness at it. Second, a column of light erupted from the top of the fortress in the mountain to the southwest.

Reginald frowned. Why would they try to shoot down one of their own boats? Unless . . .

"Kris!" Cyrus said. "She must have escaped on her own! What a woman I married . . ."

"And she's about to get a face full of angry Arch-Villain," William said, his eyes glowing blue. He must have been using *Farsight* or some other ocular enhancement spell. "It looks like Voshtyr himself is after them, and he's brought friends." He pointed to more dark dots joining the first one. "They're Minions of some sort."

Serimal looked at the column of light from the fortress. It spiraled up and pushed the clouds away. "And that looks like the P.L.O.T. Device warming up. I don't know what Voshtyr is hoping to do with it without you and your Heartstones, Cyrus, but the individual pieces can still be dangerous without the final components. One of us should take care of that."

"I have to take care of Voshtyr," Cyrus said. "If he's any more powerful than he was last time we fought, I may be the only one who can stop him."

"Slashback and I will make sure Nieva and the kitty cat are safe," Emily said.

Reginald looked up. "I think those of us who cannot fly on our own should help for Cyrus. Can we use your airship as an artillery platform?"

Serimal nodded. "It's armed to the rudder."

William touched Cyrus's shoulder. "Here, have this spell. It's sort of experimental, but I think you'll find you like the effects. It combines *Drake's Instand Wardrobe Change* and *Wings of the Air,* as well as *Hurry Up* and *Tamper with Gravity.* Well, sort of. It's more like—"

"What do you need magic for?" Reginald said. "Just get him up there so he can fight!"

William gave Reginald a sideways look. "Yes, because giving him the ability to bend the laws of momentum and energy won't give him a significant advantage against Voshtyr."

Reginald sighed. "Just give the lad the spell. He's got the best chance of any of use to take that vile demon down."

"Fine, fine," William said, and touched Cyrus in the center of his chest. "*Ignore Physics.*"

A multicolored light spread across Cyrus's body, transforming his peasant clothing into blue and silver Hero garments with a blank space on the chest where a Heroic Emblem should have been.

Reginald clapped a meaty hand on Cyrus's shoulder.

Cyrus spun away and assumed a defensive stance.

Reginald nearly stumbled in surprise. "What are you doing?"

"Just . . . wanting to be ready for anything," Cyrus said, relaxing a bit. "In case you were still angry with me."

"Well, I'm not."

"Really?" Cyrus said.

"Yes," Reginald said. "I just wanted to tell you, before we go off to battle . . . ."

Cyrus looked hopefully at his former mentor. "Yeah, Reg?"

"I'm sorry, lad."

Cyrus felt tears at the back of his eyes, but blinked them away. He hugged Reginald. "I'm sorry too, Reg. Sorry for everything."

"A-*hem*," William said. "You can make amends later. Don't you have a Villain to fight?"

"Right," Cyrus said. "That's the first thing about being a Hero. Slay the dragon first—rescue the Damsel afterward."

His hair lit up into a blazing flame, his eyes turned solid blue-white, his skin toughened into armor-like hide, and a whirlwind sprang into existence around him.

"Let's do some stuff," he said.

Reginald watched Cyrus blast off, then he turned to Serimal and company. "There are still far too many foul creatures around that fortress for my taste. If Cyrus chases Voshtyr inside, or one of us needs to dismantle the P.L.O.T. Device, we'll be swarmed if we set foot anywhere near it."

Serimal nodded. "That's probably true. But even with Emily, Koshiro, you, and myself working together, we don't have the ability to cleave through that many monsters and Villains."

"No, but I know some people who can." Reginald fished in his belt pouch and retrieved one of his Tokens of Summoning.

"Who?" Serimal asked, looking at the token.

Reginald smiled. "The Spectrum Heroes." He pressed the token. "Purple? This is Crimson. How would you like to participate in some Daring Heroics?"

"Left! *Left!*" Nieva shouted.

Kris spun the wheel to port. "What is that black thing behind us?" she shouted.

"It's Voshtyr!" Nieva said. "He'll kill us both at this rate!"

Trailing darkness like sinister cobwebs, Voshtyr blazed toward the boat, shrouded in crackling energy and flanked by flying Minions. Even from that distance, Kris could see the blazing red of his eyes. "*You fools!*" he shouted. "*There is no escape from Voshtyr Demonkin!*"

Kris looked over the vessel's side. Another bolt, this one a brilliant golden white, shot up from the ground toward the ship as well.

"Hang on to something!" Kris yelled. "Something else is coming!"

"Heavens help us!" Nieva clung to a railing.

Kris leaned back with all her might, pulling the wheel toward her. The ship shuddered and careened upward instead of sideways.

The black and white bolts collided. The world paused for the briefest of moments. It was as if every living thing in the world thought, for just one moment, that this would be the way the world ended. Whether the Balance tipped one way or another, whether it rebalanced, or if the world itself were destroyed, there would always be that one eternal moment when Hero met Villain, Light met Dark, Courage met Fear, and Time stood still.

Then Time got bored and resumed his hyperactive jaunt across the universe.

A crackling shockwave blasted away from the impact. It upended the small boat, sending Kris and Nieva plummeting toward the ground.

As she fell, Kris wondered if she'd been a fool for trusting some prophecy. After a brief flying boat ride, she was once again falling to her doom. She couldn't be the Huntress, and her cubs couldn't be the key to everything. The ground streaked closer every moment, and to make matters even worse, that gryphon didn't look too friendly.

Wait . . . gryphon?

A gryphon and rider caught Kris and Nieva as they fell, swooping to match and absorb their momentum. Kris found herself in a saddle in front of the rider, a young blond woman in military garb, who smiled at Kris. Nieva was clutched in the gryphon's talons. She looked all right, but unconscious.

"Now what're you doin' in the sky, marm?" the blond woman said with a chuckle. "Only two things are supposed to fall out of the sky: idjits and bird poo. Which are you?"

"I'll go with the latter." Kris breathed a sigh of relief. "It's less likely to die on impact." From the safety of the saddle, she looked up into the cataclysm going on in the sky.

• • •

Cyrus tackled Voshtyr with the force of ten Intercontinental Ballistic Magics. The shockwave rippled out from the two of them, knocking one of the flying Minions out of the sky, swatting away Kris's boat, and flattening trees a league away, though they were still high in the sky.

Voshtyr's three remaining escorts wheeled and began firing green magical beams at Cyrus. They wore magic-shooting gauntlets, and they flew about on strange devices made of leather harnesses and glowing crystals. In the split second Cyrus saw them before flying past, he realized that the crystals were the same kind as was on the pirate boat that had attacked him and Kris as they fled from Centra Mundi the first time.

The Minions soon had other things to shoot at, as the *Hellbat* came up to altitude and opened fire on them. They were too busy dodging and returning fire to trouble Cyrus any longer.

Cyrus and Voshtyr tumbled and fell through the air until they shoved each other away and regained their respective balances. Cyrus hovered in midair, the Elements taking over his body completely. His skin looked like shale, his hair was like a torch, his eyes glowed bright blue, and wind whipped his clothing and hair about, even though there wasn't much of a breeze.

Voshtyr's transformation was not as drastic but still disturbing. His normally high features were now pointed, and his eyes flamed red. Swirls of black shadows whipped about him, occasionally sticking and clinging to his appendages. His metal arm was different than the last time Cyrus had seen it. It was a darker grey, burnished to a sheen, and it glinted crimson when the light struck it.

"Hi," Cyrus said, grinning into Voshtyr's face as the two grappled in midair. "Looking for me?"

"Oh, look, the whelp has arrived," Voshtyr said with a malicious sneer. "You are extraordinarily hard to find, boy, but you have the common sense of a roast chestnut. I sent two crews of pirates and a whole city full of psychics to find you, and you just fly into my arms. Fool. Now I have you."

"You may have me, but you can't hold on to me." Cyrus punched Voshtyr in the face. As his fist swung forward, it hardened into solid rock. The crack of snapping bone penetrated the rush of energy around the two.

"Ow! The face!" Voshtyr said, losing his grip on the young Hero. "Why do you Heroes always go for the face?"

"Comedic effect, I think." Cyrus kicked off Voshtyr's chest and landed on the rocky underside of the Citadel of the Kinetics. He stood up. Sideways. Apparently William's spell allowed him to ignore the existence of gravity itself. "That's the first thing about being a Hero: if you can't show up an opponent, you haven't really beaten him."

Voshtyr snarled, his teeth now resembling fangs more than cuspids. "Then you're about to get your posterior beaten so royally you'll need a crown for your bum. Rraagh!" He leapt at Cyrus, the blackness around him forming into a pair of batlike demonic wings.

Cyrus leapt aside, which caused Voshtyr to crash headfirst into the spot he had just occupied. The impact knocked a crater in the bottom of the Citadel and ensured that the toilet above where he'd crashed would forever leak unless the handle were tilted just right.

"That's using your head," Cyrus said. "I suppose you're just noggin on the Kinetics' door?"

"What?" Voshtyr pulled himself out of the crater. He drew a scimitar from his belt. The blade was made of the same dull grey and crimson steel as his arm, again edged with the Shard and with a core of Darkmatter. "Was that supposed to be a joke?" Voshtyr asked.

"Of course," Cyrus said. "How can you get a head in this world if you don't get humor?"

Voshtyr growled. "By the Horrible Toenails of Beelzebub, stop it with the puns! No one thinks they're funny!"

Cyrus chuckled. "Abskullutely. Just as soon as you stop being evil."

Voshtyr roared and slashed at Cyrus with the vile blade.

Cyrus fell back under the onslaught, retreating up the side of the Citadel. He drew his new sword. "Beware, Arch-Villain!" he said, brandishing it. "You may have a blade made of coalesced ancient evil, but *this* blade was forged by a big lizard and magic'd by a small rabbit! When I strike you down, your humiliation will have no end!"

Voshtyr looked confused. "Um . . . all right?" Then his eyes burned red again. "Cyrus Solburg, you have *no* idea how long I've waited to catch you."

Voshtyr twisted his wrist. The blade hidden inside the mechanical arm whirred out, protruding above his hand. This time the blade was different. At its core was a heart of blackness, a forged and refined piece of Darkmatter. Protecting that was another layer of Hellsteel. On the outer edge, the malevolent ionic blue of the Shard glinted. It was a new weapon.

"I've waited *years* for a Hero to have such attunement to the Elements, and now here you are! The fifth ingredient in my immortality!"

"What makes you think you need me?" Cyrus asked.

"You think my younger brother is the only one with a spy network?" Voshtyr said. "You Heroes are so arrogant, you think that if you have a plan, it can't possibly fail. Well, you're wrong. You know what they say about the best laid plans? The fail, that's what! Just like you will today, you will fail, and die, and I will attain immortality and rule the world forever!"

"This sounds like a Monologue," Cyrus said, standing sideways on one of the Citadel's walls, next to a window. "Is this going to take a long time? And if your mother was doing it, would it be a Momologue?"

Voshtyr stabbed at Cyrus again. "If you're as poor with a blade as you are with humor, this won't take long at all. Now hold still!"

Cyrus reached in the window of the building he was standing on, retrieved a flowerpot containing a midget tree, and dropped it on Voshtyr. "Banzai!" he shouted.

Voshtyr swatted it away with his blade. "You know, I think it would almost be worth spoiling my plans by killing you just to *shut you up!*" Six bolts of black lightning leapt from Voshtyr's palm, spattering upward and taking chunks out of the building.

Cyrus leapt straight up, grabbing an Air line and shooting lightning back at the oncoming bolts. The lightning struck Voshtyr's bolts, sending them veering away opposite directions, trailing harmlessly into the air. "Whaddaya know," Cyrus said. "It works."

"Yes, the Philistine figured out counterspelling," Voshtyr said, his foot finding purchase on the windowsill Cyrus had pulled the tree from. "When I have my immortality, I'll find my way around that triviality."

"Immortality?" Cyrus said, shooting a second bolt at Voshtyr's face. "Is that what all that kidnapping Reg and holding Kris hostage and making me betray the Heroes was about?"

Voshtyr dodged the bolt and leapt at Cyrus. "No, those were just for fun. Part of my 'ruling the world' project. But I'm on to serious matters now. I need you and the Elemental Heartstones for my immortality project. I'm a busy fellow. Lots of projects."

The two crashed through a window and into a hallway in the Citadel. It was the first time he'd seen the Citadel up close, and it was not what he expected. It wasn't a militaristic fortress city. It was starkly beautiful. The architecture was elegant, with sweeping columns and marble buildings and rounded corners. Everything was pure white and so clean it almost hurt the eyes to look at it. Houses, some large, some small, lined the white brick streets. It wasn't just a flying fortress. It was a flying civilization.

Regardless of the caliber of civilization he saw, Cyrus was still in the middle of a fight. Voshtyr launched black lances at him. Cyrus leapt behind a corner as the scorching black beams ate troughs in the marble walls.

"If you need me for your project," Cyrus shouted around the wall, "why are you trying to kill me?"

"Oh, did I say I needed *you?*" Voshtyr said. "To be more specific, I need your soul. Generally speaking, it kills people in the extraction. I hope you don't mind."

"Fun times," Cyrus said, risking a look down the hallway. "But I'm busy that day. Whatever day it is you were planning on draining my soul, I'm busy. All those days." He leapt across the hallway and sprinted for a doorway, lashes of hostile magic crashing into the floor behind him. He leapt out the window into open air, then quickly used an Air line to blow himself back to the floating city. He crouched beneath the balcony.

Voshtyr shot out the window as well. But his fury sputtered, and he hovered there looking around, his back to Cyrus.

Cyrus leapt off the side of the Citadel and planted his sword firmly in Voshtyr's spine, just below his shoulderblades. "Voshka-bob," Cyrus said, no smile on his face.

"Aaaugh!" Voshtyr screamed, but in a different kind of agony. "That was the worst pun yet!"

"Huh?" Cyrus said, surprised Voshtyr could still speak after that blow.

Voshtyr chuckled. "Oh, little Hero, we have met again, but this time . . ." He whirled, the momentum pulling the sword free of his back, and kicked Cyrus in the stomach . . . "the advantage is *mine!*"

Cyrus crashed through the wall, through a sitting room, and into a dining room table. Two adult Kinetics and a child stared at him as he sat in the middle of what had probably been a cut of roast beef and a bowl of baked beans. It was hard to tell, because like everything else in the room, they were white. Cyrus picked himself up from the wreckage of dinner and wiped white gravy off his sleeve.

"Oh, we are *so* done with this malarkey." Cyrus felt his hair flare up, his skin harden further, and his eyes glow. "Sorry about your dinner," he said to the family. He ducked his head and ran in a rush of wind back out the hole in the wall he'd just made.

He barreled out into the sky again. He spun just in time to deflect another blast of evil magic. "I have to tell you," Cyrus said, "my puns may be really bad, but your cliché Villain lines are worse. 'I have the advantage'? What is this, quote-from-the-Villain-Handbook day? What's next, 'Now you are mine'?"

"Oh, don't worry," Voshtyr said, charging up another shot, "you won't be alive long enough to hear my whole repertoire of them. Prepare to Meet your Doom!"

"Called it." Cyrus rolled his eyes and readied himself to dodge.

This time, the magical bolt didn't perform as Cyrus expected. Cyrus dodged it, but instead of shooting past him into the air, it skidded to a halt, glowing malevolently. Then it came after him again. Cyrus dodged again. Again it followed him.

Cyrus ran. He ran along the edge of the Citadel, the blazing evil smart bomb of fire hot on his trail. Literally. He ducked in a window, out another, down a white brick street, , and up the side of a tower, then looked back. It was still following him.

He gritted his teeth and jammed his sword into the side of the tower, cutting a huge slash in the side. He pumped Air energy into himself and his sword, increasing his speed and spraying marble dust everywhere as he enlarged the slice. He ran in a circle, cutting the tower clean through at a diagonal. It began to slide.

Cyrus jumped atop the tower, the blast of fire shooting up the side of the tower at breakneck speed toward him. He crouched, and with one mighty leap, shoved the top half of the tower down at the Hero-seeking magic.

The tower exploded as the magic tore it into dust in a blast of sound and fury. Dark flames covered chunks of marble as they fell, consuming them before they hit the ground. But at least the relatively smart bomb was gone.

Cyrus skidded down the side of the tower and landed on the ground again. He wiped his brow and looked around for

Voshtyr. He was in a courtyard of the Citadel in a small rock garden, wherein all the stones were, unsurprisingly, white. A few bits of rubble still burned on the ground. It was quiet. Perhaps the Kinetics had had the good sense to retreat further into their city.

There! Voshtyr flew around the corner fifty feet up in the air, his batlike wings trailing darkness as he flew. Spotting Cyrus he charged through the air, his face twisted in rage.

Cyrus chuckled. "That the best you got, Arch-Villain?"

Voshtyr shot past Cyrus, sweeping his Shard sword in a vicious cut at his head. Cyrus parried, but the blow left Cyrus's ears ringing.

"Oh, yes, taunt the Villain." Voshtyr's eyes were black pits with no pupils, corneas, or any other eye parts. They were balls of blackness in his head, glowing with red cores. "You Heroes and your smug self-superiority. It sickens me. It's been said it will be your downfall. But no, it won't be, *I* will be your downfall. Take this!" Voshtyr slipped a ring from his finger. It enlarged into a thin coppery tube. With a flick of his wrist, he launched a blast of green and yellow energy at Cyrus.

Cyrus barely dodged in time. The shot knocked a crater in the wall behind him. Another followed, then two more. Cyrus leapt for cover, but every time he found concealment, it shattered to dust under the tube's onslaught.

Cyrus slid into a building and lay there panting. Voshtyr was too fast, and his attacks were so quick that Cyrus barely had time to dodge them, much less counterattack, even with the *Ignore Physics* spell on and plenty of Air energy.

Then Cyrus had an idea. Remembering what he had done at the Highseeker's tower before, he reached for all the ley-lines he could find. There they were. All the elements. For just a moment, Cyrus saw the entire network of them in his mind's eyes. Not just all the interconnected lava pathways, and not just the waterways around the world—but all the places touched by all the elements in the world. In other words, everywhere. They resonated and connected to the Elemental Heartstones he had acquired.

Cyrus pulled the diamond from his pocket and shoved it into the hilt of his sword, where Nath had left a socket for a gem.

The sword flared white, and a blast of invisible force exploded from around Cyrus. It leveled the building and pounded a crater into the ground beneath him. From his sword sprang a brilliant white glow that grew longer and wider until it was more than ten times the original length and width of the sword. Cyrus moved it this way and that, feeling like he was holding a tool the Creator Himself had used to carve the world like a global jack-o-lantern. Voshtyr spotted Cyrus and unleashed another torrent of strangely-colored fire from the tube at him.

Almost casually, Cyrus turned the sword so the flat of the blade faced Voshtyr like a shield. The incoming fire pinged off the blade like hail against an iron wall.

"Game, set, match, Voshtyr." Cyrus swung the pure elemental sword at Voshtyr. It cleft clean through a building and sliced straight at Voshtyr.

Voshtyr blocked it with his own sword. It stopped Cyrus's blade, but Voshtyr lost a dozen or more feet in altitude. He blocked a second stroke after throwing up his other arm wielding the tube to brace against the impact. But the third stroke knocked him to the ground.

Cyrus strode out of the building toward where he'd knocked Voshtyr down. "Your reign of terror is over, Demonkin. Prepare to taste my blade."

"Oh, and a tasty blade it is," Voshtyr said, rising from a crater. "It's elementally delicious. And besides, I thought I was the one with the clichés. "

Cyrus swung the glowing titanic blade at him. Voshtyr ducked and aimed his tube at the blade. A beam of dark energy shot out and struck the sword. It spun out of Cyrus's hand straight up into the sky, the white energy fading from the blade.

"Uh oh."

Then Voshtyr shot at Cyrus. Cyrus threw up a blast of air. It deflected the shot, barely. But Cyrus realized that the blast had stripped away all of the Air energy he had collected. Cyrus kept his eye on the sword. It was falling now.

Voshtyr fired again. And again. Cyrus blocked with a wall of ice, then of earth. The shots shattered both.

"You will die here, Cyrus Solburg, and your body and blood will be mine," Voshtyr said.

Cyrus caught his sword as it fell. The gem in the hilt flickered and faded out, as did the power extentions. This was bad. He braced to receive the attacks that would at the least Hurt Greatly and at worst could possibly put an end to him. He looked at Voshtyr as the dust settled.

But instead of seeing the Arch-Villain rising above him like a spectre from the Nine Torments, he saw a bleeding man.

Blood oozed from Voshtyr's eyes and fingernails. He looked like a slightly more hygienic Blood Wraith, only more solid. He slowly rose from the ground where he had landed, dragging himself toward Cyrus. Something was definitely wrong.

Cyrus stared. "What . . . What happened to you?"

"I ran out of souls," Voshtyr said, panting. "And since I haven't been able to hit you with the ones I had stored, I've been using bits of my own." He coughed and wiped blood from his cheek. "I'm running out of soul, Solburg, and you are running out of energy. Let's see who can win a war of attrition, shall we?"

"Instead, why don't w—"

Voshtyr fired once more, and he instantly cried out in agony.

Cyrus attempted to counter the shot with a wave of fire, but Voshtyr's shot blasted right through the unleashed fire. Cyrus flinched, making a last-ditch effort to block it with his sword. It smashed into the hilt of the sword, knocking the Elemental Heartstone free.

Almost immediately, Cyrus's Elemental enhancements, his flaming hair and toughened skin, began to fade away. He had lost a good portion of his power. But apparently Voshtyr was losing more.

Voshtyr shrieked as if in torture, but again the tube fired a shot.

The blast hit Cyrus in the chest. He reeled back and careened into an already damaged building, crashing through the wall and collapsing it on top of him.

Cyrus's world dimmed and flickered. Blackness closed in on his vision, like looking through a tunnel. His tongue felt thick and dry, and his skin was hypersensitive as if he were under the effect of a dangerously high fever.

"Mwa ha HA!" Voshtyr said, lunging forward and scooping up the Heartstone. "One shot was all I needed!" He twirled the copper tube.

"Agh," Cyrus said, clutching his chest. "You needed one shot for what?"

"This device steals bits and pieces of souls for me," Voshtyr said. "All I needed was a bit of your soul and the Heartstones, and now I have *both*! Mwahahahaha!" Voshtyr seemed to have healed from some of his wounds somehow. He staggered to his feet and held the Heartstone up triumphantly. "With these, the P.L.O.T. Device shall be complete, and I can emulate the elemental power you embody. And then I shall be invincible *and* immortal. Good bye, Hero. Stick around! I'll be back to kill you as soon as I absorb the Heartstones!"

"Wait!" Cyrus said, dragging himself out of the rubble. "What about your plan!"

"Mwa ha hack cough," Voshtyr sputtered, coughing blood again. "This *is* part of the plan! If you beat me now, I do nothing. Depressing, but hardly my Utter Defeat. But if I retreat and live, I become more powerful than you can possibly imagine. Or, wait, that's cliché again . . ." He reached into the pocket of his coat, pulled out a small book, and began flipping through it.

Cyrus quirked an eybrow as he dusted himself off. "Is that a—"

"Villainic Phrasebook," Voshtyr said. "'If I retreat and live, neither you nor your little dog will . . . ' Wait, that's no good. How about 'If I retreat and live, I can fight another day . . . ' Argh, this is difficult." He scratched the side of his head with his vile sabre. "How about 'If I retreat and live, I will find your lack of faith distur—' Oh, hang it all, I'll just kill you when I come back." He snapped the book shut and pocketed it. "Farewell—or should I say, 'Fare poorly!' Mwahahahaha!" Voshtyr leapt into the air and flew southwest across the countryside.

Cyrus tried to follow, but either his *Ignore Physics* spell had run out or it had been canceled. He slumped to the ground. "I couldn't do it," he said. "I couldn't stop him. And now he's got the Heartstones."

In front of him, Slashback and Emily and a second rider, flew up to land on the cliff, depositing a third person on the ground as well.

"Cyrus!" one of the riders shouted.

Cyrus looked up. "Kris? Kris!" He stood up just in time to be pounced back to the ground again.

Kris smothered Cyrus's face in Katheni kisses. "I missed you so much."

Cyrus chuckled. "Hey, my distressing damsel. I missed you too. What's up with the whole rescuing yourself thing?" He hugged her to himself.

"I got bored waiting for you," Kris said with a smile. "What took you so long?"

"Eh, I had to become an Everything Elemental," Cyrus said. "Though I think Voshtyr kind of stole that from me. And we need to stop him."

"Yes, yes, of course," Kris said. "But I need to tell you—"

Emily hopped off the gryphon and walked over to the two as they lay on the ground. "Hey, I hate to interrupt you two lovebirds," she said, "but a half-demon with the intention o' subjugating the world just took off thataway." She pointed southwest. "You plan on doin' something about that?"

The strange dirigible boat belonging to Serimal floated over the edge of the Citadel and landed beside them all. Reginald and Serimal got down from it—an odd couple indeed.

"Serimal!" Nieva ran to embrace Serimal.

"Nieva," Siermal said, holding her tight. "Don't ever worry me like that again."

Nieva looked up at him, tears in her eyes. "I'll just tell the next megalomaniac who abducts me that you said I wasn't allowed to be kidnapped."

"You do that," Serimal kissed her. "Because I have first claim to any kidnapping."

Reginald strode over to Cyrus. "Here, lad," he said, tossing some cloth to Cyrus. "If you plan on defeating that Villain, you need all the help you can get."

Cyrus sat up, managing to barely dislodge the amorous Kath on top of him, and looked at what Reginald had thrown to him. It was his blue floppy hat. A bit worse for wear, but still his.

"Yeah," Cyrus said, putting the hat on and pulling down the brim as he used to do. "I think it's time to save the world. Let's get to it."

Chapter 28

THE PUISSANT LIFETIME OMNIPOTENCE TRANSFUSION DEVICE

In which P.L.O.T. Device works Almost Perfectly And Cyrus Attempts to Save the World

VOSHTYR CRASHED through the window and landed in a dark, smoldering pile. "Roger . . ." he croaked. "Roger . . ."

Roger looked up from his desk, a monocle in one of his eyes. "Oh, you're back. How did the meeting with Lazik go?" He looked at the sorry state Voshtyr was in. "Not too well, I see."

Voshtyr pushed himself up and glowered at his accountant. "Solburg is back. Wearing blue and acting exactly like the kind of smarmy upstart I've been working to eradicate. But I've got him now." He held up a large diamond.

The monocle fell out of Roger's eye. "Y-you took his soul?"

"Bah, I wish I'd gotten the whole thing," Voshtyr said, "but no. This is the combined form of the Elemental Heartstones. The bit of soul is in the Destructo-Tube. I couldn't get the whole thing, but I should have enough. The last things I needed in order to make myself immortal. Mwahahaha! Fire up the P.L.O.T. Device, Roger! Tonight I become as the gods!"

• • •

The two ran to the mountain keep's basement, where the P.L.O.T. Device was set up. It looked like a giant column made of fan turbines connected to a coffin. At the front was a console made of obsidian. The console was a simple affair, with simply a lever, a button, three gauges, and a slot of some sort on it.

Voshtyr ran about connecting the cables and checking the turbines.

Roger opened a spellbook, set it on the console, and began checking another hefty tome, one with the words INSTRUCTION MANUAL printed in gold on the front of it. In smaller print, underneath the larger words, was the inscription "Instructions for Operation of the Puissant Lifetime Omnipotence Transfusion Device." Roger flipped it open and began to read the cautionary material in the front of the book.

> Wear Brotherhood of the Black Hand-approved Safety Goggles at all times while operating. Do not operate under the influence of drugs or alcohol. Do not operate without having at least eight hours of uninterrupted sleep the night prior to operation. Do not attempt to operate heavy machinery or war golems within eight hours of receiving the Transfusion.

Roger skipped a few pages to the Troubleshooting section.

> If Power gauge reads less than twenty five percent, recalibrate air turbines A and B. If this is unsuccessful, increase energy input from Heartstone

until Power gauge balances. If low levels persist, recite the Draconic Alphabet while recalibrating air turbines C and D. If low levels persist persistently, recite the Draconic Alphabet backwards while doing jumping jacks. You may also try sacrificing a goat.

After the hundreds of pages of cautions, only one page remained. On that page were the instructions for actual operation of the P.L.O.T. Device. They were short and simple: "Step 1: Push button. Step 2: Live forever." It was extremely helpful. Roger sighed and closed the book. He reached into the pocket on his robe and pulled out a set of official Mad Scientist black-tinted goggles and slipped them onto his head.

"Are you quite done fooling around?" Voshtyr shouted from across the room. He had finished connecting the cables to the turbines and was climbing into the coffin-like apparatus.

"You do realize that this isn't going to make you immortal," Roger said, turning the switch on the bottom of the console on. The obsidian lit up with purple light and glowed darkly. "You don't have sufficient connection to the elements for it to work properly. It would work on Solburg but not you."

"I have a piece of Solburg's soul," Voshtyr said. "Sympathetic magic. If he has the connection, and I have a piece of him, I have the connection as well." He grasped the lid of the chamber with his mechanical arm. "Now activate the machine!"

Roger shrugged, eyeing the coffin. "Your funeral."

Voshtyr slammed the lid. Roger placed the Elemental Heartstone in its slot on the console and threw the switch.

The turbines screamed into motion. Their roar quickly dimmed to a high-pitched keening. The cables lit up with swirling energies and thrashed about on the floor. An overwhelming brilliance lit up the entire room.

Roger adjusted his goggles to the Blackout setting and looked at the gauges. All three were at peak levels. The progress meter read one percent. Roger sighed. This was going to take forever. Which kind of made sense for an immortality process. He needed a book, and the only one in the room besides his spellbook was the manual. He grudgingly picked it up and began reading more of the lengthy cautionary statements.

"What in the Nine Torments!" Lazik shouted as rumbles and explosions rocked his city.

"Hatred, amusement, struggle," said Vel-shan, the bald man who served as Lazik's advisor.

Lazik stood with three other Kinetics in a ruined hallway in the Citadel. Something was attacking his city, and that was *not* acceptable. The holes in the walls would have to be repaired, the rubble swept away, and the scorch marks scrubbed off the walls.

"Perhaps my people will know who dares attack the Citadel," Lazik said, and closed his eyes. He focused on the eyes and minds of his people. He closed his eyes and opened them again. He looked through the eyes of one of his people. This person and his family were having dinner.

As Lasik watched through the man's eyes, suddenly their far wall burst open and a figure crashed through, shattering the table and ruining the meal. It was an Elemental, or maybe it was a man. A young man, perhaps, who seemed to be made of all the elements.

"Sorry about your dinner," the young man said. He flared up into a higher Elemental state and leapt back out of the hole he'd made coming in.

Lazik closed his eyes and opened his own. "Solburg! We must do something about this. Mar-ras! Kel-tar!"

Two of the men in the court stood up. "Yes, Tarrasshan?" they said in unison.

"The two of you take a squad of warriors and get rid of that boy," Lazik ordered. His eyes narrowed. "And if Voshtyr Demonkin gives you any trouble, remove him too."

"Welcome back, Greymalkin," William said, shaking the hand of an old, grey-furred Kath who wore mage's robes.

"I am gladdened to see you still alive, Grand Highseeker," the Kath said. "We all are."

A dozen or so mages, including an enormous black basilisk, had gathered atop the Tower of the Highseekers and were standing in front of a ring of black chairs, the seats of the Coincil. For now, they stood in a circle around William Weatherblade.

At the center of everything, where Weatherblade stood, was the Focused Lens of Focusing, Weatherblade's magical amplification device. To an untrained observer, it would appear to be a gigantic magnifying glass on a pivoting stand, but, curiously, it did not magnify light, nor even distort the images of things on the other side of it. It was a tool of magic, not of science.

It was evening, and the battle royale had already begun between the Citadel floating a few leagues away, Voshtyr's forces, Serimal's Fifth Column, and the Heroes. Sharp reports of explosions and the buzzing sounds of destruction spells carried through the breezy air.

"Thank you," William said. He turned to address the assembled mages. "Friends and fellow mages, it is a dark day for the world, and even for us, the brightest of wizards and mages. Demonkin has driven the Heroes from this world and ushered in an era of darkness and evil.

"We all know that the night is darkest smack dab in the middle of the night," he continued, walking around the circle. "But we, we are mages! And the laws of whether it is dark in the daytime or light in the night are at our beck and call! Brother mages, I ask that we pool our might in this black hour and show Demonkin that his foul sorcery is nothing compared to the hard work and study of brilliant minds. We can be the sun in the midnight sky! Are you with me?"

The assembled mages cheered, raising their fists in defiance. The basilisk bellowed.

"Now," William said, as the cheering died down, "we cannot defeat Demonkin directly. It is in our best interest to let the young Cyrus Solburg deal with that himself, as he has found the Elemental Heartstones. With, perhaps, some outside aid, but that's a matter for another day."

There was a murmur among the mages at the mention of the Heartstones.

"That being said," William continued, stopping in front of the basilisk and placing a palm on his talons, "what we can do is ensure that *that*," he pointed at the flying Citadel of the Kinetics, "does not follow him. Nor will it continue to darken our sky. Let us join together and cast it from the heavens to the sea!"

The mages cheered again, then sat in their respective chairs atop the tower and began chanting. William walked to the center of the tower and adjusted the enormous lensso that he viewed the Citadel of the Kinetics directly through it.

"Bang," William said, pointing at the Citadel. "You're dead."

The reader may be confused at this point by the number of edifices under attack in this particular section and their somewhat muddled nomenclature.

Whose bright idea it had been to separate the idea of a Citadel from a Fortress has been lost to history, but many blame Lord Colmarian the Headstrong, as it it more or less a safe bet that if it can be done wrong, Colmarian did it that way.

A citadel is a walled city, unlike a fortress, which is a military building used only for defense. As a proper noun, the Citadel is the home of the Kinetics, who at this moment were not enjoying, due to collateral damage, having an epic Hero and Villain fight on their walls.

The fortress that has been mentioned is Voshtyr's, where much of his planning and execution of the takeover of Bryath occurred. And the bright beam of light coming from that fortress is from the P.L.O.T. Device currently active within its halls.

Lastly, one may be confused about the plethora of towers and Keeps. Towers are a very standard piece of both Hero and Villain architecture, as whomever has the largest tower has the most prestige. A Keep is a fortified tower with a walled courtyard. But in this battle, there are no Keeps. The Tower of Highseekers and its wizards fight against the Citadel and Voshtyr's fortress.

• • •

"There it is!" Emily said, pointing at the fortress protruding from the side of the mountain.

Serimal, Nieva, Cyrus, Kris, and Reginald rode on Serimal's flying machine, with Emily and Slashback taking point, headed directly for Voshtyr's mountain fort.

"We'll need to be closer," Serimal said. "Down we go."

The ship veered downward and banked to port, taking them along the side of the mountain so they couldn't be seen from the tower. The ship coasted up to the base of the tower. At that moment, the swirling column of light that had been splashing out of the mountain fortress suddenly surged brighter and began to be more colors than just white. Red, blue, brown, and yellow swirled into the mix as well.

Cyrus looked up. "That's probably not good."

"Cyrus," Kris said, tugging on his sleeve. "I have to tell you something really important."

"I can't imagine *any* of Voshtyr's projects being a good thing," Serimal said. "He's activated the P.L.O.T. Device. You have to get in there and interrupt him before he completes the transfusion process, or he'll be indestructible and nearly omnipotent. I can't take you up or he might shoot down my ship."

Cyrus put a hand on Kris's shoulder. "Sorry, Kris. I'll be right back, and you can tell me when the world's not about to end, mkay?"

Kris sighed, but nodded. "Oh kay."

Cyrus turned back to Reginald. "Then let's get up there. Reg?"

Reginald drew his sword. "Sean's Sudden Springboard?"

"You know the one," Cyrus said.

"Cyrus," Kris said. "Be careful, love."

Cyrus gave her a kiss. "Twice as careful as I ever am."

Kris frowned, with a smile at one corner of her mouth. "So still not careful. Two of zero is still zero."

"Yeah, okay. I'll be a little careful," he said. "Just for you. Okay, Reg, ready, set, go!"

Reginald faced the fortress. The black rock fortification brooded in its nest on the side of the mountain. Its lone tower practically hummed with the energies coursing up through it. Reginald needed to get Cyrus inside without too much fuss, and a quick toss was the easiest way. He placed the flat of his sword across his shoulders and down his back. "*Now!*"

Cyrus leapt into the air, landing on the end of Reginald's huge flat blade, and crouched.

Immediately, Reginald rolled his shoulders forward and swung his sword with all his might.

Using the sword's momentum, Cyrus leapt. He shot into the air, collecting Air energy as he went. He cleared a dozen floors without losing momentum. Just shy of the top, he began slowing down, and he used a burst of energy to boost him up the last few feet. He tumbled across the top of the tower and came up with his sword at the ready.

Cyrus found himself near the edge of a roaring column of what felt like raw Elemental energy punching through the roof of the fortress, coursing upward and dissipating into the air. The parapets around him were all eroded, and there were no obvious stairs leading down. No matter. What Hero used stairs when there was dramatic jumping to be done?

Cyrus walked to the hole and put a hand into the energy. It felt like the Elements, pure and untamed. Cyrus breathed in deeply, then dove into the column of light.

• • •

On the ground far below, where chaos had reigned only two months before, law was now beating the carp out chaos.

The Green Falcon, the Yellow Sun, the Blue Shock, and the Purple Paladin lay about them with their respective knives, holy magic, electrical axe, and holy greatsword, scattering Minions, Henchmen, and assorted Mythologicals, and generally having a jolly good time.

"There's more of them than I thought," the Blue Shock said, frying a cluster of Minions who had been foolish enough to stand close enough together for him to bounce an ArcBolt between them. "How long do we need to hold them for?"

"Until Solburg deals with Voshtyr," Yellow said, touching and healing a cut on Green's forearm. "That may be a while."

"It wouldn't be such a problem if they weren't trying to flank us on all sides," Purple said as he brought down his sword on a chimera's heads. "If I get stabbed in the back one more time, I am going to be quite irate."

"If only Red were here," Green said. He parried a spear thrust from a Minion and whittled the spear down to toothpicks, then kicked the Minion backward into the oncoming axe of a troll. "I'm sure he could help."

At that moment, something sinister happened. The bodies of the Minions and other creatures the Heroes had slain began twitching, then standing upright again.

"Zombies!" Green said. "Where'd they come from? Where's the necromancer?" He looked around.

"They're not zombies, they're wights," Yellow said, forming a barrier around them. "They'll drain your life just by touching you. But these . . . these are different. They're glowing, and . . ."

"Oh, they won't be touching you," someone shouted over the melee. A figure in a red cloak strode forward, carrying a glowing grey sword.

"Red?" Green said, almost dropping his knives. "Red! It's you!"

The Red Death looked up with a grin. "I haven't forgotten everything I learned from evil." He gave the other Spectrum Heroes a thumbs up. Every wight that had just risen, including ones clawing their way up through the soil where battles had taken place a month ago, gave them the thumbs up at the same time. "It's time to fight fire with fire. Or Minions with with wights. It's the perfect night for a wight fight. Right?"

With that, Red joined the fray, and the Spectrum Heroes began cleaving a path through the army, straight for Voshtyr's fortress.

Roger dropped the book. "Voshtyr!" he shouted. "Voshtyr! Get out of there!" He grabbed the lever and dragged it down to the Off position.

The book fell to and came open to one final caution on the next to last page.

> Warning! Do not under any circumstances attempt to enter the transfusion receptacle while wearing any major magical items such as rings of invisibility, capes of flight, seven league boots, or pocket sized Engines of Unreasonable Destruction at risk of destroying the item, causing magical fault in the transfusion process, and/or possibly fusing parts of worn items to body. Death, severe injury, and/or

total and complete failure of your evil plan may result!

Roger was too late. The black column in the center, attached to the coffin, exploded in a massive detonation of white light. It blasted Roger back against the wall. He felt a sickening snap in his back, and he lost all feeling in his legs. The blast knocked a hole in the ceiling, and the energy poured out.

Voshtyr rose out of the coffin like a zombie. His skin was coppery bronze, crackling with a thousand colors of energy. "Aaaaauuuugh!" he screamed. He fell out of the coffin onto his knees. He clutched his torso. "Aaaaaahahahaha! Mwahahahaha! It worked!" He rose and flexed his arms. The metal one seemed to have permanently fused itself with his skin, and on his finger was the coppery ring that was the Destructo-Tube.

Roger pulled himself half off the ground. "V- Voshtyr . . . H-help me . . ."

Voshtyr chuckled. "Now why would I do that?" he said. "I'm now immortal and all-powerful. The world is mine! Whatever would I need an accountant for?" He laughed maniacally, then turned away.

Right into the face of his Arch-Nemesis.

The Citadel of the Kinetics rocked as if struck by a titanic hammer.

Lazik staggered, regaining his balance by grabbing hold of a bust of himself on the corner of a set of stairs.

Forgotten was the damaged hallway. This was much worse. Whole slabs of marble hadd been blasted loose from the walls, collapsing columns and crushing anyone unfortunate enough to be caught near the blast site. Lazik struggled to keep his balance on the stairs as they cracked and buckled under his feet. He could only hope that the Central Council Chamber was undamaged. The greatest minds for the offense and defense of the Citadel were there, and if anything happened to them . . .

"Damage report!" Lazik shouted. "What happened?"

Kel-tar materialized at Lazik's side. "The Tower of Highseekers has fired a powerful non-physical blast at the core of the Citadel, Tarrasshan," he said calmly. "It has hampered our movement and incapacitated thirty-five percent of the council. If the Tower launches another such blast, we will be unable to mount a proper defense. Your orders?"

Lazik growled. "Blast that tower until there's not one stone on top of another."

William sank to his knees and gasped. "That . . . was a little more . . . powerful than I intended."

A few of the mages who had been casting together slumped in their chairs. The only one remaining who did not look tired was the basilisk.

"I am ready for a second blow," the basilisk said. "Get up, pansies."

"Give us a moment, Rigel," William said. "That was an incredibly difficult thing to pull off. Is there something you can do to boost us next time?"

Rigel the basilisk tilted his head. "Instead of just shooting the magic at the Citadel, next time channel the spell through my breath." He breathed a splash of white flame on the ground, melting some of the stone. "It may not drive them back, but it might destroy enough of their infrastructure that they may not be able to remain airborne."

The western face of the tower shattered. "William!" shouted one of the mages as he staggered forward. "The Citadel is returning fire!"

"Five of you, cast *Grand Aegis of the Ages* on the tower!" William ordered. "The rest of you, place a hand on Rigel's flanks and cast that same spell again, tweaked to affect his breath!"

They gathered around the basilisk and began casting once again. This time, the magic visibly swirled around Rigel, and he seemed to be breathing in a mystical mist. Then he roared, took a deep breath, and unleashed a hellish hallowed beam of arcane fire, straight through the Focused Lens of Focusing, aimed directly at the Citadel.

Cyrus plummeted through the energy column and landed on top of a metallic pylon.

He found himself in a cylindrical room of dark grey granite. It smelled dry and cold, and just being in the room made goose-prickles run down his arms. The air left an acrid taste in his mouth, almost like air did after a lightning storm. The high-pitched whirring of the turbines beneath his feet was the dominant sound in the room.Cables and tubes sprouted from the top and led to turbines he'd seen before.

So this was what the P.L.O.T. Device looked like when fully assembled. He hadn't seen it since it was in parts in the Keep of Falling Stars.

Well, it needed to be *not* in one piece now. Cyrus hacked at the cables from the top. They jerked away, splashing more of the multihued energy around the room, melting holes in the floor and in the pieces of the device. An influx of power coursing through his body told him that his contact with the energy beam seemed to have at least temporarily restored his Everything Elemental state.

He jumped down from the column and saw what he had to assume was Voshtyr. The Arch-Villain's skin had changed color, and he was writhing in pain. Then he laughed and stood up.

"Hey, Voshtyr," Cyrus said. "'Sup?"

Voshtyr didn't seem to hear Cyrus over the screaming of the turbines as they tore themselves apart under the stress and damage Cyrus had caused. He seemed to be talking to someone behind the console. Then he turned around and saw Cyrus.

"Oh, good, you're here to witness my rebirth." Voshtyr's teeth were pointy, and his skin was fading from a strange coppery tone to his normal flesh color.

"And you're not wearing pants," Cyrus said, "Were you going to fix that?"

Voshtyr looked down. "Oh. The P.L.O.T. Device must not have accepted clothing as part of my person." His body blurred and reformed as himself once again, now wearing mostly black silks and leathers and a flowing black cape with a red interior. "There, is that better?"

"Much," Cyrus said, walking up to Voshtyr. "Now, you were saying something about rebirth?"

"Yes, thank you," Voshtyr said. "I have become one with the elements, as you did. And with the very power of the Torments themselves on my side, there is nothing you can do to stop me!"

Cyrus punched Voshtyr in the face.

"Ow! Again with the face!" Voshtyr whipped the ring off his finger and pointed it at Cyrus again. "Stop it with the face!"

Cyrus parried the tube aside and punched Voshtyr in the stomach.

"Oof! Gah, all right, I wasn't ready," Voshtyr said. "Run that by me again."

Cyrus grabbed every ley-line in the area and pulled them taut, drawing as much energy as he could without breaking them. He pulled it into a massive ball in front of himself, then channeled it straight at Voshtyr, blasting the Villain across the room.

Voshtyr crashed through one of the rotating turbines. A fan blade leapt free of its casing and spun across the room, glancing off walls and twisting itself with a clatter into a heap of mangled metal. With a whine like thousand creaking hinges, the white beam of energy that had been coursing upward through the roof flickered and died out.

Cyrus approached the destroyed turbine with the Voshtyr-shaped hole. "Come on, Voshtyr. You're an Arch-Villain. I know that didn't kill you."

"No, but it *hurt* like the Nine Torments," Voshtyr said, pulling himself out of the wreckage. "I was supposed to be immune to that kind of thing . . ."

"I don't think so," Cyrus said. "I broke your machine. You can't finish whatever it was you were doing."

Voshtyr laughed, long and sinister. "Oh, not to worry about that, my dear idiot." His eyes became black pools, his hair flared up like angry smoke, darker patches appeared on his skin and up his neck, and bits of metal began rising up from the floor and floating around him. "I am already complete."

"Then it is a good thing he has help." From the hole in the ceiling dropped Sir Reginald Ogleby, the Crimson Slash. "Prepare to Face Justice, Voshtyr Demonkin!"

The multicolored beam of arcane fire smashed into the side of the Citadel of the Kinetics. Immediately, the fire coated the eastern face of the city, and the castle began veering toward the ocean.

Then the coating of fire exploded. Half the eastern face rocketed into the sky and fragments rained across the ocean, plains, and mountains nearby.

"Woohoo!" William crowed, throwing a fist into the air. He waited for it to come down so he could catch it and reattach it to his wrist. Then he cheered again. "Direct hit! Good job, gentlemen. Good job indeed!"

Rigel snorted smoke at the floating fortress. "That's for trying to destroy our tower!"

The Citadel careened over the northern mountains and down toward the surface of the sea.

The panic alarm sounded again and again, the warning klaxon calling that it wasn't just something wrong, it was *everything* going wrong. The unreasonably strong beam of fire from the Highseekers' tower had slagged half of the west face of the Citadel, and exposed and damaged some of the mystic crystals that kept it afloat. The Citadel began veering down toward the ocean.

"Fear, panic, apprehension, soiled pants!" Vel-shan said.

"Shut up!" Lazik bellowed. "Everone prepare for impact!"

Lazik threw his hands forward instinctually, as did dozens of other Kinetics simultaneously. The combined force of all the minds in the Citadel parted the water to soften the impact, but still they crashed.

"*Voshtyr!*" Lazik cried as the deep swallowed his entire civilization.

Cyrus leapt back to avoid Voshtyr's strike.

Voshtyr slashed at Cyrus with his mechanical arm-blade, which crackled with electricity. On the backstroke, he kicked a fragment of shattered turbine across the room at Reginald, who ducked underneath it and rolled up to attack as well.

Cyrus flared up into his full Elemental form, though he could feel he didn't have much energy without the Heartstone or the energy that had been spraying about haphazardly. "All right, so now we're even," Cyrus said. "You have the power. We have the numbers."

"The Villain couldst not defeat the Hero by himself in their last encounter," Reginald said, leveling his sword at Voshtyr.

"Hey, is that a new sword?" Cyrus asked.

"The Hero did not think this was the time to discuss weaponry with his erstwhile apprentice," Reginald narrated. "But his new sword was named Sharp."

"Oh, you found a Weapon of Legend?" Cyrus said. "Nice."

"Aren't we supposed to be fighting to the death?" Voshtyr said irritably. "I have world-conquering to do later this evening, so can we get on with it?"

"Sure," Cyrus said. "We're pretty evenly matched right now, so can we just hash this out like reasonable people, or do you want to wreck half the continent in a Battle of Titanic Powers?"

Voshtyr tilted his head side to side. "Both sound fun. But . . . let's destroy things," Voshtyr said, his voice sounding like a half-dozen voices speaking in unison. "That's ever so much more satisfying than crushing origami."

"Wait, what?" Cyrus said, but he didn't have time to think about it, as Voshtyr rushed him.

Cyrus parried the incoming stroke, and absorbed enough Water energy to coat the underside of his own arm into a razor-edged blade of ice as a secondary weapon. As he spun to dodge, he slashed at Voshtyr with the chilly edge.

Voshtyr swatted Cyrus's arm away and *bit* him in the shoulder.

"Yargh!" Cyrus shouted. "What the Ninth?" He looked at his arm. Voshtyr had bit right through the fabric of his new tunic and left stains of black corrosive slime that were still dissolving the textile. "Yech. Don't you ever brush your teeth?"

"Thus did the Apprentice learn the perils of Poor Dental Hygiene," Reginald narrated. "The Hero leapt at the nigh-immortal demonspawn and hacked at him with his Legendary Blade!" Reginald did just that.

Voshtyr spun to parry, and discovered that it was all but impossible to parry something made of the metaphysical concept of sharpness. Reginald's blade cut the top inch off Voshtyr's weapon.

The resulting explosion, however, as metaphysical sword met Star of Anger, knocked Reginald backward into a second turbine, shattering the device and leaving only one of the set of Three Terrible Turbines intact, a lamentable catastrophe for Evil Artifact collectors everywhere.

Cyrus attacked again, but Voshtyr was ready for him. Voshtyr slashed at Cyrus repeatedly, his Shard-sword leaving traces of color in the air. Cyrus blocked repeatedly. The two danced a dance of steel and fire around the room from one shattered turbine to the other.

Cyrus no longer felt any need to posess the Shard. Perhaps it had just been the Shard in its raw, unprocessed form, an aura that made people want to use it so it could cause more destruction. But now Cyrus had no desire to posess it, especially not between his ribs, where Voshtyr seemed intent on putting it.

With his magic, Voshtyr scooped up fragments of the turbines and hurled them at Cyrus. Cyrus deflected them with blasts of Air magic and pressed his attack. Reginald leapt back into the fray as well, trying to keep Voshtyr distracted long enough for Cyrus to get a solid hit.

But whatever else the P.L.O.T. Device had done to Voshtyr, it had certainly increased his capacity to fight. The fight dragged on for a full minute. A very full minute—a minute full of wall kicks, backflips, Thompson's Tornados, and more narration than Cyrus could shake a Stick of Shaking at.

Then Cyrus noticed his energy beginning to flag.

But so was Voshtyr's. The half-demon was breathing heavily and was blocking slower than he had been.

"I don't think your machine worked," Cyrus said, taking a defensive stance.

"Yes, it did," Voshtyr said, panting. "It worked almost perfectly."

"Almost . . . is the enemy . . . of perfection," Reginald said, panting. He was holding his back with his free hand. Apparently he wasn't used to fighting without a shield.

Cyrus snorted. "You mean it wasn't supposed to explode?"

"Can't you say *anything* without trying to be funny?" Voshtyr said with a scowl.

"Yes." Cyrus said.

"That's what I . . . Er, wait." Voshtyr paused for a moment as if waiting. "That wasn't a joke. You just said something that wasn't an ill-fated attempt at humor! Will wonders never cease?"

"Of course not," Reginald said. "Now wonder at your own defeat!"

Voshtyr flared black again. "Oh, I have had just about *enough* of you and your incessant talking!" He whipped back to face Cyrus and made a gesture with four fingers, forming a box and pushing it forward. A weblike net of misty blackness burst from Voshtyr's palms and spattered against Cyrus, smashing him into the wall and sticking him there and rendering him barely able to move.

"You leave the boy be!" Reginald shouted, charging Voshtyr.

"Wait, Reg!" Cyrus said, feeling the black energy wrap around his throat. "It's a tapr!"

"What?"

"A tapr—a very confusing *trap!*"

But by then it was too late. Voshtyr slid underneath Reginald's sword stroke, and then under Reginald entirely, seeming to defy physics as the shadows around him pulled him to his feet instantly. Voshtyr reached out with his arm-blade and stabbed Reginald in his unprotected back.

"Augh!" Reginald cried.

But it wasn't over yet. Voshtyr spun, his blade still embedded in Reginald's shoulder, dragging the Hero with him. A swift kick pushed Reginald off the blade and sent him staggering toward the far wall. Reginald hit the wall and turned just in time to see Voshtyr flash from across the room to right in front of him.

"Goodbye, Crimson Slash," Voshtyr said with a terrifying grin, and punched Reginald clear through the side of the tower.

Ther Hero plummeted out of sight.

"*No!*" Cyrus shouted. "You maniac! He can't fly!"

Voshtyr turned around slowly. "No, he can't, can he? That's the problem with hating magic, now, isn't it? It solves so many of life's little problems. Like gravity, and splattery death."

He sauntered over to wher Cyrus struggled. The burning machine and the flashes of electricity from damaged equipment intermittently lit the room as he approached.

"And here ends your story, Solburg. Out of power, out of time, and out of luck. Not out of the tower like your mentor, but you are certainly out of friends to save your proverbial bacon." He lifted his arm blade to Cyrus's throat.

"And so . . . are you!"

Cyrus jerked his head to the side. The voice had come from behind the console.

Lord Roger Farella had pulled himself up onto the console, but it looked like something was wrong with his legs. In his hand rested the now brilliantly glowing Elemental Heartstone. "Cyrus . . . catch!" Roger threw the Heartstone to Cyrus.

Cyrus caught it. As he looked Voshtyr in the eyes he flared back to full Everything Elemental form. Fire blasted from around him, disintegrating the umbral webs. His Elements were once again at full power, and his sword beamed with white light. He took a step toward Voshtyr once again.

And punched him in the face.

Voshtyr toppled backward again, his black fire flickering. "Not. In. The. *Face!*" He sprang back up. He thrust his Shard blade at Cyrus's head.

Cyrus parried, but only too late did he realize the thrust had been a feint. In a flurry of robes and metal arms, Voshtyr diverted his strike and shoved the Shard blade deep into Cyrus's stomach.

Or more correctly, where Cyrus's stomach should have been.

Because his stomach wasn't there anymore. As the blade plunged in, Cyrus melded his body around it as if he were made of mud again.

"What? How . . . ?" Voshtyr tried a slash at Cyrus's neck.

Cyrus caught the blade in his hand, which was suddenly now of stone. Ice spread down Voshtyr's arm from Cyrus's hand. It cascaded down the Shard blade and up to Voshtyr's elbow.

"What!" Voshtyr said. "Stop that right now, you miserable piece of—"

"Just stop," Cyrus said. "You're done." He struck Voshtyr's Shard sword with all his might, and the evil blade shattered. Cyrus took a step back and kicked Voshtyr in the chest with every ounce of power in his body.

Voshtyr shot backward, crashing through the wall of the tower and out into the air. Cyrus followed, flying on the wings of the wind itself.

• • •

Reginald plummeted to the ground, sincerely regretting every single time he had ever made fun of mages for casting spells that let them fall slower. His last thought before hitting the ground was that a little magic would have been nice right then.

As Reginald struck the cold black rock, he could feel his spine and ribs crumple, and he almost blacked out.

Almost.

At the instant he hit the ground, a surge of healing magic coursed through his body.

Reginald gasped, and sat up. Standing a few feet away was the Yellow Sun, a magic aura fading from his hand.

"There seem to be an unreasonable number of people falling from the sky today," Yellow said. "Good to see you, Crimson."

Reginald felt his back and neck. They were fine. Better than fine. "Good to see you, as well," he said with an embarrassed chuckle. "I suppose I'll leave the flying to those with wings and magic."

"It's just as well." Yellow said. "Stay down here. We can use the help. Purple and Red have secured the front gate, and they're keeping the monsters from going inside to help Voshtyr."

"The Red Death has returned?"

"Yes, those wights are his," Yellow said, pointing at the clawed and shambling creatures. "I'm not sure how he did it, but they are somehow Healing Wights. Instead of draining your life when they touch you, they mend your flesh."

A sticky hand clamped on Reginald's shoulder, and he recoiled at the sight of a partially decomposed Minion with claws and a green glow. What was stranger was that as the Minion touched him, the remaining aches from his hard landing faded away. The Minion wight grinned awkwardly then shambled off.

"Well," Reginald said, perturbed. "Let's be about this. Voshtyr has Cyrus up there, and I—"

"Look!" Yellow pointed upward. "Isn't that Cyrus there?"

Voshtyr plummeted toward the ground. Cyrus hung in the air for a moment, watching him fall. He tossed his sword and hat into the air, then streaked down in the form of a bolt of lightning. He caught up to Voshtyr just before impact. With fists of frozen magma he slammed Voshtyr in the chest and pounded him to—and into—the ground.

Cyrus pummeled Voshtyr, delivering blow after blow to the Arch-Villain's head and torso.

Voshtyr bellowed, his fangs growing longer and his face ever more pointed and demonic.

Then Cyrus's sword fell from the sky. Cyrus caught it and plunged it into Voshtyr's chest. Torrents of black magic cascaded out of the Villain, tainting the crater around the two of them.

"*RrRraaAggGhghH!*" Voshtyr bellowed and snarled, more like a beast than a person. Despite everything, he reached up and wrapped his hands around Cyrus's throat, his clawlike fingernails digging into Cyrus's flesh.

Cyrus flinched. "No," he said, his voice like crackling flames. His entire body flared up wreathed in fire that burned the dark magic away as it cascaded around them. The fire burned hotter and hotter, scorching the skin on Voshtyr's hands until Cyrus could smell charred flesh.

Voshtyr gave one final, bestial scream as the fire inside Cyrus no longer had any containment and coursed rampant, burning everything in the crater to ash.

The scream lingered, even as Voshtyr was reduced to little flakes of grey dust.

And then there was silence.

Cyrus stood up, the elemental traits fading and receding back into his body. "Rest in peace, Voshtyr von Steinadler. Nice try at ruling the world."

With a gentle *plop* Cyrus's hat landed on his head, perfectly seated, thus completing his epic moment.

At Cyrus's feet, nothing was left of Voshtyr's body but a simple copper ring.

Cyrus stepped out of the crater and looked into the sky. The battle on the ground ended abruptly. It must have been disheartening to the Villains and their servants to see the greatest of them pounded to ash right before their eyes.

A tsunami had washed up on the beach, and Cyrus could just see the very tip of the Citadel's tallest spire sinking beneath the ocean. The *Hellbat* cruised through the air, along with a green dragon and a gryphon rider. The smoking ruin of the mountain fortress was beginning to crumble and self-destruct after Voshtyr's death, a typical Villain contingency plan.

The clouds began rolling away, and sunlight poured down on a land free of Voshtyr Demonkin.

Epilogue

BALANCE AT LAST

*In which Cyrus receives News Both Welcome and Unwelcome,
And it all comes to a Close*

THE AIRSHIP TOUCHED down on the rain-soaked ground near the wide crater Cyrus and Voshtyr had made on impact. The Hero, Villains, Kath, gryphon, and mercenary disembarked and ran to where Cyrus sat with his back against a jutting shard of rock.

"Cyrus! Are you all right?" Kris asked, kneeling in front of her mate.

"That was some battle," Serimal said. "I've never seen its like."

Reginald offered Cyrus a hand up. "'Twas indeed a fight of which they shall tell tales for ages and ages."

"Hey, good to see you survived," Cyrus said. The power of the Elements had faded from him, though he still had the Heartstone now safely re-embedded in his sword. "But what do you mean? There're no bards here. There weren't any here to see the fight, either."

Reginald snorted. "You think that matters to bards? You left a ruined tower, a beach awash in castle fragments, and a crater large enough to sleep five giants. And even with that, the bards will more than likely make up a battle greater than what you actually fought."

Kris wrapped her arms around Cyrus and nuzzled his chin. "I am glad you are Oh Kay."

"Yeah, and I'm glad you're in one piece," Cyrus said, stroking her head-fur. "I'm sorry I couldn't rescue you."

Kris purred. "I can rescue myself, thank you. It is you who needs looking after. What were you thinking, jumping out through the wall like that?"

"I might remind you," Nieva said, raising a finger, "that you just jumped out a window not two hours ago. That is hardly safe behavior for one with child."

"One with what now?" Cyrus said, glancing first at Nieva then at Kris.

Kris gave Cyrus a bashful smile and shrugged. "The King of the Kinetics said that I'm pregnant with cubs."

Cyrus gaped at her for a moment. "But . . . but that's impossible!"

"So is turning into an Everything Elemental," Nieva said. "We believe you and Kris are the Light and the Huntress from the Prophecy of the End of the World. From you two spring the Two of Balance—"

"And then a bunch of other things happen," Kris said, waving a paw. "The point is, you and I will be parents!" She squeezed Cyrus's hands.

Cyrus laughed out loud. "Okay, that's weird, but it's awesome! I'll be a dad! But . . ."

"But what?" Kris said, looking up with apprehension.

"But . . . what on earth will they look like?" Cyrus said. "I mean, Humans and Elves are kind of similar, so if you could somehow get a half-elf, it wouldn't look too different, but . . . half-Kath?"

Reginald raised an eyebrow. "I wouldn't worry about that, lad. That sounds far too strange-looking to be the result of a prophecy. Ouch!"

Nieva whacked Reginald in the arm. "Be kind. Now, let us be gone from this place and see where we can yet do more good."

"Wait!" Cyrus said, looking up at the crumbling fortress. The granite edifice was still falling apart, with occasional explosions launching fragments out into the air. "Roger Farella's still up in the tower. I think Voshtyr hurt him somehow."

"And . . . ?" Serimal said. "I've nothing against Roger, but he *was* helping Voshtyr this whole time, and he turned down my offer to work for our side. He deserves what he got."

Reginald grabbed Serimal by the collar. "Spoken just like a Villain! You save my life once, but won't help another? What, did you run out of good deeds in the blackness that is your soul?"

"Well, maybe I did!" Serimal yelled in Reginald's face. "Maybe I don't *want* to do good deeds like a namby-pamby goody-two-shoes! I'm a Villain! Or have you all forgotten that?"

"Gentlemen." Nieva put forth a hand and spraying the two with frost. "Chill."

"Let cooler heads prevail," Cyrus said.

"That would be n-ice," Kris added.

Reginald shook his head. "Again with the wordplay. You two are incorrigible."

Cyrus smiled. "Yeah, and you wouldn't have it any other way," he said. "Now can we go get the accountant out of the tower so we can all go home? Roger helped me at my Moment of Crisis, and a Hero can't forget such deeds."

"Just a moment." Kris climbed up some of the rubble from the fortress to get a better look at the ocean. There was a lot of newly washed-up driftwood,, but with the exception of some flotsam, it looked as if the Citadel had never existed.

Kris put a paw over her heart. "Goodbye, Indikos Naranai Tarrasshan. Indy. Thank you for returning me to Cyrus."

Two days later, Kris and Cyrus returned to Starspeak, with Reginald and Roger in tow. Nieva and Serimal departed for Landeralt to rebuild Serimal's family home. Emily and Slashback, after some debate, left with Serimal and Nieva to help with the Fifth Column, or S.P.I.E.S., as Serimal had begun calling it while stroking his now neatly-trimmed diabolical goatee.

Roger, they soon discovered, had a broken spine. Magic only helped so much: a *Mend Bones* spell did not restore his ability to walk. Fortunately, he retained his ability, as Araquellan nobility, to fly. So he floated around with his legs crossed under him like a scaly yogi. He'd accepted Kris and Cyrus's offer of sanctuary on Starspeak, where he could receive rigorous physical therapy to regain his ability to not only walk, but swim as well.

All was going wonderfully after Voshtyr's defeat that Cyrus, until the second week.

"What do you mean I have to *retire*?" Cyrus said, flabbergasted.

Reginald sighed and pointed at the book he was reading. They were in Cyrus's house on the shore of Starspeak Island. It was morning, and the day was just beginning to warm up to the point that Reginald had taken off his armor. Kris stopped her work at her new pottery wheel to listen to the conversation, and a curious phoenix poked its head in the window. Roger Farella, who had been staying with the Solburgs until he recovered enough to begin therapy, even lowered his newspaper to listen.

They'd had to refurnish the house, as the pirates had caused a great deal of trouble for everyone on Starspeak. But when the gratitude of a people saved from Voshtyr Demonkin had been factored in, the result was that Cyrus's house had several new furnishings, including a comfortable bench and a fine Elven wicker chair.

"Look, lad," Reginald said, "it's in the Codex Heroic. Article VII, paragraph B. 'Once and only once mayest a Hero save the world. Once it is done, said Hero must retire from the Path Heroic to become a Mentor and give the next Hero a chance.'"

Cyrus scowled. "I'm not even twenty-two yet. I've done one—count it, *one*—Quest, and now you expect me to retire?"

"It cannot be helped, lad," Reginald said. "I still have a Quest to do that you may be able to provide . . . unofficial help with, as you were always a better diplomat than I. But until then . . ." He sighed. "I will speak to the Guild about it, but they are fairly rigid on that policy. And they're not really recovered yet. After all, it is not every day that the world is in mortal peril and can be saved by only one courageous soul. You have to let someone else have a turn. Don't be greedy."

"Pfeh," Cyrus said. "So what am I going to do?"

"You could work on your Dragon Investing business," Kris said. "So far, you've invested in what, a magic rabbit and a treasure map? The returns have been Oh Kay, but . . ."

Cyrus shrugged. "But not spectacular. True enough. And I do owe Keeth some better returns. Where is he, anyway?"

"I believe he and his family are trying to contain and enforce some boundaries to where Voshtyr's empire ends," Roger said. "In the hands of his three lords, the empire has, unfortunately, survived his death."

"Great. Just when I thought we'd have peace," Cyrus said. "And I'm not even allowed to do anything about it."

"They are cowards," Reginald said. "We have them on the run now, and they've pulled back from some of our holdings, but not all of them. And we've negotiated a ceasefire with the Hereditary Evil Empire, at least until we remove what they've termed an 'upstart pretender government claiming the title of Empire but having none of the history thereof.'"

"I suppose you can focus on your business, then," Roger said. "If you could use an accountant, I would happily apply for the job."

"I don't know," Cyrus said with a smile. "There'd be some pretty stiff competition. I've seen how well my cousin Marco counts fish . . ."

Roger chuckled. "Yes, yes. I have excellent references, though. Oh, wait, you killed my best reference."

Cyrus laughed nervously. "Yeah, I kind of did. Speaking of which," he said, pulling the copper ring from a string around his neck, "I'm really not sure what to do with this. I mean, it's incredibly dangerous, right? What should I do with it?"

"I suggested destroying it, if you recall," Roger said with a shudder. "I don't want it anywhere near me. But it wouldn't melt in your forge. Perhaps we could turn it over to your Guild?"

"I'm sure the Guild would just try to find out how it worked," Reginald said. "It is magic best left in the darkness. It should be destroyed."

Roger raised a hand. "I read a legend one time of an evil ring that was destroyed in the fires whence it was forged. If we could take it down to the Deep Keep, perhaps we could destroy it there."

And so they went. Cyrus and Reginald escorted Roger to the Deep Keep, where they traveled through tunnels down to where the lava flowed.

It was fairly standard for a subterranean cave full of lava and volcanic rock. Cyrus had seen this kind of cave in several of the Quests he and Reginald had done together during his apprenticeship. Red gems provided illumination of the winding tunnels, and the pervasive smell of brimstone probably wouldn't wash out of his clothes for a week.

Cyrus looked at the ring. "It was a close one," he said. "But it's over. So long, Demonkin."

He flipped the ring over the edge, where it fell, glimmering, into the lava. The molten rock swallowed it up, and it disappeared.

"Huh," Cyrus said. "I was expecting a flash of light or a volcanic eruption or something."

"Voshtyr never got around to adding the Dramatics to the prototype," Roger said as they moved back up the tunnel. "And pyrotechnics weren't in the budget." He grimaced. "I made certain of that."

"Well, I am glad we've seen the last of him," Reginald said, rubbing his neck. "I have had enough trouble from him."

Cyrus clapped Reginald on the back. "Yeah, he got kind of boring there for a while. Started sliding into the predictable behavior of a Villain."

"And that is the first thing about being a Hero," Reginald said.

"Good may be predictable, but it always wins?" Cyrus said.

Reginald chuckled. "No, it's that you can always expect Villainy to follow the path of least resistance, even down to evil for its own sake."

"So what will you do now that you have defeated Voshtyr?" Roger asked.

Reginald scratched his chin. "I have a Blessed Quest to finish, I suppose. I still need to make some friends among each Race. What good that does me, I don't know."

"Well," Roger said, "if you'll help stop the civil war going on in Lorimar, that would probably earn you the friendship of the Elves. And it would make the place less of a financial nightmare—and earn you my friendship as well. Two Races befriended for the price of one."

Cyrus looked at Roger. "How long would it take to convince all the various factions of Elves to stop fighting?"

Roger rolled his eyes. "Well, you know the Elves. Once they set their mind to something, they have the time to make sure it is done right. I wouldn't be surprised if it took you a few years."

"Years?" Reginald said, his jaw dropping. "Years of bickering and negotiating? It will drive me insane!"

"Hey, Reg," Cyrus said. "What's the first thing about being a Hero?"

Reginald nodded glumly. "Always see a worthy Quest to its end, regardless of how difficult or time-consuming it may be." He glared at Cyrus. "I taught you too well."

Roger and Cyrus laughed the rest of the way up the tunnel. Reginald kept saying, "What?"

Cyrus paced outside the house, treading a groove in the sand.

"Young one, at this rate, you will glass that sand from all the friction," Keeth said, putting a massive claw on Cyrus's head. "Calm down. It is a routine childbirth. The best healer in the Heroes' Guild tends to Kris, a more than competent dragon and a veritable flock of phoenixes guard your house, and the Arch-Villain's defeat happened nearly a year ago. You have nothing to worry about."

"Yeah, I'm just . . . well, powerless, I guess." Cyrus leaned against the Dragon's flank. "So, how are you liking that shipment I sent you?"

"The softer gold?" Keeth said. "Marvelous. I didn't even know there were custom coins for dragon hordes designed for comfort. And those rare coins were a nice touch, as well."

Cyrus smiled. "It was easy enough to pick them up. Apparently the People's Republic of the Underground doesn't get cash inflows very often, and they need capital to expand their mining operations. Turns out they can find just about any metal down there."

Keeth scratched his belly against the sand. "And what of the other investments?"

"Well, Captain Tom finally found the treasure . . . after a big long adventure he'll probably be telling people about forever, and Quickpaw just sent me his tax info for this year. It looks like we'll be coming out several hundred thousand gold pieces ahead this year."

Keeth attempted to whistle, but merely set a palm tree on fire with his superheated breath.

The phoenixes burst out in hysterical twittering and chirping at him.

"Oh, shut it, you ridiculous birds," Keeth said. "Like you've never accidentally burned something before."

Indeed, a swarm of phoenixes rested on the roof, chirruping and calling in tune with one another in some sort of ancient birdsong. The tropical night was warm and just slightly windy, and the air smelled of growing things and cooling sand as the air flowed out to sea, bearing with it the scents of the island.

Only Cyrus and Keeth stood outside, waiting. Everyone else—Reginald, Serimal, the rest of the Fifth Column, and the Spectrum Heroes—had all gone back to restoring the world to order. The half-moon shed its light down on the sea and the beach, painting everything silver.

"Yeah, yeah, everybody keeps telling me not to worry," Cyrus said. "But one, it's not routine—it's physically impossible, not to mention really freakin' weird. Two, the Guild's lost so many members that I don't know if 'the best healer' is more competent than a first-year novice. Three, the phoenixes still make me nervous. And four, Villains still control the majority of world governments! I'm worried, all right?"

"Water line, Cyrus," Keeth said.

Cyrus sighed and took hold of a Water line, absorbing the energy into himself. He felt himself relaxing. "Yeah, okay, I'm done being panicky. Thanks. But I'm still anxious."

"That is allowed," the dragon said. "It's for one you love. It would be troubling if you were not anxious."

Emily stepped out of the tent. "Hey, Hero boy. Come in and meet your kids."

Cyrus leapt for the door.

Inside, tended by a blond Elven woman in robes of the clergy of Wanona, was Kris, lying on a reclining bed.

Cradling two babies.

Cyrus rushed to the bed and looked at the children.

"Hey," Kris said weakly, a smile on her face. "Meet your sons."

And an odd pair of sons they were. The first appeared to be a Human baby, normal in all respects, with the possible exception of having a lot more hair than most newborns. It was already a curly blond, with strange spots of black in it. His face was freckled, also an unusual trait for a baby. He looked, Cyrus noted, almost like a leopard.

The other boy was, surprisingly, entirely Katheni. The cub mewed, his eyes not yet open. He was very much his mother's coloration, but instead of Kris's blond head-fur, he had a shock of fiery-red hair running from the top of his skull between the ears down his back to about his waist. The same color as Cyrus's hair.

Cyrus looked at the children in an adoration. "They're . . . the most beautiful things I've ever seen. I can't . . . They're so . . . Was I really part of making something so . . . perfect?" He stroked the newborns' heads. "They're beautiful like their mother."

Kris smiled weakly. She lay back on the bed. "And they have quite a legacy to live up to. The Two of Balance . . ."

"Yeah, let's not go there," Cyrus said. "I am *not* raising my kids to have a Hero complex."

"So," Kris said, "what do we name them?"

"How about Erik Jacob Solburg, after my dad?" Cyrus said, admiring the tiny, perfect fingers on the Human boy's diminutive hand.

"And the other, Michael Gabriel, after the Saint and the Archangel," Kris said, licking the Kath baby's head-fur. "Enough guardian angels to protect them both."

Cyrus smiled up one side of his mouth and looked at Kris. "Yeah. That sounds good. And Kris?"

"Mm?" Kris looked up.

"I love you."

Cyrus kissed Kris.

And his hair lit on fire.

THE END

Doubleogue

A Sinister Paragraph

*In which there is a Paragraph Most Sinister
Followed by a Sentence of the Same Ilk*

A MINIATURE VOLCANO erupted under the sea, spewing black silt and magma into the pristine water off the coast of Gold Shore Bay. The silt settled into a disgusting black pile and began tainting the sand and rock around it. The volcano coughed up a single tiny object, a copper-colored ring, which settled into the silt.

And the ring waited.

Appendix

Reference and Pronunciation Guide

Araquellus: (Ah rah KELL us) *pl.* Araquellae—An Aquatic Race, skilled in mercantile interests and economics. Governed by a ruler called a Neptarch and his privy council.

Avierie: (ah vee EH ree)—Singular "Avier." The reclusive Bird Folk of the mountains. This Race has a rigid and controlling tribal structure, characterized by shyness and hostility towards outsiders and non-Avierie.

Basilisk: (BAA zill isk)—A large, draconic beast up to thirty feet long, possessing the power to temporarily turn an organic target to stone with a glare. Basilisks come in several varieties, including lesser, greater, Darkshroud, and Hooded.

Bryath: (BRIE ath)—The ruling authority of Centra Mundi, a powerful kingdom in the southern half of the aforementioned continent. *Prop.* Dynasty of Kings who have ruled the kingdom of the same name for the last half-century.

Centra Mundi: (CEN tra MOON dee)—Equidistant from all other continents, thilandmass could accurately be called the Center of the World. Its primary features are its Racial diversity, varied terrain, and the Keep of Five Flames. The seat of Human government is based here, under King Bryath III.

Greaves: (Greevz)—Trousers composed of durable cloth covered in overlapping armor-plates. *Myth.* A Saint who participated in averting the disaster of the Falling Stars during the Twenty-Minute War.

Istaka: (Is TAH kah)—Singular "Istak." A Race of sentient, bipedal Canines, native to Centra Mundi and Landeralt. They are swift hunters, and their caste-based society is steeped in Creation legends.

Katheni: (Kah THENN ee)—Singular "Kath." This Race is comprised of primarily desert-dwelling sentient Felinoids. A non-interfering race, they move about deserts such as Mir in regular routes according to the season.

Kath Magi: (Kahth MAH jee)—A Katheni trained in learning magic by absorbing spells.

Kath Sul: (Kahth sool)—A loose confederation of Katheni tribes that live in the deserts of the southern continent of Salvinsel. Mostly destroyed during slaver raids years ago.

Landeralt: (LAN der ahlt)—The eastmost of the Five Continents, geographical location of the Hereditary Evil Empire. Primary exports are Villains and Mercenaries.

Ley-line: (LAY line)—An invisible channel for carrying Elemental energy, found in the air, ground, or water. A tremendous source of magical power. Also known as "ley-lines" pronounced the same.

Lorimar: (LOW rim ahr)—The western continent, ancestral land of the Ives. 'Discovered' by Lord Colmarian the Headstrong during an expedition to find the mythical paradise island of the same name. *Myth.* The island home to the gods and a race comprised of only enlightened beings and true philosophers. As yet undiscovered.

Manticore: (MAN tih kor)—A monstrous quadruped with a human-like face. These are almost invariably employed by the Forces of Darkness, partly because of their fierce combat abilities, but also because they just plain look freaky.

Merope: (Meh ROWpe)—A thriving mercantile metropolis in the eastern fields of Centra Mundi. This town is run by a council of merchants, and each one's greed balances out the others, making for a peaceful and stable government with everyone's best interests in mind.

Mir, Desert of: (Meer)—Located in northern Centra Mundi, this desert is home to the world's largest tribe of Katheni. It is characterized by severe summer sandstorms, and relatively mild winters. Home of the Alaks Cactus and the notorious Firebelly pepper.

Novania: (No VAHN ee ah)—The Northern continent, half of which is permanently covered in snow. Ruled by the Frost King and his three sons. The world's best brandy, as well as the famous firewine and frostwine, are brewed here.

Ogleby, Reginald: (OH gell bee, REH jinn ahld)—Known as the Crimson Slash, this Hero has participated in many battles and Quests over his lifetime, such as the Battle of Three Streams, and the Nine-Day Seige.

Ransha: (RAHN sha)—A fearsome Race of humanoid lizards. They primarily live in swamps, though some varieties live on ocean coasts. Hard scales protect them from harm, and their tribal society reveres the elderly and worships their ancestors.

Salvinsel: (SAL vin sell)—The southern continent, famous for its mountains and deserts, both renowned for richness in valuable minerals. Also home to the People's Republic of the Underground, and a good number of Kathni as well.

Von Steinadler, Serimal: (Vohn STY nadd lur, SEH ri mahl)—Trueborn son of Benjamin von Steinadler. Despite his true birth, this man was second-born, and did not receive his rightful inheritance. Brother to Voshtyr von Steinadler.

Von Steinadler, Voshtyr: (Vohn STY nadd lur, VOSH teer)—The illegitimate son of Benjamin von Steinadler. Also called Voshtyr Demonkin due to uncanny magical talents, this Villain once attempted to assassinate King Bryath III, and was sentenced to death. Brother to Serimal von Steinadler. Read the first book for more information.

Spleen

Acknowledgements

This book has been edited by a man after he shuffled off this mortal coil and joined the Theatre Troupe Invisible. Thanks to Ivan Benson for his posthumous suggestions.

Thanks to Jeff Gerke of Marcher Lord Press, who put up with my laziness in getting this done until the last minute, when he also put up with my frenetic blur of activity.

Thanks also to Stephen Pool, Avery Smith, Daniel Gerber, Amanda Bauer, Arran Sharma, and Sharaya Willcock, for providing humorous material in the form of our collective Dungeons and Dragons characters and stories.

Thanks to the patients and staff of Gritman Medical Center, who ensured that I could eat food and sleep in a place with a roof while writing this book.

And lastly, thanks to you, the reader, for putting up with my aforementioned laziness when I didn't get this book out as soon as I had hoped.

Be sure to read how
the Hero Complex began:
Hero, Second Class

order online at
www.marcherlordpress.com

Be sure to catch all three
Sixth List Titles

from

Marcher Lord Press

order online at
www.marcherlordpress.com

Award-Winning Fiction
From Marcher Lord Press

By Darkness Hid
By Jill Williamson

Winner of the 2010
Christy Award
(Visionary Category)

Eternity Falls
By Kirk Outerbreidge

Winner of the 2010
ACFW Carol Award
(Speculative Category)

CPSIA information can be obtained at www.ICGtesting.com
262850BV00001B/27/P